PRAISE ...

Mrs. McPhealy's American

"Linguistically charming prose—witty and acerbic, with the hint of a lilt—animates the story's two main characters and quirky supporting cast. McDougall excels at filling in the individual backstories of a populace suspicious of outsiders and caught somewhere between the shadows of the past and a modern world that threatens to upset their ties to the earth and the sea....this is a tale told with warmth, humor, and appreciation for the uniqueness of its small enclave on the edge of the sea.

A delightfully composed and engaging read, propelled by vibrant characters."

— *Kirkus Reviews*

* * * *

"This hugely enjoyable love story is very much a Scottish-American creation by a fine writer who is steeped in the culture of both nations. Earthy yet mystical, *Mrs. McPhealy's American* recalls for me elements of the iconic movie *Local Hero*. It is graced with strong men and women who emerge out of distinctive cultural experiences and delight us with their all too human failings and foibles. A wonderful array of great characters who will stay on in your memory, such is the emotive strength of Claire McDougall's writing."

—**Billy Kay,** Writer/Broadcaster, winner of the Mark Twain award, Scots media person of the year, author of Scots *The Mither Tongue* and *The Scottish World*

"Coming down with a case of "cianalas" and longing for Scotland? With a sip of single malt scotch and a good book—say, Claire McDougall's new novel—you'll be transported to wee Locharbert, where three Tinkers, a comely midwife, and a troubled American filmmaker prove that there's no such thing as an uncomplicated life. You'll laugh out loud with libidinous postmistress Delia Crawford: 'it's just the height of nonsense, so it is.'"

—Judith Fertig, author of *The Cake Therapist* and *The Memory of Lemon*

* * * *

"Claire McDougall's writing has the lilting cadence of poetry. Her novel, *Mrs. McPhealy's American* is a charming, richly crafted tale set in Scotland that offers unique characters, exquisite detail, and subtle humor. It is rich in themes of love, legends, and Scottish history. The reader will be captivated."

—Barbara Bartocci, author *My Angry Son* and *Nobody's Child Anymore*

* * * *

"What does it mean to be "family?" Can family ever be truly escaped or erased? Questions Claire McDougall, a factual daughter of Scotland, poses in this intriguingly titled novel. The author's storytelling skills, subtle displays of humor, and ability to create exquisite word pictures combine to create a page-turner that will engage and delight readers. And possibly provide family answers.

—Patricia Schudy, author of *Oldest Daughters: What to know if you are one or have ever been bossed around by one*

"I stayed up too late reading this book. During the day, I thought about the intriguing characters and couldn't wait to continue turning the pages. As the novel reached its conclusion, I started reading very slowly. I couldn't bear for my time in this fascinating Scottish village with these deep and memorable characters to end.

Whether we live in Kansas, London, or Mumbai, the author transports us to this Scottish village and introduces us to its gritty, resilient, yearning, judgmental, poignant, and indelible inhabitants. Add in one American middle-aged man, trying to rediscover and redefine himself, and you have a story that permeates your mind and softens your heart. Plus, it's fun to read!"

—Deborah Shouse, author of *An Old Woman Walks Into a Bar*

MRS. MCPHEALY'S AMERICAN

A NOVEL

Claire R. McDougall

Sibylline Press

AN IMPRINT OF ALL THINGS BOOK

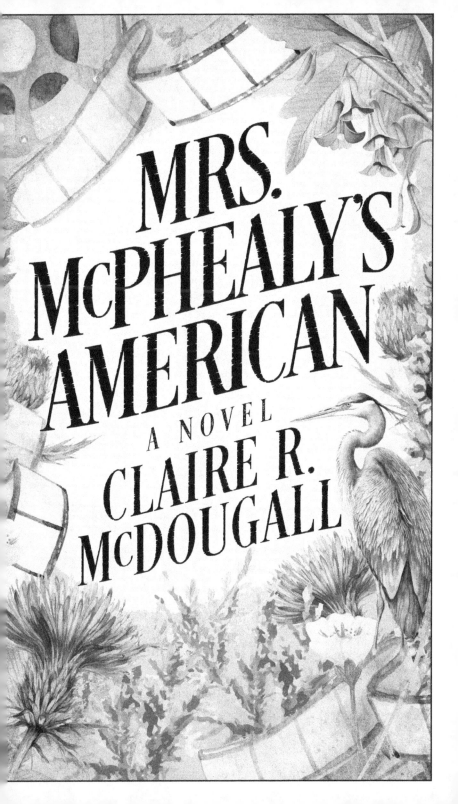

MRS. McPHEALY'S AMERICAN

A NOVEL

CLAIRE R. McDOUGALL

Published in the United States by Sibylline Press,
an imprint of All Things Book LLC, California.
Sibylline Press is dedicated to publishing the brilliant work of
women authors ages 50 and older.
www.sibyllinepress.com

Distributed to the trade by Publishers Group West.
Sibylline Press
Paperback ISBN: 9781960573940
eBook ISBN: 9781960573155
Library of Congress Control Number: 2024932642

Book and Cover Design: Alicia Feltman

PERMISSION AND ACKNOWLEDGEMENT
Original poem by Steven Charles Ward 1948-2003 used with
permission of the author

For Obadiah Duncan.

And in the end ... it matters only that you love.

There is in me a corner
        which receives this slow death,
this backache, the cavities,
        reading glasses,
which yields to maturation,
        admires dissolution,
enjoys black leaves on a puddle floor
        or the fungi on a fallen tree.
Most of me would
        keep my hair,
stay up all night,
        dance like a kite,
would fall to ground like
        un-picked fruit and
be meat for the seed contained.

—STEVEN CHARLES WARD 1948-2003

CHAPTER ONE

Every village has its idiot. Locharbert in Scotland had three. And they were brothers three, who lived together under a wooden frame pulled over with old coats and left on the shore by former sages, known in these parts as Tinkers. They were part of the scenery, the only inhabitants of the shore, the only stragglers on Main Street during a downpour. They knew the history of Locharbert, not the kind to be found in books, but who had slipped into the lives of whom and when; which farmer's tup had got into a field of another farmer's ewes; whose baby had been fathered by someone else. In these things, the brothers were as dependable as the Standing Stones left behind in the fields around Locharbert by druids.

The older inhabitants of Locharbert could put a lineage to these three, but for most folk, they were simply Murdo, Donal, and Doolie. Like the travelling folk they replaced, the brothers seldom bathed or carried out any other ablutions. In all weathers they wore army coats, whose buttons had long since been replaced by string. In the colder months, the brothers wore newspapers inside their coats. In summer, which in this rural part of the world barely counts as the warm season, they rolled back their sleeves on unwashed arms. The brothers were not triplets, but they looked alike.

Murdo was balder than the other two, but they were all small in stature, all round-faced and round-bellied, all more gum than tooth.

So, before almost anybody else, the brothers knew the American was coming to Locharbert and how he was going to be staying with Mrs. McPhealy. Because they knew the entire history of her family, the McNaughts, and they knew that the American was a far-off relative. They knew that in the distance they were related to this man, too. But he didn't know that. And they knew that he didn't. They lived along the edge of life, and the name Hollywood, or even California, belonged in their minds to the same nebulous zone inhabited by handless pipers, or the grey ladies who haunted certain bridges in the woods beyond the town.

History tells of the Druids of Kintyre, though not the history handed out to the children of Locharbert in books. John Knox and the Reformation had forged their path there, sanctifying only the Christians and damning to hell this land of godless pagans. The Christians in their pews were afraid of the stone circles that had been set in line with the rising sun, and of the Gaelic tongue, which had once been spoken hereabouts and still was by farmers.

Steve McNaught, the American, couldn't know about these goings-on, coming as he was to seek asylum from the money race and a life turned sour. He was looking for something simpler, something closer to heaven, in the backwaters of Scotland. Much as a person in a dream comes upon Brigadoon swathed in Scottish mist, Steve McNaught had come by the belief that this rural town on the west coast of Scotland, whence his ancestors hailed, would be the salve he needed to ease the kind of wounds only a successful career in Hollywood could inflict.

CHAPTER TWO

I n ages past, Locharbert had sprung up in a cove of Kintyre, a mountainous Atlantic peninsula or mull, which hung onto the body of Scotland like an adopted child. It was to the Mull of Kintyre in the fifth century that the first Scots sailed from Ireland, and here where the first kings of Scotland were crowned, on a rocky hill-fort behind Locharbert. Because of the ghosts and the weather, the people stuck to the town. Only farmers occupied the surrounding land, and, as a consequence, were wild and turned with cycles other than the clock on the church steeple.

If the brothers three were Locharbert's lowliest inhabitants, the aristocrats in the castle on a point a mile south of the town were its loftiest. If the three men were accepted on the grounds of being simple and sharing common blood with the townspeople, the toffs at the castle were not. The Duarts patronised the local shops, yes, even bought underwear from MacBrayne's, the draper on Main Street, but the toffs did not mingle.

It was to their own kind the Duarts cleaved, to the upper class in other Scottish castles and country houses. Theirs was a society of adults, where children in their boarding school blazers came in only for the holidays. They owned all of the land the farmers worked on, and had to be addressed as Lord and Lady. They ate venison and holidayed in Cyprus. The castle out at Duart Point had been their home right back to the time of King Robert the Bruce, when they were clan chieftains but no better than anyone else. Now their blood was blue, thinned out by years of marriage with the English. Their name was still Duart, but they were Saxons, the English, or what is called in Gaelic, *Sassainach*.

It was the Saxons who had usurped the Scottish throne and made the Albannach, or Scots, a people to hang their heads. It was the Saxons who cleared out the Highlands and islands for sheep, and when the Scots rose up, it was the Sassainachs who forbade the playing of the pipes and the wearing of the kilt. These days the English were a nation to be cheered against in football, to be spat against for the raising of taxes and the robbery of Scottish oil, to be hated in private as a servant hates the master who is better than himself only in name.

The single Saxon tolerated in Locharbert was the window cleaner, who was by some brilliant aberration also the eldest son of the Duarts at the castle. Peter Duart hadn't exactly been disowned by his family; in fact, he cleaned the castle windows every other Thursday. But he wasn't considered acceptable company anymore, not with that accent, which hovered midway between Fettes Boarding School in Edinburgh and Locharbert High School, but belonged to neither.

Peter had been deposited into the posh Edinburgh system at the age of seven and emerged at the other end with the emotional scars common to Britain's upper classes. To the dismay of his parents, and to the credit of a liberal English master, Peter also emerged with a firm allegiance to the Socialists. It was in this vein that he denounced his life of privilege and went to work on the island ferries, where he began to pick up the tighter vowels of Scotland's working class.

After years of wandering, Peter arrived back in Locharbert with a French wife, with whom he settled in a worker's cottage. Her name was Shefaline, and he had met her in a recent stay at an ashram on the Scottish Borders. They weren't regarded by townspeople as locals, but the couple were accepted in an amused way, as was so much of Locharbert life, as an unfathomable fact, like Tinkers on the shore or even a fine peaty whisky.

Lined up along the main street of Locharbert, from the silty sand pulled in by the Atlantic to the grey stone church at its top, were: a butcher, a baker, an ironmonger, a grocer, and MacBrayne's the draper. The café, Caparella's, was owned by Locharbert's lone Italian, and was tolerated because it sold the area's best ice cream.

Peter Duart cleaned the windows of all these establishments, while the Tinker brothers garnered leftovers from their bins. The children, let out from school at lunchtime, took the money their parents had given them for school dinners and instead bought chips or beans-on-toast at Caparella's. In a town both cold and damp, the café was a welcome steam bath of cigarette smoke and grease.

Though popular, the café was not as much a focal point for the exchange of news and gossip as the post office, which sat on the corner of Main Street and Front Street. The building, a rather grand, high-ceilinged stone affair for such a humble town as Locharbert, was run by the postmistress, Miss Delia Crawford. Not even the brothers knew Miss Crawford's history because she had been sent by the central post office in Glasgow. Already too old for the young men of Locharbert, her small round eyes and waddling bum had never turned a head. But the cleavage, when pushed up by a tight jumper, she counted her best asset. She knew it caught the eye of some male customers, as she reached down for her stamps.

Under the guidance of Miss Crawford, all the news of the town and its outlying posts was gathered and stamped. This morning, as he wiped the post office windows, Peter Duart could not tell the nature of the news being spread between the bowed heads of the women. But he knew something was abuzz, and that it was tickling the postmistress to the extent that she had slid off one of her shoes and was running her nyloned foot up and down the back of her other nyloned leg.

Not until Peter got off for lunch was he able to make a point of going into the post office to buy stamps. But by that time, Miss Crawford was already hanging her *Closed for Lunch* sign in the window, and all of the women had departed back to their own houses to discuss with their husbands the news about Mrs. McPhealy's American.

Back on Main Street, Peter ran into Murdo, the eldest of the three Tinker brothers.

"A wee bit of weather moving in," said the little man, staring off to the horizon. Murdo shifted his feet and rubbed dirty hands along his coat sleeves. "I was about to get a poke of chips, but I left my change in my other coat, so I did."

Peter had been stiffed by Murdo before, but counted out forty-three pence from his pocket into Murdo's pitch-lined palm. It wasn't enough for chips, but Peter still had to have his own lunch and it was all he could afford. A pound or more might have bought Peter the information he was looking for, but Murdo just saluted and ran off down the street to the sea front for a bag of crisps at the town's only pub, The Comm.

Peter set his bucket and cloths against the wall of the post office and crossed the street to the bakery. The door clinked back on the bell, as it slipped from Peter's raw hands. Inside, the air had a yeasty flavour. The woman standing behind the counter in her nylon housecoat stopped what she was saying to Mrs. McPhealy, leaving the air punctuated by the absence of words.

"A hot pie, please." Peter smiled, handing her the rest of the change from his pocket.

The woman picked up a pair of tongs and poked a mutton pie from the small oven at her back. She flipped a white paper bag open with her free hand and dropped the pie down in, the grease outlining the pie onto the bag. "Will that be all, now?"

Peter glanced at the tight lips of Mrs. McPhealy and knew no information would be forthcoming here. He nodded and stepped back through the chiming door. On the windy street, the pie seared his teeth; mutton grease ran off his chin. Through the window he could see the women back at it, but there was no sharp look of intent, he noted.

They weren't talking about "the news," just running over old territory: "Such a waste, him from that fancy school, and here he is cleaning windies."

"Not to mention that ponytail, for God's sake," they would say, even in the presence of his French wife, whom they assumed could not make out spoken English.

They would shake their heads and suck air through teeth tended by the dentist whose office sat above the newsagents on Front Street, but who could usually be found in the pub.

After lunch, Peter washed the windows of The Comm, even though it wasn't their day. He could see Murdo sitting by himself, pleased to have a legitimate reason for being in there. The Comm had had a long string of owners, all the way back to the point memory gave out; the general wisdom was that it pre-dated the town itself.

The present owner, Devin Ally, who had once been a teacher at the school, was a handsome, friendly man with black hair even in his forties, and startling red sideburns.

In all the centuries since Knox, The Comm had become the other "church" in town, with its one pew, its bowed heads, and grateful hearts saved by the spirit of God made incarnate in *Uisge beatha,* the water of life.

Situated on Front Street, The Comm took the brunt of the sea wind and provided refuge for those who couldn't mount the hill to Christian sanctity. Names of ancient patrons were etched on its walls. Someone had written the name of William Wallace, but no one knew if it had been the man himself or someone related to him. Perhaps one of the brothers, whose name was also Wallace.

In any case, it was a place where devils had to be drowned out by the drink and, these days, by the din of a jukebox. Many a man, escaping to the pub on Saturday night, did not emerge until after the bells had stopped their tolling on a Sunday morning, until after the minister, Reverend Campbell, had appeared from his vestibule, climbed the stairs to the black wooden pulpit and looked out at his straggly congregation, counting heads, unsurprised by the small fractions.

When Peter Duart gleaned nothing from the pub, he drove out to his old home, the castle on Duart Point. It was his last stop on a Thursday, but he wouldn't find any news out there. Gossip might circulate among the outlying hamlets because the people who lived in them could attract gossip like radio receivers, tuning into stations even in their sleep.

But Peter's family were, after all, too far removed from their ties to Scottish ancestry. A person had to listen at a certain frequency, and they had lost their receptors between Gordonstoun and Cambridge, between cocktail parties and garden parties and hunting in the Home Counties. They did not care, and so it was not given unto them.

Peter wiped a sudsy wash over the small castle windows framed in lead, trying to go easy with his ladder on stone walls that had withstood a millennium, but were still just held together with sea water and lime. The afternoon felt bitter, as though March had changed its mind and gone back to winter. He noticed the daffodils in the castle grounds were late this year. His mother and father waved to him as they passed from room to room, even offered a cup of tea in the kitchen once he had finished.

Peter took the tea, trying not to jangle the cup in its saucer, instinctively keeping the biscuit out of the cup, slipping into talk of relations, well-married cousins in respectable English counties. He found it hard to focus because his thoughts were already shifting to his wife, Shefaline, who would be home, brewing up one of her famous meat dishes, sipping on the wine that was her rightful French habit and some point of refuge in this town of surly Celts.

CHAPTER THREE

P eter drove home along the single-track road from town to Killinochinoch, the old farm on which sat his croft. He had chosen the location because he liked the name and liked even more the fact that he could pronounce it. Kulooch'noch, as the locals did.

An even older wave of Celts, the Picts, had been the first to inhabit this area, leaving burial cairns and other mysterious stone sculptures dotted about the land. The tourist board had assimilated most of these landmarks into heritage trusts, but the ancient dwelling that sat close to Peter's cottage had apparently been overlooked, entangled as it was in bramble and smothered in bracken.

It was older than the castle, round and dug into the ground. In the past, the subterranean structure had supported a slat and turf roof, but that had long since fallen and was on its way now to becoming peat. It came from before the feudal system and the Norman conquerors, when clan chiefs lived alongside the relatives they governed.

As Peter picked up speed, he tapped the speedometer lightly, out of habit from the car's younger days, when a little encouragement might send the needle to its rightful home, around twenty-five to thirty miles an hour on this narrow road bordered by hedges. It was only a small car, of the beetle variety that Volkswagen produced in the 1960s, and its odometer had already made one round and started over again. The car was too small for the ladder that balanced on the fulcrum of its blue roof, and so, as he dropped into potholes, the ladder tipped to front and back; buckets and cloths rolled about in the back seat. Sometimes he had his dog Cuilean along, but not on days he had to go out to the castle. His mother had complained about the fur.

In the far distance, Peter spotted a tractor, making him work down the gears and pull into a passing place, waiting for the rumble and the salute from the farmer with his sheep-dog loping behind.

It was still light as Peter walked from his car to his cottage, looking across into the hills where sheep grazed strangely on their knees as though in prayer. Silage assaulted his nostrils, but beneath that, the scent of ever-damp cow pats. If he stopped and turned slightly into the wind, he could pick out wild garlic from the boggy places, and even the tang of nettles already in great batches about the barns. Straining into the dimming evening, he could make out the outlines and shadows of hills. In the summer, he often walked out beyond the stone walls and the ruined crofts, beyond any sight of telephone wire or pylon. It was out there he had heard voices.

"*J'arrive!*" he called, as he came around the back door, stooping to stroke the motley dog that had been left behind today to herd chickens.

Shefaline came into the kitchen doorway, tasting of garlic and vinegar. On the oven a deep red stew spat; on the table, a baguette of his wife's own making had already been sliced into.

"You're late."

Peter hung up his coat behind the back door. "The castle today. I just about froze my fingers off."

Shefaline brought his fingertips to her mouth. "*Mon pauvre*. I would be so sad to lose your fingers." She looked at him with that coquettish smile, which isn't exclusive to French women but which is used by them to greatest effect.

Peter studied for a second the possibility of skipping dinner and going straight to bed. He kissed her, but tasted food again and his mutton pie had long since turned to fuel. Besides, there was the nagging question of that news. He reached into the high cupboard for a couple of plates and began ladling out stew.

Shefaline took a plate and sat down at the table by her glass of Merlot. Shefaline was not her given name, at least not at birth. It had been given to her by a monk in the ashram and meant *Little Blue Flower*, which she thought had more mystery to it than Sylvie. To her father in Paris she was Sylvie, but Peter always called her Shefaline. The townsfolk called her "yon Frenchie," because she had a sneaky smile like the Mona Lisa, and her clothes were a little gayer than theirs, a skirt above the knee, a silk scarf about her neck. Though they had never ventured beyond the British Isles themselves, they knew France was quite a different matter than Scotland. They had heard that in France, the sun shone for days on end, and they were suspicious.

Peter sat down with his stew and balanced a slice of bread on the side of his plate. "What did you do today?"

It didn't matter much to him; he existed at a certain level of detachment, a way of being he had fostered at boarding school.

Shefaline twirled the stem of her glass. "I went to the grocer for vegetables. How is it you say, *haricots verts*?"

"String beans."

"Ah, *bon*." Shefaline poured herself more wine, relishing the sound of the gunfire glug as the vacuum depleted. "I said *rope beans*. Nobody knew what I meant."

Peter wrapped his hand over her knuckles. He often felt guilty for the life she had to lead under Scotland's ceiling of low grey cloud. "Or pretended not to."

"They were too busy talking."

"Yes, they've been talking all day." Peter tipped a little wine into his stew, then mopped his bread absently in the gravy. "Something's afoot."

A crease appeared between Shefaline's eyebrows. "What do you mean *a foot*?"

Peter shovelled in the last of his stew. "Something's happened, or about to."

Shefaline went to the kitchen for a wooden bowl of salad which drifted in with the sting of balsam in its wake. "Who is Steve McNaught?"

"Remember, he was the director of the film *Culloden*. Then there was that strange one about Mary Magdalene." He smiled. "Where she had a whole slew of children with Jesus."

Shefaline pushed the black velvet band back on her short brown curls. She didn't share her husband's interest in films. "Well, he's renting a room from Mrs. McPhealy."

Peter laughed. "I don't think he would be renting a room from Mrs. McPhealy."

Shefaline frowned, pursing her lips.

Peter knew to step back. "Where did you hear that?"

"Mrs. McPhealy was telling Mrs. MacIver in the grocer. They don't think I understand."

Peter was trying hard to reattach himself. "But why would he stay with Mrs. McPhealy? Why in God's name would he come to Locharbert in the first place?"

Shefaline yawned peacefully, as half a bottle of merlot will make a person yawn. "I don't know. They were talking too fast."

She slid her hand along Peter's forearm. "Bedtime?"

But Peter was distracted, tapping his fingers on his forehead, trying to get his own speedometer working.

"Very strange," he said. "I only hope this McNaught fellow knows what on earth he's getting himself into."

CHAPTER FOUR

Mrs. Effie McPhealy pulled on a blue floral housecoat over her Sunday tweed and wheeled her vacuum cleaner out of the cleaning cupboard. The morning service wasn't until ten o'clock, so there was time to tidy up before she left. She was unusually fidgety this morning. These past few nights, she had been kept awake by "the news."

So much could be changed by one telephone call. If she hadn't answered, as she often neglected to, everything would have stayed the same. She would never have known that she had a relative who was famous in America. The thought, even now, made her draw in a quick breath. She knew her grandfather had had a brother who had emigrated in the early part of the century, but his leaving had been something of a necessity and any mention of him thereafter had come in spurts from between tight lips. Mrs. McPhealy, or Effie McNaught as she was then, had learned not to pursue the subject.

But here was the wicked relative all over again in his grandson. He had told her on the telephone that he had been born in Indiana, but was now living in Malibu, as if she should know where these places were.

"It's in California," he told her, sounding like no one who belonged to her family.

If only he had called while her husband Samuel was still alive. Samuel would have known what to do, more than likely sent him packing. But Effie was alone now, with only the one son in London. She didn't know how to defend herself against America.

The gentleman wanted to come and stay, and it was true she had rented the back room on occasion, but certainly not since she had been alone. She was all scattered to pieces, and the man did keep talking about things she had never heard of; his shrink had told him to take it easy since his breakdown, and now he wanted to get away altogether from the life he knew. The film industry was going to the dogs, he said, and Mrs. McPhealy couldn't think of a thing to say in response. It had been more than five years since she had been to the cinema, and that had been in London. The Cinema in Locharbert, The Empire, had no heating and was only good for the summer. It had been boarded up these past ten years.

Mrs. McPhealy allowed her focus to wander back to the vacuum cleaner. According to Reverend Campbell's creed, she shouldn't be working on the Sabbath at all. But she needed some distraction this morning, so she kept her foot poised over the ON button, arguing to herself that God would be better served without the layer of dust. Leaving it would only make her uncomfortable and on edge; each mote would clatter onto her polished wood like a plate onto the floor. She let her foot drop, and the rest of her worry was overwhelmed by the enormous rumble of an ancient machine.

Little crumbs danced nervously in the Hoover's light, seconds before being shot up the chute. Samuel had brought the contraption back from a trip to Glasgow, and after thirty years, it still performed an admirable job.

Mrs. McPhealy held the handle affectionately, glancing at the grandfather clock when it chimed nine o'clock. Tardiness was as much a vice as uncleanliness, said the Reverend, who was really just Alasdair Campbell, grown up and celibate. The Church of Scotland didn't require such a thing as celibacy, of course, but neither did it frown upon it.

Mrs. McPhealy stepped the vacuum cleaner off and smiled a little. As a child, she had played with Alasdair's sisters, back when the family owned the newsagent in Locharbert, back when their everyday shoes were clogs with metal tips that rattled on the cobbles. Alasdair was older, and he had peed in front of her once through the slats of a gate. She had tried to pretend she hadn't noticed, and in fact it had taken her a good while to realise what she was looking at. But what Alasdair Campbell had done was always between them after that. He even asked her to marry him, as though their manhood and womanhood were somehow bound together by the thing he had done.

In the end, it was as well Alasdair had joined the ministry. She had never told another soul about what she had seen that day, not even Samuel, for he wasn't the kind of man to be indecent himself. He had grown up among the *Brethren*, and they didn't even have music in their churches. They didn't have dances, and they didn't smoke or drink, for it is written that the body is the House of the Lord. They certainly didn't use their bodies for vulgar activities like peeing through gates. Samuel McPhealy had used his body on Effie only on occasion, his birthday each year being one of them, and even then he had never exposed himself. She had always kept her nightie on. Some things are not for the eyes of others, he told her. But he bought her the vacuum, the first of its kind, and she counted herself a lucky wife, as did the ladies of Locharbert who came to view it.

At half past nine, Effie McPhealy shook out her housecoat and set it on the shelf above her kitchen counter where it belonged with other aprons and cleaning cloths. She settled her Sunday hat on her hair in the mirror by the front door, and wondered what he might look like, this cousin from Malibu in America. The McNaughts had always been pale of skin with a tendency towards freckles. The freckles on her face had faded somewhat since childhood, but not on her arms, which rarely saw the sun, or on her shoulders, which never had. The men in her family kept their hair, soft but thin, like her own, which even at sixty-five showed little sign of greying.

Her Grandfather McNaught died at ninety-two with nary a grey hair. As a child, Effie had seen a picture of her grandfather standing beside another young man with a similar face. Her mother hadn't answered when she asked who it was. Every family had its scandal, and it wasn't until the end of her mother's life that Effie found out the exact nature of this family's. She hadn't told Matthew, because she hoped her secrets would die with her. But this is what her great uncle's grandson had stirred up by wanting to stay in the back room of her house. Steven McNaught was a secret himself.

She looked back at herself in the mirror. McNaughts tended to be short. She herself had never measured more than five feet. Only her son, Matthew, had grown to six feet, and no one could say where that came from. Samuel hadn't been tall. Neither did he have red hair.

Effie pulled on her dark green camel coat, picked her keys from their hook and went out onto the path that led between rose bushes to the gate. Lying in the shadow of her house, her roses always came late into leaf, but she noted with pleasure the tulips by the door bright in their reds and yellows. She waited for the click of the key in the lock, pulled her handbag onto her forearm, and marched towards the steel gate that had been erected by Samuel to keep schoolchildren out.

From time to time, her son Matthew sent her airplane tickets to come to London on a visit, but she didn't like to fly. She didn't care for the small toilet at the back of the plane, where men spilled on the floor and bright blue water gushed out the bottom of the toilet with a gasp as though hell itself had opened up. She went by railway, if she had the choice. But she didn't go that often, because London was strange to her and full of people from other countries on the buses, calling her "Darling," and "Love." She was too old, she told Matthew, to adapt to new ways. She wasn't used to foreigners.

Matthew ate foreign food, coffee in the morning instead of tea, and flaky pastries instead of bread rolls. It put her on the wrong footing for the day, she told him. His friends came into his flat without knocking. They called him Matt. His women friends wore short skirts and silky tops with the top buttons all undone. He slept until late, leaving his mother half-famished, then ate at all hours of an evening.

Matthew hadn't sent her a ticket for a while. Just as well, Effie thought, as she turned off Manse Brae and crossed the road to the church, where cars were backing into the few parking spaces, and children were waiting for Sunday school friends. Matthew didn't go to church now.

She had telephoned Matthew when the news came in. He knew the films Steve McNaught had made. It was the kind of thing he would know. He and his silky friends often went out to cinemas in London, even when Effie was visiting. She never went along, not with all the language and the nudity. She didn't like to ask if these things were in the films of the distant relative, because she had already agreed to him staying in her back room. Matthew wanted to come up to Locharbert while their relative was there. Effie McPhealy felt hurt and resented this man from America already. Matthew hadn't been back since his father died.

The organ was playing quietly when Effie came out of the light of the street into the dull interior of the church, lit behind the pulpit by a series of small stained-glass windows. She had dedicated the window on the far left to Samuel after he had passed on. He had always favoured that one of Peter's denial of Christ, the apostle's eyes pleading forgiveness, the cock at his right hand. It seemed like the best thing to do with the Savings and Loan account Samuel had left but never told her about. He had died on his bike, hit early one morning by the Glasgow bus. One day, breakfast as usual with Samuel behind his *Telegraph*, the next day his slippers by the door and no one to fill them. It was confusing to Effie. She missed him, but not as much as she might have thought.

The doors of the church clicked shut, barring latecomers, though only Reverend Campbell nursed the illusion that there would be any of those. He began every service shaking his head for the lazy ones. He had kept his red hair, old man that Alasdair looked now. It was a more faded red than it had been in his boyhood, but he hadn't turned bald like Samuel. When Alisdair lifted his head from the opening prayer, it was always Effie he looked at first. She had come to rely upon it. Next week they would celebrate the Lord's Supper, and she would be responsible for flowers. She had already picked them out. In bud in her garden now, the flowers would be bright and unfurled by then. Her relative from America wouldn't be in time to see them, as he wasn't due until a week on Wednesday. For dinner, he had said on the telephone. Matthew told her he meant tea time. Americans had their own terms: lunch for the middle meal of the day, breakfast the same, but dinner or supper, instead of tea time. Matthew didn't know what the man would call a mug of Horlicks and a digestive biscuit before bed. That's what she called supper.

It was more than she could handle, so she turned her thoughts instead to her flowers in the church window bottoms and on the altar. It would be announced in the weekly newsletter. *Many thanks to Mrs. McPhealy for this week's flowers.* Alasdair typed the newsletter himself. He would be there to lend a hand when she brought the flowers on Saturday, hovering nearby as she rearranged her vases, locking up after they had finished. He always walked her up to the corner of Manse Brae.

After "Praise to the Holiest in the Height," the congregation sat for the first scripture. Reverend Campbell had chosen the Book of Job, King James Version, of course. He had talked to Effie once, as she arranged dahlias, about switching to the Revised Standard Version, but Effie preferred the old language. It seemed holier, she said. Rev. Campbell, who wasn't sure about the switch anyway, had let her sway him.

He opened the pulpit Bible, bringing the fringed bookmark down onto the page: *Oh that I might have my request, and that God would grant me the thing that I long for. Even that it would please God to destroy me; that he would let loose his hand, and cut me off!*

He closed the book and announced the next hymn. The organist pulled out the stops and fumbled over the introduction as the congregation stood. Children dropped hymn books, not grown enough yet to know what to do with abject boredom. After the hymn, they were dismissed to their classes in the hall at the back of the church.

With the children gone, Reverend Campbell lowered his voice and spoke intimately to his flock about the trials of the faithful. Effie had heard him on the subject before, and it always consoled her, for her life had been something of a trial. Now she lived alone, persecuted by the cheeky pupils that filed along Manse Brae at dinner time and at the end of the day. Her son had become foreign to her. Her husband had been older than her by ten years. He had been dead for five, and at age sixty-five she didn't consider herself an old woman. The school children called her an old bag when she shouted at them for kicking her gate and flicking the heads of her flowers. And now there was this article from America telling her about his *shrink*, when she hadn't a notion what that meant.

After the service, she waited with the rest to shake the minister's hand. She would have to tell him about the newcomer, even though she hadn't sorted it out in her own mind. He was of her family, and so she had no choice about asking him to stay. But was he going to be like Peter Duart with a ponytail, with all his education and cleaning windows, for goodness' sake? Or what if Steve McNaught turned out to be vulgar, or worse, and him living under her roof? She was going to need the help of her minister, but she couldn't enlist him just yet.

Effie placed her hand in his, a warm hand with familiar texture and grooves. He always called her Mrs. McPhealy. He said it with a bitter tone, as though to underscore the fact that she had not chosen him. It was up to her to let go, but she took the feel of his hand into the bright Sunday morning. Even later, when she was home, removing her tongue casserole from the oven and ladling peas onto the side of her plate, it was a comfort to her. Nobody but the minister touched her these days.

REVEREND CAMPBELL CHANGED INTO HIS SLACKS and cardigan in a bedroom that was cold, winters and summers over, then went downstairs and turned the heat on under a pan of soup. His housekeeper, yon French woman, Shefaline, came three times a week, but not on Sundays. She had started coming after Mrs. MacRae died suddenly. Mrs. MacRae had always had a good pot of lentil soup going. This soup wasn't lentil, and it had that taste of garlic, same as everything the new woman made. Even cakes.

He sat at his kitchen table, trawling his soup for foreign objects, mulling over the delivery of his sermon. After church, Devin Ally's wife Anita had caught him as he came out of the vestibule. It had been a long time since he had seen the owner of The Comm in one of his pews. After a late night at the pub on Saturdays, Devin was probably oblivious to anything until after midday on Sundays.

There were five young Allys from the age of five to seventeen, and it was the oldest girl, Nicola, who was giving her mother trouble. She had long since exchanged Sunday school for sordid lessons taught by tough boys who lived further down the peninsula. Nicola had inherited all of her father's looks, Anita complained, but none of his wit. Reverend Campbell nodded knowingly and advised prayer. *Seek and Ye shall find.*

At his Sunday dinner of soup and yesterday's crusty bread, Alasdair Campbell shook his head. He knew what Anita Ally only feared; there would be a hasty marriage there sooner or later. He had served this parish for thirty years, and more marriages were forged that way than not. These days they didn't even bother getting married. Half the young children of Locharbert had fathers who were not their own.

Alasdair Campbell moved on to his dessert of trifle. Effie had brought it down a week ago, and he was trying to make it last. A sherry trifle can take a man's mind off the most gruesome of subjects. He himself had been a good, helpful boy, never was belted once at the school, though his soul was a dark place in those days. He had tried to keep his mind off the mechanics of putting a girl in the family way, but whilst serving behind the counter in his father's news agency, he couldn't keep himself out of the ladies' magazines full of bras and other female paraphernalia.

It was Effie McNaught who had tempted him, though, swinging high on his sister's swing, letting her skirts slide back to the lace around the legs of her drawers. Effie Faye McNaught. He had written her name in a corner of his attic, and once when he fought with the devil and lost, he had pulled himself out of his breeks when he knew she was looking.

He had turned to God then, promised every sacrifice known to man, if only she would keep what he had done to herself. He turned away from the body, and chose the service of the Lord. *For what is a man profited, if he shall gain the whole world, and lose his own soul?*

Reverend Campbell took his tea to the fireside, allowing himself for a second or two the image of Effie flushed and lovely as she had looked when she was stretched out with child. How badly he had wanted to place his hands on her belly. Even to this day, he wrestled with such things in his dreams.

After all, a man cannot help what he does in his dreams.

CHAPTER FIVE

The Comm was closed on Sunday nights. The rule had been instituted in days when the threat of hell held more sway, but these days was adhered to simply out of habit. At any rate, it eased the guilt of the men who spent the better part of their lives in the pub. But one night a week at home was enough to propel them back to the bar stool on Monday.

Devin Ally, otherwise an easy-tempered man, felt his patience threatened on Sundays. Once they were home from Sunday school, his children would drag him out of bed, would pester him and each other for the rest of the day. Theirs was a small council house, several children to a bedroom, seven people in a living room designed for no more than two.

"Bedlam," he called it. "The height of nonsense."

Each Sunday, he told them that children were supposed to be quiet and leave a father in peace to read the newspaper. But the children read him instead, and could push him, pulling on his legs, bouncing balls off his head.

Anita Ally sat in her chair, content that this handsome man belonged to her, satisfied to have him in his proper place among his brood.

"I hear Mrs. McPhealy's all of a whirl," she said.

Devin removed a small child from his shoulders and sat it upon his knee. "Och, she's been working herself into a state over those school children ever since we were up at the school. It's just her nature to complain."

"It's not over the school children this time," Anita said. "It's the American coming to stay at her house. He's a McNaught, right enough, but not anyone she's ever met before."

Devin reached across his head to scratch the opposite side of it, as he did in the pub when tallying up the till. "What does Mrs. McPhealy want with an American in her house?"

"He's from Holyrood," said a boy at the onset of puberty. "He made the film about Culloden."

Devin laughed. "Hollywood. Do you learn anything at all at that school?"

He scratched his head again. America was the place to which ancestors had been shipped, where they had taken on new habits and new accents, a different way of looking at the world. Nobody in America was Scottish anymore, though every so often one of them would appear in his pub, looking altogether foreign, acting in ways that put a native Scot on his guard. America was a fast lane of palm trees, big houses, and sun-tanned grins behind dark shades. No one had need of sunglasses in Locharbert. In America they had to water the grass; they had to hide from the sun. It was more foreign than France.

Devin Ally took the puzzle to the pub on Monday, standing at the back of the bar, scratching the side of his head with the opposite hand, waiting for one of his patrons to fill in the missing link. An old farmer who sat by himself knew there had been a McNaught that had gone over the Atlantic and had never been spoken of again. He said MacBrayne the draper would surely know more.

Peter Duart came through the studded door, a great gust of wind and his long-haired dog, Cuilean, trailing after him. The dog went wagging around the feet of the other customers, smelling their dogs, silage and other varieties of decomposition.

Devin stopped wiping a glass. "Peter, it's yourself."

The other men gave a glance and a quick nod. This man from the castle was still suspect.

Peter laid two pound notes on the polished bar. "A pint of cider, Devin."

Devin scooped up the money. "It's a wild night, right enough."

Devin took pleasure in the smart pull of the handle, the sharp tang of apple as the cider fell clear and amber into the cold mottled glass. It wasn't the same as the quick drop of peaty Laphroaig into the dram glass, but he enjoyed the different scents, as a dog goes after smells, and a woman like Mrs. McPhealy relishes her waxes and polishes.

He set Peter's glass in front of him. "A bag of crisps for you?"

Peter smiled, trying to get into the swing of things. "Why not? Salt and vinegar."

He popped the crisp bag open, crunching and looking around for opportunities to belong. He nodded as he named the men on the stools. They nodded back, but said nothing. They had to make a show of being annoyed by the man who was interrupting the ritual of a sombre Monday night in the pub.

Friday and Saturday nights, things could turn a little rowdy, and then Devin would be forced to say, "All right, boys," as a warning. Once in a while, two of the younger men would go at it over a faithless girlfriend or some long-standing feud. But the fights took place behind the pub, among the dustbins where no real damage could be done, except for knocking over one of the three Tinker brothers.

A police station stood at the far end of Front Street, but actual policemen were rarely seen. There were two of them, both from other parts of Scotland. At a traffic accident, of which there were few because there weren't many cars, the

policemobile flashed its lights. Nobody really knew the policemen's names, as they lived on the periphery, and the people of
Locharbert gave them little to do or think about. The policemen had moved the Tinkers off the shore, but when Donal,
Doolie, and Murdo had moved in instead, they had counted
it a lost cause and done nothing to stop them.

Seated at the bar tonight were the dentist; the janitor from
the school; a farmer; and Iain Ally, Devin's brother. Iain had
his brother's dark hair and red sideburns, which in his case
grew down into a thick beard, but none of Devin's humour.
He worked in the office at the forestry commission, but, in
his younger days, had wanted to be an actor. Actors in general were not well-tolerated among the people of Locharbert,
as pretensions were the thing in this world they hated most.

Iain went over to the jukebox and fed in a series of coins.

"One day you'll change the records in there," he said to
his brother as he sat back on his bar stool.

"Aye, a wee bit of Frank Sinatra wouldn't be bad, at that,"
said the farmer, who was old enough to have served in the
war and be grateful for Frankie on the other side.

Farmers supplied the town with milk and cheese, but
anyone living that far away from the town with a tendency
to break into Gaelic was regarded with suspicion. Another
farmer walking into The Comm tipped his hat and was welcomed by name; but he, too, drank by himself. He kept hens
and children out among the hills; he awoke in the dark and
drove his sheep across waterfalls where ghostly apparitions
were known to appear. There was altogether too much going
on out in those places for a person's sanity.

Sanity is a relative term, of course, as the inhabitants of
Locharbert knew, because a large number of them worked up
at the regional asylum. At the turn of the eighteenth century, this facility, which served not only Locharbert but all the

outlying towns and islands, was placed further up the Brae than the church and even further up than Mrs. McPhealy. It was put in the no-man's-land between society and nature, which is where most of the patients lived in their heads anyway. But even among the clinically sane inhabitants of Locharbert, there were a clutch of characters who were, as the locals put it, already "heading up the brae."

The door of The Comm opened and closed, letting in the cold wind, and, smaller than that, the draper, Willy MacBrayne, a mouse-like man of seventy who looked eighty and who kept a great stockpile of unsold clothes in a warehouse at the back of his shop: whalebone corsets, liberty bodices, crimplene dresses, X-fronts in the realm of gentlemen's underwear. MacBrayne had also, since the Free Sixties, been selling gentlemen's contraceptives from a drawer to the right of the till. Willy MacBrayne was a staunch supporter of population control. It was not known, except by Willy, which citizens ever went into MacBraynes to purchase these unmentionables, but, due to the high birth rate in the area, it was suspected that not many did. Still, he kept a lighted sign on the counter for DUREX condoms, and it was generally assumed that, in the event of emergencies, he had some custom there.

"Mr. MacBrayne," said Devin, as Willy came chest-high to the bar. Any man who had taken on the grave business of population control, not an area of expertise for a bartender with five children, deserved to be addressed with respect.

"Devin," said Willy, routing through his trouser pocket for enough change for the dry sherry that generally served as prelude to his dinner. He had been married once, and had a daughter, Georgianna, who, somewhat at the opposite end of her father's mission, was the town midwife. She was just as short as he, a hippie from the Sixties with hair down to her knees, whom he had disowned at the time, but who had come back to the town in her more sensible years and settled into delivering babies, a craft she had learned in a commune down south. Her hair, now a little thinner, a little greyer, still reached to her knees.

Midwifery had not been permitted for years in the outposts of the Highlands, ever since the doctors in the big cities had ordered highland women down to the city and the sterile hospitals properly equipped for the untold dangers of birth. Nevertheless, births in Locharbert invariably took place at home, with Georgianna (or George, as she was better known) in attendance. The trick was to give the doctor the wrong dates, which made the big city doctors suspicious for a while, especially since George was always in the vicinity just at the right time to help. But it was too far away for them to worry about, and there hadn't been a mortality yet. Locharbert in this regard, and in so many more, was left to go its own way. Willy MacBrayne would try to prevent births, and George MacBrayne would catch any that slipped through.

Mrs. MacBrayne had left on the ferry with a travelling salesman when George was just ten. George had had to find a way to survive in a house full of books on gynaecology and contraception, with a father who made her eat charcoal biscuits and drink nettle tea. She was the only one in town who addressed her father by his first name. She was strange, right enough, never having married herself and living alone in an old shack on the shore. Most families in Locharbert were on a slow plan to pay her back for her services, and so she was loved in the way a family loves its black sheep—not as well as its white sheep, but powerfully nevertheless.

Willy MacBrayne sipped his sherry with a look of pain, a remnant from his seminary years, when he was on a different mission to save the world. In his youth, he had rejected the family draper business and gone to Edinburgh to pursue a clerical career. But Willy didn't last long in the hallowed halls and was soon back behind the counter in Locharbert. He had found a wife in Edinburgh, a barmaid who would in any case never do as a minister's wife. Considering his stature, Willy considered it a feat to have found any wife at all.

She had worked in MacBraynes, and with her handsome face, drew in more men than her husband managed to do with his DUREX sign. But the locals shook their heads. A woman in high heels, four inches taller than her husband. Such a woman wouldn't last long in Locharbert.

No one was surprised when she left, and no one missed the travelling salesman either. Encyclopaedias were not great sales items in Locharbert. The school bought a subscription, but were stuck at *Ma-Mf* when Mrs. MacBrayne ran off on the ferry, and the set was never completed.

"A wild night," Peter said to Willy MacBrayne as he sat down on the stool beside him.

"It is that," said MacBrayne.

"You must have seen wilder, though." Peter was on a circular course to the heart of the news, which, as usual, he was the last to be let into.

Willy sucked in air, as though a ghost had touched his shoulder. "Oh, aye, wilder than this. In 1938, the year the war began, a storm came in off Islay that lifted whole dustbins from the back of The Comm here and left them on the steps of the kirk."

Peter began to weigh the likelihood of the story, but gave up quickly, as he had learned to do. These accounts were only supposed to approximate history. If the Loch Ness monster had come on holiday to Locharbert in 1722, and taken rooms above The Comm, it might never have reached the history books, but it would go down nonetheless in the annals of Locharbert, which is what counted. The people weren't stupid, but they belonged enough to their Druid past to know that what is real lies somewhere between what is and what could be.

"Is that a fact?" Peter asked.

Willy sucked in air again through yellowed teeth, the result of much nettle tea and pipe tobacco. "And back in 1831, a hurricane reaching a speed of one hundred and twenty miles an hour took the roof off MacBraynes and flattened the warehouse to pieces. It was the same storm that hit the Isle of Lewis and uncovered the chessmen that had been buried on Uig Sands since 1150."

"No joking," said Peter. "You're like an encyclopaedia."

Willy let out a gust of breath, which passed for a laugh.

"I was just wondering," said Peter, after a moment's pause had let Willy turn back to his sherry, "where McNaughts hail from."

"McNaughts?" said Willy, frowning and making Peter think he hadn't circumvented enough. "McNaughts hail from further north, but not since Prince Charlie marched his army to Culloden. Like most clans, the McNaughts scattered when the rebellion failed, and a branch of them ended up here in Locharbert. Same as your clan of Duart, which hailed originally from the islands."

Peter went back to his cider. He had been out to the tiny piece of land in the Atlantic called Ulva, on a wet and windy day that made him grateful his ancestors had decided to move to the mainland.

Willy finished his sherry and stood up to go. "Of course, if you're wondering about this creature from America coming to stay with Mrs. McPhealy, you'd be right in thinking he had no place here. If every McNaught or Duart in America thought fit to move back to Locharbert, where would we be then, eh? Knee-deep in caravans and tourist mugs."

It wasn't exactly abuse. It was fact. No offence intended.

"Bloody right," said Iain Ally from along the bar. A farmer

cursed in Gaelic, sending all Sassainachs and other intruders to the devil.

Peter stroked his dog's head. "Good night, Mr. MacBrayne."

Devin nodded. "Is that you away, Mr. MacBrayne?"

When Willy MacBrayne left, the men on other bar stools smiled into their glass mugs. No one got anything over on Willy MacBrayne of the Durex counter. Of course, his daughter was another matter—many a man had got the leg over there. Or so it was told. No one actually *knew* any man who had got the leg over George MacBrayne, but an ex-hippie like that with hair down to her knees was just asking for it. Living out on the shore by herself, going by a man's name, still wearing hippie clothes as though she were twenty, not forty-five. Who ever heard the like?

George MacBrayne, who had inherited her mother's round blue eyes and sculpted cheekbones, roused a little fear in the hearts of these men. None of them wanted to feature in town gossip as the man who had got the leg over her, but to a man they had weighed the possibility. George suffered no man gladly, having been set against the sex by her father. Which didn't mean she never had sex, because she did, though, contrary to rumour, never with anyone from Locharbert. She had had sex with Devin Ally behind the school cafeteria, when they were both seventeen, but only the once, because she was on her way out then to the Sixties which was happening everywhere but in the Highlands and Islands of Scotland. Devin had waited for George a year or two, but Anita MacDonald was persistent and he had married her one summer when he was home from the university in Glasgow.

When George came back to Locharbert, it had set Anita on edge for a while, but George had by then cultivated an edge of her own, which she would take out on enemies, and even on her clients. She had been known to thrust a packet of condoms into a father's hand after a difficult birth. She had done this to Devin Ally the last time, and so it was with a little sinking of the heart that he saw her walk through the door of his pub.

George stroked the dog, unbuttoned her trench coat and nodded at him. "Dev."

He winced a little, because no one else had ever called him that, and it brought to mind their limby encounter on the worn grass behind the school kitchens.

"How are you doing there, George?" he said.

Forty-five or no, she was still a handsome woman. He was happy enough with Anita. He had never demanded much of life. Still, there was that memory, which popped up in dreams now and then. Unlike Alasdair Campbell, he knew he was responsible for those.

George sat down next to Peter on the stool her father had just vacated. She smelled of a Catholic church, and was surprisingly bright when she let her dull oversized coat drop off her shoulders: a yellow and red striped cheesecloth shirt gathered loosely by drawstrings at the neck, an orange skirt. Wellington boots.

"I was just talking to your father," Peter said.

She gave him a quick, uncommitted smile. "In for his sherry, was he?"

Peter winked, making the other men at the bar roll their eyes. Only a man unused to the women of Locharbert would wink. George knew he meant nothing by it. Sometimes she wished he did.

"I was pumping him for some local history. Here, let me get you a drink."

It wasn't Peter's habit to splash money about, but he knew George only scraped by.

She smiled at him, meaning it this time. They both looked at Devin who knew what she would have, then down at the dog. Cuilean had met George only on occasion but had an animal's instinct for kindness.

"Aye," she said, "Willy is the one to pump. He could write a book. In fact, I think he's writing one."

Peter smiled. "I bet he is, the sneaky sod."

"Of course, mum's the word." George tossed her hair over her shoulder, making the other men look at her, then at each other. The Comm wasn't the place for a woman, they were agreeing, even one with a man's name.

Devin wiped the bottom of the glass before setting George's martini down in front of her. She didn't look up.

"What were you asking him about?"

Peter sighed. "I was just being nosy. I was trying to find out why this Steve McNaught chap is staying with Mrs. McPhealy, of all people."

George sipped her Martini. "Her grandfather had a brother who went to America. Steve McNaught is his grandson. I've seen his films. Misogynist git."

Peter nodded, not knowing what she meant.

"American women think they're that liberated," she said, "but they flock around famous men like brainless pigeons. All the women in his films are cardboard props for men. It's a form of pornography, when you think of it."

Peter tried to get his mind around the proposition, but he had reached the bottom of his glass and conclusions weren't going to come easy. He reached down and patted his dog's head.

"He made that film about Mary Magdalene, though."

"So he did," she said, "so he could put her under Christ Almighty. Or wandering after him, washing his feet, making his food. I don't know what Bible he's reading out of."

Peter laughed. "Yes, but it's a nice twist. I mean, a woman's the best thing that ever happened to most men."

George tried to catch Peter's eye to see if he could be wavered on his commitment to which particular woman he owed his life. But she could tell he could not, and she softened into a friendly smile. "How come I never meet any single men like you?"

Peter fumbled for an answer, the thought dawning on him suddenly that she might have more than a passing interest in him. He couldn't make sense of it if she did. She was ten years his senior, and after Shefaline, he had pulled the sluice gates shut. Not even a smile like George's affected him where it was meant to.

George finished her martini quietly.

"Anyway," Peter said, "it's not every day a Hollywood director walks into Locharbert."

George shrugged. "I'll be more interested in the day he walks out."

He watched her stand up and pull her coat back on, enveloping her colourful self in army green. He noticed the other men at the bar watching, too. He could tell she saw them, too, by the deliberateness of her movements, the way she tossed her hair out from under her collar.

She patted Peter on the shoulder. "Thanks for the drink. Chivalry's not dead yet."

After she had left, Peter played with his empty glass on the uneven bar top. He had always loved films. For a while after school, he had thought about studying film production at an American college. McNaught wasn't his favourite director, but he did think George had been unfair.

At any rate, Peter had the answer to his question about McNaught and Mrs. McPhealy, and his thoughts were turning now to Shefaline who had been heading into the shower when he left. Soft and powdered in her Chinese robe, she would be reading by the fire. It gave him nothing to say to anyone else tonight, even if they had had something to say to him. He pushed his glass towards Devin, clicked for his dog, and headed out the door into wind that was swinging the metal pub sign above the door.

Apart from that, the town was still, in the way Locharbert could be silent but full of human bustle nonetheless. In Locharbert, silence was just another form of discourse.

CHAPTER SIX

Nicola Ally tossed her reddish-blonde hair from her forehead, the better to see her face in the bathroom mirror. Her eyelashes, normally fair and invisible, were about to receive a coat of mascara.

Her father Devin banged on the bathroom door. "Are you going to be in there all day?"

Nicola tutted. The trials of being seventeen were legion. Not only did she have to share a bedroom with two much younger sisters, but she couldn't find a moment's peace anywhere.

"It's because of all the bread I've been eating," she called.

Devin turned back down the landing. "Oh, thanks for the information."

Nicola went back to the mascara. She had heated it up in a sink of hot water, so it would glide onto the lashes without clumping. Clumping meant that later in the day she would have black flakes on her cheeks. Boys didn't care if they messed up her make-up. In moments of passion, she didn't care either. It was afterwards, when she had to get the bus home and endure the stares. Everyone knew what smudged mascara and messed-up hair meant. She was getting a reputation. She could tell her mother knew about it by the looks she got whenever she dressed up and was heading for the door, whenever her mother said, "You're not going to be late, are you?"

Nicola brought her face close to the mirror, inspecting her wide-eyed look; the lashes curled up and outwards. She sucked in her cheeks and brushed the hollows with busy strokes of rouge, as they did in the adverts on the television. Her father had a song to sing about the marriage of the painted doll every time she came downstairs in make-up. Well, she wasn't twelve anymore; she wasn't even a virgin. Those boys from the towns further down the mull had you out of your knickers before you knew what was what. She worried about getting those diseases they gave slide shows about at school. But she wasn't going to get pregnant, because George MacBrayne, who had delivered her, was handing out Durex when she asked.

Her father knocked on the door again. "Bread or no bread, I'm going to have to shave before I go to work."

Nicola stood back from the mirror and adjusted the wire in her bra to give her the most lift. Not that Mrs. McPhealy was going to care, and it was to her house she was going. But it was a warm day and boys on the street might whistle, make her curse them even though she was glad for the attention. They expected to be sworn at; it would make their day.

She flushed the toilet and opened the bathroom door. "Patience is a virtue, don't you know?" she said to the man whom she alternately loved and hated.

Devin Ally walked into the perfumed air of the bathroom. "The height of nonsense," he muttered, as he flipped the tap on and filled the basin.

Nicola sat down at the large table that swallowed the kitchen. Around it were six chairs and a high chair off at one corner.

"What time is Mrs. McPhealy expecting you?" Anita asked.

"Where's the Shreddies?" said Nicola.

Her mother said, "Eaten by early risers."

Nicola put her elbow on the table, her chin on her hand. "Brilliant."

"There's cornflakes," Anita said, wiping from the table remnants of all the breakfasts that had already passed through the kitchen that morning.

"I don't like friggin' cornflakes."

Anita lifted Nicola's elbow and wiped beneath. It was her way of showing annoyance. She didn't want to encourage any outright rebellion, like running away from home or coming home pregnant.

Anita told herself Nicola would grow out of it. She told Devin one Sunday, but Devin couldn't fathom his daughter, and was overwhelmed, he said, at the thought of having to go through it all again with the other two girls.

"The minister says we should pray," Anita said.

Devin scratched the side of his head with the opposite hand and squinted as though into a blinding sun, which in Locharbert wasn't that likely.

Anita watched her daughter leave the house in trousers that hung below her navel and laced up the front as though she were just asking for someone to untie them. Nicola had turned out bustier than her mother. Anita assumed it came from the Ally side of the family. Everything about Nicola was of Devin's stock, down to her lack of modesty. But what would you expect from a family that counted an actor among their number.

EFFIE MCPHEALY PULLED BACK the curtains to see if she could spot the Ally girl. Now that Effie was running a bed and breakfast, it seemed as though she would need help. She didn't think it would be her job to rifle through the belongings of a fifty-year-old man, picking underwear off the floor to vacuum the carpet. She had put out for a girl before, but only now had she got any response. And not just from one girl, either, but half the girls at the school, and the postmistress, who said she had been looking for a bit of extra work on the side. Effie didn't trust the postmistress around any man, let alone her house guest, and she wasn't about to hire one of those cheeky girls from the school, picking her roses when she wasn't looking. So she opted for Nicola Ally because Nicola's father had grown up in the town, and because the last time Effie had taken any notice of the girl she was still in Sunday school wearing a white dress with a pink sash and patent leather shoes.

The thought of this strange man in her house was beginning to creep up on Effie. It hovered over her shoulders as she went about her life. She could feel it under her fingernails, in the catch of her breath. She didn't want it mentioned in the baker's or the post office anymore. She didn't want any more questions about the man. She had never clapped eyes on him, and wouldn't know him if she fell over him in the street. Yet here he was arriving the day after tomorrow. Here he would come, using her bathroom, leaving his slippers at her door, eating off her plates and cutlery, reading newspapers at the table like all men do. She wasn't sure she was ready for another man in the house, especially one under the care of a psychiatrist. Locharbert had enough of his type up in the asylum.

When Effie heard the gate clang open and shut, she went to the door to wait for the bell. When she opened the door, she found a delinquent on her doorstep.

"Nicola Ally?" she asked, implying that it had better not be.

Nicola had been schooling herself all along the road in how to put up with the old bag they knew at school as Old Feely Drawers. She wasn't enamoured of the idea of cleaning, either. But she knew that the American who was coming was famous, and that was enough for her. Everyone said she was pretty, so maybe he would put her in one of his films. It had been perhaps a year since Feely Drawers had asked her dad if she would help out on Manse Brae. At the time, she had curled her lip and looked as though he were delivering an insult instead of an invitation.

Devin took her answer and told Mrs. McPhealy that Nicola needed all her time for homework. And that was a joke, because Nicola had made a career at school of being a numbskull. Nicola couldn't see herself belonging to the swots, teachers' pets, following in her father's footsteps to Glasgow University. What good had it done him, spending his life down at the pub? She resented his absence and his dissimilarity from the fathers on television. Inside her school portfolio, it said she swore and she smoked. She had snuck a look once when she had been sent to the headmaster's office but had had to wait. She snogged with boys at school dances, for the minute or two before one of the patrolling teachers came to break it up. In her portfolio, it said Nicola was a rebel.

But she didn't really fit in with the crowd she had chosen, either. She knew they weren't bright. Every so often, she would say something that would make them look at her blankly. She was tired of the excitement over half-bottles of vodka stolen from the off-licences in the bigger towns. She liked the oblivion of drinking, of feeling really empty and on the level of her peers. She liked the relief of it. But she didn't like the way it felt later. She didn't like smelling of smoke and booze, of having to carry toothpaste so the parents wouldn't suspect anything. It wasn't really the life for her, the boys that took what they wanted and left, the stealing, the plain stupidity of it all. She was waiting to see if there was another option.

Nicola Ally, standing on Mrs. McPhealy's doorstep, looked as confused as the old woman herself.

"Hello, Mrs. McPhealy. Am I late?"

Mrs. McPhealy kept looking at her, as though something should occur to rescue them both from the situation.

"No," she said. "Well, just a wee bit. You'd better come in."

Nicola stepped through the door into a house in a different category from the houses she knew. The smell of cooking in this house was a small hint contained far off in the kitchen behind a mottled glass door, and overwhelmed by polish and other cleaning agents. The floor was not a well-worn carpet, but wood that squeaked when you set a foot on it. A Persian rug, with tassels all in perfect symmetry, lay in the middle of the floor. The other rooms were behind doors; the stairs didn't run carelessly upwards, but stood at attention, every corner dust-free and beaten into silence. There were echoes in this house, like in the church.

"Everything looks very clean already," she said, pleasing Effie into asking her to remove her shoes, and thereby accepting Nicola Ally as the new cleaning girl, instead of a serious mistake.

Nicola untied her platform shoes and lined them up like soldiers, not a habit she was used to, but instinctively aware that anything else would not pass muster. She stood like a soldier herself, as Mrs. McPhealy went to her apron shelf for a large wrap to cover the girl's front, which was not the kind of front Effie wanted in her house. Without her shoes, the girl was much smaller, more like the one Effie remembered from church. And with the apron loosely bound, Nicola began to look like a girl Mrs. McPhealy could use.

"Now," she said, "My guest will be arriving tomorrow in time for tea, or *dinner*, as the Americans call it."

Effie led her to a bedroom to the left of the kitchen, where her boarders had always stayed. She wasn't planning on asking her relative for board and keep, but she was expecting something of the sort. Americans were rich, as anyone knew, and this wasn't just any American.

"And if he needs change for his dollars," Delia Crawford had said, "the post office offers a handsome exchange rate."

Dollars. Effie didn't like to think about it. It was a word that belonged on the television, not in the space of her home. What if the man handed her a wad of dollars? What if he had them stashed away in her drawers?

The room where he would be staying was blue, a good colour for a man, she thought. The counterpane was light blue, and the wallpaper provided a blue backdrop for pink roses; the curtains were dark blue, for shutting out the light and keeping shadows on the inside where they belonged.

"Very nice," said Nicola. She went to sit on the bed, but recognised in time that dents on the counterpane would sit ill with a tidiness she had only seen in magazines. "It'll be nice and quiet for him, eh?"

It wasn't a big room, but Effie didn't want her relative getting too comfortable. If he was used to big houses in this Malibu place, he would begin to feel cramped in her blue room after a while.

"I've tidied the room for today," she said. "But you'll need to come in before school to vacuum, and dust, and help me with the breakfast."

Nicola had only ever got up that early when her family went on holiday and there was Glasgow traffic to beat, or an airplane to catch. She smiled stoically. She wouldn't be looking her best at half past six.

Mrs. McPhealy fetched a dustpan and a long brush for reaching under the bed. She explained that her bad back stopped her from bending over. Nicola swiped the brush under the bed, trying to look industrious, or even like she had done this before. Feely Drawers was watching her. Nicola strained, trying to find something under the bed. Under her own bed, wads of dust and dog hair drifted out without even being asked, but under Mrs. McPhealy's beds, there was only stubborn floor, yielding nothing.

Nicola pulled the brush free and shrugged apologetically. Mrs. McPhealy said, "Mmmm," as though she didn't believe the child had tried hard enough. As they left the blue room, Effie closed the door quietly behind them. If there was one thing that shattered her nerves to pieces, it was slamming doors.

Nicola followed her into the kitchen, a strange kitchen where no food or evidence of food was visible. "I will be giving Mr. McNaught a cooked breakfast in the mornings." She pulled her fridge open and took out several packages. "Bacon, sausage, eggs, and fried bread. You'll need to cook it, as I can't abide the smell of grease that early in the day."

Nicola made a mental note to quiz her mother on the finer points of frying.

"He'll be served at this table." Effie showed her how to release the wing and affix it underneath so it didn't wobble. "I'll make the tea myself in this teapot."

She lifted a brown teapot off the shelf and set it by the kettle. It was still a day and a half until the man came, but she didn't want to be thinking of details at the last minute.

"You must pick up the food with these tongs," she warned the girl, "and you must wash your hands before and after."

"Right you are, Mrs. McPhealy. Is there anything else for me to do today?"

But Mrs. McPhealy was already on her way back to the bedroom to tidy up a matter she had forgotten. It was how to make a bed. Nicola gave her half her attention, noticing from the corner of her eye the way the sheets had to be folded at the corners and tucked way under the mattress, as though a person were in danger of falling out. With the rest of her brain, she was entertaining the possibility of lying in the bed herself.

"Are you listening to me?" Old Feely Drawers wanted to know.

"Yes, Mrs. McPhealy."

Mrs. McPhealy pulled the sheets free of the bottom of the bed again, indicating it was Nicola's turn. Nicola performed a fair approximation of the task, one which made Mrs. McPhealy go, "Hmmm," as though she belonged to the bee family and was contemplating an attack.

For the rest of the morning, Nicola reordered cupboards, wiped shelves clean that were already clean, and stayed at the end for a "wee cup of tea and a biscuit." By "a biscuit," Mrs. McPhealy meant exactly that. There was one tea biscuit set by her cup and no others even in sight. Mrs. McPhealy drank with her, but didn't take a biscuit herself. Nicola felt awkward for the small indulgence.

Walking down the path to the iron gate, Nicola was a woman freed from jail. It made the rest of the day much sunnier, and she was even nice to her mother when she was learning how to make a cooked breakfast. Add a little salt to the fat, and the sausage won't stick to the pan. It was a little mantra she began to repeat in the next two days, the first of its kind to enter Nicola's consciousness, perhaps the first piece of religion ever to affect her.

EFFIE DROPPED HER TOP TEETH into a jar in the bathroom, as she did every night before getting into bed. She waited until after her prayers, of course, for a person shouldn't appear before the Lord in an undignified manner. She sucked her gums on the way back to bed. A seed from her homemade bramble jam had worked mischief under her top plate. Under the care of the town's inebriate dentist, there weren't many people her age who still owned their own teeth. By and by the teeth of Locharbert were replaced by what were known locally as *wallies*, coming from a piece of vernacular which meant wall tiles. Most of the older inhabitants of Locharbert sported wallies, except for Devin Ally, who had inherited teeth with the strength of walrus tusk, attractive, though, nonetheless. The Allys had always had good teeth, which is perhaps why he bore less resentment than most to the dentist who sat on his bar stool, drowning his lack of expertise in dentistry in a bottle of Glenfiddich.

Effie's son Matthew had joked that her teeth were like the stars that come out at night. But that was only half true, and she was proud that she could still lay claim to a row of bottom teeth. Alasdair Campbell had parted company with his teeth in his early thirties. Effie's husband Samuel had been fitted with a full set just a month before the incident with the Glasgow bus. At the time, Effie had wondered about cashing them back in, but he needed them for the funeral.

Effie McPhealy pulled the covers up to her chin, crossed her arms and ankles, and settled in for a sleepless night. She had been on tranquillisers once, just after Samuel died, but they had made her so sleepy, she could hardly keep her eyes open during the day. She had gone down to the shops a couple of times and completely forgotten why. It was no way to live. She came off them without the doctor's recommendation, preferring nervous tension, pouring anxiety into every inch of her habitat, especially the bedroom.

In her bed of white flannelette sheets, she both longed for and dreaded the light coming up behind the curtains. The Teasmade beside the bed would shudder into action at six o'clock, waking her, if she wasn't already awake. It had been a birthday present from Matthew to his father, and, Samuel, being a man for new fads in machinery, had installed it at

Effie's side of the bed. Samuel always wanted his breakfast by a quarter to seven, so the six o'clock alarm was useful in those days. And a wee cup of tea together before the day began set things in good standing. Breakfast was the best meal of the day, Samuel always said: bacon, sausage, eggs, and fried bread. It was the kind of indulgence he didn't otherwise allow himself.

Effie had slept better in those days. The gurgle of the Teasmade was more like a friendly nudge to get on with things. Nowadays, it felt like a brick over the head. She had dropped a teabag into her cup and filled the machine up to the water line from the bathroom tap, before starting her bedtime routine. She had flicked the switch to red, so it could commence its nighttime countdown. Now it was half past ten, and she was running through her inventory of sheets and towels, setting some aside for the guest, some for herself.

Steve McNaught was running around her head again, as though asking her to catch him up. She set her heart firmly against washing his sheets. Nicola Ally would have to do that. Her thoughts were entering a groove from which there would be no return for the next few hours. She wouldn't put up with any American behaviour. Nor would she be used as a doormat for anyone with grand ideas about himself. Especially since he belonged to the dark area of the McNaughts' past that needed to be forgotten but now never would.

By two o'clock in the morning, Effie had decided she wasn't going to change anything about her life just because this shady relative had seen fit, or his psychiatrist had seen fit, to look her up. She wasn't running a castle for tourists. She wasn't even running a bed and breakfast, though, Lord knew, that was what he thought he was coming to.

Effie explored every corner of malevolent intent until, finally too tired to accuse anyone further, she drifted into sleep about an hour before the Teasmade started coughing and hic-cupping like a mad man.

On this day of the arrival of her relative from America, Effie McNaught greeted the day with little more than an hour's sleep, for the window cleaner was to arrive at eight o'clock, and she would have to have everything tidy, in case he had to come in and use her bathroom; just in case he looked in her windows.

CHAPTER SEVEN

S teve McNaught peered through the airplane window at Glasgow, emerging rapidly from under a solid layer of cloud. He had never seen Glasgow before, but it made him smile, the red brick, stone walls, traffic streaming down the other side of the highway, rain streaming down his window. On the spectrum of cities on planet earth, Glasgow looked just about as far from Los Angeles as a person could get. He smiled at the flight attendant. She obviously didn't know who he was, but then that was one of the advantages of being a director and not an actor.

He was in First Class, so she had been attentive to him throughout the flight, leaning down and speaking softly when the captain was expecting a little turbulence on the descent into Scotland and was asking the passengers to buckle up. Once the plane hit the runway, and it seemed safe to get out of his seat, he went into the galley, where the flight attendants were strapped into special safety seats, and asked the woman to join him for a drink.

Her name was Sandy, and she hailed from Cleveland, Ohio. She was good-looking only in the way a girl should look when you introduce her to your parents. He took her to the airport bar, because she was due to fly out later that day, but found nothing exceptional to talk about. He had never been to Cleveland, and he didn't want to impress her with his career. He told her he lived in Los Angeles, where, it turned out, she had attended college. They swapped the names of streets and restaurants, failed to find any people in common, and then she went to "catch a few Zs," before her flight out. He told her she was a nice wholesome girl and offered Mrs. McPhealy's address. She said he was nice to talk to, quiet and not pushy like the pilots she normally drank with. He waved as she walked off, then turned back to his Diet Coke. He was off alcohol; he was learning to take control.

In the airport lobby, Steve located his car rental company, but wasn't quite prepared for the left-hand drive. He had been in Ireland once, so he had encountered the concept, even though he had never had to drive. But negotiating the traffic circles leaving the airport made him grip the wheel hard, and quite soon he began talking himself through the turns. It was easier once he left the city and settled into the straight trek northwest around Loch Lomond. He settled back in his seat and shook out the stiffness in his back. He took deep breaths, letting the oxygen circulate up his spine and over his head, as he had learned in meditation.

Rounding a bend, he let out a "Whoa!" as a snow-dusted Ben Lomond rose out of cloud at the far end of the loch. Indicating first the wrong way, then getting it right, he pulled the car over on the shoulder. Nothing but dark forest covered the far side of the water, and no structures dotted the islands at the loch's centre. He crouched at the water's edge and skipped a stone across the surface. It jumped a couple of times, then hit a metal statue of a boy about thirty feet offshore. Steve glanced behind to make sure no one had seen. Obviously, the boy had drowned there. It hadn't been that long since Steve had felt like he was drowning himself.

He didn't know how his life had soured, almost as fast as his first marriage. He had a son by that early marriage, who was now a thirty-year-old guitarist with a band in Bloomington, Indiana. The wife still lived there, but she had hated him now for almost thirty years. They had met in the Sixties, tripped on psilocybin and mescaline, dropped out of college, holed up in the woods of Brown County with other trippers and gurus of one stripe or another. But when they found themselves on the other side of the trip, there wasn't much to say, except she was pregnant, and he was already on his way to L.A., if not in actuality then at least in intention.

From his more recent marriage, he had two more sons. These he had actually lived with, gone through with the teething and the long nights. Still, he had been out of the house a lot. Even when he wasn't filming, there was always another project in the offing, another opening, another ceremony. He had been nominated for two Oscars, but was still waiting to win. He had assumed the nominations would pave his way, but he found Hollywood had a short memory, and he hadn't secured funding for his pet venture, a semi-documentary story set in the psychedelic Sixties. The studios weren't interested. He struggled with endless drafts of the script. But Hollywood was Hollywood.

"It has no action," they said. "It's mostly just dialogue."

Their biggest audience, they told him, was twelve-to fourteen-year-old boys. That demographic wasn't interested in the Sixties. Or dialogue. They didn't want to know.

Steve's wife, a restoration artist for a prestigious interior design company in Beverly Hills, had hired a young intern about that time, and soon Steve was beginning to get suspicious. When he found them together on the floor of her studio, he moved out. In return, she slapped him with a divorce suit that took the better part of his savings and made it imperative he launch a new project soon.

Steve abandoned his own script and took on other people's pet projects. His life began to spiral into shades of grey. He was stuck with scripts that said nothing, only provided fodder for the entertainment machine. Explosions, chases, a hand on a trigger here, on a breast there, films that ran for two weeks, then dropped out of sight. Films he didn't want his sons to see.

All of a sudden, his wife didn't want their sons to see him anymore. She called him *psycho*. He was drinking; he was a bad example. Steve didn't have the will to fight her. He had walked out on one marriage; leaving this one almost felt like a habit. He missed his sons, but his wife made it hard for him to visit. The boy she was living with was always in the background, sporting a braid that fell to his waist. Steve named him "Hairball." The boy was tall and wearing his first scraggly beard. Steve was five foot seven inches and wearing some of his last hairs. Unlike his father, he had lost his hair early. In an attempt to hide it, he had started having his head shaved close.

By the water's edge on Loch Lomond, Steve ran his hand over his stubble head and chin. He hadn't shaved since yesterday morning. He probably looked like he had looked in those first weeks in the rehabilitation centre. Drink had got him in the end. A beer or two for breakfast before the real drinking began, Scotch mainly. Empty bottles of Glenfiddich lined up next to his trash. He never remembered drinking that much; after about two o'clock in the afternoon, he didn't remember anything at all. He looked in the mirror and told himself he looked like shit: red eyes, sallow skin, stubble shadows on his head, life shadows everywhere else. Steve told the shrink they wouldn't let him make his movie. The shrink told him to find a new life.

So here he was, looking for something else, a little heaven instead of hell. Here he was, Loch Lomond water on his fingertips, moss on the rocks, clouds like a halo on Ben Lomond. When he could find no meaning in his life, he had poked around in Clan almanacks. He had vague recollections of an old man with a sing-songy way of speaking, of the grandfather who had died when Steve was five.

The old man and Steve's father had not been close, so Scottish ancestry rarely came up. It had taken some work to trace a ship passage back to Liverpool, a train to Glasgow, and then farther north and west to Argyll. Steve possessed Argyle socks among his collection, but he didn't know how to conjure Argyll, Scotland. He expected it was like Ireland, and indeed it was, he realised now, looking out over the loch and the forested hills, the occasional tread of tires on the road behind him. It was the same, but craggier and higher, somehow lonelier.

Steve looked across at the boy in brass standing in the water and wondered how long he had been there. He wondered about Mrs. McPhealy. On the phone she had seemed distant, not necessarily pleased to be introduced to her great uncle's grandson. But she had offered the room in her house. They shared the same blood, and he was good with ladies, even old ladies. He didn't anticipate any problems getting along. He would just go about his life, quietly, whatever his life was supposed to be nowadays. He would stay with the widowed Mrs. McPhealy and keep her company. The future was vague for Steve McNaught, as he crouched at the side of Scotland's famous loch. He tossed a stone farther out, watching it skip six times.

Back in the car, he drove over the pass known as *The Rest and Be Thankful*, where the mountain slopes were forested, but the rounded caps bare of anything but a thin yellow grass. He pulled over at the windy top and sat in the plastic smell of his rented car, surveying this barely populated land of his ancestors. No highway here, no bumper-to-bumper cars, just a pencil mark of a road insinuated through hills and lochs where, it felt, man had never dominated; just a wind shaking the ton of metal in which Steve sat like a rattle in the hand of a baby.

On the downside of the pass, Steve stopped in a small town of white houses, which seemed to be a signature of the rural northwest. He pictured Mrs. McPhealy waiting for him in a whitewashed house like these, thick stone walls and tiny windows like he had seen in movies made about Scotland. He couldn't remember when he had told her he would arrive, but he knew he was hungry now, so he found a tourist shop with an adjoining café and took up a menu.

A waitress of no more than sixteen years was suddenly and silently at his side. He looked at her kindly and asked her advice. She talked to him, pointing to lines on the menu with her black-polished nails. He barely understood a word.

He caught "bacon," not from her, but from the smell behind the door that led to the kitchen.

"Bacon. Eggs. Sunny-side up," he said.

He automatically fell into monosyllables, as it had always worked in Mexico when he couldn't be understood. He added, "Orange juice," as an afterthought. It was already the afternoon, but for his clock the middle of the night, so he ordered breakfast.

He looked around at other patrons as he waited. Nobody met his gaze, and he didn't like to push it, because he suddenly felt the foreignness of this land.

He studied the plate the black-nailed waitress brought, but couldn't match it to his idea of breakfast. Alone in the middle of painted flowers sat a bread roll with gristle hanging off the side.

"Eggs?" he said, hopefully.

The waitress lifted the top off the roll to reveal on top of the gristle, a collapsed and over-cooked egg.

"Oh," he said.

She sighed. He thought it best to say nothing, as she set a glass of thin orange drink with bubbles and a straw next to his plate.

He winked and said, "Thank you," wondering if he was going to have to learn another word for this gesture, just as he had taken on "*Gracias*" for Mexican trips. She tutted and left. He didn't know what he had done to cause her chagrin, but he determined not to take it out on her tip. He lifted the greasy bun and ate it like he ate hamburgers, in circles around the edge until he reached a dollar coin-sized middle, where the smashed yoke sat and which he ate whole.

He wiped his mouth with the napkin, decided it wasn't a bad meal after all, and ordered another. He left the orange fizz and asked for water. On his bill, he was charged 75p. But he wasn't going to let that bother him either. It was the cost of bottled water in L.A. True, this water was from the tap, but it was probably purer.

Around another loch and then the long stretch of another, the road seemed to narrow. Steve flicked on his headlights, which cast an eerie look into banks and banks of rhododendrons running off into dark hillsides. It seemed like he was the only one on the road, the growing darkness interrupted only by his own lights and the occasional presence of another car seen from a mile away and heading past him on the road back to Glasgow as though illuminating his only way out.

Hamlets of whitewashed houses came and went, the signs driving him on along the last of the lochs down towards the Mull of Kintyre to "Locharbert." To date, it had been only a tiny scrawl on a map for him, but now was looming, thirty-two miles away according to the green signs, then eighteen,

nine. One last hamlet, and there were the lights of his destination, the land of his forebears, crouched at the base of hills
that looked like they were moving in and a sea that threatened to take it out altogether.

Steve crossed the town boundary, where a sign gave the
name both in English and Gaelic. He slowed the car along
the side of the empty front street, fighting with fingers and
teeth to unravel his page of instructions. He laid the page out
on his steering wheel, but was distracted by this first encounter with Locharbert. Without the few parked cars, the town
could have come from any era in the last century, no super-
markets, nothing modern here at all. The stone of the houses,
where it was not whitewashed, was the same stone that jutted
from hills all about, as though it had rolled into town of its
own accord. Steve sat in his car and felt the silence, as though
no people inhabited this town, at least not the noise-makers
he was used to, but some less massive stage of human existence, a whisper instead of a shout.

The car clock in red digital read five forty-five. Steve
glanced at his instructions, and took the right turn up Main
Street, past a row of small shop fronts towards the grey stone
church at the top. Lights in a cafe window indicated life. A fine
drizzle, one for which Steve couldn't find an appropriate wiper
speed, had been falling for the last fifty miles or so. It glistened
on the windows of the café and on the faces of three short
men with string around their coats who emerged from an alley
smiling, though not at him. This wasn't a rain such as might
fall on L.A., more a San Francisco fog. Yet, he could see clearly
enough to turn right past the church, then another right, and
read the street sign for Manse Brae, also in English and Gaelic.

He had only been able to doze during the flight over, and
now at the end of his journey, with the light fading, tiredness
began to drag on his shoulders. He stopped the car, suddenly

jittery from his escape from the familiarity of one country and the novelty of a land of low clouds and mist. The night, the hills, this town with its strange edifices and empty streets, the Gaelic words, the steady drizzle, all seemed to crowd him out. Yet he had nothing in America to go back to. He had two ex-wives and three sons, but the person who was Steve McNaught was just a collection of fragments refusing, in this moment, to pull together.

Steve looked along Manse Brae as far as he could until it curved and headed a little uphill. People here probably were born and died in the same houses, barricaded in stone against the elements, existence not simply given but fought for. There was a fine thread leading him to one of those houses, but all of a sudden he felt like a director again, standing in the wings of another director's movie. How could he walk onto this stage as an actor? He didn't know the story. He didn't know how it should be played or filmed, hard focus or soft.

He lifted his foot off the brake and let the car creep along the sidewalk, noticing the numbers on the gates increase in odd numbers. When he got to 23, he pushed his foot down on the brake. Effie McPhealy lived at 25 Manse Brae. The address had jumped around in his head ever since the last leg of his ancestry search had thrown up her name. But now the configuration of letters, odd words he had looked for in the dictionary, only somewhat matched what he had conjured for himself. The windows on Mrs. McPhealy's house were larger than most, and the stone walls, rather than being whitewashed like the houses nearer the shore, were a patchwork of different coloured stone.

He could see the lights in her front window, her high gate, tulips and roses up her garden path. For a moment he thought he saw the curtain sway, and for a long moment he could muster no inclination towards that house. But he let the engine die and slid the key into the palm of his hand. Perhaps he had already been spotted.

The back of the car was full of his boxes. He left them there, touched the cold steel latch of the McPhealy gate, and walked past its whining to the door with the mottled glass oval and the doorbell. Retreat was no longer an option, so he ran his hands over his stubble head, sat his sweatshirt back on his shoulders, regretted not bringing flowers and absently picked one.

He hid the flower in his hand as the door began to open.

Mrs. McPhealy was smaller than he had expected, with hair the colour of his own but under a fine-mesh net held on with clips. She wore a hand-knitted cardigan over the kind of crimplene dress one saw little of in L.A. The Steve McNaught who had pitched screenplays to production companies and regarded himself as a good talker, could come up with nothing for the woman who stood in front of him waiting for him to speak. Something about her containment warned him about who she was and who he was not, and that the boundaries should be carefully observed. He flicked the flower back into the bed before she had the chance to see it.

He held out his hand, still moist from the flower. "Mrs. McPhealy." Addressing her formally seemed to come naturally with the territory. He awarded himself a point for observation. She didn't exactly smile at him, but she didn't look mortally wounded either. He preferred not to consider how she would react when she found the plucked flower on the ground in the morning.

She took his hand and said, "Steven McNaught," and then, almost as an afterthought, opened the door to let him in.

"Steve," he said. "Everyone calls me Steve."

She closed the door behind them, her hands nervous and giving her away.

"I've been keeping your tea warm," she said. "I hope it's not spoiled."

"I'm sorry," he said, "the plane was late getting into Glasgow."

She tutted. "You can never trust an airplane. I never fly myself." She led the way across her Persian rug, turning only to ask, "Did you bring a pair of slippers?"

Steve glanced down at his wet sneakers, expensive, but a little soiled from his stop along Loch Lomond. "I'll just leave these by the door."

As he untied his laces, he caught a faint aroma of beef, and at the same time registered the presence of two bacon and egg rolls still sitting heavily in his stomach. He followed the woman out of her clean hall into her tidy kitchen, but hung in the doorway as Mrs. McPhealy went to a small closet containing a bucket and mop, and pulled from a high shelf a pair of old-man slippers made from what looked to Steve like carpeting.

She handed them to him. "These belonged to my late husband, but there's still plenty wear left in them."

Steve thanked her and slid a foot into the grooves and worn patches forged by a much wider foot than his own.

Mrs. McPhealy turned to pull a loaf of brown bread from a steel bin onto her wooden counter. Behind the smell of beef, under the odour of clean surfaces lurked the hint of something old, mould perhaps. He ran his eyes along the yellow roses of the wallpaper, talking himself into a beef sandwich. The woman was already fussing around her oven, pulling out a tray of some kind of rolled beef that he dreaded was going to require the company of more than just bread. A glass dish at the back of the oven confirmed his suspicion.

"I made you Beef Olives," she said. "I hope they're not tough. Of course, I was expecting you for tea at five o'clock."

"They'll be fine," he said, "no worries."

She seemed appeased. He was doing all right now. If he knew what Beef Olives were, he would be doing even better, but the main task was to get through them, not identify them.

"My husband was partial to a Beef Olive," she said, setting the tray on the counter. She forked three of the five Beef Olives onto a plate. "I'll give you three to start with."

He sat down at her formica-topped table already set with utensils and a folded cloth napkin in a silver ring. She set his plate neatly between the knife and fork, then added both a mound of boiled potatoes and a pile of peas. Everything looked a little curled. He couldn't remember promising to be there by five o'clock, though he might have mentioned dinner. Now he had it, and had to eat it. As he contemplated taking the first bite, a green water oozed from the peas and surrounded the Beef Olives like a moat. Mrs. McPhealy, keeping sentry by his left shoulder, left for a moment and came back with a set of glass salt and pepper shakers.

He shook salt and pepper on, which did nothing to encourage his stomach to accept what lay before him like a piece of ancient torture. Below him, on the floor, his feet sat in their slippers, looking like something that didn't belong to him.

"Very nice," he said. "Aren't you going to join me?"

"Oh, no," she said. "I always take my tea at five o'clock. But I wouldn't mind a cup of tea. You must be ready for one yourself, after all your travels."

She left to put the kettle on the oven. The flame blew into action, bringing with it a faint aroma of gas. He thought to argue that he was a coffee man, and that tea held little appeal for him, but he wanted to start on the right foot, and he did know, from being in Ireland, how attached to their hot beverage the British were.

"Eat up," she said, "or your dinner will be getting cold."

Steve lifted his fork and sliced into the Beef Olive with the side of it. It took a little sawing, but the first piece came free, revealing at the centre of the roll of meat a stuffing with the consistency of wet bread.

"Look at that," he said kindly, poised to take his first bite. "Is this a traditional dish?"

Mrs. McPhealy was back at the counter in a cloud of steam, pouring boiling water into a china teapot. "Oh, no, not at all. I didn't want to serve you anything too strange on your first night. Do you eat Beef Olives in America?"

"All the time," he said.

He had worked through one and a half beef rolls by the time Mrs. McPhealy poured the tea.

"It's best to let it brew for a few minutes," she said.

She poured milk into the cup, giving him no time to object. The dark brown tea followed, turning the mixture the colour of weak coffee.

"I'll just away to the sitting room and bring in the trifle."

She left, closing the door behind her, her distorted image retreating to a small cube in the glass, then disappearing altogether. He heard another door open and shut. He sighed, let his jaw drop and stuck out his tongue. He stood up and sat down, hoping to move the food further down his gullet. When she came back holding a large glass bowl with various shades of Jello and whipped cream on the top, he asked if he could use her restroom.

She set the trifle in front of him. "Pardon?"

"Bathroom?"

"Oh," she said, "I thought you meant the bedroom." It didn't seem to amuse her, what he meant. "The second door to your right."

He left the kitchen, closed the door, opened the bathroom door, then closed it behind him. Romans, he remembered from school, made room for other courses by throwing up their last. It might only have been jet-lag that brought him to this predicament, but it seemed he faced little by way of alternative. He emptied his bladder, then knelt over the bowl and stuck his fingers as far to the back of his throat as he could manage. He had expected a fountain of potatoes and half-masticated beef, but only managed a little of each. Peas were more cooperative. Probably every pea he had eaten was now floating in the toilet bowl, clashing with the pink toilet paper that hung at his side. He stood up, satisfied he had created enough room for Jello and cream, grateful to the Romans for their ingenuity.

Flushing peas, especially recently boiled peas, he found a harder task. The ancient Romans didn't have flushable toilets, and Mrs. McPhealy, he discovered, didn't have a very efficient one. He waited for the cistern to fill again, glancing every so often under the heavy porcelain lid. But the second flush didn't have much more effect than the first. The peas danced on the surface, laughing, because they had been cooked by Mrs. McPhealy, and they knew what kind of woman she was. Even now she had left the kitchen and was listening outside the bathroom door.

On the third flush, Steve McNaught was talking to the peas. "Go down, you little bastards. Go down! God damn it!"

Mrs. McPhealy tapped on the door. "Is everything all right, Mr. McNaught?"

He looked around for escape, but there were iron bars on the outside of the window. "Everything's fine, Mrs. McPhealy. I'll be right out."

He shut the toilet lid and listened carefully on the inside of the bathroom door. Perhaps his way was clear, perhaps it wasn't. He heard no breathing except his own. He opened the door, and there she was.

Was the toilet acting up for you?" she said.

He cleared his throat.

She walked into the bathroom and stood over the closed toilet. "The tank doesn't always fill up that well."

Steve decided that leaving was his best recourse. He had got to the kitchen door when he heard the toilet lid go up and then quietly back down again. He sat in front of his bowl of trifle, idly studying small pieces of fruit and a kind of cake embedded in Jello.

When Mrs. McPhealy returned, she was moving quickly and efficiently, like any person who had just suffered an insult. When she went to the sink to scrub the willow pattern off her plates, Steve took a healthy spoonful of his dessert. His stomach was feeling quite empty all of a sudden.

"This must be a traditional Scottish dessert," he said.

Mrs. McPhealy turned slightly, still unable to confront the man. "Trifle? I wouldn't know."

Steve McNaught, on his first night in Scotland was sent to bed for misbehaviour. She didn't spank him, except with a look she gave when he finished his trifle and stood up to be excused. She covered the trifle bowl with a shower cap, and slid it into the fridge, he suspected, for resurrection the next day.

Awake under his blue counterpane, in his manly blue room that first night in Scotland, Steve McNaught resolved that whatever the days to come might bring, he would leave regurgitation to the birds.

CHAPTER EIGHT

E ven before she opened her eyes to the light of morning, George became conscious of waves thumping onto the sand. It was the kind of thing she lived for. Her shack on the shore, however, wasn't among those things. It was only a stepping stone to Rose Cottage half a mile down the shore at Achnarannoch. She often walked along the sand, because she had lived there with her father and mother before the advent of the encyclopaedia salesman. She knew in the end she was going to get it back, but on her meagre earnings, she didn't know how. George's father had sold the cottage quickly after his wife left, but George still had memories of waking up and running down to the sea, of those yellow roses over the door.

It was a cottage, not a croft, as it had no arable land attached, save what had already been taken over by bramble and rhododendron along the path up to the road. Over that path great chestnut trees spread their limbs and in autumn dropped their spiky fruit. As a child, George had gathered them for the soft brown conkers that could be found within.

To the front of the house, a scrubby garden, always threatened by the encroach of sand, had produced peonies close to the house, then an assortment of hardy flowers down to the gate, on which George had swung when she was still

Georgianna and still small enough to fit her toes through the iron lattice.

Beyond the gate, grass had spread in lonely tufts with the odd sea pink adding a little colour, before the shore became shore proper and encouraged nothing but shells and dried seaweed. It was a coarse grey sand all along this shore, sand that did not sift through the fingers as sand in an egg-timer did. As it met the sea, the wet sand held up driftwood and articles once part of some long-abandoned boat: a faded red buoy, a sea-smooth remnant of coloured glass, a toothless comb.

Beyond the sand, the waves kept their timeless rhythm, easing their way into a young mind, for they say the sea is exactly as salty as the fluid that buoys an unborn child. For an adult there are still echoes and drumbeats as if from some distant land, where we once lived like natives before the encroach of the missionaries. In this way, George was bound to Achnarannoch, where she had once swung from the gate and where her mother had lived, like all mothers, never with any hint of leaving.

Rose Cottage had been occupied off and on over the years, but had stood empty now for two. With rotting beams and windows and crumbling stone, it would take a buyer more than the cost of the land to renovate. George was undeterred.

George lay for a while on her mattress on the floor that was partitioned from the rest of the room by hanging shawls and cheesecloth wraps. She pulled her quilt over her ears, resisting the need to move out of the warmth to her gas heater. It would have to be primed like an ancient car, but took longer to warm up; its gas canisters were cumbersome and hard to replace. Her only running water flowed through a hose from a spring on the hill; a tiny water heater above her sink clicked and hummed before dripping out in a paltry stream. It wouldn't fill a bath, if she had one. Cloths and basins of warmish water had to make do.

George didn't own a watch or a clock, and had become quite adept at pinning time down to the slant of the sun or, on cloudy days, by the tides and the degree of light. She had an oil lamp for the evenings, but her days started early, calling through the thinnest of curtains, which were really just more of the same cloths that separated her bedroom from the table where she ate and the couch where she read and napped. The toilet was an outside affair, supplemented by a chamber pot found among her father's stores. Some nights were just too wild for dashing to the outhouse, some mornings just too cold.

In the commune where she had once lived, she had followed a macrobiotic diet: rice, couscous, vegetables, and fruit in season. On coming back to Locharbert, she had modified the diet to include fish and potatoes—fish because they were free, and potatoes because they were still the only vegetable to be counted on at the greengrocers. Other items came and went in her diet, dependent on whose baby she had delivered and what currency they were prepared to pay. Rabbits had been popular this last winter, after she delivered a baby on an outlying farm. She had been promised a lamb later this spring. By necessity, George was slowly shifting towards the omnivore end of the culinary spectrum.

She had no real reason to get out of bed this morning, other than her cats scratching at the door. They normally slept on her bed, but with the moon waxing, they had gone out mousing and now were back, anxious for their morning milk. They were two sibling Abyssinian mixes rescued from an animal shelter, amber, thin-faced Egyptian felines, quite out of place with the motley local cats. They were George's one luxury, the steak of a macrobiotic life.

It was the cats that made her get up in the end. She pulled her trench coat over her flannelette pyjamas, thrust her feet into sheepskin slippers rejected by her father, opened the door

a crack for the animals to slink through, put a match under
the kettle, switched on Joni Mitchell, then hurried back under
the covers. Her hands would welcome the warmth of a mug of
tea half-hidden under the covers. The cats, knowing their milk
would have to wait, had already buried into the warmth left in
the bed by her body. The tickle of their fur on her legs was as
close to a sensual pleasure as she had had all winter.

"You moggies," she said, finding her groove in the mattress again. Her father didn't know why she had to have
two cats in such cramped quarters. He had been out to the
shack only a few times; he said the place smelled of cat pid-
dle. But George said the cats were good for her soul. At very
least, they were good companions for a lonely existence on
Scotland's western shore. Most of the time, lonely was good.

But she was forty-five now, and the men who had come
and gone during her middle years were tending these days
more towards the gone than the come. Unmarried sailors
and globe-trotters gravitated towards the young set. Some of
them were young enough to be her sons. She wasn't proud of
it; besides, she liked the older ones who were more comfortable in their skins, for whom sex wasn't a mad dash from here
to there. Men like Peter Duart, she often mused, though he
was still younger than she.

George had friends who went with grey-haired grand-
dads, but she wasn't yet there herself. She felt vital, square in
the face of the world. There was a little grey in her hair, but
her face had escaped so far any major sags, the skin still taut
across her cheekbones, any looseness in the eyelids falling
discreetly behind her deep-set eyes. Her eyes were still white
and blue where they should be, no merging of colours, no creative diversions into red.

Her father had wanted her to marry Devin Ally, because
it seemed at the time of his leaving for Glasgow University

that he had a future. George had always insisted that she had her own future and didn't need someone else's. She was grateful that Willy's prophylactic for her one encounter with Devin behind the school kitchens had prevented her from becoming another Locharbert statistic. These days, with Devin in the pub, Willy was glad his daughter had had her own ideas about marrying.

Of course, Devin Ally had always been a handsome man; even now the fact was not lost on George during her trips to The Comm. But she had never wanted children. She still didn't, except for the moments when she did. She had to keep wrestling with the notion, although she usually came out on top. She told herself it was simply her age talking: impending menopause, the prospect of a lonely old age. Her father had been trying to hide from her the prophylactics she had earlier taken for her own use, but which now she supplied to some of Locharbert's teenage girls. If George was facing menopause, Willy was staring straight at life-pause, and he had told George that a little one would brighten his life. He said *her* life, but she knew he meant his own.

As the heat spread through the small space of the shack, George sat up and reached for her book, *The Story of Scotland*. She was the only person she knew, apart from her father, who took any interest in the events that had shaped her land. Her father knew a lot of history, but it was mainly local. George was interested in the broad sweeps, the tones, the drones, the abiding forces. She knew the history of Kintyre, the peninsula on which Locharbert sat, as well as anyone who had turned it into dry-bone fodder for history books. She knew that she was really Irish, descended not only from Willy MacBrayne, Locharbert draper and supplier of prophylactics, but from a Fergus MacErc, father of Kintyre who had come over in the sixth century from Ireland. This is how George MacBrayne saw herself on a Saturday morning, reading a book in a shack on a windy shore in the middle of Argyll.

She read until the cats woke up and batted her arm for milk. But a second cup of tea took her back to bed and another half hour's snooze. The sun, hanging just above a thin layer of cloud, read close to ten o'clock, when she pulled her coat back on and trod barefoot over the bank of seaweed to the ocean's edge. The early morning noisy waves had given way to a gentle lapping. The sea rarely grew wild here, buffeted as it was by the islands of Jura and Islay. On this morning, she could barely see any island, just a faint outline under a bank of cloud.

On a sandbank a heron watched her without moving its head, its great grey wings folded around its back, its black eye shifty, suspicious. She loved the wildlife around her, even the screeching gulls and the diving gannets. From time to time an otter ferreted through the weed on the shore, making her want to put her fingers into its sleek coat and cuddle it like one of her cats. Roe deer came down from the hills sometimes, miniature replicas of their red cousins who stayed higher up. She knew without these creatures her heart would turn hard.

George took the presence of the heron this morning and played with it for a while, watching it lift its hefty wings and waft away to the other side of the bay, voiceless, saying something she wished she could hear.

She went back to dress, pulling a grey woollen jumper over her pyjamas, slipping on embroidered jeans which she had been fastening with a safety pin since the zip gave out. Porridge with brown sugar served as breakfast, tasting all the better for the salt air and the puny flame that had struggled to perform against all odds.

She had finished half her bowl when a knock came on the door. She had a couple of ladies at seven months, but none due. At seven months, a baby was really asking to end up in a Glasgow hospital. George went to the door, hoping not to find the anxious face of a father on the other side. What she found was Nicola Ally, hanging back from the door, the hood of her jacket falling over her eyes, looking in the shadow like her father had looked twenty-five years ago.

"Want some porridge?" George asked.

Nicola sat down heavily on her table. "What do you live all the way out here for? I'm so knackered after I've walked all this way, I haven't any energy left for the things I came to get in the first place."

George laughed. She already knew why the girl was there. It was the only reason any teenage girl walked the two miles from Locharbert to see her, MacBrayne the Draper's Durex counter really only an option for the men of the town. But George enjoyed Nicola more than most. She was Devin's, after all, and could have been hers.

"I thought you'd stopped running around with those wild boys," George said, sprinkling sugar over another bowl of porridge.

"I have," said Nicola. "But boys aren't exactly what's on my mind these days."

George set the bowl in front of the girl. "You've lost me."

Nicola's spoon hovered in the steam above her bowl. "Maybe I have my eye on something a little more mature."

"Define *a little more mature?*" George asked, hoping she wasn't about to hear what she suspected. She had heard Nicola was working for Mrs. McPhealy. She was also aware that Mrs. McPhealy's relative had arrived from America and that his hostess had even somewhat warmed to find him less American than she had feared. Miss Crawford in the post office was passing out the news, even though she had taken the huff when Mrs. McPhealy had passed her over as potential cleaning help.

Nicola looked away through the window. "Nice weather we're having."

George took her porridge back, leaving Nicola's spoon dangling in mid-air. Nicola had never seen George's face set like this, her eyes fixed and challenging. She had heard it said that George MacBrayne was not a person to rub the wrong way, but until now the woman had seemed like the big sister Nicola had never had.

"Look, you. I've never asked questions, and the condoms have been free till now, but I hope this mature person hasn't given you any encouragement. He's probably married, and he must be fifty-five if he's a day."

"Fifty."

George went to the sink and swilled the porridge down, a bad notion, since the sink dumped onto the sand and she'd have a flock of seagulls any minute making short work of the slop.

"That's older than your dad, you silly wee girl."

Nicola laughed defensively. "I haven't even done anything."

George took a slow breath. "Have you signed up for those night classes yet?"

"Not yet."

George sighed, studying this younger version of herself, all the same restlessness, but with no movement like the Sixties to syphon it into.

"You're going to, though, eh?"

Nicola shrugged. "I don't know if I want to go to college. I mean, what's the point?"

George's back was beginning to stiffen and hurt. Her hands agitated to grab and shake the girl, or was it just herself she wanted to shake? She didn't know, and it was making her breath waver when she exhaled.

Nicola squatted to stroke the cats. George watched her short shirt part company with the trousers and ride up

a stretch of pink back furred with light down. In a thir-
ty-year-cycle, clothes had come back around to the kind
George's own father had cast a disapproving glance at.

"Mr. McNaught's friendly," Nicola said. "There can't be
any harm in that."

"Well, I won't have anything to do with this," said George.

She turned her back as a sign for Nicola to leave. Friendly
indeed. George knew about friendly American males. Nicola's
sullen departure, the empty click of the closing door, was a
first. George's shoulders stiffened. She half went to call the girl
back. After all, she wasn't angry with Nicola. It was that man,
that callous American moving in where he didn't belong.

George thought about talking to Devin, but she knew
enough about young girls to know that opposition would
only spur Nicola on. She had no recourse but to sit still and
hope nothing occurred. There must be integrity to be found
somewhere in Hollywood, she reasoned. But she wasn't holding out much in the way of expectation.

A little while later, George was pushing her boat out into
the waves. She hopped in, drawing in the oars as she sat
down. Her cats paced along the edge of the shore, knowing
nothing was worth risking the evil water. Her fishing rod lay
in the bottom of the boat, but she wasn't any great fisher-
woman, and today she wasn't in the mood for waiting hours
for a bite. She pulled back hard on the oars, caught a crab,
and swung back into the bottom of the boat.

"Buggar!"

She sat for a moment, trying to breathe her way out of
her anger.

"Stupid girl," she said. "Let her get pregnant. It's no skin
off my nose."

Only it was.

Her easy approach to life was running up against limits on all sides these days. It had all worked fine as long as she was the centre, and forces ebbed and flowed around her, as long as she didn't have to move at all. But now she was moving out of herself. The face in her scrap of mirror was telling her different stories from the ones she learned when she was easy in summer skirts and the moral imperative was just a way of pinning a person down.

For one thing, the face in her mirror wasn't as easy to see; she had to squint a little, which made her look different. Her skin took longer to go flat after a pinch. The furrow between her eyes was becoming more of a permanent feature, not only because of the squinting, but because things seemed of bigger consequence these days. She had meat in her diet and worries that kept her awake, stirrings under her nightie that weren't as easy to satisfy because she wasn't the draw she had been and even when she was, she had too much dread of the morning after to enjoy the night before. Life in her forties was becoming much more of a moral proposition than it had been in her twenties, and she couldn't do anything about it.

She rowed hard, fighting the sea because she couldn't fight herself. She would suffer tomorrow, wake to aching shoulders, but for now it was therapy. And if she rowed all the way around to Crinan Harbour, there was a baker's wife who owed her, so she could expect a bowl of hot potato stovies and a cup of tea before the journey back. By then she might even be in the mood to catch a mackerel for her cats' tea.

It wasn't a mackerel but a whiting she caught, and she did feel better, after sitting on the harbour wall with her sausage roll, as it turned out, and a pint of cider. After all, these were the moments she lived for. When she got home, the cats went wild for the fish, arching and purring.

"If you come from Egypt," said George, "how come you like Scottish fish?"

George felt glad to be tilting towards silly as the evening drew down across the sea and the horizon lit up in its final show for the day. She ate part of the whiting herself, fried in one of the eggs which were her weekly fee from another farm. A bowl of fried tatties afterwards went down well with a smattering of ketchup.

Her father had never permitted any such stuff, and then, being macrobiotic, she wasn't allowed the sugar. But it certainly oiled the tatties; it certainly made her smack her lips, then lick her fingertips afterwards. That and the salt. But she preferred not to think about the salt at all. It wasn't even in her cupboard, as far as she was concerned.

The sun finally dipped like the last eye wink before sleep, shutting the world into darkness. George sat on her couch beneath her oil lamp, cats on her lap, trying to focus. *The instability in Scotland created the ground for political change.* George kept her eyes on the words, but her thoughts kept flying off the page. She wondered how a forty-five-year-old woman could suddenly be so enraptured by a plate of fried potatoes.

Books on such topics were abundant in her father's curiosity shop of gynaecology: oral gratification in place of clitoral. Of course, her father, suddenly deprived of a wife, had quite naturally fallen into the intellectual study of the female. It had been a wonder to George that he had never re-married. It seemed to his daughter that he wasn't that bad looking. It must have seemed that way to the postmistress, too—on Hogmanay, young George heard the two of them groaning in the bedroom next to her own to bring in the New Year.

The instability in Scotland created the ground for political change. Willy had tried to convince George the next morning that Miss Crawford had had to stay the night due her inability to hold her New Year's drink. But the thirteen-year-old George was informed enough to distinguish the groans of a single woman's dreams from a bad stomach.

The instability in Scotland created the ground for political change. And, of course, the little packet rolled in toilet paper and deposited in the kitchen bin the next morning gave the game away right there and then.

George closed the book. The instability of the ninth century in Scotland would have to wait. She had had enough of her father's sexual antics. Though there weren't many more to contemplate, she didn't want to contemplate them now. She was only glad that he had kept them out of his marital bed.

Next Hogmanay, the same scenario played itself out. George was only fourteen then, but she saw enough in her father's dusting and preening to know that he had high hopes. Doors in those days had their locks, and George made a point of locking the spare bedroom and hiding the key inside her diary. This place, she was sure, never passed the scrutiny of her father's eyes. She was wrong about this, though she didn't know until she was in her thirties, that her father had read every word, and that this was why he had been anxious for her to marry Devin Ally. It was why these days the daughter and father rarely spoke.

"That's it," George said, standing up and sending the cats off her lap.

She reached for her trench coat, pulled on her wellies, and was off to the pub along the dark road before she could argue herself out of it.

Along the road to Locharbert, George remembered how on that Hogmanay with her father and the postmistress locked out of the spare bedroom, she had hidden beneath her covers, listening to her father curse.

"God damn it to hell." But God apparently didn't, because "it" took place willy-nilly on the sofa in the living room, and it was a long time before George would be able to sit down in that place again.

"Come and sit down, will you?" her father would say, because it was the best place for watching *Bonanza* on a Friday night together. It was probably then she developed the habit of sitting on the floor, which might even have predisposed her, she mused, as she walked through the doors of The Comm, to the Buddhist tradition of meditation.

Devin Ally, wiping glasses, nodded at her, as she sat down at his bar. He reached for the Martini.

"I'll take a dram tonight, Dev."

"Right you are." Devin took it easily, though he squinted as though he were wondering about the change.

"Life's a bugger," she said.

"Right." He wiped the bottom of the dram glass and set it before her.

She didn't really like whisky, but it took its effect swiftly and without question. She downed half the glass.

Devin was watching. "Crisps?"

She shook her head. "No, but I'll take another of these."

Other men in the bar were tapping each other on the arm. Strange things were happening in the pub tonight, women knocking back the whisky, the American sitting by himself in the corner with his Coke. At the end of her first dram, George noticed the stranger, too, but passed him over as a tourist. Most strangers were English, coming in expecting a Scottish public house to be like an English one, beer and lunches on tap, friendly chatter. This man in the corner had probably expected to get a meal, and had had to resort instead to Devin's five-year-old crisps.

Devin had been to a Cash and Carry once, and he had been trying to get rid of the evidence ever since. Beef-and-onion flavoured crisps had gone first, then prawn cocktail. But sausage-and-bean had been the hardest to move. By the look on the tourist's face, the flavour was not a hit with him either.

It is entered somewhere in the chronicles of Locharbert, under the section *Interests and Activities of the Scottish Male*, how many whiskies it takes a woman to smile and how many to submit her will altogether. But these rules depended to some extent on the time of year (Hogmanay versus Easter, for instance), and the place (lavies and closes, of course, but the single bed of a spare room promised a better outcome).

There were knowing smiles, as the wild woman of the shore started in on her second whisky. At this point, an interested male might step in and buy the woman a Laphroaig which has more of the ancient peaty taste and is reputed to send the woman's senses back to a time before the influence of John Knox.

But none of the men in The Comm that night had drunk enough, and in any case, the American, whom Devin had been able to identify by his accent and from his daughter's description, had just looked over in George MacBrayne's direction.

George turned and looked back at him. She liked to fix a man with her stare, and the whisky had given her courage. He was already bringing his crisps over to the bar when Devin whispered, "McNaught," at her back. George turned back and was staring straight ahead by the time he was level with her at the bar.

"A Diet Coke," he said to Devin.

Devin shook his head, "Sorry."

"Okay," said McNaught, "How about an orange juice? But nothing with fizz."

"Right you are." Devin reached deep under the counter where he kept bottles of orange juice for tourists.

Steve McNaught tried to catch George's eye. She could feel it on the periphery of her vision, but she was keeping herself focused on the yellowed poster of McEwan's Beer behind Devin's head.

"Hi."

It was a friendly enough *hi*. It almost made her want to turn her head and look at the man up close as she said, "Hiya," back.

"I'm Steve."

She came face to face with him this time, looking into his tanned face, his brown eyes, taking in the appealing grin. At the same time, he was just another tourist, a small man, shaven of head, a little unusual in these parts but not outlandish, normal clothes, jeans, and a sweatshirt that had *Sundance* written on the left breast. This wasn't Steve McNaught whose credits rolled after a movie, Oscar nominee, bastard chaser of women. This was just an ordinary stranger.

"George," she said.

He turned his body in her direction and leaned on the counter. "I'm staying with Mrs. McPhealy."

She looked away. "So I've heard."

He took a sip of his orange juice.

"Don't you drink?" George asked. She wasn't looking at him.

Steve had thought she was giving him the eye until he got up to her at the bar and he could see she was icy. After two weeks in Locharbert, Steve had concluded that the people of Scotland weren't really that friendly. No one went out of their way to notice you or ask you about yourself. You were either there or you weren't. But he wasn't going to let himself be put off. In a way, this is why he had come.

Mrs. McPhealy had got over the incident with the peas and never served him Beef Olives again, though trifle was a regular feature. He almost welcomed it when he saw what other puddings were on offer, stodgy pastry covered with custard, lying like lead in his stomach at night when the bushes outside scraped against his window.

In the evenings, he had to get away from the McPhealy house, relieve himself of the silence. He told her he was going for walks. He didn't yet understand the workings of a town the size of Locharbert, how news is not only what is spoken outright, but what is hinted at, what the wind carries, what the walls absorb. Mrs. McPhealy knew right away that he was going to the pub. She meant to have Reverend Campbell talk to him this Sunday when he came for dinner. The two men would be alone while she was in the kitchen.

But of this, Steve McNaught was blissfully ignorant, and the pub had come to provide something of a refuge.

Steve said, "I don't drink these days. But I'd be glad to buy you another."

The men on the other bar stools nudged each other. A woman like George MacBrayne with three whiskies in her would surely stop at nothing.

"I'm not much of a drinker myself," she said, "and I almost never drink this stuff."

Steve smiled. "Hard day, huh?"

George went to smile, but thought better of it. "Yes, as a matter of fact."

And then, because it had been in her head all day, and because two whiskies is too much for most women, she said, "Stay away from Nicola Ally, all right?"

Devin Ally, who had been talking to the men down the bar, came to attention. Everyone in the room seemed to stop what they were doing.

Steve held up his hands. "Whoa!"

George said, "I'm just saying, this isn't Hollywood here. That's all."

"Okay," said Steve. "Who's Nicola Ally, for God's sake?"

The excitement over, everyone went back to their drinks. Only Devin kept near, pretending to tally figures. But since he didn't scratch his head, everyone knew he was doing nothing of the sort.

George looked into her empty glass, suddenly focused and completely unaffected by two whiskies.

"People talk around here," she said. "You had better be careful."

Steve laughed. "But I haven't done anything, except clog up Mrs.McPhealy's toilet. I've behaved since then, honest. No, I lie. I left half a glass of piss masquerading as orange juice."

George couldn't help but smile. Everyone smiled a little. They had heard about the peas and had already had a laugh about it. They didn't know about the orange juice, nor did they know what he meant.

"Okay, fine," said George. "As you say, I've had a hard day."

"More crisps?" said Devin.

Steve regarded his empty packet sitting on the bar and shook his head. "Thanks all the same."

"Don't worry," said George, "he's been trying to fob those sausage-and-bean crisps off on strangers for years."

Devin batted the air about George's head. "It's an acquired taste."

George ducked, laughing, aware that Steve was watching, aware that in the past men had called her smile "pretty." The other men at the bar tutted, annoyed because this was what happens when women started coming into the pub. They were only put out because it wasn't happening to them.

"So what brings you to Locharbert?"

Steve shrugged. "Had to get away."

She was trying to size him up, this American of few words. She looked into the back of his eyes and saw that he meant no harm. As his smile fell under her scrutiny, he looked away. She studied his face, the dark stubble on his chin turning redder by his ears, a feature he shared with most of the men in the bar;

the pores around his nose; the brown eyes. He had white and even teeth, but then that was an American feature and one that set him apart from most of Locharbert. Except for Devin. George had always liked a nice set of teeth on a man.

Steve was used to being stared at, but not through. He held onto George's blue eyes until he felt beaten and had to look away. There was too much that he didn't even permit himself glimpses at. He didn't quite feel safe with her; like a man suddenly faced with dancing the woman's part, he didn't know when to step backwards or forwards.

So he stepped forward again. "How about you?"

George took her eyes off him. "I went away for a while," she said. "But I was born here, and this place has a way of keeping its own."

"Maybe even bringing its distant own back to itself?" Steve asked.

George shook her head. "I doubt it." She looked at him and smiled, maybe with a flirting glance. "I don't give you very long. Malibu is one thing. Locharbert is quite another. You're not going to find what you're looking for here."

He smiled back briefly, showing those teeth. "But you don't know what I'm looking for."

George stood up. Enough of slipping into niceties with this man. He did, after all, belong to Malibu and the American way of being, which has as much in common with the West Highland way of being as a fish does with a dog.

She said, "Great peace, great Scottishness, great communion with the elemental? How am I doing?"

"Not even close," he said.

"We'll see," she said, and then she left.

One of Locharbert's travelled few, George had actually been to Malibu, California. She had driven along the coastal road from Los Angeles, north to San Francisco, with a boyfriend at a time when their relationship was in its wane. Their first night out, they had stayed at Malibu Beach campground. He went out to a bar called Paradise; she bought essentials at the Superstar Supermarket, sat by the fountain in the square, bathed in jasmine, watching the floating figures of those who don't appreciate the small things. It was all she could remember about Malibu, but it was enough.

She pulled up her hood. The rain in mid-Argyll would get Steve McNaught, if nothing else. George had lived in a squat in London for a while, so she knew of other types of rain, rain that came and went with clouds; rain that could be sat out, as in, "We'll just wait until it passes."

Rain on the western coast of Scotland was more like a character in a book, not an occasional one but a constant feature, so that any director making a film here would have to mention *Rain* as a character in the credits. *Hills*, too. And *Forests*. The credits would have to mention *Sky*, not a Californian sky but one that moved just above the head. What Americans thought of affectionately as "Scotch mist," was really just *Sky* coming down to see what was going on. People lived and died under this sky, the same conditions under which the Druids had lifted their great stones on the land that hereabouts had later been divided into fields for sheep.

George wandered home along the dark road, her feet instinctively following the dips and curves, in much the same way as bleating lambs find their way to their mothers in the night. An animal ran off the road into the rhododendrons, a small deer, by the scale of it. But nothing startled George, not even ghosts.

She was annoyed by this American, by his need to find icons and archetypes here. Men like Steve McNaught had happened before and would again, while the tides ignored him, while teenagers bore children and then became grandparents, while a small piece of property went in and out of the MacBrayne family.

It was for these small things George lived: for the small lap of waves, for the heron standing silent but sentry, for roses over a cottage door.

CHAPTER NINE

M rs. McPhealy had always enjoyed her drink of Horlicks before bed, which Steve learned was a sort of hot malt shake. Fortunately for him, her late husband had gone in for something a little stronger: it looked like Horlicks, steamed like Horlicks, but tasted of whisky. Steve wasn't about to count a milky nighttime drink subject to his ban on alcohol, especially since he needed to be encouraged each night into slumber. Mrs. McPhealy had pointed out that the mattress upon which he slept was made of horsehair and had come down through the family McNaught. It is possible his grandfather had once slept on it.

"It's so much more comfortable than the beds these days," Mrs. McPhealy had told him.

The mattress sank in the middle, which is where he found himself each morning, a little prickly in the bare legs and backside, but rested nonetheless from whisky and cream. Due to the absence of pyjamas in his daily wash, Mrs. McPhealy had laid several pairs of Mr. McPhealy's pyjamas on his bed. Steve pulled them on if forced to the bathroom in the night, but never went to breakfast in them.

By the time he got up of a morning, the day was already new and being spanked into shape by Mrs. McPhealy and her vacuum cleaner. He could feel the vibration even through six inches of horse hair.

Over breakfast, Steve asked Mrs. McPhealy about George MacBrayne, but only got "ochs" and tuts in reply.

"Any decent woman," she said, "would take herself off to a hospital to have her baby."

Steve assumed from the comment that George must have had a baby at home, and reasoned, therefore, that there was probably a father on the scene. He missed his own sons enough to welcome the thought of playing dad to someone else's child, but he knew from experience to proceed cautiously. He had once carried on a brief affair during a shoot with a makeup girl who claimed her marriage was over, but whose husband decided to visit one weekend. Within days, it had been all over the tabloids. According to his shrink, it was part of his downward self-destructive trajectory.

He couldn't ask Mrs. McPhealy if George had a significant other. So he asked the window cleaner, an Englishman who was also an outsider, whose way of being chimed only about a semitone below his own. Peter Duart didn't turn away or refuse to answer, didn't consider the question none of Steve's business. Peter simply shook his head and smiled the kind of smile that one man passes to another and means the topic has to do with sex. Steve sat on a chair just outside Mrs. McPhealy's back door, watching Peter go over the kitchen windows with a chamois. The window cleaner's dog sat at the car window, following his every move.

"But she has a child, doesn't she?" Steve said.

Peter came down his ladder and sloshed his rag in the soapy bucket. "Not that I'm aware of. She's the local midwife. Not exactly legal but in hot demand."

Suddenly, Steve's day looked a little more promising. A weak sun drifted out from behind a lace of cloud.

"How often do you clean Mrs. McPhealy's windows?' Steve asked.

"Once every two weeks. But the minister is coming for Sunday dinner this week, so she wanted to make the extra effort."

Steve watched Peter remount his ladder, considering the kind of culinary effort Mrs. McPhealy was likely to launch for a minister. He hadn't been to church with her yet because he hadn't got up in time. But with the minister coming for dinner, he resigned himself to going this Sunday.

As a gesture to the life he was leaving behind, Steve had brought one suit, an Armani. He had supposed that women everywhere would respond to a well-tailored suit. But he hadn't factored in going to church. Mrs. McPhealy had presented him with her late husband's tweed three piece, but, though about the same in height, Mr. McPhealy had far outmatched Steve McNaught in girth. So, the tweed suit, like the coarse wool dressing gown and the thermal underwear, went back into Mrs. McPhealy's wardrobe.

It was customary for Mrs. McPhealy to offer the window cleaner a cup of tea after the job was finished. A pot to warm the hands around was, after all, half the pleasure of the national beverage, a point not well understood by visitors from more temperate zones. Peter usually excused himself to his next job, but today he accepted the tea, much to the disappointment of his dog.

But Peter had been watching the director from a distance, and he was curious to see what the man was like up close. He had already gathered that McNaught had his eye on George MacBrayne, though there was nothing unusual in that. The only woman ever to venture into the pub, the only woman with hair to her knees and flouncy skirts above her wellies, was sure to attract attention. From what he had heard down at the pub, George had not exactly ignored the man, either. This fact would go down in the annals, and colour or dis-colour the events to follow, in what was already becoming a saga for the ladies in the Locharbert post office.

The two men sat outside Mrs. McPhealy's kitchen with their tea, and a plate of buttered pancakes at their feet.

"So how are you surviving in Locharbert?" Peter asked.

Steve had lived with Mrs. McPhealy long enough to know that she would always be within hearing distance. "Oh, fine," he said. Lowering his voice, he added, "Some things take a little more getting used to than others."

Peter smiled nervously, knowing better than the American how little voice-range affected the transmission of news. "But you've been to Scotland before," he said, "when you made the film about Culloden."

"Not strictly true," Steve said. "The way things worked out, the film had to be shot in Spain."

Peter laughed, "Oh, God. Don't tell anyone that."

Steve shrugged. "I haven't been making any great friends anyway. I don't think anyone likes me here, except for the three little guys, but somehow I don't think they count."

"It's not that," said Peter. "Around here, it just takes a while for people to get used to you."

Steve sighed. "Yeah, about two hundred years of a while."

Peter smiled. He knew the feeling well.

"There's always George," Peter said, but immediately wished he hadn't. He wasn't sure McNaught was up for George MacBrayne. She had always been affable towards Peter, but he suspected it was only because she wished Shefaline wasn't in the way. With George, other people always felt one step away from being cut into pieces.

"Do you think I stand a chance there?" Steve asked.

Even before he had finished the sentence, he became aware of Mrs. McPhealy moving about in the kitchen behind him. Peter had noticed, too, and responded with a quiet shrug.

A couple of seagulls had been flying overhead, optimistic for their chances of finishing off the pancakes. Steve was unused to pancakes slathered with butter and no prospect of maple syrup. As hopeful as the seagulls, the three brothers suddenly stopped by Mrs. McPhealy's back gate.

Steve held the plate up, encouraging them to do what they had never done before: mount the steps through Mrs. McPhealy's dahlias to her back door.

Peter said, "Whoops," and stood up to collect his buckets, as Mrs. McPhealy began rapping sharply on her kitchen window.

The pancakes were enticing, but not enough to overcome the natural fear of motherless men for fierce old ladies. The three of them turned in unison and headed back down towards the gate, making Peter's dog bark for the sudden action.

ON SUNDAY MORNING, the windows were sparkling, and the birds were joined together in chorus on Steve's window sill. He pulled the covers over his ears, but the alarm at his shoulder drew him back. The last time he had gone to church had been to a wedding. These were the only occasions in Steve's life for Christian rituals. He had tended, anyway, since the Sixties, towards the eastern traditions. Hallucinogens in the cult of Nirvana seemed a more obvious step for him than the cult of *Forgive us our trespasses.*

His busy schedule had eventually squeezed out the new practice of meditation, and without the classes, religious ritual eventually found itself on the outside of Steve's life. He still had his meditation mat, and had even thought to bring it on this trip. He had his bell, and his incense, and the picture of his guru. But he hadn't come out of his downward spiral enough yet to think of taking on board anything outside of himself. And the thought of church didn't help.

A tap on his door made him reach for Mr. McPhealy's pyjamas. Mrs. McPhealy usually stayed away when there was any question of him being in bed, but today she probably expected him to be already fully clothed. He chucked the bottoms and buttoned on the pyjama top in a hurry. Under the circumstances, it was better to stay under the covers.

"Yes?"

Not Mrs. McPhealy, but her cleaning girl put her head around the door. The famous Nicola Ally. She smiled and looked around his room, before saying, "Mrs. McPhealy wants to know if you'd care for a cup of tea."

"Do I have to?"

Nicola chewed her lip and nodded. She let a little more of her torso appear from behind the door. "We used to call her Old Feely Drawers at the school," she whispered, letting the door swing open to reveal her whole self, wrapped in a large apron. She was just tugging the wrap tight across her chest, when Mrs. McPhealy called her name.

Steve smiled. "Tell her, no thanks."

After Nicola had closed the door, he lay back in his pyjama top. So, that was the Nicola from whom George had warned him away. After his wife left him for the boy, he had tried out women of all ages, even one as old as Mrs. McPhealy, although in Los Angeles, women that age were trying to look as young as Nicola. It didn't matter that much to him, who she was. He was on the run and didn't want anything that could cause him grief. Nineteen or sixty-five, he took on nothing that would last longer than a month or two. And, in his defence, the sixty-five-year-old woman had been a director of some renown, in need of someone herself.

Nineteen-year-olds were fine to look at, he found, a boost to be seen with, but, after a few dates, the conversation tended to thin out. In the end, he had lost the will to sleep with anyone. His shrink told him loss of libido was a normal facet of depression. But Steve wanted more than just to be up and running again. He shied away from the notion of marrying, but he had begun to wonder how it might feel to be safe again.

As he shaved that Sunday morning, two and a half weeks into his stay in Locharbert, Steve McNaught wondered about buying his own place. The small mirror above the bathroom sink was split down the middle to provide access to the cupboards behind. Steve could see one half of his white-foamed face on one side and more than half on the other, making him look like Santa Claus with mumps.

What passed for a shower was a small white electric box on the wall over the porcelain bath, with a small shower head sticking out from it at an angle almost impossible to stand beneath. Mrs. McPhealy had explained to him how to make the contraption work, though she said she never used the thing herself. She had had it installed for the bed-and-breakfasters. A cord had to be pulled, and after ten minutes, the shower sputtered out its spray by the tablespoon. The white box had a dial with an arrow pointing from *cold* to *warmer*, though there was no earthly way, Steve discovered, to find a balance between the two.

Being used to a wake-up shower every morning, Steve had stood beneath this needle-point spray each morning, his feet on cold porcelain, his knees barely wet, getting ever closer to the realisation that he was simply ill at ease living in the McPhealy house. He had wanted to wait and see how life in Locharbert worked out, but he determined that morning in the split mirror that the following day would see him at the real estate agents, just to see what was on offer.

Nicola served him his muesli and grapefruit. She had been able to perform her new-found skills with the frying pan only a few times, before Mrs. McPhealy had called a halt. Her guest always left his fried bread and other remnants at the side of his plate, and she wasn't about to incur the extra cost of a cooked breakfast for someone who didn't want it. Muesli and grapefruit was what her son ate for breakfast in London, and by extension, this was what Steve McNaught was served from then on.

It suited him fine. The cooked breakfast of grease-toast, fried tomatoes, sausages, and a strip of some kind of animal innards, left him wanting to go back to bed.

Nicola hovered, trying to think of something to say.

Mrs. McPhealy called her back to the sink.

Before church, Mrs. McPhealy gave Nicola her instructions. She had never left the girl alone in her house before, but it would be better not to make the men wait for their dinner once they all got back from the service. She schooled Nicola in the way of building a fire in the living room. The girl didn't have a fireplace in her own home, and it left Mrs. McPhealy nervous. The chimney had been swept recently, but there was always the chance of a chimney fire.

"Only use half a firelighter," she told Nicola, breaking a whole brick of the petrol-smelling substance with her rubber-gloved fingers to show the girl what she meant by "half."

"The beef is already in the cooker," she said at the kitchen door, "put in the potatoes at half past eleven."

Mrs. McPhealy waited for her guest by the front door. She was wearing her fur coat today, fox, not mink. She had pulled out her old faux crocodile-skin handbag from the mothballs at the back of her wardrobe. Inside the bag, she found gloves to match the colour of the coat. She had already be-gloved herself and released her hair from its net at the mirror on the coat stand by the door.

She could hear the man moving about in his room, could see his shape come and go in the mottled glass. She didn't mind him being in her house as much as she had thought she would. After all, he was a quiet American with good enough manners. He didn't slam doors, didn't make undue noise in the night, and, if he only could get up of a morning, she wouldn't have much in the way of complaint. She hoped Alasdair Campbell would be impressed by her American relative.

Steve McNaught emerged from his bedroom, straightening the navy blue tie set against a pin-striped shirt and dark navy suit.

He raised his eyebrows for approval. "A bit much for church?"

Mrs. McPhealy smiled. "That's fine."

Though bald, he looked like the men on her father's side of the family, with his freckled skin and hair the colour of her own, now that he had stopped shaving his head and she could see it. He wasn't tall and gangly, as her own son had turned out to be. People gossiped about how he had inherited that trait, though it was true a person in Mrs. McPhealy's mother's line had long ago married an Englishman. Perhaps the height had crept in that way.

Mrs. McPhealy handed the door key to Steve as they went out, indicating that he had moved up in rank and was now fit to take on the responsibility of her house.

"We won't lock the door today on account of my cleaning girl," said Mrs. McPhealy, who had grown to like ownership of her fetch-and-carry, much in the way some owners take pride in their dogs.

They were halfway down Manse Brae before Mrs. McPhealy realised that Steve still had the key in his hand. "Would you prefer me to keep it in my handbag?"

Steve offered the key back. "The suit," he said. "It will spoil the lie of the pockets."

Mrs. McPhealy dropped the key into her bag. She wasn't sure if such concern over his clothes wasn't a bit effeminate. She had heard about men like that in America, even in London, men taken to wearing women's clothing and the like. She walked a step or two behind him, just to make sure he didn't have the walk. He didn't. She caught up with him and settled into his stride.

"Reverend Campbell," she said, "has been a friend for a very long time. We were children together." A flush came to her face. "He was a great comfort to me when Samuel passed away," she said.

Her walking companion nodded his head in understanding, a trait, she considered, not often found in a man.

"Which church were you brought up in yourself?" she asked.

"Quaker," said Steve.

"Oh," said Mrs. McPhealy, not really knowing how to respond. "I'm not at all familiar with the Quaker Church."

Steve shrugged. "Just another American denomination. Started by women, I believe."

Mrs. McPhealy said, "Oh," and they arrived at the church.

Alasdair Campbell had brought out his Easter sermon for the occasion. Effie was pleased; it was one of his best. And though she had heard it often herself, she thought it apt for a man who had not been to normal Sunday school as a child. She opened her King James at the reading and held it between his lap and hers: *He that believeth on him is not condemned: but he that believeth not is condemned already, because he hath not believed in the name of the only begotten Son of God.*

Steve began to suffer from the early morning and his birdbath of a shower. After the second hymn, he felt dizzy and was grateful to sit back down. With a tinge of longing, he watched the children dismissed to their Sunday classrooms.

Reverend Campbell cleared his throat and began to preach.

Steve picked himself up, widened his eyes, opened his ears, and told himself to listen in case there was a quiz later. He noticed Mrs. McPhealy's eyes fixed on the preacher. He had told her he had been brought up Quaker, because it was the first thing that came into his head. Now, he realised, he had confused Quaker with Shaker, a sect of celibate women that had died out in the early nineteen hundreds. He didn't know all that much more about Quakers, but he suspected now the movement hadn't been started by women.

Christianity was such a confusing religion, with its violent split between Catholics and Protestants, and then all the minor denominations in between, the doctrines of which he could never get straight. This one believed in christening, this one in baptism, this one in the Holy Ghost, this one in God knows what. And the whole combined bunch of them with a fundamental split with nature. No wonder the Sixties happened, Steve mused, as he watched the minister jawing and wagging his finger. He made a note to make the point in his pet movie.

Steve had spent three months in Rome directing the Mary Magdalene film. A well-known actor had written the script and put up the money for the film himself, so Steve had little investment, though he had taken a particular fancy to the actress who played Holy Mary, Mother of God. Unfortunately, she was sleeping with Judas. Her son, Jesus (who chain-smoked and had seven children) had green eyes, so had to wear coloured contacts, which fell out during the scene in Gethsemane. And there were hundreds of Italian extras clothed in togas, trying to look Middle Eastern. Still, Italians know how to throw a party, and it was rumoured that Jesus fathered another child on the night they wrapped. A brown-eyed one this time.

Steve looked around the congregation. This was not the southern type of European, not the partying European he had encountered in Italy, not even the happy drinking species found in Ireland. Here was sombre Europe, beaten down Europe, a people in the shadowland. He tuned back to the pulpit speech, and wondered why Mrs. McPhealy had a smile on her face. *No man cometh to the Father but by me.* Steve didn't feel as though he needed another father. The first one had been bad enough. He had come and gone during Steve's childhood, depending on how much forgiveness his mother had on hand.

There was a two-year stretch when he was there for breakfast and dinner, but there was always another secretary, another mother at the school, another phone call taken under the breath. Steve's mother and father had divorced when he was sixteen, and even now he couldn't understand his hurt about it. He had never really had a father to lose, much less to love. Steve's shrink said divorce was a manifestation of society's general fatherless malaise.

It was when his father had died of a heart attack in Tucson, Arizona, that Steve started to pick up the pieces of his family history. There had been numberless generations of Hoosiers on his mother's side; Scots on the other.

Steve felt himself stand up again. When he looked down, Mrs. McPhealy was pointing to hymn 158. The organ ran through its introduction, with more of a plod than a run. Steve didn't recognise the tune: *There is a green hill far away, Without a city wall, where the dear Lord was crucified, Who died to save us all.* Steve took the time to wonder why a green hill would ever need a city wall, but by then Mrs. McPhealy was already pointing to the last verse. Amen.

Steve and Mrs. McPhealy waited outside the church door for the Reverend to lock up. When he came round to the front, he took Steve's hand in his own.

"Now," he said, "Mrs. McPhealy tells me your grandfather hailed from Locharbert."

It took the walk home along Manse Brae to explain how Steve had come to find Mrs. McPhealy. As they walked along the street, Steve noticed the minister walking along the edge of the pavement, presumably to protect the woman from oncoming cars, of which there were two, both speeding by as the company reached Mrs. McPhealy's gate.

The minister turned to Steve. "Mrs. McPhealy keeps a beautiful garden."

The way Mrs. McPhealy smiled, the look that passed between her and the minister, the way the minister was bouncing compliments to the woman off the third party, made Steve begin to wonder about the exact relationship between this widow and her reverend guest.

NICOLA ALLY AT THE WINDOW knew the occupants of both vehicles that whizzed by. Boys from further down the mull had heard she was working up on Manse Brae and, with the café closed for Catholic Sunday, had been driving by like thunder all morning. She had waved to them a few times, but now she straightened her apron for Mrs. McPhealy and guests. Steve McNaught looked just like a film star in his suit.

She had lit the fire, to her surprise and satisfaction, in the living room, where the guests would eat. She had added the boiled potatoes to the beef, used the toilet and wiped the seat to remove any trace of herself. And with a half hour to spare, she had snuck into McNaught's room, to see what he kept from the eyes of others, anything that might bring her on the inside of his world.

She had found nothing lying on the floor or under the bed, of course, because she had hoovered the room only the day before. It was with a lazy gesture that she pulled a drawer open and ran her hand among his boxer shorts, not a thing she had ever seen worn, but had noted in American films. T-shirts lay haphazardly in a drawer beneath. She lifted a faded light blue one to her nose. It had the words *Independent by nature* embroidered on the left breast and smelled of Mrs. McPhealy's washing soap.

The bottom drawer yielded more treasures: an address book, a pad with names and doodles; a few pictures of Steve with small boys; a photograph of a woman; a bell; a thick black cushion of some kind; and a box of incense sticks. Nicola didn't know what they meant, but, because they were strange and exotic, she assumed they had to do with sex. She closed the drawer quickly, sat on the bed, and noticed his toilet bag on the table by the door. She glanced at her watch and knew she had a good fifteen minutes.

Nicola carried the bag to the bed and laid each of the items out on the counterpane: a can of shaving foam, a toothbrush and toothpaste of brands she didn't recognise, nail clippers, a small pair of scissors, and a bottle of aftershave with *Givenchy* in gold letters on the front. She unscrewed the top and sniffed. It was a heady, musky scent and smelled just like Mr. McNaught when he left for church earlier. She took another whiff, resisting the urge to splash a little on her wrists, then replaced everything. She had left the small zipped pouch to the end. She pushed her fingers in and pulled out a string of five condoms.

She covered her mouth and glanced at the door. She held them for a moment, laid them on the bed, and then in a quick gesture, pulled up her apron and slid them down into her jeans pocket. She replaced the bag to the table by the door, her heart thumping hard, not knowing if she could carry out the deed until she was on the other side of the door and heard Mrs. McPhealy opening the gate.

She went to the front window to make sure, set the guard up to the fire, then retreated to the kitchen to check the oven. When Mrs. McPhealy came into the kitchen, Nicola stood up and clapped her hands together the way her father did when he couldn't think of anything to say. It was the first time she had ever felt any connection to him.

"It's a nice fire you've built, Nicola," Mrs. McPhealy said. "But it will need a shovel of coal now."

Nicola went outside to the coal shed, the little plastic packets working lower into her pocket, crinkling near her crotch. She dug into the heap of dusty black pebbles until the shovel was almost too heavy for her, then staggered back into the house and through to the front room, where the men sat on either side of the hearth.

Mr. McNaught jumped up. "Here, let me help."

As he took the shovel, his hand brushed against hers. She smiled for this intimacy, the brush of hands, the communal condoms. He tipped the coal around the flames, making sure not to extinguish them altogether. When he stood up, he handed the shovel back to her with a smile.

"Thank you very much, Mr. McNaught," she said.

He came close and said, "Steve," in a low, soft voice.

She blushed.

He was taking his jacket off when she left. The minister still sat in his black cassock, sipping the sherry Mrs. McPhealy had poured before going to the kitchen.

"Nice girl," Steve said, laying his jacket over the back of the chair and carefully rolling his shirt sleeves to the elbow.

The minister was sucking in air, indicating disapproval. "The mother is fell anxious about that one."

"Really," said Steve, not really wanting to know why.

"It's what happens to the young people of this town, always the pull away from the straight and narrow. It's a dark place to live, Mr. McNaught, and no place darker than that public house on the Front Street."

Steve picked his sherry from the hearth. "Young folks just need a little room to maneuver." Steve cleared his throat. "My son Eli is at a similar stage."

"Oh," said Reverend Campbell, "I wasn't aware you were a married man."

Steve pursed his lips around the sherry glass and glanced at the door for Mrs. McPhealy. It was the first time he had ever looked to her for rescue.

There was still silence when Mrs. McPhealy appeared, saying, "Gentleman, if you'd care to take a seat at the table."

Steve eased his napkin out of its silver ring, wondering how to make his twice-divorced status any less shocking in a town where marriage appeared to be of the swan variety. Since Steve's recent history with women was better likened to the practices of a tom cat, he decided instead to ask about Nicola's family. Reverend Campbell was able to fill him in up to four generations of Allys, ending with Nicola's father in the pub and his brother Iain attempting to be an actor in London.

"We had high hopes for Devin," said Mrs. McPhealy, setting a tray of sliced melon in the centre of the table.

"Please," she said, "help yourself."

It was the first time Steve had realised any connection between the cheerful bartender and the friendly girl who brought his breakfast. Now that he thought about it, he could see the resemblance. And it gave him another reason not to regard the girl in any light but as an employee of his host. She had blushed when she brought in the coal. She was a funny mix of innocent and worldly.

The melon was so ripe and juicy, Steve was almost tempted to take another slice. But he didn't know what else lay in Mrs. McPhealy's kitchen waiting to be moved onto this white-linened tablecloth, something perhaps less pleasant.

He decided to wait. Mrs. McPhealy and the minister were talking for the time being, leaving him to his thoughts. He watched the way his hostess dabbed her mouth while the minister was speaking, the shift of her knees under the table. He noticed how the minister had to look away every so often while she was speaking.

It would have been written into a script as, *As the man and woman exchange small talk, their body language belies their true feelings.* He had directed a scene like this between Bonnie Prince Charlie and Flora MacDonald during their passage over the sea to Skye. That, too, had been filmed in the Mediterranean, where there was less risk of death if the actors fell in.

Nicola brought in a platter of roast beef surrounded by roasted vegetables. Steve looked around for a bottle of wine, but the only drink forthcoming was another glass of fizzy orange juice. Mrs. McPhealy still thought it was his drink of choice.

Still, the meat was tender, the potatoes crisp and salted just enough. A large gravy boat was passed, eliciting a tasty brown coat over everything. Steve sat back to enjoy what was, after all, universal food, something his mother might have concocted in Indiana. He wouldn't have been able to accept the glass of wine anyway, but its presence would have rounded things out, the cheerful tinkle as it hit the crystal glass would have brought something to the occasion. Steve missed being able to drink, even with the loophole he'd found in his nighttime milk. He had accepted the glass of sherry out of politeness; it was after all more sugar than alcohol.

Reverend Campbell sliced through his meat in a way that Steve couldn't, since Mrs. McPhealy had decided from observation that a fork was all an American used. Steve had watched the British pushing food with their knives onto the backs of their forks, and had just given in to what he was used to, plain old American fork-eating.

Of course, meat was a different proposition. A steak knife was what was required, but he got the feeling that Mrs. McPhealy took pleasure in watching him struggle. For this meal there was a plate of bread on the table and a small floral saucer holding butter that came with a small knife. Steve took the butter knife when no one was looking, but it was proving next to useless.

"Mrs. McPhealy tells me you're involved in the film industry," the minister said.

"I have a few movies to my credit," Steve said. "Or discredit." He laughed shyly.

"And," said the minister, "I'm told one of your films concerned itself with the life of Christ."

The minister rolled the "r" in Christ. Steve could feel himself backing up already. He set the butter knife against the edge of his plate. "The life of Mary Magdalene, actually."

"I'm told the actors spoke in Hebrew," said the minister. "And I'm wondering why, since Our Lord spoke not Hebrew but Aramaic."

Steve felt the space around him tighten. It was so damned long since he made the film, he couldn't remember who spoke what and in what language. Italian was his main impression. Maybe it had been Aramaic. After enough wine, all languages become one.

"And I hear it is your opinion, Mr. McNaught," the minister said, "that Mary Magdalene was Our Lord's girlfriend?"

Reverend Campbell leaned on the word *girlfriend* as though it were a poison he needed to eject forcefully from his throat.

Steve held up his hands in defence. "I didn't write the movie, only directed it."

"I see," said the minister

The scrape of knives on Mrs. McPhealy's willow-patterned plates tried hard to fill the silence.

"Of course," said the minister, "Our Lord led a life of celibacy. Of that there can be no doubt. He didn't need girlfriends, Mr. McNaught."

Steve decided to play ignorant. His fork was tussling with a particularly tough piece of meat.

Mrs. McPhealy jumped up. "Och, Steven, did Nicola forget to give you a knife?"

She took the butter knife from his plate and hurried out to the kitchen, closing the door behind her. She wasn't given to calling him by his proper name, so Steve figured he was on the right side of the war for once. Both men chewed, staring at their hostess's knife and fork propped against the side of her plate.

"Of course, I don't go out to the films very often," Reverend Campbell said. "But I remember the young folk talking about your film *Culloden*."

"Yes," said Steve. He could feel his neck go against the cold steel of this man's guillotine again.

"It must have been gye cold making the film way up in the northeast of Scotland," said the minister.

Mrs. McPhealy returned, setting a serrated knife at Steve's left and the newly washed butter knife back in its saucer. Steve hoped this would be distraction enough for him to disregard the question, but the minister was still looking at him.

"Mrs. McPhealy," said the minister, "I was just asking Mr. McNaught about filming the Battle of Culloden."

Mrs. McPhealy said, "Och, Steven, we're not giving you a moment's peace to eat with all this chatter."

During pre-production, Steve had argued for using the land that had been preserved as an historical site to the south of Inverness. But the prospect of constant bad weather won the argument in favour of shooting the film in Spain. It was nothing personal, just part of the movie process.

"It must have been cold in Culloden, was it not?" said the minister.

Steve smiled, "Especially for the men in kilts."

The sound of knives on plates took over again. Jokes about kilts and related body parts was not fit talk for Sunday dinner, especially with a woman over sixty present. Steve gave up, settled into enjoying the food, and smiled at Nicola, his only ally, when she came in with pudding.

"Pudding," when it was not trifle, ran the gamut from soggy canned fruit swimming in a pool of nasty-tasting milk from another can, to doughy pastry spread with jam, rolled several times and served with bright yellow sauce. The overriding feature of pudding, Steve had decided, was "soggy." But this time Mrs. McPhealy surprised him. In Nicola's hands was a tray balancing three sundae glasses, containing ice cream, raspberries, whipped cream, and chocolate wafers tucked into the top.

It cheered up the dinner no end.

"This is wonderful," Steve said, making Mrs. McPhealy look pleased and Reverend Campbell suspicious.

"Alasdair has always been partial to a dish of ice cream," she said, making the minister clear his throat.

Steve began to relax. The ball had just been volleyed into his court. "Mrs. McPhealy tells me you have known each other since you were children."

The minister patted his lips with his napkin. "Mrs. McPhealy was friendly with my sisters."

Steve scooped ice cream from the top of his glass. "And you must have known Mr. McPhealy well. Did he also grow up with you in Locharbert?"

It did not go undetected by Steve that a look was exchanged between Mrs. McPhealy and the minister.

The minister said, "Mr. McPhealy was from the Isle of Bute in the firth of Clyde." But the way he spoke the name Mr. McPhealy had "rival" written all over it.

"Really?" asked Steve.

He could have left it at that, moved on and talked about the hollyhocks swaying just over the edge of the window. But he figured he was on his way out of this house, anyway. And he didn't much feel like playing the pawn in this age-old match of chess.

He turned to his hostess. "So where did you and Mr. McPhealy meet?"

Again the glance to the other man. "My husband was an engineer and was sent over to Inveraray when they built the bridge there by the castle."

"The stronghold of the Campbells," said the minister.

"He couldn't find a church to his liking in Inveraray, so he would catch the bus down to ours every Sunday morning. Of course, Reverend Campbell wasn't the minister in those days."

Spoons in glasses. Steve smiled undetected, for both of the other heads were looking down.

"Of course," said Alasdair Campbell, "this was all long after your grandfather had left Locharbert."

"True," said Steve, willing to concede the truce and finish his ice cream sundae in peace. "I've never been quite sure why he did leave."

There was something in the way they didn't answer that made Steve push a little further. "Do you know, Mrs. McPhealy?"

She shook her head quickly and looked down at her sundae accusingly.

"It's like I was telling you, Mr. McNaught," said the minister, "the youth of this place are always falling into dirty ways."

Steve wanted to ask the exact nature of the dirtiness his grandfather had fallen into, but the agitation of Mrs. McPhealy stopped him.

"This really is a great sundae," Steve said.

The rest of the meal was given over to similar emptinesses. After dessert came a plate of shortbread and a cup of tea. Steve had reconciled himself to the brew to the extent now that he could almost enjoy each sip between bites of the shortbread, which he had come to know as a wonderful Scottish invention.

"I hope to see you next week from the pulpit," Reverend Campbell said later in the afternoon, as he took his leave at the door. Steve noted the absence of any handshake between Mrs. McPhealy and her guest. Steve went into the kitchen to leave the two by the door together and found Nicola in rubber gloves at the sink.

He came to her shoulder and said quietly, "He has the hots for her, doesn't he?"

Nicola giggled. "Hots?"

Steve picked a tea cloth off a hook and began drying plates. He didn't notice Nicola glancing at him as she set the dripping crockery on the drying rack; he didn't even notice her rubber finger tips brush against the back of his hand. Steve was staring out the window at the coal shed, wondering what his grandfather could have done to bring such shame on the house of McNaught.

CHAPTER TEN

George MacBrayne washed her morning cup and porridge bowl at the sink. An ache between her shoulders made her lift her elbows to shoulder height and expand her chest. It used to be that ache followed a long birthing night on her feet or afternoons of searching for whelks on the sands, but now it was almost constant. Forty-five wasn't being a kind year for her. Forty-five saw its role as reminding her of her mortality.

George's two cats rubbed their backs against her ankles.

"All right, you sleekit wee beasties," she said, slipping her feet into her slippers and going outside for the milk; it kept better in a little dugout she had made and covered over with a piece of corrugated iron. The air was warm, but low fast-moving clouds were moving over from the island of Islay and looked likely to vent themselves on the mainland. A fine drizzle sprinkled her hand as she carried the plastic jug of milk inside.

"Looks like that's in for the day," she said to the cats, which didn't care much what the weather did. They had prowled the night after rodents, eating all but the bitter green gall. A day on George's bed after a saucer of milk was right in line with their plans.

George was just as content to stay put, too. She sat at her window, watching the swell of the pock-marked sea, unable to see any of the islands now. She was still under a cloud herself, thinking about Nicola Ally.

George had been around Nicola's age when she and Devin had ended up together at the back of the school kitchens. Devin was skinny in those days, showing barely any promise of what he would become. It had been after a Valentine's dance in the school gym, the loud music still deafening their ears. Out of the DJ's turning sparkle lights, the Cinderella dance hall had reverted to the sweaty gym.

Newly attached couples had dispersed from their last kiss to the playground where tired parents sat in parked cars. George, who had left before the snogging slow dance, lit up a cigarette at the back of the school, wanting to face her father like she wanted a firing squad. He had pushed on her the facts of life, as if she hadn't gleaned what she needed from the school toilets and boys with twenty-five hands. She listened, because it was easier than explaining why she didn't need to. She let him urge the birth control upon her.

He said, "Take it. Someone's bound to need it."

It made her wonder what he had got up to in his own youth at school dances, but she didn't wonder for long. She knew the man was oversexed. And she didn't want to take after him in any regard, especially not this. Still, Devin Ally had surprised her with how he looked in his jeans with the cuffs rolled, his shirt open at the neck, leaning on the outside edge of his trainers at the back of the school. She stubbed her cigarette out with the heel of her lace-up boot.

"Aren't you going home?" he said.

"Would you," she said, "if you had my home to go to?"

He shook his head and laughed, showing those teeth that would defy even a drunken dentist.

"I didn't see you leave the dance." He stepped a little closer. "I was looking for you."

She studied his face, realising she had missed the prelude to this moment, the furtive glances of a skinny boy who was clever enough to help her with her maths, but not noticeable enough to fancy. In the dark behind the school kitchens, George, who was still Georgianna in those days, looked past the few pimples and saw a handsome face, at least one that would become so.

"Come here," she said, as though she were used to ordering boys to her. As though her stomach wasn't flipping and threatening to empty crisps and pop and other dance fare onto the sparse grass at her feet.

He walked over, but he didn't come close.

"Do you fancy me, then?" she said, remembering the flunky in her pocket, and deciding in that minute, that now was as good a time as any to use it.

He stepped into her space and said, "Aye, a bit."

She reached her lips to his, and knew then, and in the half hour afterwards, that "a bit" didn't come close to the feeling Devin Ally had been harbouring in those jeans. She thought to pull on his reins a little, but, *What the hell*, she thought. *They do this all the time in films.* No questions asked. Natalie Wood and James Dean in *Splendour in the Grass*, for a start. And Devin was a nicer boy than James Dean. George found herself hanging onto his collar and calling him "Dev." Dev didn't know how to use the condom. When George realised she didn't either, she sat back on the grass, one leg out of her trousers, and laughed.

It made her smile now, as she stood at her window, mindful of her purring cats, the rain splatter on the roof. She took a sip of her second cup of tea that morning, wondering if Devin had managed to fit the contraption on properly in the end, or whether she was just not that fertile.

Nicola Ally had been born nine months after Devin and Anita had married. Anita was a church-goer and must have held out for the wedding night. Willy had never taken George to church. Sex had definitely triumphed over religion in his case. Sex hadn't led George to any religion, although the Tantric yoga she had learned in the commune had added a new dimension. Hers was the God of small things, of small epiphanies, and then something close to the profound when she watched the sun stripe the sea red as it descended beyond the islands into its dark velvet bed. It was the quiet in all of those things that hinted to her of something present but unseen.

George sighed. Nicola was trying to find her way, just as George had. It didn't look as though she stood any chance with the director, anyway. Nicola would get over him and move on. In the best case, she would emerge untangled onto her own path, as George had had to do.

George dressed quickly, shut the door on her sleeping cats, and made off in her raincoat down the road to Locharbert. She took the main road, instead of the path, in hopes of a passing car. With her last three condoms in her pocket, she was on a mission to get to Nicola. She had taken a box at New Year from her father's drawer, dallying with the possibility of a cuddly Hogmanay herself. The holiday had seen her supply depleted, to a teenage girl here, another there, all friends of Nicola's, and Nicola herself at one point making off in a car, wearing thin-strapped sandals and a body-hugger, waving thanks.

Hogmanay used to be called the "daft days" and was designed for the expression of all manner of daftness, especially sex. It was the reason the church slammed its door in Hogmanay's face. Last Hogmanay, George had gone home alone. Sleeping by herself was beginning to feel like her natural state; nothing daft about her these days.

A car slowed and crept behind her, its headlights making the rain shine on the road in front of her. A ladder swaying on the top of the car came precariously close to her head as she ran back and opened the passenger door.

"Peter, you're an angel," she said, climbing in and slamming the door that hung at such an odd angle it needed slamming. "I was about to drown."

Cuilean licked her face from the back seat.

Peter let the Volkswagen roll back onto the road. "I didn't know you believed in angels."

"Are you joking?" she said, "I'm in the business of delivering angels."

Peter chuckled and looked back at the road. George's face was ruddy with the walking, and the rain had curled the hair that fell from the sides of her hood. For a moment he played with the notion of saying how attractive miserable weather could make her look. But he left it alone quickly. He and Shefaline had their own groove and these days were in a conspiracy to bring George and the American into a liaison of the Hogmanay variety.

"Just drop me at the café," George said.

In Locharbert, Peter pulled over beside the windows that streamed but never got washed. Only the three brothers stood outside.

George put her hand on the door handle. "Thanks a bunch."

Peter and Shefaline had never had George out to dinner before, and he didn't quite know how to get to the point of asking.

"How about dinner?" he said. George cocked her head, as though weighing what the invitation meant. "Shefaline and I would really like for you to come to dinner on Saturday."

"Oh," she said. "All right, barring any sudden appearance of angels."

"Quite." Peter laughed, as the door swung from her hand and she climbed out into the rain, the dog at her heels. "Barring that."

She chased the dog back into the back seat, and was just about to slam the door shut, when he shouted, "Seven o'clock!"

George heard. Inside the café, they heard. With such a woman as George MacBrayne, it wasn't surprising, said the nods. It wouldn't be surprising if Peter's wife knew and approved. You could never be sure with these continental women. Some of the more subdued whispers were already toying with the notion of three-to-a-bed.

George walked right in and headed for Nicola Ally. It had been a safe bet to find her here amid the pie-and-beans and raspberry ices.

Nicola was still sulking from her earlier rejection and didn't look up.

"Your mother wants you," George said, nodding at the door.

Nicola smiled to herself, knowing this was no messenger from her mother. She plied herself from the booth of rebel girls and randy boys, and went outside with George into the rain.

"Here," George said. She held her fist out, palm down. "Someone might need these."

Nicola took what was offered and went back to the chatter and the society of smokers.

Steve McNaught caught sight of George in the rain as she turned off Main Street and onto Front Street. With a raincoat that came almost to her ankles, she looked like a walking tent. He thought she was funny, anyway, and looked forward to some flirting and repartee on Saturday night at the Duart's house. He had already decided against wearing his Armani suit, but he had a Norwegian sweater to wear over jeans for a classy yet casual look.

He had just been at the real estate agent's office and picked up a couple of brochures, over-inked pictures of available houses. He flipped through them while he was standing in the close, waiting for the rain to stop. Coming from California, he still counted it a possibility that the rain would stop.

He had already decided he didn't want to live in the town itself; he didn't want any neighbours spying on him. A cottage had caught his eye. It was a few miles out of town along the shore. In America, they would have called it a "fixer-upper." But he liked the idea of being able to hear the waves at night and in the morning when he woke. He liked the yellow roses that had grown up around the door.

CHAPTER ELEVEN

T hrough all Steve's years of dining in plush restaurants, he had garnered a respectable knowledge of wine. He and his second wife had toured a few wineries in Sonoma County, and he learned the correct procedure for sniffing and quaffing. It made him look more of a connoisseur than he was, but it impressed the ladies when he could tell a fruity Rioja from a Pinot Noir. He could put a taste to most of the names on any wine list.

Steve McNaught stood in Locharbert's one off-licence on Saturday afternoon, picking through its wine in disbelief. Scotland had obviously come late to the notion of fermented grapes. He picked a riesling and a white zinfandel, not because he liked either, but because he recognised the vineyard. Vaguely.

The bottles sat in a brown paper bag on his dresser, while he stepped into his jeans. In this rainiest of countries, the appliances in Mrs. McPhealy's house didn't stretch to a dryer. In the short space between downpours, wet clothes were dashed from the washing machine to a sagging outside clothesline with wooden props. On a very good day, the clothes would take only an afternoon to dry. Nicola would fold them, jeans and boxers alike, and lay them on his bed in a pile resembling carefully laid-out planks. After their stint on the washing line, the clothes, Steve wrote in letters to his sons, could stand up and walk off by themselves.

Thrusting his legs into stiff jeans was something Steve was taking his time getting used to. When he moved into his own place, he told himself, he would install a dryer. In another new phenomenon, his shirts were always ironed here. He wasn't used to creases down the arms, which, under his sweater, no one could see anyway. As he pulled his wool sweater over his head, he noticed it had taken on a heavier, more pungent quality since being in Scotland.

In the bathroom's split mirror, Steve ran a deodorant stick under his clothes into his armpit, lending a fragrance that in this damp climate also seemed sharper. His cropped hair had grown too long to keep standing, and had begun to turn over. He now looked like an army deserter slowly reabsorbing into civilian life. He was even losing his tan. He brushed his teeth, then went to report to Mrs. McPhealy, who was knitting on three needles by the fire.

"Do you do much knitting?" he asked.

"Och, no, not at all. In fact, I haven't done any since my son was wee."

Steve noticed the net was gone from her hair, and it wasn't even Sunday. It was very fine hair, like his own, not the kind to grow down into a ponytail like the one sported by the hairball his wife had run off with.

He weighed a ball of grey wool in his hand. "What are you knitting?"

"Just a pair of socks," she said. "Is that you away to the Duarts, then?"

Steve nodded. "Too bad Peter doesn't still live at the castle. I wouldn't have minded checking that out."

Mrs. McPhealy sucked air through her dentures. "Such a waste of a life."

When Steve turned to leave, she said, "You'll not be late, though."

It wasn't quite a question, but Steve did think to ask how late was late. He suspected "late" meant just after dark.

He said, "I doubt it."

She looked up from her knitting. "I'll have your supper ready."

"Right you are," rolled off Steve's tongue without a thought. Stiff jeans and the odd colloquialism were becoming par for his course.

Steve climbed into his car, which he rarely did these days. It was still on rent from Glasgow Airport and must have run into hundreds of dollars at this point. Still, it was a comfort, smelled like any new car, without any trace of mould, and, if he was honest, promised a last escape out of here.

The afternoon rain had left an unseasonably warm breeze. In the fading light, small colourful birds of varieties that Steve wasn't used to swooped daintily across the path of his headlights. He rolled the window down an inch. Ever since his arrival he had been impressed by the smells, at first because they weren't familiar, but now just because they were so overwhelming. The air in Los Angeles didn't smell of earth, the grass didn't smell green. Bracken, which is what the locals here called a type of tall fern, had a smell acrid as sweat. Even the ocean here smelled saltier, somehow fishier.

Steve passed a sign for Oban at thirty-five miles distant and Killinochinoch at five. On this single-track road it mattered little whether he tended more to the left or right. He slowed the car, realising he was driving fast, as was his habit. Before a compact hump-backed bridge he almost came to a stop and noticed, in doing so, a small deer-like creature drinking at the side of the stream. It bolted; Steve drove on and passed the ruins of a castle outlined on a hill with a pinkish sky behind. How often he had worked hard to recreate scenes like this on film. No wonder so many battles and momentous events had taken place here—the landscape almost demanded it. It was certainly hard to understand why his grandfather had ever left.

Steve hadn't thought to wonder if George might be in need of a lift out to Killinochinoch. He had simply expected to find her there, in the manner he was used to finding people. The need for other people's transportation wasn't a question in his land of independence and six-lane highways. So, driving up behind a small ambling tent two and a half miles along the road caught him unawares.

And it only occurred to him, as he passed George, that she wasn't walking for the pleasure of it.

He pulled up sharply and wound down his window. "Need a ride?"

George smiled sarcastically. She climbed in.

"You should have told me," he said, pulling back onto the road.

She said, "In Scotland, we walk."

She looked out of the window. Steve glanced at her, but didn't know how to proceed. Like so many visitors between countries that share a common language, he felt he should be conversant in the idiom thereof. But he was at a loss. Was she angry that he hadn't just shown up on her doorstep and offered her a ride? He didn't even know where she lived. Was she just tired from the walk? Perhaps she felt awkward in the confines of his car?

"So you grew up here," he said.

She didn't look at him. "My father owns the draper."

Steve slowed as they drove past the yellowed-tin sign for Killinochinoch. The lit windows of the first few houses announced the bend in the road that Peter had told Steve to take.

"You seem different from the regular locals, though."

"I'm not."

The road grew narrower as the car rumbled off the tarmac and onto a dirt road, at the end of which sat Peter's house pushed back a little against the hill.

"This is cool," Steve said, as he parked by the wall. Through the window, they could see Peter's wife moving around the kitchen.

George didn't answer. She just got out and started walking into the small courtyard at the back of the house. Steve followed her, the evening suddenly looming ahead of him like the hills.

He petted Cuilean's head on the way into the cottage. He hadn't met Peter's wife before.

"Shefaline," she said, taking his hand and smiling in a way most un-Scottish when he handed over his brown bag of wine.

"Not much of a selection, I'm afraid."

"Isn't it terrible?" she said.

He smiled and patted her arm. She landed a *petit bisou* on his cheek. He gave her one back. Such is how lonely travellers greet each other in foreign lands.

In the small living room by a fire, George was talking to Peter, who was wearing a leather waistcoat and a scarf sportily tied about his neck, a different Peter from the window-cleaning version. And the living room was different from others Steve had encountered in Scotland, particularly that of Mrs. McPhealy. This one resembled certain houses in America lived in by adults who had been teenagers in the sixties. *Funky* was the American word used to describe such places. *Messy* was how Mrs. McPhealy and the rest of Locharbert would view it.

Steve studied the large watercolours on the walls, local landscapes mostly. He noticed *Shefaline Duart* written small in the right hand corners of the paintings. Within his peripheral vision he noticed George, who was standing alone now with a sherry glass in her hand, looking out of place and annoyed. The gateway to George-dom was looking on the verge of slamming shut.

"I like your paintings," he said to Shefaline, as she came from the kitchen with a plate of fish slices on cocktail sticks. "Perhaps I could buy one for my new place."

"You're moving out of Mrs. McPhealy's?" Peter asked.

Steve shrugged. "Well, sooner or later."

There was no point in starting rumours yet. They might reach Mrs. McPhealy's ears before he had had time to tell her himself. But the picture of that rosy cottage had stayed with him, even though it was run down and would need a lot of work.

"What do you say, Shefaline?" he asked. "Something for over my fireplace?"

Shefaline reached for the painting over her own fireplace. "Here," she said. "No charge."

Steve had liked this one in particular. It was of a simple, crumbling, grey stone wall, with grass growing on top. The light from an evening sun made a person want to reach out and touch it.

"I couldn't just take it," he said.

"Not at all," Peter said. "It's a house-warming gift."

Steve said what he was supposed to say in such circumstances. "I don't know what to say."

What he wanted to say was, "George, what do you think?" But she was making a point of not paying attention. Out from under her raincoat, she looked slender in a blue dress with the bodice and ties open at the neck. Tiny bells on the ends of the ties fell to her waist and made a tiny sound as she crouched and fussed over the dog. Under the window, a table had been set with a batik tablecloth and a large candle striped with long drips from an earlier burning. A vase of daffodils sat in the window bottom.

Steve propped his painting carefully against the wall, then took another fish hors d'oeuvre from the table. Peter went to help his wife in the kitchen, winking at Steve as he left.

Alone with George, Steve studied the rain on the window. He took another piece of fish.

"These are tasty," he said.

George stood up and looked at him for a moment. "Razor fish."

Steve took a closer look. "No kidding."

She almost smiled. Peter came back with a dish of small potatoes floating in butter, and, by the smell of it, garlic. Shefaline followed with a platter bearing a leg of lamb.

"Sit, sit!" she said, gesturing with her free hand for Steve and George to take places opposite each other at the window end of the table. "Darling, don't forget the *haricots*."

Peter came back and set a bowl and a board of braided bread on the table, his wineglass tucked under his arm. He dimmed the lights, then put on some music.

It took only a moment for Steve to recognise it as the film score from his *Culloden* movie.

"You've seen at least one of my movies," he said.

"I heard you make films," George said. "Any good ones?"

Steve tried not to show his pleasure.

"Indeed," Peter said, pouring wine into four large glasses.

Steve went to place his hand over the top of his glass, but he hadn't felt this good in a while. Even when drinking Mrs. McPhealy's nightcaps, there was always a little guilt insinuating itself into the bottom of his cup.

Steve smiled. "A few of them made a buck or two."

George reached for the heel of the bread, as though she might throw it at him.

It took Steve well into his third glass of zinfandel for him to contemplate taking George on. The lamb had been too good to leave at a first helping, but after the plates had been cleared and cheese brought to the table, he was beginning to wish he had had more reserve. The cheese, Shefaline told him, had been sent by her father and was a kind of Brie, but the crust thinner, the centre more gooey. Steve couldn't leave it alone. He toasted the French. He toasted window-cleaning, and then he toasted the art of midwifery. George, who had passed on the zinfandel but drunk a good amount of Shefaline's French wine, even smiled.

She lifted her glass. "I propose a toast to America. No, to Steve's wife."

Of those awkward moments when the right word can move the proceedings into a more comfortable zone, this was not one of them. Steve's first thought *Which one?* was superseded by a confusion as to how George knew about any wife. He was taking one of his first lessons in intra-Locharbert communications.

"Oh, God. The minister," he said out loud. "Of course."

And then he began to laugh, perhaps because of the wine and the fact that it had been a while since his liver had had to process three glasses of wine. Perhaps because weeks of tiptoeing around Mrs. McPhealy had finally got the better of him. Perhaps because he had finally let go of his latest marriage fiasco and was safely on the other side. But he put his chin on the heel of his hand and laughed, quietly at first, and then in a silly but noisy sort of giggle. The dog came to him, wagging its tail.

"For your information," he said, "there have been two wives."

He no longer cared what the midwife thought. He might regret it in the morning, but he had had it with Locharbert rumour-mongering.

"Which one would you like to toast? There's the one I married in college, or the one who ran off with a hairball?"

George lowered her glass a little.

But Steve was undeterred. "And while I'm at it, there are more secrets. *Culloden* was not filmed in Scotland, but in Spain. I fought it, but in the end I sold out. I had an affair with the hairstylist on that set and was beaten up by her husband in the tabloids. What can I tell you, folks, I am a loser of the first order."

"*Non,*" said Shefaline. "*Tu es chouette!*" She blew him a kiss. "We all have our confessions."

Peter looked at his wife quizzically. She merely shrugged.

"I had an abortion once," George said suddenly.

George looked Steve in the eye and tried to smile. Any witticism that might have saved the moment was stubbornly evading him. She hadn't dropped her dress, but she seemed oddly bare, and he was scrambling to cover her up.

"The father already had a family." George took a swallow of wine. "He didn't want another."

Peter asked for the potatoes to be passed.

Under the table, Steve rolled the edge of the tablecloth around his finger. "Well, he was crazy."

Flirtation was familiar ground to him, but this felt more like a body rescue. George finished her glass and held it out for a refill.

Steve poured her more wine. "It's a good thing I'm taking you home tonight."

George withdrew her glass. "Is that what you think?"

"Well, not 'take you home,'" Steve said, wondering how he always managed to get on the wrong side of her. "Just that I'll be driving."

They talked through three courses and the same number of bottles of wine, but Steve was on edge, uneasy over what had happened. They wanted to know about Hollywood, and he told them a little about his breakdown and the forces that had been at play.

"That's what you get for making silly films," George said.

Steve sighed. In a way she was right, but he didn't want to defend himself tonight. After the wine ran out, Peter brought out a bottle of Ardbeg whisky. And the clock on the mantel, with balls that spun dizzyingly beneath, passed midnight and trotted on to two antemeridians before any of them noticed how late it was.

"I'd better be getting back," George said eventually. She looked over at Steve hopefully.

He glanced at his watch and stood up. "So you do want me to take you home?"

"I'd just like a lift," she said. "That's all."

Steve went to the bathroom on the way out. It was a small wood-panelled room with thick towels hanging from a wooden rack. Steve's head was already heavy from the whisky. The effort of standing over the toilet made him want to lie down on the floor and go to sleep.

In the car, George was quiet.

"Nice people," Steve said.

She turned in her seat. "You're not that bad yourself. For an American."

He smiled. "You're not that bad either, when you're not accusing me of running after teenagers, or polygamy, or whatever bee it is you have in your bonnet."

She laughed. "Very funny. And, besides, the warning about Nicola Ally still stands."

Steve shrugged. "For this trip I thought I'd give up teenagers."

He saw her go to speak but stop herself. The road was dark, lit only by the searching headlights. Stands of trees in early leaf ran off into the dark shapes of hills. It all seemed to demand a quiet. George gave him directions, but said no more until he pulled over at the back of her house. When he pointed to a large leggy bird sitting on her wall, she told him it was a heron.

He turned the engine off, leaned back in his seat and sighed. He did want to talk to her, and he didn't want to go back and face Mrs. McPhealy.

He glanced at her a couple of times before venturing, "I hope I didn't put you off with the talk of my failed marriages, the breakdown and all."

She shook her head. "You're entitled to your life."

He laughed. "Yeah, my life. I suppose you think I have sold my soul to the Gods of Entertainment."

George looked over at him, and their eyes engaged for a moment.

"You might be right," he said. "Perhaps all I've ever been is some damn cog in the Hollywood fodder machine."

"Very poetic," she said.

She put her hand on the door handle.

"You don't need to be so defensive," he said.

She looked back at him. "I'm not defensive. It's just that I have made it a rule never to go out with Americans."

Steve didn't know what to make of George. It was true that in high school, he hadn't been the kind of boy girls secretly fancied. He had been short and pimply, the head of the school literary magazine, not the first with a date to the prom. But he had grown used to fame and the fringe benefits that came with it. These days he wasn't used to out-and-out rejection.

"Is that right?" he said. "Well, just for the record, I don't date women over forty."

George pulled hard on the handle. "That's a shame, because I was about to ask you in."

She slid from the leather seat, taking herself and her smells out of his presence, then leaned back into the car. "But, anyway, you'd probably just trip over my walking stick."

When she slammed the door, Steve jumped a little. He turned the engine back on, and in the glare of the headlights watched her walk to her door, the cats that came running and weaving about her ankles, the heron that flew off her wall and landed by the shoreline.

"God, she's a pain in the ass!" he said to the steering wheel, which he was gripping as though he intended to throttle it.

Steve pulled back onto the deserted road and turned the car around. He was confused. It was obvious George didn't like him, except for the small suspicion that she did. There was something, sometimes, in the way she glanced in his direction. He would have called it *coy*, if it hadn't been so fleeting. But it kept him from dismissing her altogether, as he drove back to Manse Brae and readied himself for a blast of McPhealy disapproval. In addition, there was the nagging fact that of all the houses offered in Locharbert Realty, he had picked the cottage closest to hers, even without knowing where she lived.

CHAPTER TWELVE

George waited in the dark until the lights of Steve's car had disappeared down the road. She turned on her music, one of those Sixties women with their guitars, and then sat on her bed without any light, her cats nudging her to feed them. She had noticed all through the meal how Steve had watched her. Everyone knows stolen glances do not go unnoticed, because of an invention in nature called peripheral vision. But the person who steals the glances always thinks he has got away with it because of a thing in human nature called denial.

Still, it had pleased her. She had known right away what Peter Duart and his wife were up to. She didn't know whether Steve was party to the scheme. But she had already made up her mind before going that she wouldn't go along with it, especially after hearing the rumour that Steve had a wife in America. George needed to dislike the man, so she hadn't thought too hard about the status of the wife. And then when she found out otherwise, that initial decision to rebuff him still lurked and needed a place to go. She had let it out in the car, and he obviously hadn't known how to field the volley. With another Scot, she could have shrugged and called it teasing. But Americans didn't seem to know about teasing. He should have smiled or tried to take her down playfully, not come at her with such nastiness.

"Anybody would think I was an old fogey," she said to her cats in the dark.

And without any warning, her voice cracked, and then came the tears. She did like him, but she knew about these Hollywood types, and didn't want to be another lost woman in his history. What's more, he hadn't even filmed *Culloden* in Culloden. And what about affairs with hairdressers? And emotional breakdowns? she had enough weight in her own life for her not to want to take all that on.

He hid it all well beneath that friendly veneer. But she had been fooled by Americans before. Some solitary Yank off a yacht in the hotel bar would make a play for her and end up under her cheesecloth sheets. Next morning would bring the same story of the girl back home with whom he had had an on-and-off relationship for years, but whom he supposed he would probably marry. She'd started avoiding Americans, wary of the friendly smile and the easy manner, turning away before she got bitten. Steve McNaught was obviously more dangerous than most Americans because he was quiet and deceptive in that way. So she should keep her distance, as planned. Still, when his hand had gone to the gear stick close to her knees, she had felt herself yearn a little.

With her music still playing songs about pretty bows and life's illusions, she lay back on her bed and fell asleep. She had often found sleep to be the best antidote to confusion. It was a warm night, and she didn't need the covers; besides, the cats curled into helpful warm bundles at either side. She had done enough of this, she realised; she was weary from the effort. Her trysts with flighty men, taking what she needed and waving the rest goodbye, wasn't going to work anymore.

BY THE TIME HE PULLED UP OUTSIDE Mrs. McPhealy's house, Steve had already written George off. In the morning,

he was going to have to come up with excuses for his hostess. But now all he craved was rest and some space to sort
things out. As he walked slowly down the path among shadows of roses, he thought of George in her bed in the little
tumble-down shack on the shore.

He turned the door handle, expecting it to give and to
find himself back in the spit and polish, creaking his way quietly across the hall rug to the mottled glass of his bedroom
door. But nothing gave. He tried again, resting his shoulder against the door this time, in case something was stuck.
Nothing. All the lights were out, even, now that he noticed,
the small yellow light over the door.

Steve took the flagged path around the back to the kitch-
en, where sprigs of mint growing by the coal shed lifted warm
and pungent. But the back door, too, was shut, like a mouth
that will never speak again.

He said, "Fuck," but quietly to himself, aware that if he
cursed anywhere on McPhealy property, the disturbance of
her moral biome would get back to her, like the flap of a butterfly wing stirs the universe.

He went back to his car, reclined the passenger seat to its
maximum forty-five-degree angle, and tried to sleep. But the
street lamp directly above the car made him screw his eyes
shut, a position not conducive to rapid-eye movement, and so
neither dreams nor dreamless sleep were forthcoming. Besides,
he knew he had blown it with Mrs. McPhealy and that he was
going to have to stretch his talents to win her back.

Arguments for his defence started to compete. Not having noticed the passing of time was one that he reckoned she
wouldn't give much credibility to. But his car might have had
a flat tire, except that if it had, there would be evidence sooner or later at a local garage and the news would come back. If
he slipped through his bedroom window, he could argue that

he had been there all the time and hadn't wanted to disturb her when he came in. Of course, there was the small obstacle of bars on the outside of the downstairs windows. And, in any case, could he break and enter without someone on the brae noticing?

Steve fought with sleep for a while, then left his car and walked down through the town, past the deserted café, to the shore strangely absent of the flit and cry of seabirds. The sea moved only its dark self, unsleeping, lapping the island somewhere out there in the night and lethargically eroding this shoreline. It had a life all itself, quite apart from the people who regarded it askance by daylight but who lay asleep now in the town behind it. Steve chucked a few flat stones along the surface of the black water, heard them skip once or twice, then sink.

He kept walking until he was on the edge of Locharbert's proper houses and was approaching the roughly assembled houses of Tinkers. Steve had noticed them when he had driven out to see the cottage, but from the road they had looked like mounds of trash. As he drew near, he could see that they more closely resembled yurts.

For a while, Steve stood back. The waves kept lapping on the shore, a watery moon peeked from behind dark clouds. Finally, he came close and lifted the vinyl tablecloth that served as a door.

From out of the clutter on the floor, one figure sat up, then two more.

"Is it the policeman?" a voice wondered.

Steve thought to retreat, but another voice said, "It's yon American."

"Hi," said Steve. "How are you all doing?"

Steve still couldn't distinguish one man inside the tent from another. A grey rise in the floor said, "Come away in and have a cup of tea."

Steve felt the first patter of rain on the canvas. Someone struck a match and illuminated the inner circle, which gave Steve an idea of where to put his foot. The flame travelled through the air and lit a small gas ring just inside the doorway. Murdo balanced a kettle on it, while Steve scratched his stubble chin and wondered where he should park himself. Steve was not a tall man, but there was no part of the tent that afforded standing room. Donal and Doolie, shuffling aside to make room, seemed more embarrassed by the intrusion than Murdo, who was evidently the social member of the crew.

Steve sat on his haunches, watching steam start to drift from the kettle spout. Murdo produced an array of chipped mugs from behind him.

"Have you always lived here?" Steve asked.

"Oh, no," said Doolie, who seemed to be second in command. "We lived out at Auchnotroch, right enough. Our father minded the graves out there until he was put in one himself. Then we came to live on the shore."

Steve accepted the cup that Murdo handed him. The handle was missing, but with rain battering on the canvas roof, the cup was useful for warming the hands. "And what about your mother?"

All three heads went down, like sheep in the grass hoping to escape a dipping. Murdo answered without looking up. "Our mother took ill after Donal was born. She died of the milk fever."

Steve felt he had trespassed on holy ground and wanted to move on quickly. He worked up a general question about the town, but Donal had got up and was fishing about along the edge of the tent. Eventually he brought a box that had once held a clock, and in it found a picture, which he handed to Steve. But it was in black and white, and there was next to no light. Murdo came over with a match which he tore from a card, and for a flash Steve could make out a stern-looking woman in an apron, her hair in a bun, standing beside a man in a long coat and Wellington boots.

"This is your mother and father," Steve said. "They look like nice people."

It was all in the training, the making of vacuous comments. But in this small sanctuary with its holy people in a clock box, it felt like blasphemy.

He took a mouthful of bitter tea. "You must have loved them a lot." This chord rang truer, but the men couldn't answer. In their universe, the last significant event had been the passing of the parents. It wasn't anything they could ever get over. There was nothing else to move in and take its place.

Steve finished his tea, feeling for the first time in a long time that he wanted to help. He had given to charities over the years. He had hired an agency whose sole purpose was to match clients with appropriate causes. He had saved the ocean, given to children in drought-ridden Africa, and to cancer research, but he hadn't felt need as palpably as he did now.

The rain, which had been doing a fair tap dance on the roof, turned into a heavy wash, dwarfing the sound of waves from the near distance. The wind was picking up, too, shaking the sides of the tent and sifting through the weave of Steve's Norwegian sweater.

Doolie picked up a coat and tossed it to him. "Are you feeling the cold?"

Even in the breeze, Steve could smell the mould on the fabric, but he put on the coat and, in the absence of buttons, pulled the belt tight. This was clearly one of the better coats owned by the brothers three.

"Just the job," said Murdo.

Steve set his cup by his feet, then stood up to go.

"Och," said Doolie, "you'll not be going out in this weather."

Steve knew he was right, and, when the brothers laid their heads back down, his followed shortly after. There was something comforting about the rain and the nearby waves, and the wind. It was almost like belonging to a family. He pulled the collar of the coat about his ears, listened to it all for a while, began to hear snoring after another while, and then found himself drifting into senseless thoughts. His leg jerked, the forerunner to any sleep, and the next thing he was aware of was the gentle slapping of waves on the sand not far from his head.

It was light but Murdo was nowhere in sight. Doolie and Donal were on their elbows, watching him. He didn't have to blink twice, and he didn't feel groggy, as he so often did upon waking. He had a perfect sense of perfect rest, and his first impulse was to smile.

"Where's Murdo?"

"Here I am," said Murdo, stooping through the door with a bag in his arms. "You'll be staying for breakfast."

When the thought dawned on Steve that he still had to make amends with Mrs. McPhealy, he ran his hands through his hair and lay back down.

A blush ran over Murdo's face. It was possibly the only time in his fifty-so years that he had ever had to prepare breakfast for a guest. But he had brought potatoes and cheese from town, probably not in an honest sale, but it all smelled good frying in lard on the gas stove. Last night's dinner felt oddly distant.

"I will have to go after breakfast, though," said Steve, accepting another helping of fried cheese potatoes. "Mrs. McPhealy is mad at me enough already."

"Och," said Donal, the quietest of the three. "She's always got her knickers in a fankle, that one."

The other brothers laughed. Steve laughed, too.

"I was eating at the Duarts' house last night," he said. "They're good people, aren't they?"

"Oh, aye," the brothers said.

Doolie seemed less sure. "Not that the wife will last at all long in Locharbert."

"The wife of Willy MacBrayne was the same way," said Murdo.

Steve scratched his chin. "She was French?"

"Oh, no, not French," said Doolie. "Not at all. But she was different, you understand."

Steve wasn't sure he did understand, but he nodded his head knowingly. "And George MacBrayne?"

Murdo laughed, but looked away. "Oooh, she's a wild one, right enough."

Donal giggled. Doolie picked up a rolled newspaper and smacked his brother's head.

"Wild," Steve said, not sure he wanted to know, "how so?"

"Ask Devin Ally," said Donal.

This, spoken softly, was clearly meant as the end of the conversation. But Steve's heart sank, and he couldn't help himself. "Is she having an affair with the barman?"

"Not just him," whispered Donal. "Not just the one."

Steve might have dismissed this if he had heard it from anyone else.

Doolie whispered, "Ask the sailors."

"Sailors," Steve said, sure that he didn't want to know. He took off the coat the brothers had given him the night before and handed it to Donal.

"Just the young ones," said Murdo. "Of course, she's a good-looking woman and no mistake."

Murdo was trying to have a man-to-man talk. He smiled, revealing his tooth pegs, waiting to see how he was doing.

Steve nodded, though he felt of a mind to go straight to George and hold her to account. Her with her moral airs.

Murdo grinned for the privilege of being allowed to be a man with an American. He'd seen films, especially when The Empire was still going. In the cold cinema, no one could smell that he hadn't washed. American men always got the woman, so being in the know with an American man far outmatched any such thing with fellow Scots, who only sometimes got the woman.

Steve started to leave, promising to come back, though the brothers didn't look hopeful. He left a twenty-pound note tucked into the tip of the kettle spout, making a note to himself to bring more.

He told them he had to go and make his peace with Mrs. McPhealy, and the thought of the woman with her knickers in a bunch helped as he walked up to Manse Brae and prepared himself for an encounter. But what was really occupying him was George MacBrayne. He had naturally given her the benefit of the doubt, since she had grown up in Locharbert. He had felt low and guilty for his ex-wives and his tom-cat record with women. And all along, she had been the guilty one, offending him with who she would and wouldn't go out with.

When he arrived at Mrs. McPhealy's, Steve instinctively slipped around to the back door. There was no need to announce his arrival. He had already worked that one out on his way up from the shore. Nicola was over the sink at the kitchen window, blue rubber gloves up to her elbows.

He put his head around the door. He could hear the vacuum cleaner out in the hall.

"All clear?" he mouthed the words, not because Mrs. McPhealy could hear, but to show that he knew he was in trouble.

Nicola was relieved to see him. Mrs. McPhealy had already told her that this would be her last day, and she knew she didn't have much time to make her move. She walked

142 I CLAIRE R. MCDOUGALL

to Steve and put her arms around his neck. His face was all rough. "I was worried about you."

Steve gave her a quick squeeze, then let go. "Is she really mad?"

Nicola said, "Oh yes, everyone knows she's a lunatic."

Since Steve was smiling as though she were his only friend, she slipped her fingers into his hand. "She already told me to strip your bed."

Steve held her by the shoulders. "Oh, God. Do you think I'm really out, then?"

In Locharbert, men didn't touch women unless they meant something by it.

She kissed his cheek softly. "Don't worry. I'll stand by you."

Steve untangled himself, but not angrily. "Nicola, what are you doing?"

She didn't understand. He wasn't telling her to go to hell.

Instead, he kissed her on the forehead and said, "You're a sweet girl."

She didn't have much time. She had to show him how sweet. She was sinking in Locharbert, and this was her last chance. She opened her mouth and pressed it against his, feeling the moistness of his lips and the warmth of his tongue.

He took her head between his hands and lifted it off his face.

"Look," he began to say, but she didn't want to hear.

He had always been so nice to her. She ran her rubber-gloved hands up the back of his sweater and pulled him against her chest. She didn't even notice that the vacuum cleaner had dropped everything into silence and that the door handle was being turned on the opposite side.

When Nicola saw Mrs. McPhealy standing before them with her mouth open, she didn't care. But this was why she had taken the job in the first place, and she was determined it wasn't going to be just another dropped dream, another hard fact of life in Locharbert.

Steve stepped back, banging his head against the broom cupboard, the very cupboard out of which Mrs. McPhealy had pulled her husband's slippers when he first arrived. He wasn't even going to try to talk himself out of this one. He was almost as confused as Nicola, except he was blaming himself for not having seen this coming.

Mrs. McPhealy's eyes kept running up and down the length of them, and it was a moment before she could find the words, "Mr. McNaught," in her vocabulary. She lifted a wagging finger and made to walk towards him, but Nicola blocked her way.

"Don't touch him, you old bag of drawers!"

Steve sank against the cupboard door and hit the floor with his tail bone, just as Mrs. McPhealy shouted, "Out of my house!"

Nicola glanced at Steve for reinforcement. Steve merely shrugged. Nicola untied her apron and threw it at her employer's feet, and, then, as a second thought, pulled Steve's condoms from her pocket and threw them at him. Mrs. McPhealy gasped. The front door slammed shut.

Steve didn't want to touch the condoms and claim ownership. He simply stood and walked past Mrs. McPhealy into his bedroom with its bare mattress. The condoms simply lay on the kitchen floor, leaving a spot of sin that would take Mrs. McPhealy weeks to rub off.

CHAPTER THIRTEEN

At Mrs. McPhealy's house, Steve's suitcase had already been pulled out from under the bed; his empty boxes were sitting on the floor, waiting to be filled. He picked up his stiff pile of laundry and eased it into the suitcase. He was reaching into his top drawer for his underwear, when he noticed on the floor a piece of lined paper torn from a notepad with writing in Mrs. McPhealy's hand.

Saturday night: Please telephone Sandy Row at The Comm.

Steve stuffed the paper into his jeans pocket, more concerned for the moment with retrieving his belongings and getting out of the house than with the question of who Sandy Row was.

Driving down into town, Steve passed Nicola, began to slow the car, but thought better of giving her a lift. He didn't know where he was going, and kept on not knowing even when he turned out of town in the direction of Glasgow. But he hadn't gone far before he pulled over and got out. He knew he would have to go back and explain to Nicola's father what had happened, or, more to the point, what hadn't happened. And that rosy cottage could be his if he wanted.

Then there was George. Even though things hadn't gone well with her, he still wanted to see her again. He was reaching for other reasons not to go back to California, when he remembered the note in his pocket.

He read the name again. It sounded familiar. *Row, row, row your boat, gently down the stream.* It came to him suddenly that Sandy Row was the flight attendant on the plane from Los Angeles. He looked at the paper again. What was she doing at The Comm? He had invited her, but an American invitation isn't supposed to carry any more weight than "How's your father?"

He turned the car around and headed back for Locharbert. He stopped at the petrol station to place a call to the flight attendant. When Devin picked up the phone at The Comm, Steve could tell news had already travelled and that he was going to have to have a very well-rehearsed defence when the time came.

Devin redirected Steve's call to Sandy's room, but his breathing remained on the line. It was such a relief to hear an American accent on the other end, Steve couldn't help sounding more enthusiastic than he would normally have felt. He arranged to meet Sandy outside the church at six o'clock, because it seemed like the least likely place to be noticed. Steve drove to the grocer for food, bread and cheese, and a miniature Glenfiddich. At the till, he added a bar of Cadbury's Fruit and Nut, but the air was frigid with judgement, even though he was outnumbered in the shop by only one other customer.

He ate in his car, then went into the real estate agent's, and, because his brain was telling him he couldn't stand another day in Locharbert, he put a down payment on the little cottage by the sea. Perhaps George might warm to him a little more if he was her neighbour.

"It's going to take a lot of work," said Mr. Wallace.

Steve registered the resemblance of the agent to the three brothers on the shore, but he didn't like to mention it, since this one was in a suit and was trying to seem important.

He asked, "Are you sure you're up for it, Mr. McNaught?"

"Sure I am," said Steve. "But let's keep this quiet, okay?"

Mr. Wallace cleared his throat to stifle his pride.

He held out a pen. "Would you be so kind as to sign here, Mr. McNaught?"

On his way out to the cottage, Steve munched on the bar of chocolate. Like his life in general, his new home really was a mess. At some point the stone walling had been covered with wallpaper. But a gash in the roof had allowed enough moisture in to save Steve the effort of peeling back most of it. He wandered around, challenging himself to learn what he needed to put the place back together again. He could already feel a hint of the satisfaction of living in a place he had built himself. He had fond memories of the small house in Brown County, Indiana, which he and his first wife had patched and painted in sober intervals between trips. That one hadn't been made of stone, but surely he could find a mason to teach him the basics. How hard could it be to build in stone blocks?

He barely made his appointment in front of the church, and had to speed a little on the way to make up time. He had never seen a cop yet. Along the way, he tried to conjure how Sandy had looked, but he finally realised an American woman of any sort was going to stand out.

And there she was in Wrangler jeans like his own and a turtleneck under a sweater that Steve knew came from L.L.Bean, because his wife had owned one, too.

"Well, howdy-do!" he said, as the passenger window rolled to the bottom. She was prettier than he remembered, with bangs down to her eyes, and a little bob of a ponytail. And she was smiling, which right now was as much as he wanted from anybody.

She opened the door. "Should I?"

"Climb right in," said Steve.

She got in and hugged him, the first person to do so, Steve realised, since he had left the airport in L.A. Not counting Nicola, of course. Steve had conveniently shut that memory down until he could think of what to say to her father. Sandy's hug wasn't, in any case, anything close to Nicola's. The type of hug Sandy gave him was of the filial order. And she didn't smell of Palmolive dish soap either.

Steve was anxious to get going. Mercifully, there had been no one else on the street when he picked her up, but he would feel safer with her out of town limits.

"So, are you on vacation?" he asked.

He started driving out the road he had just come. The cottage might be a conversation point, and, after all, it was his.

She laughed dismissively. "Just passing through on my way to the Isle of Skye. I'm meeting some buddies for a biking tour."

Even not knowing much about the geography of Scotland, Steve guessed Locharbert was out of her way. "Well, I'm glad you looked me up."

She loved the cottage. She said it was right out of a romantic Scottish novel. Steve was surprised to notice how it grated on him when she said, "Sca-ttish." She said she had spent the first night in "Glas-cow," and that she was ending her trip in "Edin-burg." He corrected her each time, and that grated on him, too, because he was normally an easy-going fellow as far as language was concerned.

They ate what was left of Steve's lunch on the grass above the sand. There was no way of knowing if George was at home. If she was, then it served her right for rebuffing him.

Sandy pointed out the heron standing in the shallows, but called it a stork. He let it go, and offered her half of his small bottle of whisky instead. They took a walk along the beach, not in the direction of George's house but further down the mull, where they watched a pair of otters slither in and out of banks of seaweed.

"I can see how you like it here," she said.

"I don't, though. I really don't. Today I just wanted to get the hell out."

They turned and started back down the water's edge towards the cottage.

She slipped her hand into his. "Why didn't you?"

He glanced down at his fingers intertwined with this stranger's. After months of no women, suddenly everything was happening fast.

He said, "Well, you were here, for one thing."

Steve had played this game so often, the words slipped out on automatic. George be damned. It was a role he could easily slide into, narrowing his vision into this one little bay where the siren sang. She put her arms around his neck; he ran his around her waist. He found the hollow of her spine and worked his fingers up until he reached her bra. But he was still distracted by the otters, and it was a moment before he realised they were kissing.

"We could go back to the hotel?" she said.

He looked back at her face and noticed how symmetrical her eyebrows were. "I'll have to take the back way in."

She laughed. "Are you wanted by the cops?"

Steve nibbled her ear, making her groan. He took this to bode well for the night's proceedings, and knew he would have to find a way up to Sandy's room, even if only because the thought of a shower after a night with the Tinkers, even a drippy Scottish shower, made his toes curl with longing. He kissed her neck and undid the clip on her bra.

"Wait, you naughty boy," she said in a little girl's voice which irritated him.

She took his hand and led him over the grass to the car, where she sat, fastening herself back in and waiting for him to drive her to her lodgings. Steve hesitated by the driver's seat, then got in and drove back to Locharbert, talking in the way of a couple who has already decided on intimacy and is casting about for enough details about the other to make the coming action warranted.

She had been married once, she told him, for a total of sixteen days. It had been an impulsive decision to marry a frequent flyer businessman out of Seattle.

"Impulsiveness is my worst trait," she said.

Steve drove on, wondering if he could take advantage of someone's worst fault.

"Perhaps you're just a free spirit," he said.

"I suppose I am," she said, smiling to herself. She laid her hand on his thigh. "You, too, huh?"

Steve felt a little honesty was called for. "My shrink says I just don't know what I want."

She squeezed his leg. "Do you want me?"

She laughed in a here-I-go-being-impulsive-again way.

He nodded. It was all he could muster. He was heading into sex with a piece of cardboard, which wouldn't have bothered him in the past, but today he could feel himself beginning to drag. He let her out at the post office, then pretended to drive off in the direction of Manse Brae. After he had left his car in the empty parking lot of the old Empire Theatre, he doubled back on foot and ran into Murdo and Doolie at the Comm's back door. He smiled at them as he brisked by. Words weren't called for.

He had to move quickly and take what was being offered. Sneaking up the stairs, he could hear the jukebox below, the orders for pints and drams. He had to knock on Room 4 quickly and be out of sight before any of the patrons decided to wander up and take a sleep in one of the other rooms. In all, there were only six doors off the landing.

Steve stood in the middle of the small room, taking in the décor, which looked as though it had been outfitted from a thrift shop: gingham curtains which shut out none of the streetlight, a few prints of famous Scottish places in plastic frames, a taupe polyester bedspread.

"I hope they're not charging you much," he said.

Sandy shook her head. He noticed, then, that she had changed out of her clothes into a pair of short pink pyjamas. The breast pocket was decorated with a poodle wearing a collar of plastic rhinestones. She had let out her short pony-tail, so that he could see there were blond streaks in her light brown hair. He wanted to touch it, bring the softness of this woman, any woman, against himself and let the strands of her hair fall through his fingers.

He reached out and kissed her, undid her buttons and felt his watch catch on the rhinestones. He walked her over to the bed and laid her down.

"I have my period," she said.

Only then did Steve think about his toilet bag in the car with the rest of his things, not that it would have done him any good, since his condoms lay on Mrs. McPhealy's kitchen floor.

"Do you mind?" she said.

He kissed her nose. "It's the best thing that could have happened."

He had fathered enough kids, and now at fifty, he didn't need any new responsibilities. He had often thought it would be nice to have a daughter, but not out of a one-night stand on a polyester sheet in The Comm.

"Where's the bathroom?" he said.

"Down the hall."

"We're going to need a towel."

She pulled her top back on and went out. He undressed and got into the bed. It was just as well for her not to see that part. His stomach had seen fit to rearrange itself further down these days. He laid back, his hands behind his head, studying the paint strokes on the ceiling the way he did in doctors' offices while waiting for the doctor to come in. When she arrived, she noticed his clothes on the chair and stood for a moment hugging the towel.

"Cute tattoo," she said.

Steve put his fingers over the tattoo just over his heart that he had had since his early twenties. He had got it because he had at the time some vague awareness that he came down from Celtic people, and he liked the claddagh heart between two hands. He thought it would endear him to the ladies.

Sandy kept standing in the middle of the room.

"Everything okay?" he said.

"Close your eyes."

He didn't really close his eyes, but left enough of a slit to see her emerge from the poodle pyjamas, the triangle of dark hair, her breasts swaying as she lifted the covers and arranged the towel.

She sat on the towel, hugging her knees. "Okay, you can open your eyes."

He ran his hand down the taut skin of her spine, then almost instantly found himself getting out of bed. It wasn't a case of cause and effect. He was moving away before he made any decision to do so.

He stood by the bed and said, "I'm really sorry."

She pulled the covers up. "I'm not tying you to anything."

"I know you're not," he said. He sighed. "It's just that there's this George character." He laughed sardonically, running a hand through his newly-grown hair. He hardly even knew George.

Sandy reached for her pyjamas. "George?"

Steve shook his head. "Someone I've met since I've been here." He laughed, almost light-hearted now to realise that George was a force he was being driven towards, whether he liked it or not. "Isn't that ridiculous?" He thought of her in her tent raincoat, meeting Devin Ally round the back of his pub. "It's unlike me to feel this way, but there's no way around it. I just do."

Sandy got back under the covers. "Have there been any other *Georges* in the past?"

"No, this is completely new for me."

Realising he was naked, he walked to the chair for his clothes.

"You should leave," she said.

"I can't," said Steve, pulling his T-shirt over his head. "I've got nowhere to go."

She turned over and feigned sleep.

"Please don't feel offended," he said. "I've just been going through a lot of changes lately."

Sandy looked up long enough to say, "No kidding."

Steve studied the worn carpet, then opted for the chair. He stretched his feet out, folded his arms and knew he had done the right thing. It was quite liberating. But, more than that, he had brought George into focus, and he knew now he was going to keep zooming in until he saw what he had to do to make her want him.

Perhaps she was more than she seemed, more than the angry Scot, a deliverer of babies, a woman with affairs, more than a dweller on the shore. She was the soft touch of lips on his cheek, the challenge in her eyes, a trace of incense, that smile that lit her face. Lovely little lady.

CHAPTER FOURTEEN

George knew it must be close to three o'clock because the waves were that much closer than they had been when she had put the cats out and gone to bed. But sleep wasn't any closer.

She rolled over and flicked on her music. She had been in the post office when she heard the news. She couldn't remember who was dispensing it, only that it had come clattering into her ears like a trumpet hitting the wrong note. Anita Ally was in line behind her, so what was being said must have some truth to it: Steve McNaught had tried to rape Nicola Ally on Mrs. McPhealy's kitchen floor, and then he had gone and spent the night with an American woman in one of the rooms at The Comm. The cleaning lady had found a folded towel in the bed, and that could only mean one thing.

"The beast."

"Only interested in one thing."

"And him fifty and a married man. Someone should tell the police. Not that she hasn't been asking for it, mind."

The postmistress had been notably quiet. A sexpot in the town, and she was only just finding out about it. She tugged her jumper about her hips, revealing more of her cleavage. Surely if the man had had a chance at a proper woman, he wouldn't have gone chasing after wee girls.

George had bought her stamps, working hard on her face, for she knew it was being gauged. The husbands of these women had told them how she had smiled at the American in The Comm, and McNaught's car had been seen driving out from George's way in the early hours of the morning. Something would register on her face sooner or later.

George knew the game and kept it all in until she was walking home along the shore path. She sat down at the side of a gorse bush. When would she ever learn? She should have married Devin Ally and settled down early with a good man. Now she was making a fool of herself all over again. She should have paid more attention to the heron and been on the lookout.

When a thin line of light crept under the horizon, George got out of bed, wrapped a blanket around her shoulders and went out into the wind. The only thing worth talking to in the end was the sea, and it did calm her down for a while, making sleep almost seem possible. But in bed again, she was back to tussling with her covers. What made it worse was that, eventually, she could have wanted that man in her house. She could have seen him coming and going from her future, two old mismatched hippies finding refuge together. She looked about for the heron this morning, but saw only curlews and shags. So she set off in the direction of Rose Cottage. When she lived there in the future, with memories and ghosts for company, she would feel less like a raft come loose from its mooring. She pulled a few weeds from around the roses, smiled because there were more blooms this year than last, and took it for an omen.

She couldn't have seen Steve's car, because it was parked in the trees up by the road. But inside, she did come upon a form in a sleeping bag in what used to be the back bedroom. She took a step towards it, for squatters, though common in London, were not usually encountered in the middle of

Argyll. She got close enough to see the eyes flicker open in the semi-dark, but it was a moment before she realised who she was looking at.

In her night wonderings, she would have welcomed such an opportunity to do damage to him. But, seeing him lying there, looking up at her out of his sleep, only had the effect of getting her back to the water's edge as quickly as she could. From there, blanket flailing, she was heading for her own house, when she became aware of him running behind her. He even called her name, but the more she reminded herself of the kind of man he was, the more her bare feet pounded on the cold, firm sand.

He caught her blanket, before he caught her arm. She let the blanket go, and he stood for a while holding it.

"Wait!" he called.

It was now almost light, and George's shack was in view. Her back was hurting, though, which made him able to finally gain ground and stand in front of her.

"Stop," he said, "just let me explain."

She hadn't meant to talk to him at all. She was Scot enough to know the kind of weight silence can carry. But he was panting, and her retort stuck in her throat. She went to walk around him, but he put his hands on her shoulders.

He said, "Just tell me the charges."

She pushed him out of the way. "As if you didn't know."

He came running after. "I know what I did and what I didn't do. I know it's not what you have probably heard."

She turned back to him. "Take your lying gob back to Hollywood. That's where you belong, among other lying gobs."

She said it with the kind of sting that usually worked on men. But he kept following.

He grabbed her arm. "Perhaps you don't know everything, Georgianna MacBrayne, or whatever your name is."

She didn't want to listen. All night long she had refused to give him the benefit of the doubt. She could have excused the Nicola story, because of what she already knew about the girl's intentions. But there was no way around the towel in the bed at The Comm. She stopped walking and sighed, which was all the encouragement she intended to give.

He took a deep breath and began to tell her about leaving her off at her house after the evening at the Duarts' and how Mrs. McPhealy had locked him out. He told her about his night with the brothers on the shore and that Nicola had let him in the next morning.

"Nicola knew I was about to leave," he said, "and for some crazy reason, she made a play for me, right there in the kitchen."

"Because you had encouraged her."

Steve shook his head. "I did not, though perhaps I confused her by being friendly. Sorry, I didn't know *friendly* was a crime in Scotland."

George folded her arms tightly across her chest. She was beginning to feel cold and shivered a little. "*Friendly* isn't a crime. But *solicitous* is."

Steve threw up his hands. "I give up." He was going to walk away, but there was the matter of what the Tinkers had told him. He had forgotten all about that during the last day.

"Anyway," he said, "Don't think I haven't heard about you and your affairs."

George laughed nervously. She knew she was the object of much conjecture in the town. She had always feared the extent of it. "With whom?"

"Nicola's dad, for one."

George sighed, hoping that was all he had heard. At least this was ancient history.

"We were seventeen!"

"Oh." Steve looked confused. "Well, what about all the young sailors, then?"

The way George smiled let Steve know she felt cornered. The youngest had been in his twenties, which was still a far cry from a seventeen-year-old. Still, she wasn't proud of the fact. She let him continue with his story of how Mrs. McPhealy had slapped Nicola and how he had not sprung to her defence.

"So she threw her apron at Mrs. McPhealy and condoms at me."

George was about to find this amusing, since she assumed the condoms were the ones she had given Nicola. And, anyway, she had already half-dismissed the rumours about Nicola even before she found Steve in her cottage. What had really been keeping her awake was the evidence of that damned towel. "I suppose you're going to tell me the American in The Comm was your sister."

Steve took a moment to catch up. He felt he would never get used to the velocity of news in Locharbert. "She wasn't my sister, but I slept in the chair, for your information."

Steve caught the fist that was heading for his head.

"Then why was there a towel in the bed?"

Steve started to laugh. This town was truly something for the big screen.

George turned and marched on.

"Come back," he called. He was still laughing. "It isn't what you think."

"It is what I think," she shouted, "because what I think is that you're full of shit."

She reached her door and went in, hoping in an almost unrecognisable part of her heart that he wouldn't go away.

He didn't. He knelt at her door and talked through the crack. "Georgie Peorgie, Pudding and Pie, I didn't kiss the girl and made her cry."

She wished he wouldn't do that. She didn't want to be snookered by an entertainer.

"Look," he said, "I don't deny I was going to sleep with her, and why not, since you have been spitting at me ever since I got here? She was having her period, so we put a towel down. I was feeling very alone, but I couldn't go through with it. Maybe I'm growing up, who knows?"

"Maybe you just don't like the sight of blood," she called from her place along the wall at the back of the door. But she knew she was spinning webs.

"I couldn't go through with it," he said, "because what I really wanted was you."

George went to call out, "Aye, right," but she stopped her tongue with her teeth. Perhaps he was telling the truth. She came close to the crack on the other side of the door. "Why were you sleeping in the rose cottage?"

"Why were you wandering around it in the middle of the night?" She could feel his warm breath through the gap.

There was an answer to the question, which she would tell him about in the days to come. For now, it was enough that he was turning out to be who she hoped he was.

"Do you want to come out here," he said quietly, "or can I come in?"

Steve wasn't hanging too much hope on her doing either. He was surprised when the door handle turned and she was there, smiling in the way that made him feel like his kingdom had come. He handed her back her blanket.

"I'm still not going out with you," she said.

"Okay," he said. The words didn't seem to matter anyway. "Can I kiss you anyway?"

"But I'm over forty."

The crease between her eyebrows deepened. He stepped over the threshold and felt his stomach come up against her nightie. "In your case, I'll make an exception. But just this once, mind you."

He caught her fist before it pummelled its way into his heart. He lifted her hand and kissed each whitened knuckle. "Over forty is my favourite age."

That smile of hers flashed along her front teeth. Lines formed at the sides of her mouth and stopped just under the bowls of her cheekbones.

She said, "Over fifty is okay, too."

She spread her hand along the line of his jaw. It had been so long, the roughness took her by surprise.

He kissed her. "Just fifty." He kissed her again, and this time didn't want to stop. He felt her waist through her night-ie and wanted to discover how she felt everywhere, but he didn't know if the Scottish mating game moved to different steps. He didn't want to get it wrong. He held her against him, curving his back into the hollow of her hands.

Kissing had always just been a prelude for him, a minor step along the way. Somewhere in the back of his mind, he still thought of sex in the childish terms of bases. Kissing was first base, as it had been in junior high. He had made it to home plate by the end of his first year in college. And he had been going round and round ever since.

This felt different. He didn't care if he hung about first base all day. He didn't know if it would ever go any further, and he wasn't hoping. Her skin smelled like cats and bracken. There was peace between them, a small plateau where they could take a rest from the climb and simply be.

"Would you like a cup of tea?" she said.

He laughed. "Sure, why not?" But when she turned her back to fill the kettle, he wound his arms around her and kissed the back of her neck. "To tell you the truth, I don't like tea that much."

She set the kettle down and turned back to him, not kissing this time, but each feeling the contours of the other's back. When, after a while, he arrived at the slope of her backside, he reached a hand around one buttock and simply let it rest. He hadn't engaged in so much foreplay in an upright position since he was a teenager. She kissed him again, running her hands over the seat of his jeans, coming to rest with her hands in his back pockets.

"I like the way you smell," he whispered.

But she hardly heard, because the rough engine of a truck or tractor stalled and stopped not far from the house. She pushed Steve into the corner of the kitchen, then went to answer the door almost before anyone knocked.

Steve could make out a man's voice. "I think you know why I'm here."

George's voice was deliberately slow. "When did she start?"

"Her waters broke three hours ago. You have to come, George. She's puffing and won't talk to me."

"Don't panic, Ginty, I'll change and be out in a second."

George didn't come back to the kitchen. Suddenly she was by her bed, pulling her nightie over her head.

"This could take a while," she called.

Steve leaned out and saw her stepping into a pair of loose purple cotton slacks. Her back was bare, with all the grooves where they should be, according to his earlier exploration of it. Only a mole to the left side of her lower back was a surprise.

She turned her head suddenly and caught him looking. "I told you I wasn't going to go out with you."

He smiled. "When will I see you again?"

She slipped a purple T-shirt over her head. "You can stay here until I get back, if you like. Just don't park your car by the house, or we'll have Reverend Campbell over, casting out demons."

She pulled a bag out from the side of the bed, then came over and laid her cheek against his. He wanted to hold her, mould the shape of her into his hands, in case this moment never came back. But her body was agitated.

"You'd better go to the puffing wife," he said.

She kissed him lightly on the lips and was gone.

He stayed in the kitchen for a moment, looking at what she had imprinted of herself there. He lifted the kettle, then set it down. He studied photographs on the wall, jealous of the people in them who had more claim on her than he did. He saw her when she was young without the sparkles of grey in her dark hair, without the lines beneath her eyes when she laughed. He saw her holding babies at bedsides beside exhausted mothers. There were pictures of men with their arms about her shoulders, which he preferred to think of as husbands to the weary wives, but who he suspected were sailors.

He sat on her mattress, feeling that he was trespassing. He wondered if this really was the stage on which the next part of his life would play itself out, or whether she would only ever let him twist himself around her heart. He wondered how many other men had sat here waiting for her to come back from a birth, anxious to worm their way back into her arms. The film of how he had come to be here at all kept playing through his mind. But, unlike his own films, he had no desire to alter anything. The dialogue was anything but terse, but it was most of what had gone on between them; it was her and it was him, and he wanted to leave it alone.

He thought about walking back to his car, about buying food, but something held him right where he was, as though leaving would break the spell. He might go off and come back to another angry scene, instead of the kissing scene from earlier. It wasn't a scene that would play out well on celluloid anyway, because there weren't clear bookends, and a kiss on camera can only last so long, a matter of seconds before the audience tires of what is essentially silent dialogue.

He picked up her nightie off the bed, the kind of ancient flannelette type his grandmother might have worn. But it smelled of her, a sweet smell, perhaps of lavender, with a faint aroma of leaves. He wrapped it around his neck, laid down and let his eyes close. His short night on the cottage floor had not been comfortable, so it wasn't long before he let his thoughts drift. The rain picked up and spattered hard on the roof. In the vague land between waking and sleeping, he had the sense of breathing very deeply into a place he had never been before, but a place that was safe.

A scratching at the door broke him out of his sleep. Cats, obviously more at home here than he, meowed their vexation at being left in the rain. His boys had had a dog, Buster, and the task had often fallen on Steve to feed the large and brainless hound. But Steve wasn't well-versed in cat care, so hardly knew what to do but watch when the cats came in, shied from him, then settled into the spot where he had been lying. He scoured the small room for a clock, but there was no way of telling how long he had been asleep, nor how long George had been gone.

He went through her two cupboards for cat food but found only oatcakes and oatmeal. He wasn't about to try and make oatmeal. His area of specialisation, as he often explained to women, wasn't cooking. He made movies, made love, made a complete mess of his life, but he didn't make food. It was a story that had become a point of tension in both his marriages, but he stuck by it.

He hated the whole process of cooking, the enormous effort to peel, trim, and cut, to measure exact amounts, and get the heat just right. On the few occasions he had been forced into it, he hadn't been able to enjoy what he had made

anyway. After his last marriage folded, he had eaten in restaurants. The maître d's knew him, gave him his specials. He
didn't want to have to think about food, just turn up when
it was ready.

The oatcakes weren't bad, but they were dry and needed
liquid to wash them down with. He made a cup of tea and
surprised himself by looking around for milk. He couldn't
find any, so he walked with his cup to the stone wall outside
her door and watched the sky race, not yet decided if it wanted to empty itself again before moving further inland. The
sea was choppy after the storm, but it didn't seem to bother
the large grey bird, which stood at the water's edge a little
further down the shore. It turned its head slightly towards
him. He had seen egrets on Malibu beaches, but they were
smaller, more timid, and didn't lurk like this bird.

His sons were always reading fantastic tales of portals to
other layers of reality. It occurred to Steve, as he sipped his
tea, that the tall hunched bird at the water's edge looked as
close to such a portal as possible. It was standing here and
now, looking at him, but it might just as well belong to a
there and then.

CHAPTER FIFTEEN

George set her bag of tricks, as she liked to call it, by the door of the bedroom and went in to Ginty's wife, Maven, who was not so much on the bed as kneeling beside it. She stroked Maven's hair from her forehead and listened. Listening was the first rule of midwifery.

Maven let her gaze wander up to George. "Is this it?"

George smiled. "If it's not, it's doing a fair impersonation."

Maven managed a smile, before another contraction.

"Breathe deeply," George said. "Breathe into the pain now."

Ginty stood in the doorway, nervous and helpless. The couple was in their late twenties, and this was their first baby. George glanced over at his face, not a pretty one, and neither was his wife's, but they had been together since secondary school and no one could think of one without the other.

"Come here," George said. She pulled him down to Maven's side and led his hand to the base of her spine. "When she starts a contraction, press firmly here."

Ginty kept his hand at the ready, stroking his wife's back with the other.

"Do it now," Maven said. Her face began to scrunch. When Ginty pressed, she nodded. He kept pressing; she kept nodding until her body relaxed.

She turned to George. "How much longer?"

George shook her head. When she had first started, she kept track of each stage: one centimetre dilated, then three, all the way up to ten. But it always bothered the women and made them think too much. It wasn't a question of dilation, but of energy. George could tell when the limits had been reached and the woman was going inside herself. Then the birth would happen, as a kind of unconscious pact between mother and child.

Her best instrument was the rhythm of nature. Only if there was delay did George call on technology. She had never had to transport anyone to the hospital yet. The doctors in their steel-gilded hospitals would have cringed, for they told their horror stories, led women by fear to yield their power to men in green suits. So much could go wrong, they said. But George knew the worst thing that could go wrong was for a woman not to find her own strength. In her experience they always did.

After a while, she got up and went for her bag. Little bottles clinked around the bottom: oil of primrose for dilation, pulsatilla for excessive bleeding, dandelion for coagulation. She brought out her wooden horn and, during a rest, listened to the baby's heartbeat. This one had always been a little on the slow side, probably a girl. George liked to guess—it nearly always worked. The little heartbeat was somewhat elevated now, but then whose wouldn't be on the brink of birth?

George sat back on her heels and listened to Maven's breathing, hearing now for the first time in several hours something deeper in the sound. No need to tell a woman when to push. A few more contractions and Maven bore down.

"I can't help it," she said, looking to George for solace.

George mopped the blood that had begun to trickle onto the towel between Maven's knees. "Then don't."

Ginty looked at George anxiously.

George said, "How are you doing, Maven?"

Maven didn't answer. Her eyes were closed.

George crouched low to the floor by Maven's knees. "Your baby has lots of black hair. Maven, have you been having it off on the side?"

Ginty laughed, but Maven was starting another contraction. Hot water and blood spewed onto the towel. George noticed part of the cord coming out alongside the head. She slipped her hand into a latex glove and eased the cord back in.

"Help me move Maven into a squat," George said.

Maven moaned as they shifted her onto her feet, but it was a moan from a far-off place. The next time she pushed, a small face emerged like a little goblin from its hiding in the woods. Another contraction tightened itself around the baby's body, squeezing fluid in a fountain from the nose and mouth. Air rushed in and came out as a cry. Another squeeze and the body tumbled out wrapped in a blue cord.

"She's beautiful," said George. "You're beautiful," she said to the slimy blue-pink creature she wrapped in a towel and handed to Maven.

She wasn't beautiful, nor were her parents, but at that moment it was clear what beauty really was. It was this, and this was why it made all the difference to George. In a life that had had its tough shells and its grit, here was the pearl. Maven sat on the towels, the baby in her arms still attached by the pulsing cord. Ginty dashed off to the kitchen to make tea. George would wait until the placenta was expelled before doing any cutting. The blood from the cord was still sending nutrients and oxygen to the baby, and George always waited until the last minute to sever the connection.

Maven had taken a sip of tea and had to hand the baby off to her husband when the exit of the placenta caused her to bear down again. The red heart of life plopped onto the towels, its job done. George would stay long enough to fry it up with onions for the mother, give her back some of the energy lost in the birth. If she was lucky, she would be permitted to take a little home for herself. She wrapped it up and told Ginty to put it in the fridge, and was on the way to putting baby to the mother's breast when she found the job already done. Nature had provided the urge; sucking would shrink the uterus back down.

This was the best time of all for George. The drama was over, and she had time to observe, drink her tea, put together the hanging scale, and weigh the newborn. George could tell this one was going to be hefty. After catching this many babies, her hands were as good a judge as any mechanical contraption.

George wiped the baby and wrapped it in a blanket, before placing it in the scale and hoisting it up.

"Nine pounds, two ounces. A big, healthy girl."

Night was coming on by the time she and Ginty left the council house, which stood among other council houses all the same. She would have to return the next day to check that all was well. As they drove through Locharbert and out towards her shack, she thought for the first time of Steve waiting for her. She worried first that he was there, and then that he wasn't. She wondered for the first time since she had left in the morning what he had been doing in her house all day, and whether he had let the cats in. His car wasn't in sight when Ginty pulled up.

He handed her the placenta package. "Thanks, George. Get some sleep."

George watched Ginty drive away, knowing payment for the birth would come in trickles from these two. She stood outside her own door, noticing no cats. Her heart began to race, as she opened the door quietly and waited. Something stirred on top of her sheets: a pair of jeans, the same jeans she had had her hands in that morning. She came around the end of the mattress and saw him sleeping with a cat on either side, just as she did. The smell from the placenta in her package woke the cats.

"This is too good for moggies," she whispered.

Steve got up on an elbow, ran a hand over his face.

She said, "Hello."

He asked, "What time is it?"

She shrugged. The cats stood on their back paws and stretched up her legs.

Steve sat up and swung his feet onto the floor. "You must have something tasty in there."

She held out her hand. "Want some?"

He took the package, grease-proof paper wrapped around a plastic plate. He opened it and sniffed. "Is this some kind of traditional Scottish dish?" George smiled. "There's nothing more traditional in all of Scotland than that."

"Really?" He sniffed again, then, glancing at her, tried a small piece. "Tastes like Mrs. McPhealy's breakfasts." He took another piece, then another. "I'm half starved, aren't you? All I could find around here was a couple of dry place-mats made out of oats.

"You could have made some porridge."

Steve shook his head. "I don't do porridge."

"Is that right?" she asked. "Then it's about time you learned."

He held out the plate. "Here, you'd better grab some of this before I eat it all."

"Help yourself," she said, "I'm fine."

When he had finished, he set the empty package on the floor for the cats. "They like it, too."

"Oh, aye," she said. "A little placenta slips down a treat."

She hadn't planned to laugh, but then she hadn't seen an American try to pretend that everything was all right and retch at the same time.

He said, "Tell me you're kidding."

She laughed again, the kind of laugh that rumbles up from deep down and needs to come out.

"It's very rich in nutrients," she managed to say, but was already doubling over and tears were running down the sides of her face.

He caught her by the waist and shook her, laughing himself. "What kind of sick joke was that?"

"It wasn't a joke," she said. "I eat it all the time. I'm serious, it's very good for you."

"But it was just inside a woman this morning."

George stopped laughing. "Do you have something against the inside of a woman?"

Steve held up his hands. All he wanted to do was touch her, but he was a small boat trying to read buoys in the mist.

She sighed. "I'm really knackered."

Steve searched his mental encyclopaedia for *knackered*, but came up empty. It didn't sound like the kind of thing that was going to lead easily into the note they had left on that morning.

She kicked her blue clogs off and climbed under the sheet in the spot where he had lain.

"Let the cats out, will you," she said, sleepily. "After that placenta, they'll probably have the skitters." She closed her eyes and smiled.

He sat down by her feet. "Thanks a bunch."

He watched her chest rising and falling under the sheet, the smile slip from her expression as her breathing slowed. He didn't know whether she was pushing him off or inviting him in. But there was a certain intimacy now between them as she slept and he sat and watched. It was odd the way she could come and go, whether out of the house, or just out of his presence, as she was now, somewhere off in an interior world with its own parameters and logic. Watching a woman sleep wasn't something he had done much of. He considered beds to be for sleep and sex, and if the latter hadn't happened, sleep would ensue, and if it had, sleep would ensue.

Sexual arousal for women, on the other hand, seemed to propagate general arousal, and he had often drifted up from sleep in the middle of the night to hear a woman walking around his house, flushing toilets, eating from his fridge. It was one of the inexplicable differences between the sexes. He was a little out of his milieu, sitting by George. Her face didn't twitch, nor did her eyes move beneath her eyelids. He wondered what kind of dreamless sleep she was in; she gave nothing away.

He got up and took a seat on her chair, twisting into a position from which he could still make out her face. He picked up the book he had noticed earlier splayed across the arm of the chair, with the title, *The Story of Kintyre*. He hadn't picked it up before, because he hated history books. He had never actually read about Culloden outside of the screenplay. He had let the writer take the brunt of criticism for any historical inaccuracies.

Steve read the first page and found the writing comfortingly unacademic. It talked about the Neolithic occupants of the peninsula. It reminded Steve of what he knew about Native Americans, their communion with all beings, the importance of the sun and moon in their calculations.

He glanced at the sleeping woman and wondered how much of these early ancestors still lived on in the modern occupants of Kintyre. George was strange to him. All the

people here seemed far more different than he had expected, considering they spoke the same language. He used to
think they had customs in common, too, but living with Mrs.
McPhealy had disabused him of that belief. These people really were different from him. He had grown up in Indiana,
and the lightheadedness of California had taken some getting
used to. But the differences there had never felt like a gulf; he
had always known he would grow into them.

Now as he read about the strangers from Ireland who
had crowned their kings on the top of nearby Dunadd Hill,
he could glimpse why these modern descendants kept themselves wrapped inside inner cloaks, why they whispered and
struggled so fiercely to keep their mythic selves intact, even if
it now only took the shape of gossip and rumour.

He looked at her sleeping face and understood why it had
so little difference from her waking one. These people were
subterranean from the start, descendants of folk who had
climbed down ladders into dwellings sunk close to the living
heart of the world. He had come down from these people,
too, but the drumbeat of their existence was much paler in
him, a distant echo was all.

He looked over when George yawned.

"I'm famished," she said.

He smiled. "I'd offer you some placenta, but we're
clear out."

She smiled back. He closed the book. He had read three
chapters, without noticing he had been tilting the page to the
fading light.

"Did you let the cats out?"

They looked over at the door where the cats were patiently
waiting.

Steve got up to open the door. "I'll treat you to dinner at
the Locharbert café, if you like."

George got out of bed. "Don't make me laugh." She slipped her feet into her clogs. "Besides," she said, nodding towards the darkened window, "it's not open now."

"The Comm, then?"

"Oh, aye," she said. "You're popular in there."

Steve had forgotten he needed to make amends with Devin over his daughter. He tried to forget again. "Well, I'd like to take you out someplace."

She pushed past him towards the door. "You don't need to splash your money around, you know. This isn't Hollywood. I'm not for sale."

He followed her out. The storm had left a pleasant warm breeziness behind. He found her kneeling over a pit, to the side of which she had pushed a piece of corrugated metal.

"Is that what you think being with me would be, selling yourself?" he asked.

She pulled out a variety of roots and set them beside her knee. "I'm scared it would be."

"Why, because I have money?"

"There's that," she said, picking up her bundle and making back for the house. "And I know your type. Everything has to be at your disposal."

He followed her in and shut the door behind them. "That's not fair. So far, you're the only one who's been calling the shots." He placed his hands on her shoulders as she skinned the carrots with quick, rough movements. "You don't need to be scared."

"Neither do you," she said, handing him a knife. "Cooking isn't going to take away your manhood."

He looked down at the cold handle of the knife in one hand, the bulbous root she handed him in the other. She was tying her hair up into a messy bun, waiting for his move. So much of what he had counted on as himself had undergone renovation lately, it wasn't a huge leap to lay the knife against the root and begin peeling.

"What is this anyways?" he asked.

"Turnip."

Mrs. McPhealy had served him "neeps," which he had discovered was the Scottish name for turnip. She had served a mound of it next to a pile of haggis, which had turned out to be more edible than it smelled. He knew that turnips were a root, but he wouldn't have been able to tell it apart from celery root or rutabaga. Steve sniffed the yellow flesh.

George laughed. "Welcome to the dark ages."

Steve felt belittled. After all, Malibu wasn't exactly Disney World. He shopped at Ralph's Supermarket for bread and cereal, fundamentals he wouldn't walk to a restaurant for. Perhaps they sold turnips there. He didn't study the vegetable section much. For the first time, his philosophy of specialisation began to feel like a limitation.

He handed her the peeled turnip and took up a leek. "What do you want me to do with this?"

She took the leek from him, sliced it long ways, and told him to wash under all the layers. He was beginning to feel like a player in a charade.

She said, "Are we having fun yet?"

"No." He ran the leek through the water, picking out the dirt until his fingers squeaked on the flesh.

George pulled a pressure cooker from under her sink, threw the vegetables in, a handful of lentils and stock.

She tightened the top, glancing up at him. "Sherry while we wait?"

He nodded. He needed a reward for letting one of his chief principles slide. She picked two small crystal glasses off the top of her cupboard, a blue bottle from the countertop, and headed out the door to the wall that portioned off her garden from the scraggly sea grass. He leaned against the wall and felt the stones shift slightly.

"You're sulking," she said.

She was right; he knew it. "I am not."

She nudged the tip of his sneaker with her toe. "Tell me about your breakdown."

He warmed to the contact of the small nudge, but she was like the tide, splashing over him, then running back before he had time to stand back up. She brought her toe against his shoe but didn't move it back this time. He sighed. No matter what he said, he felt she would use it against him.

"I don't know," he said. "I reached a point where everything I touched just seemed to turn to ashes. Two wives, three sons, my efforts to make just one film of any significance at all."

He stole a glance at her by her stone wall, the ends of her hair sprouting from the bun like a little brown fountain. She was looking straight at him, expecting more than he could comfortably give. The story he had given to tabloids and serious documentaries, to women, if they asked, was only a version of the details. Over twenty years, his shrink had pried more from him, but Steve had kept the tender part of it close to himself.

She said, "Go on."

He cleared his throat, looked away into the dark where the sound of waves was a soothing presence.

"My first car, when I was eighteen was this beater, 250,000 miles on it, rust everywhere. But it was an ancient Saab, and I loved her."

Geroge's face broke into a smile. "Her?"

He shook his head. "Yep. Just about the only reliable Her in my life." He ran his hand over his head. He cleared his throat loudly, because something was suddenly constricting his airwaves.

"It was in that car I drove out to L.A. for the first time. And I kept it, even after I was making enough money for any car I could want. I had them all, Mustang, Mercedes, MGB GT. When things got bad, I used to drive up to the top of Griffith Park in my old car and sit there, looking out over L.A. I had everything money could buy, but I had lost so much along the way, none of it seemed to matter much."

When Steve paused, George laid her hand over his along the top of the wall, which was cold and rough. She was pushing him forwards, when all he wanted to do was run away. But fleeing had never got him anywhere, so he decided to stay.

He couldn't look at her, though.

He blew out through his mouth. "I wasn't living in the house anymore with the boys, and I was drinking heavily. One afternoon, after a morning of bingeing, I found myself in a hardware store next to a shelf of PVC pipe. Without really thinking about it, I bought a length, got some duct tape, and somewhere in there made the decision to 'end it all,' as they say."

When Steve looked over at George, she was staring out to sea. He thought he should probably stop his account, but he had come this far, and somehow the story that had been kept inside his head for so long wanted to run out, like a streaker at a football match.

When she turned back to him, it seemed like he had no choice.

"So," he said. "I went back home, parked the car in the garage, taped the pipe to the exhaust, fitted it through the window, taped up the window, turned on the engine and waited to fall asleep."

He felt like dirt, like something George would scrape off her shoe at any minute and discard.

She said, "But you lived to tell the tale."

He smiled. "It was a diesel car."

She looked confused.

He said, "No carbon monoxide. I'd written notes to my boys about how I'd messed up my life, how they would be better off without me, and I sat there, waiting for the poison to kick in. But it didn't. Perhaps it had been long enough since my last drink by then, but I was thinking more clearly at that point, and so I turned the engine off, ripped up the notes, threw all the piping and duct tape in the trash, and no one was ever the wiser."

George smiled. "Except you, right?"

He nodded. "Yep. In a funny way, I think my old car saved me."

"No," she said. "I think you saved yourself."

He said, "I'll take that credit, if you're handing it out."

They stood for a while longer, watching nothing, looking back at the path their discussion had come along and whether it was all right to proceed.

She said, "You Americans are so in thrall to dollars and the glitzy life. It's no accident Las Vegas is in America and not in Scotland."

"Yeah," he said. "In Scotland it would be called Loch Vegaloch. Doesn't have the same kind of ring."

He nudged her when she laughed a little.

She said, "There's more to life than money and fame." She took a step back and looked at him for longer than made him comfortable.

"I know that," he said. "I didn't grow up in Hollywood. Once upon a time, I had parents, although my dad was a drunk who never kept a job for more than a few weeks. He drove vans mostly, for local companies in Indiana. When he did work, he drank the money. When he didn't, he screwed my mother's friends. You know, your classic American childhood."

When he looked back at her, he noticed the furrow between her eyebrows. "My grandfather was a drunk, too," he said. "I come from a long line of substance abuse."

George nudged him again. He liked the intimacy of her elbow against his ribcage.

She said, "Don't worry, I come from a long line of sex abuse."

Steve was confused. "Your father abused you?"

"No," she said. "He only abused the postmistress. Or she abused him. Or they abused each other. Something like that."

Steve wanted to smile, too. He had stood in line with everyone else for stamps, stared down Miss Crawford's cleavage like every other man. "What happened to your mother?"

He hadn't seen George look as vulnerable as she did at that moment. She tried to smile in the direction of the ocean, but it didn't come.

She let out a breath. "Mum ran off with an encyclopaedia salesman." She tried to stop her mouth from turning down. She cleared her throat. "I tell you, they're all sexpots in my family."

Steve watched her for a moment. "Are you a sexpot, too?"

George laughed, relieved for the diversion. "Me? I wouldn't know. It's been too long."

After a moment, Steve said, "Me, too." It was an admission he found surprisingly hard to make.

"Oh, come on," said George. "You're stringing me along."

Steve lifted both hands. "I swear. I had my fill, then it all seemed sort of pointless, and I gave it up."

George laughed. "I'll have to call you Father Steven next."

They turned from each other and listened to the sea, the dark now almost entirely engulfing the horizon. George needed a moment to digest this new Steve, a Steve who was working his way through his own life, trying to make sense of the forces that had fashioned him, reaching an age where sex, or even being close to another, wasn't necessarily the answer to personal woes. She thought of him in The Comm with the American woman and understood better what had happened there.

"Don't you miss your sons?" she asked, and, then, seeing his eyes fill, she reached over and curled her hand into his.

When he wiped his cheeks, she worried she had been pushing him too hard. It was a relief when he lifted her hand to his mouth and kissed the fingertips.

"Of course, I miss them. In fact, when I get set up in my own place here, I'm going to have them over for a vacation."

George placed her palm against his wet face and the facial stubble of two days.

"Have you found a place?" she asked.

He hesitated before he said, "Not really."

She wanted to tell him about her dream of living in her family's cottage, but this man, even stripped of his pretensions, was still too strange. He might not act like the Hollywood director of films she scorned, but he still sounded like one. She caught herself hoping there were yet miles down the road for talk of such things, but it didn't feel like now.

"I want to kiss you now," she said.

Steve said, "I don't know if you should, if it's going to make you feel like you're selling yourself."

She went to say something, but the pressure cooker sounded off with a gust of steam, and George went running inside. Steve stayed by the wall, but could hear her moving around, the hiss of the cooker as it hit cold water, the scraping of furniture.

He did feel uncomfortable, to the point of shuddering a little. He didn't find the breeze cold. In fact, it was soothing, sifting through his new length of hair, flapping inside his shirt. What was cold was the suspicion that he was scared. She was scared of selling herself, and he was scared of her uncovering him. He wasn't in control in the way that he liked to lead his dance with women. At first, he had wanted her to give herself to him, but now he recognised the cost. The cost was himself, and he didn't know if he had gathered Steve McNaught together enough to be able to afford it.

After a while, he smelled candle wax and incense. She drifted out to him quietly, without him noticing at first. She laid her face against his back. "Ready for some soup?"

He turned round to face her. He needed so badly to have his cheek against her hair, which she had let drop from the bun and draped over her shoulders.

She took him by the hand and drew him to a knee-level table, where she sat down, waiting for him to do the same. He glanced at the door. Now was his last chance to disentangle himself and go back to things as he had ordered them. The broth steamed in brightly coloured bowls beside a plate of oat-cakes and cheese. He glanced at her in the lilac dress she had changed into. He sat down and didn't notice the door again.

"Any body parts in this?" he asked.

She smiled. "Just the bodies of vegetables."

He ate two bowls of soup. He placed chunks of sharp crumbly cheese on the oatcakes, and understood why they were treasured. They drank more sherry because she didn't have any wine, and, afterwards, when she brought out a bar of what she called "tablet," a sugary kind of fudge, he ate twice as much as she. He didn't even object to the cup of tea after-wards. A thin suspicion of light was inching under the door when they cleared the table and took the dishes to the sink.

"Shall we wash them tomorrow?" she asked.

He pulled her to him and worked his hands into the groove of her waist. "It is tomorrow." When she yawned, he asked, "Are you *knackered*?"

She slid her hands under the band of his jeans, "Not yet."

He hoped he was reading on the same page.

She took his hand and led him outside, up beyond the back of the house, where sheep were stirring after a night under the trees, and dew on the long grass wet the knees of his jeans. Even after she had dropped his hand, she kept close to him as they began the ascent of a hill. They came to a gate, which she cleared easily, even with the handicap of a dress and clogs, and then they were on a small trail through the bracken to the summit. It was light now, and as far as Steve could see behind them into the dark masses of hills, no electrical or telephone line marked the land. Before them, the sea stretched out flat and glistening to the islands. She stopped by a large rock, her eyes closed, breathing deeply.

Steve held her from behind. "It's beautiful." He turned her round into a kiss. "So are you."

The hesitation of the former morning in her kitchen didn't apply up here. A pair of hawks, caught on an early morning uplift, called from above the trees. Up here, the wind in the trees drowned the lap of waves, making of it a silent partner, a mere observer of events as they happened: the wrap of clothed bodies in the lee of the rock, the sweet sleep that descended like sky, the total absence of words.

They slept, and it was much warmer by the time they awoke. The silent trees stood sentry above them; the light made their eyes flicker as they opened. They got up and walked down the hill through the bleating sheep to the shack, to a bed, beside which they hovered for a while, not knowing if this was the language they should be speaking. She climbed in first, in her lilac dress, pulled the covers over her shoulders, closed her eyes and drifted away from him. He looked back at the door, then climbed in himself, not too close, because there was nothing here that would easily save him, no hawks, no trees standing guard. He lay on his back, listening to her breathing, then to his own, and when he awoke, the bed and their bodies were warm.

He couldn't see her well in the dark, but he could feel in his half-sleep her in her half-sleep, too, a foggy zone in which all defences had been dissolved. No one had to decide anything. There simply was, slowly and as though matter had assumed a new fluidity, the mutual slide of one entire person into another.

They had no prophylactic against this. It was an outcome that had planted itself on bar stools in The Comm, back at a dinner table under a rainy window in Killinochinoch. All their real prophylactics had passed through the hands of Nicola Ally.

In the morning, when Steve pulled his T-shirt over his head, George laughed at his tattoo.

He put his fingers over it. "It's a claddagh."

"I know what it is," she said.

He said, "I thought you would have liked it since it's Scottish."

She spread her hand over the tattoo and his heart. "It's Irish."

When she pulled the lilac dress over her head, he felt it in his groin, but more than that, he wanted to hold her against the vulnerability he could see in her face.

"It's okay," he said.

He lay in her and was rocked like the strange fusion of child and adult that man is, thrusting back to where he came from. He lay on his back afterwards, running his eyes over the patchwork ceiling.

She was awake, looking off to the window. When she sat up and the sheet fell off her back, he knelt up next to her and kissed each vertebra. He kissed the mole on her lower back.

She said, "Tell me about your sons."

He lay his cheek against the taut skin of her back and liked the way she smelled of trees and outside things.

He smiled, because he was being asked to really think of Eli and Tanner, not as sons of an absent father, or pawns in a marriage break-up, but who they were as people he loved.

"They're doing all the usual adolescent stuff," he said, "screwing around, being a general pain in the butt. They're great. Tanner's a bit more like me. Eli's a goofball." He ran his finger down the line of her ribs. "Do you wish you'd had that baby?"

George shrugged. "Me? No. I deliver babies. I don't have them."

Steve laid his face against her stomach. "Who was the father?"

"Someone I was with for five years. He was this English actor guy. That's why I got dragged over to California. As far as I know, he never landed a part."

He didn't like to think of her with anyone else. He ran a hand over his head. "Speaking of babies, should I worry?"

She told him it was all right, because she hadn't bled in many a month and the time for such things was passing her by.

Over breakfast, Steve said, "I've always thought I would like to have had a daughter." He poured more milk into the depleted moat of his porridge. "But I've got enough on my plate. Plus, you just get too old for it: diapers and teething and sleepless nights, all that jazz."

George's gaze shifted to the window.

Steve gestured at the heron standing by her wall. "Spooky, huh?"

George shuddered. Yet, it wasn't cold inside; it wasn't cold outside. It was warm and it was light and it was beautiful. It was raining and it was still beautiful. Sitting across from George in her flannelette nightie, eating creamy porridge on The Mull of Kintyre, home to the kings of Scotland, Steve had all of a sudden turned into royalty himself.

CHAPTER SIXTEEN

S teve liked to watch George sleep, travelling by proxy to wherever it was she went when she closed her eyes. Even though the rain was usually hammering on the roof and waves were pummelling the shore, it felt to Steve like the quietest thing he had ever heard. It didn't have to do with decibels, only with the insignificance of humans in the landscape. In America, people had made it their goal to dwarf nature, to build cities where there had been only desert, to make parks out of wilderness. To be the force in play. His house in Malibu had been fairly rural, but he was always only ever a highway's drive away from human industry.

In this shack with one other person under a domineering sky, beside a brooding sea, he was only another prop of nature, like the heron at the water's edge or the otter ferreting in the sand. It seemed like a place he should always be.

Not in this shack, which wasn't big enough for two and had no plumbing or real heat for the winter, but perhaps in the cottage he had bought along the shore. He had been thinking about having it worked on, then taking George there as a surprise. At any rate, he wasn't going to mention it yet.

Steve lay back down. This life with George was far from the life he had led with his wife. They had built a glass house, with views of the Pacific from almost every room. It was in this house that he had found his wife on the floor with the hairball. His breakdown had taken place in someone else's house, in Santa Monica, during a party, with needles and lines of cocaine sniffed up on little mirrors. He had fallen apart in the master bathroom with a couple going at it in the master bed.

All those parties and barbecues, the clubs and limousines, the glamour of that life, had no relevance here. Probably it had no relevance anywhere, but just as L.A. had carved itself out of the desert, so it had built its own system of belief and value. The odd thing was the way the rest of the world filled their lives with news of it, consumed the invented lives of stars and paraphernalia, kept the whole machine oiled and working.

Some of the parties and barbecues Steve and his wife had attended had been in the houses of actors who earned enough money in one performance to feed an African country for a year. Steve had money, but not that kind. And it hadn't brought him anything he valued. It always stood like a wall in the way of his kids being normal kids. The price of money was an obscured view. For a long time, his fingers hadn't been able to feel a pulse on anything he touched. It all went dead on him.

And here he was in life again: the woman, the rain, the ocean, the heron, and the man.

When the light came up, George opened her eyes. "Is it raining?"

Steve caught her hand under the covers. "It's always raining."

She rolled over and kissed his shoulder. "Will you leave in the end because of the rain?"

He pulled her warmth against him. It was beginning to feel like a familiar niche. "I like the rain."

"You say that now," she said, "but it'll get you in the end."

He rolled over on top of her, sliding his bony knees between her fleshier ones, his flat chest onto her softer one. "The only thing I want to get me in the end is you."

She wrapped her arms around his neck and resolved then to let him in, not just to her body but to herself, to the part of her that was vulnerable and could be threatened.

Over a breakfast of porridge, she said, "Maybe it will be the people that get to you in the end."

He lifted her hand from the table. "I weathered Mrs. McPhealy, didn't I? How much worse can it get?"

George sprinkled brown sugar into her bowl.

"But, for all her sins," he said, "I think Reverend Campbell is in love with her."

George finished her mouthful of porridge. "If you only saw Matthew McPhealy you'd know how much."

Steve started to laugh. "You're kidding!"

"Well, he didn't get his red hair from the McPhealys or the McNaughts. He didn't get his height from them either."

Steve fell back, laughing. "My God, this place is like a bad soap opera. Someone should make the movie." He started to ponder the possibility and lost himself for a minute in an old groove that had nothing to do with his life here.

When George touched his hand, he came back to her and smiled. "Do you know why my grandfather had to leave Locharbert?"

She shook her head. "Willy probably does. Why?"

He shrugged. "Seems to be some kind of scandal to do with it. At least, when I asked Mrs. McPhealy about it, she got that look on her face."

He made a face and made George laugh.

"It probably just means he left his dirty underpants on the floor," she said.

When Steve laughed, she explored every facet of it, the way his lips thinned, the exact line of his teeth, the way his ears moved up. After breakfast, she led him by the hand up the shore to her cottage.

"Why are you bringing me here?" he asked.

She squeezed his hand. "I used to live here with my mum and dad. I remember waking up in the morning and running out here on to the sand. In the summer, there were always yellow roses over the door."

Steve shifted his feet. "Who owns it now?"

"Nobody," said George. "Who would want it except me?"

She took him inside and showed him which rooms had been what, where she had slept under an eave in one of the two small upstairs rooms. He seemed reticent, she couldn't understand why, but she kept talking, because she had lain awake at night so often, thinking these things through, and she wanted to let Steve in.

"I'm going to bang the two bedrooms into one," she said. "The kitchen wall needs to go, too, to make one open dining area."

Steve nodded, as though he hadn't already inspected every corner with Mr. Wallace, the little man from the real estate office. He had to keep catching himself, so he didn't mention the dry rot in the roof, the windows that ought to be replaced, the foundations that would need more support if further rooms were added

Outside again, she pushed open the rickety gate to a pen overgrown with brambles. "I'm going to have goats in here."

She paused to see how she was doing. "What's the matter?"

Steve shrugged. "What if someone buys it before you get the chance?"

She put her hand on his shoulder. "It's really mine already. I believe that."

"Except for a few legalities," he said.

She took him to be mocking and walked out to the sea. It was the only other living thing that knew her secret.

Walking back along the shore, Steve pulled her to a stop. "Let me buy the cottage for you, then you can be sure of having it. You could start work on it right away."

George kept on walking. "You just don't get it, do you?"

"No," he said, "I don't."

He watched her hurry down the sand, then dawdled after her. She said no more about it. He decided to let it go. But the idea of living in the cottage with her began to creep in between waking and sleep, between loving her and watching the heron lift off the sand. He wanted to hang nothing on it, but it was there all the same.

He drove to Locharbert and brought back bags of groceries, too many to fit into her two cupboards. It was all new to him: cats eating food out of tins, boxes of cookies, and bags of bread made and sliced in Glasgow. He bought cereal and other foods in cardboard and plastic, and soon George's bin was too small. He bought big plastic bags to put the rubbish in, then hauled them to the dump on the far side of Locharbert.

"I haven't lived like this before," she complained.

But there was much about her new life with Steve that was not for complaining about. It was warmer in her bed with the man there, and warmer in her heart with him there, too. It had been so long since she had invested any feeling in the men who came and went from her life that it made her ill at ease. She had loved the man she had been with for five years in England, though she had long since decided she had only been a convenience for him. She felt bitter about the abortion, especially because it seemed to sum up the lack of anything substantial in that relationship. She had missed one or two of the other men after they had left, but she had not come close to this feeling of need when she rolled over and looked at Steve McNaught in the middle of some nights. She even loved his Irish tattoo.

His weren't movie star looks, but he had a way of smiling suddenly that caught her unawares, a way of running his hand over the top of his head that made her want to catch it and kiss the palm. She even liked it when he called her Georgie. His stomach hung a little over the band of his jeans, but she never stopped wanting to spread her hand around the seat of them, or watch him sit on the side of the bed and tie his sneakers. She laughed at his Americanisms, belying the kind of ache they made her feel. They were him and he was who he was, and who he was didn't seem as though it could settle for what she was and where she was. Surely time and differences would launch him out of this space, just as it did the heron from the edge of the shore.

When he drove off to Glasgow to trade in his rental car for something more permanent, George stayed for a lady who was due. She went to the birth and came back to find him asleep on her mattress. His new car was a sportier kind of vehicle than the one he had rented from the airport. Red and shiny with a sunroof. In the back seat, she found a small video camera.

She knelt beside him, and he seemed strange to her. He had only been gone for a day, but for a moment he was back to being that other person whose name rolled up with the movie credits. She leaned over and kissed his freckled shoulder. She kissed the small inked heart on his own heart.

He pulled her across his body and tucked her in beside him. "Placenta for breakfast?"

"Two, as a matter of fact. She had twins."

Steve opened one eye. "You're kidding."

She inched back from his face, so she could study his eyes. "What's the camera for?"

He smiled, but his eyes weren't smiling.

"You can't make a film of Locharbert, you know," she said. "This isn't a film set. It's the lives of real people."

Steve lifted his hands. "I'm not doing anything. I just bought a little toy to play with. Okay?"

She said, "I'm just warning you."

She had to say it because it was a matter of principle. That was the problem, there were principles and other factors that could force their way in and sidestep this man out of her life. It wasn't all up to her. Her mother had gone when she was ten. She had had no say in that either. Nobody had asked her. She had merely had to find a way of moving on.

After Steve's sporty red car had been parked on the road outside George's house for more than a couple of nights, the town had started talking. It was said in the post office that Mrs. McPhealy was all a frenzy. Devin Ally had made it known he was quietly displeased, first with his daughter, now George. Reverend Campbell had disseminated judgement among his congregation; a car living outside George MacBrayne's house could only mean the driver was occupying her bed. It was unsanctified, and it was a sin.

Steve could make soup by himself now. He tried variations on stock. He had bought George a bread machine in Glasgow, forgetting the lack of electricity. He went with her now and again to the Duarts for dinner. They climbed hills and took picnics. He waited out due dates with her, and came to a familiarity with her body, with the placement of each freckle, the mole on her lower back, the scar on her little toe where she had all but severed it with a chainsaw.

He never told her he loved her, and neither did she tell him. It seemed to be an intrusion on what simply was. They had come alongside each other, and there was nothing more to say about it, no clichéd gestures. He came to know her pleasures and lost himself in the discovery of more.

Steve tried not to think about filming, not while they were in bed or even over porridge. But in the simple act of buying the camera, he had placed the director's cap back on, and he couldn't help thinking about the possibilities. He had been thwarted in his efforts in Hollywood to make a movie about something that was real, and had had to give up his idea of a movie about the Sixties.

But here was a whole town of characters, especially the three brothers. It could be half-documentary, half-fiction, a new genre altogether. He could pay the little men, and pay the townsfolk for being extras, give them a little financial mobility. He had made a pledge to help the brothers, and perhaps this was the right vehicle.

The camera in his car was only for himself. Only a toy. That's what he had told George, though it itched in his hand and led him, during one of George's absences, to the Tinker tent, just to film the outside. He filmed the tent's door flapping in the sea breeze; he caught a thin layer of tissue dancing in the wind outside. He took the camera out at night and caught the essence of an empty town, the puddles golden with lamp light, the trees ringed in yellow hoar.

One secret life often leads to another, as Steve's shrink in Los Angeles had once pointed out. When he received a royalty check from Los Angeles, he asked a contractor to give him an estimate on the work for the cottage. He was a carpenter, called Ginty, who had a fair knowledge of stonework, too. He could come after hours, he told Steve, begin to replace rotten beams and floorboards, clear away some of the debris, cement down stones that had crumbled off the walls. It was a small step, one that might have gone unnoticed, except for the fact that Ginty also had a job repairing the stage at the high school, and friends of Nicola Ally had seen him head out of Locharbert every day after school to the cottage at Achnarannoch. The news soon circulated that the property had been bought and was in the process of renovation. When the news reached Willy MacBrayne, he cycled out to discuss it with his daughter.

Steve found George sitting at the water's edge, hugging her knees. He crouched beside her and pulled the hair from her face. "Are you crying?"

She wiped her nose with the back of her sleeve. "There's a contractor out at the cottage. Someone must have bought it."

Steve stood up, as guilty people do. "Who?"

George shrugged her shoulders. "I'll find out tomorrow. It doesn't matter, though, does it? It means someone else is going to be living there."

Steve picked up a stone and tossed it into the waves. "Maybe not."

He had fought this long enough, and was almost relieved for the end of the deceit. George wiped her nose again, then looked up at him.

He sighed. "The truth is, I bought the cottage. But I swear it was before I knew it was yours."

The furrow between her eyebrows deepened. "What?"

It was a bitter word, not even a word, just an expression of contempt.

Steve winced. "Isn't it better that I own it than some stranger?"

George got to her feet and looked into his face. "You are a stranger. When I took you over there, you acted as if you knew nothing about it. You're a very good actor, do you know that? But why am I surprised?"

She turned to walk away. He caught her arm. "You can't blame me for buying a piece of property that was on the market. How the hell was I supposed to know you wanted it?"

She kept walking. "You've spoiled it."

Steve laughed. It was his only recourse. "But it's yours," he called. "I'm giving it to you."

He was surprised to see her stop and turn around. But it brought no truce or kiss. He had not seen this look on her before, so he wasn't ready when she walked back to him and swung her arm. The blow hit his shoulder.

"I told you I wasn't for sale."

"Good," he called after her, "because I wouldn't want to buy you anyway. You're way too ornery, you damn vicious Scot." He watched her go, rubbing his shoulder. "No wonder the English got tired of dealing with you."

She carried on in the direction of the shack; he walked on towards his cottage. His mind was black. When he reached the door of the croft, he kicked it, bringing a loose board down. "Fuck."

It was a word he had often used in his old profession, but which had hardly seemed necessary in Locharbert. Inside the cottage, he was distracted for a while by what the carpenter had been doing. The corner of the floor was pale and shiny from new wood. He scanned the room. It would be much brighter in here with wood panelling. He cursed George and decided to go ahead with it anyway. She would surely come around when she saw it so improved.

After it got dark, he walked along the road to get his car. He had already changed his mind and decided to give the cottage back to the seller. When he got to her shack, the cats came running and wound themselves about his legs. He peered in the windows at their life together, the sheets still ruffled, cups he had drunk from still by the sink, the gap under the mattress where they kept the condoms. An entire movie had played itself out within those walls, a perfect arc of character and plot. Now, as it eventually always turned out in his life, it seemed, he was back on the outside looking in. Always on the outside of other people's stories, and on his own life, too. Just like the film he had made about Mary Magdalene, it was all Hebrew to him. He didn't understand; he hadn't done anything wrong. He sat on her step, his chin on the heels of his hands, watching tears drop into the faded wood.

He didn't know how long he had been sitting there before he noticed George out on the sand, walking back from the direction of town. He watched her turn and head for the shack, loving all those small things about her that were her and nobody else, the way her bun never quite came under the restraint of the clasp, the way the arms of her sweater hung lower than her hands, the ridiculous safety pin she tied her jeans with.

She started when she saw him.

"I'm going to give the cottage up," he said. "You can have it back, earn it in your own way."

She shook her head and walked towards the door. He stood up and stepped aside.

"I know you've been filming," she said. "Everyone knows."

Steve sighed. He was obviously a slow learner when it came to Locharbert communications. He ran his hands through his hair. "It's not going to hurt anybody. It can only help."

He noticed now that her eyes were wet.

She said, "Like I said before, I don't go out with Americans, especially not the Hollywood variety."

Steve was going to laugh, but she passed him on the step and went through the door with her cats, closing the door behind her, not slamming it, but clicking the lock with a finality. With such a silent step is the curtain brought down.

Steve went to his car and drove back to the cottage, guilty in the same way he felt he had let down his sons. He hated how easy it had been to deceive her. He had simply disembodied himself and disembodied her, then argued himself to the place he needed to be.

Reason had got him other places, he knew, to the conclusion his sons didn't really need him on a daily basis, perhaps even to the place where his wife was lonely enough to turn to another man. Reason, the great disembodier. Reason had smiled on his decision to take on projects he didn't believe in. After all, said reason, this is the way the industry works, after all the bills had to be paid. Getting on a plane to Scotland had been different, more like a blind man in the dark.

At the bottom of one of his boxes lay an old family quilt, which he had had on his bed as a small child. The stitching was coming out in places, and the colours in the little windows of cloth had faded, but it had a certain smell and comfort about it. He took it out of his car and made a bed out of jackets and sweaters in the attic room where George had slept as a child. As he lay, wrapped in guilt, he found some satisfaction in deciding to go ahead and restore the cottage. He'd buy a dishwasher and a dryer. If he had to, he would send back to the States for a decent shower. On the edge of sleep, he even decided to get a goat. It might not bring George back, but it surely couldn't hurt.

CHAPTER SEVENTEEN

G inty wasn't spending as much time with his new baby as he would have liked, but the extra work out at Achnarannoch had pushed his bank balance into the positive. He hadn't expected to be able to pay off the midwife this early, and so he made a bit of a ceremony of it, when he drove out to her shack to pay off half the bill. In an Arran sweater Maven had knitted during her pregnant months, he stood on George's doorstep, clean and combed, with a bunch of irises in his hand.

When George opened the door, she couldn't help smiling. "God, Ginty, did you win the lottery?"

She hadn't felt well earlier in the day and had wondered if she was coming down with the flu. But by evening she had been feeling a little better. Ginty handed her a wad of fivers. She tried to hand it back. "You can't afford this."

"I'm doing a little overtime," Ginty said, and he curled the notes back into her hand.

George went to put the kettle on. "Where are you working?" She pushed the notes between two of Steve's boxes of cereal.

Ginty was still holding the flowers. "Just down the road at Achnarannoch."

She looked out the kitchen window and noticed the heron was back. Blasted bird. "What kind of work?"

"Just knocking down a few walls," he said.

George stemmed any impulse to inquire further. She had thought she could count on Steve. But, just like her mother, he had let her down. He had lulled her into revealing what was sacred, the part of her that could be beaten down. And all the while he was keeping himself secret; how long had her mother nursed her secret, before she ran away? Now Steve was laying a trap to lure her back. But she couldn't trust him. He said one thing and intended another. If only she had taken what she had learned from midwifery and applied it here, if only she had listened.

She had retreated to the place where love could do her no harm. It was a reflex to gather her defences. The night before last, she had heard Steve moving about the back of her shack. And now, just before Ginty arrived, she had seen him out on the sand. She lit her spare lamp, so that if he were still out there, he would be able to see her alone with a man holding flowers.

She walked over to Ginty. "Are you going to hold those until they wilt?"

Ginty turned them over with a red face. She took them and hugged him, embarrassing him more, because only his mother and Maven had ever hugged him.

George always had her music going, not bands, but women and their guitars.

Ginty dropped his arms, not sure at all what was going on here.

She said, "It's worth a fiver to you to hug me back. Don't ask why."

Because he held George in high esteem, he leaned over and held her tightly around the waist. But even for George, this was turning a little strange.

She offered no explanation when she stepped back. She pulled one of the five pound notes out from between the cereal boxes and tried to slip it to him when she handed him his tea. He shook his head.

"How's the baby doing?" she asked.

He nodded. "Fine."

He slurped his tea, and she could tell he wanted to get away. She still didn't know how she was going to get away with this.

"Did Maven knit that jumper?"

He nodded. He had finished his tea and was waiting to be excused. George could count on him not telling Maven or anyone else. This wasn't a man for gossip. He had grown up on one of the outlying farms, had played bagpipes in school, and was still regarded as a bumpkin, a *teuchter.* But the confusion on his face when he left bothered her and put her in a storm for the rest of the evening. *The best laid schemes of mice and men* and all that—she didn't even know if Steve had seen.

George packed the cereal boxes, together with the rest of Steve's belongings into plastic bags, and the next day took them down the shore to the Tinkers' tents. Murdo was shy to accept goods from the hands of a woman. Donal and Doolie ignored the woman and set right into the boxes, the likes of which they seldom enjoyed, especially not still in their wrappers. Even Murdo became agitated at the sight of caramel wafers.

"Will you stop for a cup of tea?" Murdo asked.

But he saw the look on her face and knew he had no experience in the appeasing of storms.

George sighed. "Murdo Wallace, I'll thank you not to go telling my affairs to strangers." She began to walk away. "I'm sure Devin Ally will thank you, too."

The brothers watched the woman march off on her warpath, and under their breath they thanked the powers that be for never having put them in the married state.

As the wafers were unwrapped and the ceremony begun, Murdo said, "She's a piece of crumpet, all the same."

The brothers unveiled teacakes from their foil wrapping and smashed them on their foreheads, as they had done as children.

"Yon American's been looking awful dour these past weeks," said Donal.

"He has quite the crew out there at Achnarannoch," said Murdo. "Supposing we should pay the man a visit."

Murdo rocked back, picking slabs of broken chocolate off the marshmallow, peeling the marshmallow in its entirety off the biscuit. He was pleased at the thought someone might need his company.

"We might have to take the man's things back," said Doolie, finding in the bottom of one of the bags a handful of loose change and several notes.

"Och," said Donal, "he's got more where that came from."

The three nodded their heads in relief.

"Besides," said Murdo, "we don't want to offend the man."

Donal said, "Davies has a wee Loch Ness Monster for one pound on the counter."

As there was no tourist shop in Locharbert, Davies, the ironmonger, sometimes offered knickknacks.

Murdo reached for a second teacake, cuing his brothers to do the same. "A Loch Ness Monster." The brothers lifted the teacakes and smashed them against their foreheads, adding another layer of sticky residue to the first. "Just the job."

"And what about a half bottle of whisky," said Doolie.

Murdo licked the chocolate off the marshmallow. "How much did you count in the bag?"

"Three pounds and fifty-four pence," said Doolie.

Murdo wedged his tongue under the marshmallow. "A bottle of Irn Bru is only fifty-two pence."

He hadn't gone to school that often, but he knew whisky would take a larger chunk of their new wealth. With the money left over, they could surely buy a few bags of chips.

It was a kingly day. The sun even inched out from behind the clouds and lit the faces of the brothers, as they finished off the chocolate goodies. They rolled up their sleeves, as happy as barnacles.

Later, they trooped up to the ironmonger and asked for a Loch Ness Monster.

"Have you got the money to pay for one?" Davies asked.

Murdo nudged Doolie, who by dint of having discovered the money, had taken on the role of banker. Doolie produced a pound note from his pocket and set it on the counter.

Davies stared at it. "Who've you been robbing this time?"

The brothers looked guilty. They had done nothing wrong, but a lifetime of being suspect left them nothing to say in their own defence.

Davies took the pound note and handed over the Loch Ness Monster, which was made of glazed clay and came in three parts, the head and two humps.

Outside on the street, Donal wanted to know if it was broken. "Not at all," said Murdo, who had at first wondered the same thing. "It's for a table, to look as though it's swimming."

"Right enough," said Donal, who, not being all that familiar with tables, couldn't quite picture what his brother meant.

Donal was grinning, as they set off for the grocer.

"Gentlemen," muttered the lady at the till as she watched the three walk in.

It wasn't exactly a term of endearment, rather an excuse for not saying, "Get out, you stinky wee men."

She would later tell anyone who was interested that was what she had said.

In they waltz, like they owned the place, asking where I keep the Irn Bru, if you please. I say, "Have you got the money to pay for it?" whereupon Doolie pulls out a pound note

and sets it on the counter. I say, "So, who have you been rob-
bing?" Then off they march up the road to Achnarannoch, Irn
Bru sticking out of Donal's pocket, a Loch Ness Monster's
head out of Murdo's. It's a shame for those three when you
think about it.

On their way out to see Steve, the brothers headed off
the main road and down to the shore where they felt more at
home, though the tide cut them off at certain points. Still, it
was summer, and damp shoes would only mean chaffed feet,
not pneumonia. They trudged along in their army coats on
this most unusual of days, when even the sun had stepped out
of character and thought to shine on mid-Argyll.

Halfway to Achnarannoch, they were thinking of taking
off their coats.

"It's gye warm," said Donal, who had the extra burden of
the bottle of Irn Bru.

"It is that," said Murdo.

They had had such a conversation a few years back and
it had almost led to the removal of outer clothing. On that
occasion, however, clouds had moved in and saved them the
bother. They looked up at the blue sky and felt a little dizzy.

"A person could do with a wee drink of something," said
Doolie.

"Not a chance," said Murdo. "Yon Irn Bru's for the
American."

"But supposing," said Donal, "supposing we each took a
wee tiny swig and filled the bottle up with water."

Murdo squinted at the sun, as people in vast deserts do.
"Right enough, the man is a foreigner and probably doesn't
know the taste of Irn Bru. A wee bit of water might not make
all that much difference."

Donal pulled the bottle from his pocket and set it on a
rock. They sat and looked at it.

"After all," said Doolie, "he'll probably never open it anyway, a man like that with so much money doesn't need to be drinking Irn Bru."

Donal and Doolie looked to Murdo for the decision.

Murdo said, "It's a shame to waste it, when there are children starving in Africa."

He reached for the bottle and quickly unscrewed the top. He could never decide, when he thought about this days later, what had been the greatest mistake: allowing Donal to carry the bottle in his pocket, so that the fizz inside was fit to explode, or whether it was the fact that Doolie took two swigs instead of just the one. Either way, the brothers were left with half a bottle of Irn Bru before they knew it, and funnelling sea water into the bottle proved not an easy task.

STEVE WAS DRIVING BACK FROM LOCHARBERT, where he had gone to deal with unfinished business at The Comm. Things had been a little icy between him and Devin ever since the incident with Nicola. He had put off speaking to Devin, but one morning after another night on his own, had felt propelled over to the pub to catch the owner as he was opening up.

It was a tricky business.

"Nicola is a lovely girl," Steve said. "But I'm not a sick man. Things got a little confused out there at the McPhealy's, but I want you to know I never had any designs on your daughter."

In the end, Devin had shaken his hand, but, driving back to Achnarannoch, Steve wasn't sure he had told the truth. Lying seemed to be second nature to him. Perhaps he was a sick man. He was drinking again. What Locharbert lacked in wine, it made up for in its whisky selection. It seemed that every town and island hereabouts had its own distillery, and Steve was working his way through the collection. His shrink had warned him about blaming people. The last time he had gone under, it had been his wife's fault. Steve's psychiatrist had talked him out of that, but Steve had never been fully convinced. In the end, he had taken to blaming the studios.

Now his mind was set against George. For weeks after the split, he could think of nothing else, especially because, when he walked out to the shore in front of his house, he could see the lights from her shack, where most of his belongings still lived. He had walked over once or twice in the dark, watched her go about her routine.

The last time, he had seen her with her arms about some man, probably a sailor, wooing her with flowers. Steve had walked away fast, and now there was a line of whisky bottles by his bin, accusing him, telling him he should have done himself in properly the first time. He was back on his best story about how he would never amount to anything. Driving back from The Comm, he was already reaching for the glasses above his sink.

He wasn't expecting the three brothers, but there they were as he pulled into his drive, waving like a welcoming committee. As Steve got out of his car, Murdo was coming towards him, balancing something in his hands.

"It's a wee Loch Ness monster," he said.

Steve looked down at the green head and two humps. "No, guys, some other time, huh?"

"It's a present," Murdo said.

Steve looked at their faces and knew he had no choice. "Okay, come on in. Everybody come on in. What the hell."

The trio followed happily, Donal with the Irn Bru behind his back. They had decided just to leave the drink somewhere without mentioning it. That way they couldn't be blamed, but they might be praised. Steve opened the cupboard and his hand went around the smooth cold glass. He fit his whisky bottle, from a distillery in Oban this time, between his knuckles and took everything over to his new kitchen table. The three brothers shifted uneasily where they stood by the front door.

"Grab a seat," Steve said. "See my new dryer? Neat, huh?"

A washer and dryer had been Steve's first purchase. Next, he had special-ordered a showerhead that pooled the water before releasing it in a goodly stream. A large-screened television stood on a table by a leather couch. The walls were still without panels, and the couch was still in its plastic wrap on account of a new hole in the roof. But the place felt lived in. The brothers sat down and pushed buttons on the television until the screen lit up. Steve stood with his back to the fireplace, above which hung Shefaline's landscape.

"There's still no reception out here," he said.

He went over and slid a video tape into the player at the side of the television.

It was his own tape of *Culloden*, four hours long, the director's cut. The brothers settled back. It had begun to rain, and he knew they weren't going anywhere soon. Steve found the bottle of Irn Bru and read the label: sugar, colours, flavours. He pushed it to the back of his bottle collection, and poured shots. The brothers drank silently, eyes forward, undisturbed by a low rumble of thunder. Steve sat on the arm of the couch. This scene hadn't made the final cut: Prince Charlie is hiding out in a cave. His army has just faced devastating defeat. He is desolate. It is twilight and he is watching a spider laboriously spinning a web. He realises then that his mission might take a long time, but he is renewed in his commitment to see it through. But twilight is costly to film, and so they had had to shoot it in the morning with special lighting. Prince Charlie kept squinting instead of contemplating the spider dolefully. The scene was cut, though Steve argued vehemently that it was pivotal.

The brothers were impressed with the scene. With every scene. They sat for the full four hours, and even until the tape ran out and started to rewind. By then, Steve was having trouble holding himself up. Doolie looked around for more tapes.

"No," Steve said, trying to look as though standing weren't a problem. "That's all, folks."

He laughed. The brothers laughed, too.

Steve sat down. "I made that movie."

"Away you go," said Murdo.

It's not that he didn't know Steve made films. The entire town knew it. Murdo just hadn't grasped what it meant until he had watched one.

Steve nodded. "I did. Every flaming six months of it, and Bonnie Prince Charlie was a royal pain in the butt, let me tell you. Talk about a prima donna."

Steve poured them all another dram. He knocked his off in one gulp. The brothers followed suit.

"Flora MacDonald was something else," Steve said, but really only to himself. "I kept hoping she'd rescue me, but I was a married man at the time. Kids and all."

Murdo nodded knowingly and held his glass out for another shot.

Steve filled Murdo's and all the other glasses. "Women."

The brothers grinned. They knew nothing about women, except what they had seen through windows, down the closes and behind the school. Behind the church, for that matter.

"In the beginning, God made man," Steve said, "then he offered him a wife, who was absolutely gorgeous, someone who would dote on him and never cause him any grief. Man was pleased, but wanted to know how much such a wonderful mate would cost. 'An arm and a leg,' said God. 'Oh,' said man, 'that's a high price. What could I get for a rib?'"

Steve laughed with his head in his hands. The brothers laughed, too. They didn't get the joke, but it was nice to be laughed beside instead of at.

Steve stared down into his glass. "I'm going to bed."

It wasn't really dark, and, left alone, the rain wailing on the roof, the brothers didn't see any great need for parting. They found another tape with *Mary* on the side, and, although they got the machine to produce a picture, they couldn't get the sound right and never did understand what was going on. When it was over, they snuck upstairs and found Steve sprawled on a large bed with four posts and curtains. Back downstairs, they fell asleep in chairs and on the floor, strange as it was for them to lie down among corners and edges.

CHAPTER EIGHTEEN

For a moment, on her way back from town, George regretted giving Steve's belongings to the Tinkers. Especially the Rolex, which he might have valued. But she cursed him for only valuing things in terms of money and reminded herself that he had enough to cover a new watch. She wished instead that she hadn't used Ginty to make him jealous.

She had heard about Steve's drinking. Peter Duart had made a point of crossing the road to tell her Steve wasn't doing that well. As though she could do something about it. She hadn't put his Sundance T-shirt into the bag for the Tinkers. His change had gone in, his watch, his packets of Fluffer cookies. But she couldn't give up that T-shirt. George had sat on her mattress the first night and cried. It was unlike her to cry. Sadness generally got siphoned through the angry channel and came out in a verbal sword fight. But here she was, walking home, wiping tears off her face. She wondered if this is what menopause felt like.

She went out to the toilet when she got home. She had been needing to go a lot lately. Up in the night, not producing much. Of course, not having a mother who ever reached menopause, she didn't have any real guidelines. But her body had been feeling different lately, her breasts rubbing uncomfortably under her clothes. Walking had made her pelvis feel heavy, and so she was sitting in the draughty shed, waiting, cursing the passing of her fertility. She gave up and went over to the house to let herself and her cats in.

The place was just as she had left it, back to being hers, with nothing of Steve about, neither his shoes nor his packets of convenience foods. Even the T-shirt was out of sight under the mattress.

When she lay down to sleep, she kept her music on, because the sound of the waves was suddenly too lonely.

STEVE DIDN'T WAKE UNTIL NOON the next day. The thought of George didn't make it easy to get out of bed.

Downstairs, he found the Tinkers still asleep. Four hours of silent biblical drama had had an unusual soporific effect. The air smelled of stale whisky and unwashed bodies.

Steve nudged Murdo awake. "Time to get up, bud."

"Right you are," Murdo said without opening his eyes.

Steve nudged him again. "No, really. At least go take a shower."

Murdo had heard of showers. He might even have seen one on television. But his clothes were another layer of skin to him, and the thought of peeling them off didn't come easy. Steve pointed to the back of the kitchen where the shower had had to be installed for fear of backing up the lines. "Leave your coat here."

Murdo wouldn't give up his coat, but he went into the shower room. After a while, Steve heard the run of water. The shower went off, and then back on again. He fished in the back of his fridge, another present to himself, for a bottle of beer. He levered off the top and went out to the sea, leaving two brothers asleep and one in an unnatural state of wash.

The day was dark with clouds, the sea choppy. It was a strange kind of ocean, with no surf, a dark, unjoyous kind of sea, like the people it surrounded. Somewhere out there, sat the mound of an island, rarely ever visible. George had told him it was there, but it wasn't like Catalina Island off California. People actually went there for fun. The Isle of Islay or Jura or whatever it was called was just a dark presence. Along the beach, George's shack was dark, too.

He finished his beer and went back in. The shower was off, so Steve knocked on the door. "Hand out your dirty clothes. I'll put them in the washing machine."

For a moment nothing stirred, then a foot pushed out a heap of rags. Steve picked them up gingerly. Western man is not used to the animal smell of his own species. Dogs, cats, mice, he could tell blindfolded. But a person can go an entire lifetime without encountering the raw state of unwashed and unperfumed man.

Steve walked right past the washing machine and dumped the load in the trash, an extra-large dustbin he had had to special order at the ironmongers. He was hard pressed to find anything that would fit Murdo among his own collection. But T-shirts from film festivals only ever seemed to come in extra-large sizes, and he had quite a collection of those in the bottom of one of his boxes. He picked out one from the Aspen Filmfest, which read *Independent by Nature* across the chest. A pair of stretchy sweatpants could be rolled up at the cuff and would have to do until other arrangements could be made.

Those other arrangements were beginning to bloom in Steve's brain like vapour in the inner atmosphere. He had wanted to help these poor men, and here was where he could begin. His psychiatrist had often talked about taking that important first step. Murdo came out of the shower, looking like a judge at a premier film festival. His two brothers followed suit, until Steve had an entire panel on his couch, waiting for breakfast and another film. Steve tied his bag of garbage and set it at the end of the drive for the trash men. He fried up eggs and bacon, squeezed oranges on his new juicer, and sat through *L.A. Guns* and its sequel.

Willy MacBrayne jumped nervously when Steve and his troupe of T-shirt-clad brothers came through the door of his shop like a company of Jehovah's Witnesses. He wasn't well disposed towards the American because of the way his daughter was acting these days, but he had long regarded the brothers of the shore a useful, if not unfortunate, historical resource. Willy stood defensively behind his Durex sign.

Steve set his cheque book on the counter. "Mr. MacBrayne, I'd like you to outfit these gentlemen."

It was an historical moment that would surely not be forgotten in town annals, so Willy MacBrayne started taking mental note: *Independent by Nature* on Murdo's chest, *Pickaflick* on Doolie's, and *Rendez-vous des Etoiles* on Donal's. Willy led the way through his shop to the warehouse at the back, glancing behind him at the three Wallaces and their benefactor. He could remember their father, who had been a small man, too, and a Tinker, to boot. Even when the family was moved by the council into a house, they still made their living going door to door, selling pots and pans.

Willy had just sold a school blazer the day before, so the padlock on his warehouse wasn't as hard to budge as it sometimes got, rust settling quickly in the salty air. He had to gesture to encourage the others to follow him, the mothbally space admittedly a little dim with only the one light bulb.

Much of the inventory Willy had inherited from his father, but a lot of it was older than that. He ought to have given it all to charity long ago, except that the smell of camphor in which the clothes were preserved had been with Willy since childhood, and it was hard for him to let it go. Some of the army coats felt like old friends, and now and again a youngster would come in asking for one of these relics. At nineteen forties prices, the wool coats were a bargain. And Willy harboured the suspicion that much of what he was holding onto would again find its place in the cycles of fashion.

Murdo, Donal and Doolie went straight for the heavy coats, fingering the buttons, commodities long since vanished from their own. But the American was pulling them away towards a rack of suits.

They were a little baggy, the trousers of those suits, a little turned up at the bottom, as was the style in nineteen fifty.

Willy tutted. "What in God's name would they do with suits?"

Steve McNaught went to a different rack. "A sports jacket, then."

He pulled three off their hangers and handed one to each brother. These were a little more modern, from around the nineteen sixties, when intellectual types sported tweed and smoked pipes. The shortness of the brothers' arms had not been counted on. Murdo turned his up at the cuffs; the others followed his lead.

The American seemed satisfied. He turned back to Willy. "Pants, then."

Willy led them back through the shop and scurried about behind wooden drawers with brass fittings. He found what he was looking for and laid upon the counter a pile of men's underwear.

Steve McNaught laughed. "I suppose we'll be needing those, too." He looked to Murdo, who shrugged. Such things had been worn in childhood, but had gone out with the era of the mother. "What do you say, boys? Four apiece?"

Willy's stack only amounted to ten, but the American wanted them anyway. He took a couple in his own size, too. At the end of the spree, three jackets lay on MacBrayne's counter, together with six Viyella shirts, three pairs of tweed trousers, ten pairs of underpants, three bowties, and three pairs of suspenders.

"I don't suppose you carry shoes?" Steve asked.

Willy disappeared into the back again, brandishing the key to a padlock. He took a while coming back, which allowed the brothers time to try on their new clothes. Willy MacBrayne came back to a shop full of professors.

He set three pairs of army surplus boots on the floor. "The teenagers like these. I wasn't sure I had any left."

Willy licked the tip of his pencil and began the task of tallying up the bill. Steve's eyes wandered about the shelves, hoping to discover signs of George. A ladies' bust sat on the far corner engulfed in a large bra. Not the kind George wore. For that matter, George didn't wear any. The groove of her spine ran up smooth to the fine hair on her neck, uninterrupted by bands of cotton and steel clasps. No doubt the man who had brought her flowers had already discovered that.

The brothers pulled their new boots on. The boots may or may not have fit. The brothers didn't care. It was going to be a year or two before this smart leather began to leak.

"That will be two hundred and sixty-three pounds, and thirty-nine pence," Willy said, setting his pad on the counter. He had never racked up such a bill, and he hoped he didn't look as incredulous as he felt. He studied Steve McNaught's face; his reaction to the bill would be a key point in the retelling of this story. But in this regard, there was little to tell. The American simply bent over the counter to fill in his check, tore it off and handed it over.

"Thanking you," is all he said, before he turned with his troupe of princely tinkers and marched out of the door.

Steve drove the brothers back to their tent and left them with bags of fish and chips. On his way home, he smiled to himself. George was wrong about money, and here was the proof: he had made three lonely souls a little happier. And it gave him a lift, too.

What's more, his new roof hadn't leaked, though it had rained through the night. The wood panelling gave the place a homey feel, and the satellite people were coming up from Glasgow to install a dish out of sight on the back corner where no one could get for brambles. He was now accepted back in The Comm; even though the local men were all married, they could admire from a distance a man who took a woman, then scarpered. Such was the stuff of poets. Besides, George MacBrayne had a thing or two coming.

At home, Steve dialled the familiar 310 area code. It didn't seem as though it should be humanly possible to talk to California from the mid-section of Argyll. As the rings clicked into an answering machine, he pulled the telephone away from his ear. He didn't want to hear his wife, even though he had to listen to know when to speak: *"Terry, Eli, Tanner and T.J. are not in right now. Please leave a message, and we'll get back to you. Bye, and have a great day."* T.J. Even the hairball was included these days.

Steve waited for the beep, trying to re-muster enthusiasm. "Hi, you guys, it's Dad. I want you to come visit. I have this great place on the beach in Scotland. You're going to love it."

He told them living in Scotland was like being in a time warp. He said the people were friendly and the food wasn't that bad. He asked Eli about summer camp and Tanner about his new level in karate. He finished by saying, "I love you guys," then hung up and sat on his plastic-wrapped leather couch, wiping his face with the heels of his hands. He hadn't realised how much he had missed them.

WILLY MACBRAYNE CLOSED SHOP, got on his bicycle and headed out to Achnarannoch. He had lived through enough storms to see one coming, and it was his duty to tell his daughter about this one. He found her in her chair, listening to her songs. She made him tea, while he told her the story in its every detail, flicking cat fur off his flannels as he spoke.

"It starts here," he said. "He thinks he'll be putting Locharbert on the map, but it won't end here. The man has enough money to do a lot of damage."

George handed him a mug. "I don't know why I'm so tired."

Willy turned the cup around to a place where there were no chips, and slurped the tea noisily. "What's the man going to do next?"

George lay down on her mattress. "Willy, I think I've hit the change of life."

"Nonsense," said Willy.

"I'm tired and hot," she said. "I feel like the bottom's about to drop out of my pelvis. I can't eat and I'm not sleeping well."

Willy set his tea on the floor and got up. "It's a tonic you need."

She sighed after he had gone outside with a tea cloth for protecting his hands against stinging nettles. When he got into his potion-mode, he would not be leaving soon. It had been a long time since she had asked her father for anything. She had been rattling around by herself out at Achnarannoch since Steve had left, and she didn't mind the company. She turned over and tried to sleep. She had given Willy a mission, and he would be a while in the picking and the brewing.

She had been watching the lorry loads of lumber driving out to her Rose Cottage. People in town said McNaught had installed a Jacuzzi that had come on a lorry all the way from Glasgow. She didn't want to think about it. She would never be able to undo what he was doing. Her little rose-covered cottage was gone, as sure as if it had drifted out on the tide. It didn't matter what else he did, she thought. Let him make his movie. Let him dress up the brothers; let him dress up the whole town. He had cut her off at her most vital point, the place from which she dreamed.

Willy pulled up a stool and watched her pick her way through the plate of boiled nettles, just as he had always done when feeding her things of dubious gustatory value.

"Every last piece," he said, when she took a moment's pause. It should have irritated her, but this time she found some comfort in it. Just for now, she needed to curl into this caring hand.

"I hear the man's pining after you," Willy said quietly. "The word is he's drinking."

George pushed the plate into her father's hand. She slumped back down onto her mattress. "I suppose you know what he's doing to our cottage?"

"I know fine," said Willy. "But then that cottage was never the saviour you thought it would be."

George groaned. She wasn't up for one of her father's lectures. "Yeah, but I thought it was mine. I thought it was something I could count on." She turned away from him. "Not like Mum. Not like you."

"Is that fair?" Willy asked. "Wasn't I the one who stayed, the one who looked out for you?"

George turned her face to him. She did love this small man with his oddities. "I think I looked out for myself." She saw him wince, but, then, it only seemed fitting for him to hurt, when she was. He was the only biological extension of herself around.

"What do you think I was doing," she asked, "when you were going at it with the post mistress every Hogmanay?"

Willy's voice was almost inaudible. "Sleeping."

George sat up. "Fat chance. Even when I locked the door of the spare bedroom, you just moved into the living room. Why do you think I never wanted to sit on the settee?"

George watched him for a moment, watched the clouds come over his idea of himself. She felt venomous and constricted. But she had said all she had to say, so she pulled a cover over herself. "Let me sleep, Willy."

He went to the door slowly, more fallen than she had ever seen him.

"Dad?" she asked, "Why was it that Steve's grandfather had to leave Locharbert?"

Willy stood a little taller. "Oh, well now, it wasn't so much having to leave as not wanting to stay. As I recall it was a Sheila MacNiall he put in the family way, and the shame of it drove the poor girl to the asylum. Being a bastard, her daughter never was allowed into the school; when she grew up she married a Tinker. She died young and left three wee boys behind. And that's all that's left of that sad tale."

George heard her father leave, imagined him hooking his bicycle clips around the bottoms of his trousers. She closed her eyes, hoping for sleep, but finding after a while, her eyes brimmed with tears. She reached under her mattress and pulled Steve's T-shirt against her face. It almost didn't smell of him anymore. It almost smelled of Tinkers.

CHAPTER NINETEEN

The leaves were already succumbing to colder weather, springing up in surprising hazes of yellows and oranges, as Steve made the trip down to Glasgow Airport to pick up his sons. The days were still warm, but mornings had Steve on his knees in front of his new woodstove, feeding in logs which he had spent some time splitting in the past month. It was as good a therapy as any he had tried. He was drinking less, too; he didn't want his sons reporting any deviant behaviour to his ex-wife.

Besides, he was feeling better. Locharbert was a small town, but he had managed to stay out of George's way. Except for in the distance, he hadn't seen her all summer. He had kept her roses over the door and planted more along the front path. He had brought in the three brothers to clear the patch of land beside the croft, but they had worried about spoiling their new clothes and Steve did most of the work himself. He had wished a time or two at the end of a hard day for his chiropractor back in Malibu.

But it had all come out right. He had bought a goat, a young brown and white kid that he kept in the cleared pen. When he had to pay for feed for the animal, he wondered why he had gone to the trouble of clearing the vegetation in the first place. A few goslings were promised to him from a farm out by Peter Duart's.

Peter and Shefaline had been his best allies in his time since George. Shefaline, who had her suspicions of George anyway, had taken a special interest in Steve's welfare. She brought him bread and cheese, and when her father came to visit from France, kept back a bottle of cabernet for Steve. He was saving it because he had the notion that he would have some people over for a cookout when his boys came. Apart from going to the airport, he had it in mind on this trip to pick up a grill. His culinary skills still weren't formidable, but he could grill a hamburger or a sausage. The bakery made astounding fresh cream cakes which could serve as dessert.

Steve drove around Loch Lomond, its curves and farther shores more familiar to him now. He had made the trip several times, for commodities that couldn't be bought in Locharbert and environs. He had built a kind of life for himself. The telephone hardly ever rang. People still wanted to reach him, but he had given out his phone number to a mere few. He suspected his ex-wife must have handed out his address, what with the number of scripts still arriving. To save the postie, who in America he had called the mailman, he had chained a broken-down shopping cart to the fence up by the road. A hundred-page script didn't fit through his letter box anyway. He left every one unopened. Packed tight in their envelopes, they made good fire starters.

Steve threw his coins into the toll booth at the Erskine Bridge. He drummed on the wheel with the tips of his fingers. In the night, he had felt the approach of his sons as an unease in his stomach. He wanted to be comfortable with them, but he hadn't seen much of them in the past two years, and he didn't know how it was going to be, living in the same house. The drive to the airport took three hours and he'd figured he'd pick up something to eat at the airport. From the bridge, he could see planes spiralling in. He was an hour and half early for his sons' flight.

While he was still angry with George, on lonely nights he had given a few moments' consideration to other women. In the middle of the night, it helped him get back to sleep. But when he awoke in the mornings, the little goat bleating below his window sent his thoughts right back to George. Peter and Shefaline had broached the subject of George a few times over dinner, but he steered the conversation away, letting them know they were on unwelcome ground.

Steve parked his car in the airport lot and walked to the terminal, clicking his key chain between his fingers. His boys had sounded friendly on the phone, but he suspected the terms might have changed during the planning of the trip, the wrenching from friends and familiar places. He waved to them as they came up the jetway, unexpectedly melted by the change in them: Eli about six inches taller, Tanner with much longer hair.

Eli had always been more like his mother Terry: square face, blond and leggy. Tanner was more of Steve's line, smaller and freckled with darker hair than his brother. It was the first time Steve came to below Eli's eye level when they hugged. Eli was seventeen and tanned with sunny streaks in his hair. Steve rubbed his knuckles into Tanner's scalp and called him "Boo," as he had done when they were still a family.

As they walked out of the airport, Steve told them about the party and about finding a grill before they headed up into Argyll. "There's some pretty neat folks I want you to meet."

"Any girls?" Eli asked.

Steve made a mock punch to his son's stomach. "What are they?"

Tanner pulled the chest of his shirt out with his fingers and started to walk with a waggle.

Steve put an arm around each of his boys. "It's really great to see you guys."

Eli and Tanner slept most of the way up into the Highlands, even past Loch Lomond, which Steve had wanted to show them. Further along the road, he stopped at the café where he had had his first encounter with Scottish food. The same black-nailed waitress stood at their table.

"Three beefburger rolls, two Cokes and a fresh orange juice," Steve ordered.

The waitress scribbled on her notepad and left. Eli's eyes trailed her into the kitchen.

"Beefburgers?" said Tanner.

Steve smiled. "Don't even ask."

"What's your house like, Dad?" Eli was curious.

Steve cleared the table for the waitress to put the drinks down. "It's small. You guys will have to share the other bedroom." The boys looked at each other. "But it's real cozy. I just got a satellite dish last week."

"Yeah, well, I hope so, Dad," said Eli, "because I have a ton of friends I have to keep in touch with."

"Chicks," said Tanner.

"I actually decided not to buy a computer," Steve said.

"What?" The boys were shocked.

The waitress returned with their plates. This time she glanced at the beach boy and smiled. "Are you wanting any sauce with that? Tomato? Brown?"

"Dad, I want ketchup," Tanner said.

The waitress brought them a plastic bottle in the shape of a tomato from one of the other tables.

This time she lingered. "Any pudding?"

Eli was looking at her in the open-faced way of American youth. "What kind?"

"Crumble, jam roly-poly, bread and butter."

Tanner and Eli looked at Steve.

"I think we're fine for now."

When the waitress had gone, Tanner leaned across the table. "Why are you speaking like that?"

Steve shook his head. "Like what?"

"All up and down, like the waitress."

Steve shrugged and told Tanner to get on with his beef-burger before it got cold. He hadn't noticed the lilt in his accent, but his sons sounded so American to him, he recognised there must have been some shift. It pleased him even more that he didn't know how to fix it.

As they drove through Inveraray, Steve nudged them awake to show them the castle.

"Wow!" said Tanner, sitting forward in the back seat. "Just like at Disneyland."

"This castle has stood here for hundreds of years," said Steve. "It's made of stone and has an inside. It's definitely not like Mickey's castle."

"All right, all right," said Tanner, sitting back.

Steve glanced over his shoulder at his youngest son. His head had sunk and his arms were crossed over his skateboard T-shirt. Eli wouldn't have sulked this way, but this was Steve's own genes looking back in the mirror at him.

"Sorry, Boo. I just don't want you to think Disney, okay? This is the real thing."

Eli punched Steve's arm lightly. "Like Coke, huh, Dad?"

Eli started to laugh. Even Tanner in the back smiled.

Steve shook his head. "You guys!"

He hadn't realised how much he had missed the boys. Already he saw the two weeks' vacation as too short. He should have written to them more. He should have called more. For an entire year when he was on his slide into oblivion, he had hardly seen them. But he was going to make it up to them now. They were going to keep coming back to see him in Scotland, and he was going to leave them this cottage in the land of their ancestors. It had been an experiment of his forefathers to leave the inner circle and try life in the New World, but now they were back in the old, Steve and Elijah and Tanner McNaught.

They didn't reach Achnarannoch until dark. The croft seemed to be hunkered down into the shadows of the rhododendrons and the pines at the back of the house. Steve wanted to say to his house, "Be nice. This is family."

"Spooky," said Tanner, as they pulled up.

Eli stood in the living room and said, "Cool."

Tanner quickly found the goat and untied it. Steve let him chase around with it on the sand, knowing the beast would find its way back to its food source eventually. Steve unloaded his grill, and came back to find Eli asleep on the couch, drool collecting in a dark spot in the leather at the corner of his mouth. Steve grabbed a towel from the kitchen and tucked it under his son's head. Outside, Tanner was still at the water's edge with the goat. Steve grabbed a jacket and went out to him.

"This ocean smells different from ours," said Tanner as Steve came level with him. "It's more fishy."

Steve sniffed the air. "I didn't name the goat. I thought you'd like to."

Tanner smiled his childish smile that had always been his own, right from the start. He had bigger teeth now, but the same dimple appeared on one side of his mouth, his top lip curled upwards in the way it had always done.

"Thanks, Dad." He squatted down to the goat's face. The goat nudged his forehead, sending him off balance for a moment. "How about Butthead?"

Steve said, "We're going to get some goslings next week."

Tanner's smile broadened. "Goslings? You mean like geese? Sweet!"

"You must be dead beat," Steve said, tugging on Tanner's ear. "Why don't you go to bed?"

Steve had to remind Tanner to clean his teeth, something that had irritated him when he still lived with them in Malibu, but now made him feel like a real father.

"Look after those teeth," he said, watching Tanner squeeze toothpaste from the middle of the tube. "You won't get a second chance."

He wiped Tanner's face with a cloth, then kissed his head. Even after so long away, some things were still a matter of routine. "Good night, Boo."

Tanner went up the small flight of stairs, leaving Steve to sit in the chair opposite his other sleeping son. He had already planned pancakes for next morning's breakfast. His kids had always liked pancakes, especially the estranged oldest one who played guitar in a band in Bloomington and whom he hadn't seen for three years. Maybe he would give him a call. John McNaught. He was part of the clan, too.

Steve went back out to see if the goat had found its way home. But there was only a solitary seagull hunkered down against the wind. The waves were making little splashing noises, as though trying to keep from waking anyone. He could make out the faint light of George's kerosene lamp along the shore. He turned back to the cottage. Ginty, who had finished most of the work on the inside of the croft, had engraved a wooden plaque for over the door that read *Rose Cottage*.

Back inside, Steve poured himself a drink. One solitary drink. He had brought it down to this. A little nightly schnapps to bring on sleep. He was determined not to drink in front of the boys. He sipped it slowly, standing in the doorway, watching darkness cover the sea. When he got upstairs, he found Tanner asleep in his bed. So, no one would sleep in the bunk beds this night, the cherrywood beds he had brought in and the sheets with the cartoon-character print. He lay down next to his son, guilty for ever having pulled out on his family. Somehow, he always turned out to be the father on his way out. Even when he had been living at home, he had spent long stints on location. It was just the nature of the movie beast. No one but he seemed to understand that. His sons had never seen him make pancakes before.

In the morning, Tanner ran off down the beach in search of Butthead.

Eli raised his head from the couch just long enough to ask, "Butt who?"

Steve went ahead and mixed up the batter. But when Tanner came back, he wanted cereal. Eli just kept on sleeping.

Steve put his batter in the fridge. "What kind of cereal?"

"Lucky Charms," said Tanner. "Hey, I found Butthead down at that lady's hut on the beach."

Steve shook his head. "Sorry. No Lucky Charms here. How about Special K?"

Tanner shook his head. "What's her name?"

"George," said Steve.

Tanner took the box of cereal. "You mean like those guys in L.A. who dress up like girls?"

Steve shook his head, but couldn't help smiling. "Her real name is Georgianna. They just call her George for short. Are you going to eat this Special K?"

Tanner studied the box. "I guess so."

Steve stepped in the direction of the fridge. "Because I could make you pancakes, if you want."

"Maybe later," said Tanner.

Eli slept until the afternoon, and when he woke up, he wanted tacos. Steve shook his head. He had forgotten all about Mexican food. "Look guys, this is Scotland."

Eli stretched and scratched the sides of his head. "What do they eat in Scotland?"

Tanner stuck his tongue out. "Beefburgers."

Steve opened the door to his pantry, formerly a broom closet off the kitchen.

"Beans," he said. "They eat a lot of beans."

Steve picked out a bag of marshmallow teacakes. "Wicked Fluffer cookies, though. Or I can make a killer soup."

Steve hoped they didn't opt for the soup, because his soups hadn't been so killer without a pressure cooker. He had one on order at Davies' the ironmonger, but he wanted a special one, stainless steel not aluminium, so it had to come from Switzerland.

Steve decided to take them to the café in Locharbert. As they drove past the Tinker tents, Steve was hoping the three brothers would stay inside. He wanted to wait until later to introduce his sons to those characters. At any rate, they were on his list for the party. Since it was already halfway through the afternoon, the café was empty but for a small group of teenage girls. Eli immediately woke up. The girls took note. Sun-tanned California boys were not a thing ever seen in the Locharbert café.

Steve noticed Nicola among them.

He said, "Or, we could just skip the café, get some groceries and go home."

But the owner, Turo Caparella had already appeared from the kitchen. He fit into Locharbert, in that he was a small man, but his hair was white and his Italian accent worked over English with a heavy slur. "You want to eat?"

"Yeah," said Eli, who was already sitting down at the table opposite the girls and waving his brother and father to do the same.

Steve nodded in Nicola's direction. "How are you doing?"

Eli nudged his father for an introduction.

"This is my son, Eli, and my other son, Tanner," said Steve. "This is Nicola, who used to work at Mrs. McPhealy's where I lived when I first got into town."

Eli waved and smiled. "Hi, you guys."

Tanner played with the salt and pepper. They ordered corned beef rolls, but Eli wasn't paying attention. Tanner ate only half, because, he said, it wasn't like any corned beef he had ever eaten.

Outside the café again, Eli said, "Dad, you have to invite that girl to the cook-out."

Steve didn't answer. He was good and cornered. He was going to have to give Eli his version of the Nicola story, before he heard it elsewhere. But it would have to wait. He wasn't going to say anything in front of Tanner.

The party was scheduled for the weekend. Steve had already done his inviting before Eli and Tanner got there. His list had extended slightly beyond those Steve could strictly count as his friends. Devin Ally's brother had been included because of being related to Devin, and because, being an actor, he was friendlier than the other guests. The postmistress was also on the list, because she liked to talk when Steve was buying stamps. Mrs. McPhealy, he suspected, wouldn't put in an appearance, even though he had sent her an invitation. The Duarts would bring the minister who wanted to keep an eye on the doings of his flock. The brothers were to come, of course, resplendent in their university gear. Willy MacBrayne had been invited. George had not.

When Steve took the boys to the pub for a cider the next evening, Eli noticed straight away the resemblance between the girl in the café and the man behind the bar.

"Is that her dad?" he whispered. "Tell him to let her come over."

Steve mentioned it to Devin because he had no choice.

Devin noted the eager look of the California boy and scratched the side of his head with the opposite hand. "I'll let her know you asked."

"Excellent," said Eli, nodding his head enthusiastically, as unaware as any teenager that he was giving himself away. Other men in the bar nudged each other. Like father, like son, they were saying.

The butcher wasn't invited to the party, but he was pleased to be able to wrap four pounds of mince and two pounds of sausages in white paper. Steve wanted steak, too. Sirloin. The butcher didn't have enough, but would order it on the truck that came on Fridays. The bill came close to fifty pounds. The butcher's wife was pleased with him all night. When Steve went in to pick up the steak on Friday, the butcher's pleasure was written on his face.

"Is there anything else at all I can do for you?" asked the butcher. "A wee bit of back bacon for breakfast?"

Steve nodded. What the hell; he needed to make as many friends as he could.

"I've got some lovely black pudding," said the butcher.

Steve shook his head. He wasn't exactly sure what it was, but if it was attached to the word "pudding," he wasn't holding out any hopes.

"A haggis? I make them myself."

Steve took a haggis. He hadn't the foggiest notion how he would cook the thing, but he didn't want to insult the butcher. He paid for the bacon and the haggis, leaving the butcher with another smile on his face. His wife would be glad for the extra income. A grateful wife is a marvellous thing, even in a land where John Knox still holds sway.

Paper lanterns had often been a feature at parties Steve attended in Malibu, but the ironmonger only shook his head when Steve asked.

"What if it rains?" said the ironmonger.

Steve hadn't counted on rain. In fact, Steve had taken the notion of summer cookout from California and moved it wholesale onto the sands of Achnarannoch.

"Does anybody rent tents around here?" he asked.

The ironmonger sucked air through his teeth. "Planning a wee camping trip, are you?"

"No," said Steve. "I mean, to put on the beach, in case of rain."

The ironmonger shook his head. He wasn't pleased that he hadn't been invited to Steve's party. "You mean a marquee? There's nothing like that around here."

So it was established. Locharbert had neither paper lanterns nor marquees, but it did have Christmas lights, and those were what Steve and his sons strung, one set to another along the borders of their garden and out to a post propped in a hole in the sand dug by Butthead. Steve's goat had learned that he could ram the gate loose and squeeze between the gap. Steve had planted the gate posts himself, but didn't know about tamping them down properly. The goat could take off down the shore at full gallop, and only come back when Tanner went down to George's to retrieve him. It seemed he had discovered her outside food storage, and, Tanner reported, the lady with the long hair to her bum wasn't too happy about it.

On the morning of the party, Steve went out to secure the goat by rope. But when he got to the pen, there was nothing but a thistle, some scrubby weed and a few half-eaten nettles. Steve leaned against the fence and felt it give slightly.

"Damn," he said once for the fence, and "God damn it," for the sake of the runaway goat.

Tanner came running, eating one of the bacon rolls Steve had made them for breakfast. Even Eli was up early this morning, occupying the bathroom, which he wasn't used to sharing, counting his chin hairs in case one more had sprouted in the night. Steve had given up trying to shave and come out to check on the goat.

"What's up, Dad?" Tanner asked.

Steve clicked his tongue noisily. "You'll have to go get Butthead again."

Tanner shrugged. "Okay, but I don't think George will be up yet."

Steve tapped Tanner's shoulder. "Just go anyway, Boo. He has to learn he can't just go running off down there whenever he wants."

He waved to his son as he went off down the sand in his bare feet, throwing bits of roll to the seagulls.

Tanner found Butthead grazing at the back of George's shack. He had saved his last piece of crust for the goat and sat down on Georege's steps, waiting. After a while, George came out in one of his dad's old T-shirts.

"How did you get that?" he asked.

George sat down beside this miniature Steve. "It's complicated."

Tanner recognised this adult speak as a warning. His mother said her relationship with Hairball was complicated. But in that case, her younger son didn't really want to know how. In this case, he was a bit more curious.

He asked, "Did you swap it for something?"

He didn't understand why George found that funny. When she placed her hand on her stomach, he noticed the bump under the T-shirt.

"Are you okay?" he asked.

George plunged her feet into the cold sand and watched it sift between her toes. "No, not really."

Tanner threw off his shoes and socks and played with his toes in the sand, too. The goat liked the activity and came closer for the bait.

"How do you like your dad's new house?" George asked.

Tanner shrugged. "It's a bit small."

He reached out for the goat's tether and grabbed it. George helped to steady him against the struggling goat by holding his shoulders. The goat submitted to its fate. But George kept hold of Tanner.

She smiled and brushed the hair off the boy's face. Tanner had his father's eyes, and they were studying her in the way children have of knowing what hasn't been said.

Tanner got up. "I have to go now."

She waved and watched Steve's son walk back along the shore, pulling the unwilling goat at his side. He walked like his father but wasn't going to be as short. George bent over her knees, feeling like she had reached that point in the morning when the retching might start.

Back inside, she lay down on the couch and turned her music up. It was the only thing that was going to get her through this day. George had heard about the party from just about everyone, but most recently from her father who had received his own invitation.

"The nerve of the man," Willy said. He didn't look as annoyed by the man's nerve as he would have if he hadn't known the postmistress was also invited.

"Don't get yourself in a fankle," George said. "Steve McNaught has nothing to do with us."

Willy knew better. He had tried his nettle tonic on George, but she hadn't seemed to get any better. When she told him her condition felt like menstruation that kept refusing to begin, he remembered something his wife had said forty-five years earlier, and he began to suspect that "the change"

George was experiencing had less to do with infertility than fertility. He made her take a test. He was still her father, after all. When the test came out positive, he had tried not to show his pleasure. George saw it anyway.

When she told the heron, it didn't even turn its head. She knew she had been given plenty of warning. It wasn't the bird's fault if she had chosen not to listen. The heron slowly lifted across the bay. She went out to the water's edge and looked along the shore to her rose cottage, cursing Steve McNaught without meaning a word of it.

Morning sickness was common, she knew, because she had offered all kinds of advice about it to her clients. She was almost enjoying this unexpected turn her life had taken. And she loved this child already.

The sun awoke her with singing, and everything in the world was sharp and tingling. Only the shadow of Steve fell sometimes across the plain of her joy. She knew she couldn't ultimately keep this secret from him. But she could keep it folded in her pocket for a little while longer.

CHAPTER TWENTY

A banging on the door made George groan and turn over. It had the sound of an expectant father. They always had the same look, these men, like little boys suddenly in the middle of a lot of trouble. When she closed her eyes and tried to ignore the sharp knocking, she heard her name from the other side of the door. She got up and answered it.

Steve was standing on the doorstep, looking nervous. She suspected why. The nausea that had begun to flood her mornings suggested she be seated, but she kept standing by the door. "Lost your goat?" she asked.

Steve glanced behind him, as though a battalion might be waiting to come to his rescue. "George, why are you playing games?"

She felt his will against her and resented it. She said, "I hear what you're doing to my house. The word is, you have a sauna over there."

"I put in a shower," said Steve. "Is that so strange?"

George didn't want to stand up any longer, but she didn't want Steve to leave either. "What was wrong with the bath?"

Steve took a step forward. Behind him the tide was creeping over the sand. The clouds were unusually high, lighting the shores of Jura and making the sea shine.

"Baths went out with the Scottish monarchy," he said.

She didn't like the way he was smirking. She never wanted him to have anything over on her again. She took hold of the door and went to shut it. "So did I."

His foot in the door stopped her. "Why does everything have to be a battle for you?"

She looked down at his foot. He had large feet. "I have nothing to talk to you about."

She heard him sigh. She heard his difficulty with the question. "Tanner came back from your house saying something about you being pregnant."

She laughed. She didn't know why. But it didn't seem to please him.

"Are you?"

She laughed again. She liked having something over on him for a change. "Wouldn't you like to know."

"Yes," he said. "I would."

He was breathing quickly. It served him right. If he could have her cottage in secret, she could have this baby in secret. See if he liked being on the receiving end. "Then I'll tell you when I'm good and ready."

He lifted his hands. "Okay, if that's the way you want it." He punched the door hard enough that she winced for the sake of his knuckles. "If that's the way you want it, then fine."

She watched the back of him moving away just as his son had done earlier. One of his jeans pockets had a frayed hole in it that hadn't been there the last time she had run her hand over it. It was only then that she noticed she was still wearing his T-shirt. She tugged it down over her stomach and read *Sundance* over the sensitive nipple on her left breast. He was already halfway along the shore between his house and hers.

STEVE THOUGHT ABOUT CANCELLING the party. The clouds were moving faster, meaning they would soon be coming down to about head level. He cursed these Scottish skies that would never leave a person alone. He looked back at George's house and felt himself go limp inside. He had concluded on his walk home that she wouldn't say anything about the baby, because she probably didn't know if it was his. By the time he reached his garden, where the captive goat was bleating loudly, he was ready to reach for the first line of Christmas lights and yank them down.

Eli was standing in the doorway, sniffing the open bottle of Irn Bru in his hand. He had eaten and showered, and the day was full of flowers and bees and the prospect of girls. He held out the bottle. "What's this, Dad?"

Steve unhooked the lights from the post. "It's some Scottish thing."

Eli screwed the top back on. "What are you doing?"

Steve stopped and let the lights coil around his feet. "Eli, I have to tell you something." He looked about for Tanner, but there was no sign of him. "That girl you like used to work for Mrs. McPhealy when I lived there."

Steve was letting his voice drop, so that Eli had to leave the door and come closer. He looked puzzled. "Yeah?"

Steve looked into his son's soft-cheeked face. "Way at the beginning, she had the hots for me and tried to kiss me once. Mrs. McPhealy saw and soon the whole town was yakking. I got thrown out. It was a mess. They probably thought, probably still think, I raped her."

Eli put his head down and came back laughing in disbelief at his father. "So, she's pretty hot, huh?"

Steve couldn't help but laugh, too. The relief was too much. "I guess you could say she's pretty hot stuff."

Eli turned and went back towards the house, shaking his head and laughing. Steve would never understand him, this child of the sun. He would never understand himself, for that matter. His tight nervousness must have come down the Scottish line and somehow eluded Eli altogether.

Eli turned back at the door. "You didn't hump her, though, did you, Dad?"

Steve lifted his hands in defence. "So help me God."

After Eli had gone back into the house, Steve restrung his Christmas lights. He still needed a punching bag, still needed to knock the stuffing out of a swinging bag of sand. But instead he went into the house and started forming hamburger patties on his new granite countertop.

The minister was the first to arrive at the party, and Steve noticed right away his grey-knitted socks, the ones Mrs. McPhealy had been knitting on the night of the terrible misunderstanding. Woman was always leading poor man around in her dance. Man liked the contact, but he was soon dazed and wondering why he had come in the first place. No matter how much men strutted their stuff on all the stages, women were the ones who wrote the script. Steve led Reverend Campbell to the drinks table and left him there.

Willy MacBrayne arrived, much to Steve's surprise, shifting his feet until the postmistress appeared in a large flowery dress, a bag of shortbread in hand. Steve noticed Willy watching her as he introduced his sons to other guests, including Devin and Anita Ally who arrived with Devin's brother but no daughters. Eli went to stand with Willy.

When the three brothers appeared in their new clothes, they stood outside for a while among the other guests, but seemed not to know what to do with their arms and legs. As if with one will, they drifted inside to watch another of Steve's videos. With a squeeze, they managed to fit arm against arm on the couch.

Peter Duart arrived with Shefaline and the dog, Cuilean, who was immediately interested in herding the goat and had to be put back in the car, where he sat whining. Peter went off to mingle, while Steve took Shefaline inside to show off her painting above his fireplace. He served her the French wine she had brought him when he had first broken up with George. He couldn't forget about George, not even after several glasses of wine and trying hard to be the lively center of the party. It was a role he had slipped into many a time.

By the time Nicola Ally arrived, in a slinky dress with straps as thin as blades of grass, Eli had joined the Tinkers and was perched on the arm of the couch. He had taken a few swigs from the bottle of Irn Bru. The brothers were too engrossed in *L.A Guns 11* to warn him not to.

"Is it supposed to be salty?" Eli asked. No one answered.

It didn't sit well in his stomach, no matter what was in it. But he forgot about that when Nicola walked into the house.

She was moving slowly and deliberately, trying hard to be nonchalant. She only glanced at Eli. "Where's the lavvy?"

Eli jumped up and directed her to the back of the kitchen. No longer interested in the film, he stood by the bathroom door until she came out again.

"Want to see my bedroom?" he asked, grinning.

Nicola tried not to smile. "That'll be right."

She went back outside slowly, asking to be caught. Eli wanted to follow, but the quick jump from the couch had unsettled the Irn Bru in his stomach even more, and he had to dart into the bathroom instead. He didn't know whether to sit or stand, so he sat down on the toilet and cupped his hands over his mouth.

"Oh, God."

Nicola came back in and picked up the bottle Eli had left outside the bathroom. She sniffed, then looked at the label. She smelled it again. "What the hell is this?"

She put her ear to the bathroom door. After a while, Eli came out, trying to smile.

But he only got as far as the brothers on the couch, before he lost the Irn Bru together with the hamburger he had eaten earlier. The brothers lifted their feet to avoid the swill.

Tanner came running. "Dad!" he called. "Eli just barfed all over the floor." And then, because it suddenly seemed like a good idea, Tanner ran off to fetch his father's camera. He hoisted it onto his shoulder and clicked the shutter open, just in time to catch Eli losing another load.

"Get lost!" Eli shouted weakly.

Tanner kept shooting while Steve ran in. The brothers kept watching the video, their feet in the air. A huge explosion took out a multistorey building. Fire engines and police cars rushed to the scene.

Nicola handed Steve Eli's bottle. "Take a whiff of that."

Steve put the bottle to his nose. It didn't smell good, but then neither did haggis. Perhaps he had let it sit around for too long. Perhaps his wife would use it as evidence against him, when her son ended up in hospital with botulism.

Steve placed a hand on Eli's shoulders. "How are you doing, Bud?"

Eli groaned. "A little better, I think."

Mrs. Ally came in and reflexively started mopping up the mess, tutting because she had to work around the feet of the Tinkers on the couch. Steve helped Eli up and led him outside.

Shefaline turned Eli's face into the light. "He needs ginger. And parsley."

Steve had noticed a bunch of parsley growing at the back of the house. Shefaline went off to make a *tisane*. When Devin walked over, Steve handed him the bottle.

Devin sniffed it. "Where in God's name did you get this?"

"I don't remember," Steve said, though he remembered well enough. He knew he had already pushed things far enough by having the brothers at the party at all.

"I think I'd like to take a walk," said Eli, glancing at Nicola, who was hovering, looking concerned and pulling the thin straps back onto her shoulders with her pinkies.

Devin scratched the side of his head as his daughter led Eli out from under the Christmas lights into the dark, where many things happen that wouldn't in normal light. When Shefaline came back with her cup of parsley tea, the two figures were already faded dots in the distance. Steve felt obligated and drank it on Eli's behalf. It tasted like the green soup around the base of Mrs. McPhealy's overcooked peas. When Shefaline went back to join her husband, Steve tipped the rest on George's yellow roses. Tanner caught it on film.

The critics had often praised Steve's directing for its trademark realism. He had picked it up early from a European film professor, and had been only too glad that his colleagues had been slow to follow suit. Tanner caught the far-off look in Shefaline's eyes while her husband talked. He followed his brother up the shore and caught the couple lying between two dunes.

Back at the party, the Tinkers' movie was over and they were shifting together around the outskirts of the lit triangle, cramming in hamburgers and sausages. Tanner crouched beneath them, recording their uncanny shuffle. Behind the house, Anita Ally was reprimanding her husband for ever telling their daughter she was invited to the party.

Devin called the American boy "the height of nonsense." Anita was appeased. At least, that's how she looked through Tanner's lens.

Steve waved Tanner away. "Put that camera down before you drop it."

Tanner moved away, but he didn't put the camera back. He filmed guests going in and out of the toilet. He caught Murdo, Donal, and Doolie taking a collective leak onto the parsley patch. He went back along the dunes and caught his brother kissing Nicola. He even managed to catch for a while his brother's pursuit of him. But Eli had given up the chase quickly. Back at the house, only the Tinkers remained. Steve had drawn from them the history of the bottle of Irn Bru, and he would have been displeased if he hadn't been making his own way down a bottle of Bowmore single malt.

Only Murdo felt a pang of guilt. The other two simply knew they were in trouble.

"No harm done, eh?" said Donal, as Eli came in, trying to look as though he hadn't just been kissing.

"What's up, Dad?"

Steve gave up. His sons were out of order. The house was a mess. When he went in later to brush his teeth, the toilet was in an even worse state. The brothers fell asleep on the couch. Tanner was filming Eli flexing his muscles in the mirror, when Steve looked into their room to say goodnight.

"Great party, Dad," Eli said.

Steve said goodnight. He rolled himself up in his quilt. His sons were happy, but he wasn't. His head hurt. He had been trying to shake the thought of George all night. If the baby wasn't his, he didn't know how he would cope. Even if it was, he wasn't sure he had enough of a handle on his own life to withstand the upheaval.

CHAPTER TWENTY-ONE

S teve had given up telling Tanner to put the camera down. The two weeks of the boys' vacation was nearly up, and it seemed as though his youngest son had experienced it all through the lens of a camera. Steve couldn't blame him for that. Since Eli had hooked up with Nicola Ally, Tanner had been for the large part on his own. There was Butthead the goat, of course, but Butthead's only personal goal seemed to be to break free and make his way to George.

Steve had driven Tanner along the peninsula to collect the half-dozen goslings he had ordered. For a while they had delighted in them, a box of cheeping cotton balls, but they had grown fast, and wormy goose turds lay all about the garden. There were already green stains on the new living room rug. Butthead didn't like the goslings, nor did Steve much. Eli came in for some meals and to sleep, and the glibness of the young in love was beginning to wear on Steve. He had brought his boys over to be with him, not with Nicola Ally, and not constantly behind a camera.

With only a few days to go, Eli announced over his midday bowl of cereal that he was going to stay with Steve and go to school in Locharbert. He had already run the idea past his mother. Eli put her on speaker phone. Steve hardly had time to gather a defence before his wife started shouting. She kept calling them "my boys," which made Steve's neck hot. But he knew in the way that she had always been with her boys, that they were hers more than his. With his drinking past, the odds were stacked against him ever having the boys.

Afterwards, he explained it all to Eli, and for the first time in the visit, Steve watched clouds come down over his eldest son.

"You just want to stay because of Nicola," Tanner said.

Eli sent his foot flying under the table and caught Tanner around the shin. Steve shouted at both of them.

Tanner ran to the door. "You just want to hump Nicola."

Eli pursued but was too slow even for a twelve-year-old with a bad leg. "What if I do, you little creep?"

Eli sulked, and even Tanner accused Steve of not wanting them to stay. Steve tried to explain, but his reasoning was no match for the simplicity of the young. He did want them, but not every day. He was trying to get his life on track and he wasn't up for the demand of their lives on his. Still, he could hover over his sleeping youngest son; he could watch Eli spruce himself for an evening's "walk" with Nicola, and love him for every silly new hair on his chin.

Steve leaned against the bathroom doorway. "I hope you're being careful," he said.

Eli licked his fingers and smoothed his eyebrows.

"Are you listening?"

Eli started to walk away. "Chill, Dad."

"No, you chill," Steve called after him. "In fact, empty a whole goddamn ice tray down your pants."

Eli didn't turn back. Steve sat down on his couch, oddly free of little men, and played with the seam at the end of the armrest. He knew he was jealous; if he couldn't make love work, why should a seventeen-year-old with surf in his brain?

Steve got up and poured three shots of whisky into a wine glass. Tanner filmed him through the bars of the banister.

"Don't tell your mother," Steve said.

It was something he had heard a lot from his own father. Mum was always the word when it came to his father's quick dips into bars, or rides in the car with other women. *Don't tell your mother.* He never had. He was a good soldier, his father said. A soldier paid off in candy and five-and-dime toys. Of course, his mother knew his guilt, both his and his father's. Women always seemed to know, and perhaps that's why they lead the dance.

Steve looked guilty now. It couldn't be missed, even on celluloid. Tanner shut off the camera and went to his room, to the dinosaur sheets his father had bought him, thinking he was still five years old. He didn't really want to stay in Scotland. He just wanted to be like his brother. Life seemed to be a lighter load for Eli. Tanner didn't want to go back home and live with his mother's boyfriend, but he did want his mother now. In the loneliness of his small upstairs room, with his father drinking down below, he began to cry.

Steve didn't fight his ex-wife over Eli staying. He told his boys he loved them, then drove them down to the Glasgow airport. Nicola, Eli informed him in the car, was to follow soon. She and Eli had made a teary departure outside the Locharbert post office. Eli had some money of his own and would find a place for him and Nicola to stay. Perhaps she could even work for his mother. Steve didn't contradict, even when Eli told him they were going to get married.

Tanner was quiet in the back seat. When Steve asked him about going into sixth grade, he shrugged his shoulders.

"I can't keep you here, Boo. The courts have already said you need to be with Mommy for now."

Tanner said, "I guess," and went back to window-staring.

Steve bought him chocolate in the airport. He bought Eli a car magazine. He didn't want to lose them, but he hated the ordeal of saying goodbye. There was still an hour, even though he had cut it as close as he could. He took Tanner for a sandwich while Eli went to call Nicola. They sat in the cafeteria, pushing their food around, unwilling to eat.

"Maybe Mom will let you take a film course this semester," Steve said.

Tanner shrugged.

"I think you'll make a good director one day." Steve patted the back of his son's hand.

A smile flickered and died on Tanner's face. Eli came back, looking tortured.

He sat down heavily and picked up Tanner's sandwich. "This isn't fair."

"Eat up," said Steve. "We'd better get over to the gate."

Steve didn't know how to say goodbye to his boys, so he hugged them and punched them on the shoulder. Eli slid a silver ring off his finger and told Steve to give it to Nicola.

Tanner said, "I left you the film, Dad."

Steve was surprised. "You did? Well, should I send it to you when I've looked at it?"

Tanner shrugged. "Nah."

Steve caught his son in a half-Nelson and kissed his dark hair. "Thanks, Boo."

Steve watched the plane lift into the grey skies over Glasgow, then turned away, relieved and guilty. He walked out to his car feeling empty. He could never love enough or father enough. He could never be anything enough to satisfy who he was supposed to be. He drove back along Loch Lomond, returning to his life in Locharbert, where he could never be Scottish enough, either.

When Steve got home, his cottage seemed as though he had never lived in it. He poured himself a drink and took it out to the water's edge. It was too late for seabirds, and the sun had already lain itself down behind the islands. From where he stood he could make out the lights in George's house. He remembered kissing the mole on her back; in the memory of his fingertips, he could still feel the grooves of her spine.

He walked along the shore with his glass and his bottle and stood at the side of her house, watching her through her window feeding her cats in her nightie. Her hair was wrapped into a knot on the top of her head, and he knew the sensation of it loosened and falling over his hands. He kept walking, finishing the bottle eventually and tossing it out to sea. Like himself, an empty vessel; no hidden message within.

He wandered into the edge of the town, came upon the shore dwellings and stopped there. He listened for a moment and heard coughing.

"Who's there?" Murdo called out.

Steve lifted the flap and stepped in. "It's only me."

Donal sat up among the dark heaps on the floor. "I thought it was the policeman."

Steve lay down on the floor, finding something in the darkness to pull over his legs. The nights were getting chilly. On the other side of the tent, Doolie's cough was hard and raw.

Steve closed his eyes. He had walked a long way and the drink was drifting him off like the bottle he had sent out into the waves. He didn't want to go back to his black hole of a house.

"Good night," said Murdo.

Steve could hear the satisfaction in Murdo's sigh as he lay back down. For some reason, the ground was never hard under the Tinkers' tent. Right now, with the waves not twenty feet away, and the wind sifting through the canvas, it was all that was needed. Steve didn't hear anymore until he awoke and found himself watching the undulations on the inside of the tent roof. There was no one about, and rain was tapping slowly on the sides of the tent. Steve closed his eyes and let himself fall away.

When he came to again, he looked at his watch. Half the morning had gone. He got to his knees and peered out from behind the flap. The rain had stopped, but the sky still looked dark, as if the day didn't want to wake up. Coming along the beach from the direction of the town were the three brothers carrying plastic bags. Steve climbed out and waved to them. The clothes he had bought them had lost their newness; the bottoms of their trousers were beginning to fray. Doolie was coughing.

"You'll be staying for some breakfast," Murdo said, when they came near.

Steve thanked them, but his stomach wasn't up for food this morning.

"You'll be missing those boys of yours," said Donal.

Steve smiled. He wished he had done a better job at the airport. By now his sons would be back with their mother, laying out the details of the vacation for her scrutiny. By now she would know that her seventeen-year-old son was intent on marrying, and Steve could expect a phone call any time. In the meantime, he had to deliver the ring to Nicola.

He found her in the café at lunch with a few other girls with a multitude of rings on their fingers and scorn on their faces. He stood by the door, waiting for her to notice. Turo Caparella came out of the kitchen, wiping his hands, so Steve took a seat and ordered coffee. She didn't come over immediately. The other girls glanced at him and left in a clutter of cheap jangling jewellery. Nicola took her time coming over. She slid into his booth, but didn't sit opposite.

Steve worked Eli's ring out of his denim jacket pocket and set it on the table in front of her. It had the letters of runes engraved in the silver.

Nicola picked it up. "What's this, are you trying to marry me now?"

Steve took a sip of his coffee, the colour of tea. "Eli sent it along for you."

Nicola slid it onto her fourth finger, although it was too big, and she had to squeeze her fingers together to keep it from rolling off.

"I'd like to talk to you," Steve said.

Nicola looked up distrustfully. But now that he had her attention, he wasn't sure what he wanted to say. When Nicola looked away, he cleared his throat.

"Eli still has to finish high school," he said. "I think it would be better if you waited until next summer to go out there."

Nicola dropped her jaw in exaggerated fashion. "Next summer? No friggin' way." She turned the ring on her finger. "There's nothing for me to do around here. I'd just be sitting on my thumb."

Nicola was looking at him, as though he should make her an offer. But he didn't understand what. "Help me out here," he said.

She picked up the salt and pepper shakers and stood them side by side. "What about that film you're making about Locharbert?"

Steve shook his head. "Tanner was making the film, not me."

Nicola switched the salt and pepper around. "Eli said Tanner was only doing it to get you to like him."

Steve ran his fingers through the short stubble hair he couldn't be bothered shaving anymore. Of course, he had mentioned to the boys that he had had notions of filming in Locharbert. He had even shown them the first reel he had shot of the town at night, with no one about, just the wind and the stray tissue. But he had not made any connection to what Tanner was doing, and it caught in his throat now the sacrifice of Tanner to the unlived life of the father.

"I'm good at acting," Nicola said. He wasn't looking at her, but he could tell that she had turned away to say it. "My Uncle Iain used to be an actor, too. It kind of runs in the family."

Steve lifted his hands in defence. "Wait a minute, I didn't come here to make movies."

Nicola looked straight at him. "But it's what you do, isn't it?"

Steve chewed the inside of his lip.

"Anyway, you'd be doing my dad a favour," Nicola said. "It could put Locharbert on the map."

Steve took the salt and pepper from Nicola and set them back at the end of the table. "Some people think Locharbert is just where it should be on the map."

Nicola smiled her Devin Ally smile with all its attendant good teeth. "Go on, it'll give me something to do while I wait for Eli to finish high school."

Steve drank up his coffee and counted a few coins onto the table. "I'll think about it."

Nicola smiled and made to rise from the table, but Steve caught her arm. "About that thing that happened at Mrs. McPhealy's."

Nicola sat back down, but she wouldn't look at him. "What about it?"

"I just wanted to say that I understand, that's all."

Steve tried to get up out of the booth, but she caught his sleeve. "What is it you understand?"

Steve didn't sit back down, just hovered, bent in the middle until he could slide out. "You know, that girls sometimes develop infatuations for older men."

Nicola laughed. "Not me, if that's what you think." She stood up beside the table. "I just felt sorry for you, that's all."

Steve sat back down. He would always be at the butt end of some woman's tongue. He still had to go home and face his ex-wife, but he could ignore her for a while longer. It was for reasons such as this he hadn't installed an answering machine. For now, he wanted to settle down in front of Tanner's two weeks of shooting and see what he had come up with. He waited in town for the bus, then took its long and winding tour out to the outlying farms and finally ended up at Achnarannoch.

The house was as he and the boys had left it, down to the stain on the bathroom tile where Tanner had missed the toilet. The smudge on the carpet from the geese was no less green than when it had left the bottom of Eli's foot. He fed the goat and the goslings, then washed the plates he had used the morning before with the boys. The plumber had advised against a dishwasher, as the shower was already taxing the system. Steve lifted a bottle down off the top of the fridge, grabbed a glass and set Tanner's film ready to play.

WHEN DONAL WALLACE WAS TAKEN into hospital for walking pneumonia, Steve McNaught was blamed. If he hadn't taken away their old clothes, it would never have happened. Still, everyone knew that a few nights in the comfort of a hospital ward with nurses in attendance was probably as close to paradise as Donal was likely to get on this side of the grave. So no one complained too loudly. And it was said in the post office that Steve McNaught visited Donal Wallace every day in the hospital and that he had purchased three greatcoats from MacBraynes to see the Tinkers through the winter. It was also said that he had been seen giving a ring to Nicola Ally in Caparella's Café and that she had been out to his house several times since his sons had returned to America.

George MacBrayne complained to her father, who gave her an ear, but, since Steve McNaught was the father of his grandchild-to-be, he was these days more in the way of feeling gratitude towards the man.

"He belongs in a bloody soap opera," George said, washing the lettuce for dinner at her father's house. Becoming a mother had made her think more about her own mother, and she had started coming over, working her way through a trunk of her mother's belongings that had sat in the attic since the week the woman had left.

George even found a couple of maternity dresses, which she didn't quite need yet, but she tried them on anyway. Since she took after the MacBraynes in height, the dresses were too long. She had Willy measure them and chop them off at the knee, leaving enough fabric for a headscarf to match.

"You're just like your mother," said Willy. "Floozy-ing around and then blaming a man for putting you in the family way."

George turned the tap off and watched the lettuce leaves swirl around her hand. "Did Mum not want to have me, then?"

Willy laid a hand on her shoulder. It's what he had always done when he talked to George about her mother. "She did, in her own way. But she complained about the stretch marks and the veins, the sickness, all that kind of thing. She blamed me for not taking proper care."

George turned round to him. She had never regarded herself as a piece of failed birth control. "Is that why you started foisting 'proper care' on other people?"

Willy's hand dropped.

George tried to focus on her lettuce circle dance. She felt she was too old to find out new facts about her life.

Willy put his hand back on her. "I wanted you that much."

A tear ran off the end of George's nose and splashed into the water. She turned and smiled. "Steve knows how to take care of Steve McNaught," she said. "Counting on a man like that would be setting myself up for a fall."

Willy patted her shoulder. "Not everyone is like your mother, you know, Georgie."

George shook her head. "I know he'll leave. Eventually he will leave."

"Would you like me to talk to him?"

"God, no," said George. "Just you stay out of it. I can manage on my own."

She hadn't meant to cut him down, but her tongue had always had a way of getting away from her. He took a cloth and wiped the counter where the water had slopped over from the sink, and then he left her in the kitchen. She could hear him messing about with his books in the next room, banging the dust off them, putting them away on shelves. It was what he did when he couldn't cope.

George made an extra effort with the salad, chopping in a crumble of white cheese, roasting pine nuts in garlic and sprinkling them on top. But she felt like an assassin. She gave herself the best defence, and argued that Willy had always been a nosy old nuisance.

"Why are you so set against giving the man a chance?" Willy asked over the salad. He had had time to talk himself out of his hurt.

"He's meddling," she said. She isolated a pine nut and stabbed it with her fork. "Look where it got Doolie Wallace. Look at Nicola Ally. He thinks Locharbert is just another of his film sets. He's tinkering with us, moving things about."

Willy set his fork against the side of his plate and chewed. "It looks like he moved you about all right."

George impaled another nut. "It only looks that way."

It was already dark by the time they had finished their pudding and had a cup of tea while they watched the news on television. George looked out the window.

"Och, I think I'll just stay again tonight." She knew it was the best she could do to make things up to her father. Willy went into the kitchen to fill a hot water bottle, as he had done for her every night of her childhood.

It was halfway through the night when a banging at the door had Willy up in his dressing gown asking through the letterbox who the intruder was. He went to get George because it was a father come for her midwifery services.

She didn't have her purple birthing outfit with her, but anyway it had become a little tight around the waist. She got in the tractor with the prospective father and drove out to the croft, where the wife was crouched against the side of her bed. When she told George she couldn't do this, George told her she could and to go into her monkey self. The father laughed, but the wife found no humour in it.

George resisted the impulse to give the woman her hand. Every woman was alone in this moment, and the more she settled into that aloneness, the quicker this would go.

But this birth felt different to George and made her attentive in a new way. Every stage, every small victory along the way, was going to be hers in a matter of months. She saw the pain in the mother's face and tried to climb inside it. When the baby tumbled down, George held this new slip of life longer than usual. In a matter of a few months, she would be looking into her own child's sweet face.

CHAPTER TWENTY-TWO

When he first heard the rumours about George MacBrayne, Peter Duart had not believed them. But from the top of his ladder outside the bakery one day in autumn, there was no denying the bulge under George's trench coat.

Shefaline had been more able to believe the "news" that was running up and down Main Street with the fallen leaves, but Peter had not wanted to find Steve McNaught guilty of such a crime.

Shefaline had laughed at him. "Crime? It's just the way of men, *mon pauvre*."

Peter began to insist that Steve should do the right thing by George.

"You are sounding like the minister," Shefaline said.

"It's not for religious reasons," said Peter. "It's just a question of common decency."

Shefaline ended the conversation there. There were times when her husband fell back on the morals he had been fed at boarding school. She didn't want to accuse him of not thinking for himself. It would be too much of a challenge to the way he saw himself. And, in any case, there was a sense in which what he had been taught was right.

Still, Shefaline wanted, as wives of other men often do, to keep this other man within her allegiance. She had invited him for dinner several times since he had split with George, and he seemed glad for the distraction of good food, wine, and flirtation. Peter, floating that much higher over life than most, hardly seemed to notice. But now he wanted to invite Steve over, with the intention of pointing out to him some rights and wrongs.

Steve arrived with a good shiraz. When Locharbert's off-licence failed to supply any decent wine, he had sent away for it. It came by the crate and gave the postie some difficulty on days he had to haul it from the back of his van down the drive to Steve's back door. Just once, the postie had left the wine up on the road, and it had never been seen again. Some in Locharbert had dined grandly in the following weeks, though who those people were was a secret never to be told to an outsider. Which meant that neither Peter nor Shefaline ever knew, and not even the postmistress, who was, after all, from Glasgow.

Shefaline had come into two dozen oysters from a boat that had docked in Locharbert with a Frenchman aboard. Shefaline didn't know him, but he was happy to unload some of his cargo in exchange for a baguette and a dish of ratatouille. Steve hadn't had oysters in so long; he was excited by the prospect. He handed the wine to Shefaline and kissed both of her cheeks.

"I brought something to show you, too," he said, holding up Tanner's video.

Steve had never had quite so much garlic on his oysters, but the bread and salad offset the sting. He glanced at Peter, who seemed ponderous and had barely met his eye as they ate.

"Okay," Steve said, as Peter stood up to clear the dishes and Shefaline brought in her platter of cheeses. "Let me have it."

Peter sat back down in front of his pile of dirty dishes.

"Well," he said, "everyone knows George MacBrayne is in the family way."

Shefaline laughed to hear her husband's speech so stilted.

Peter glanced a warning at her. "You see, people around here are different from the way they are in America. They expect a man to do the right thing."

"*Mon oeil*!" said Shefaline, sawing through the crusty layer of bread into its warm inner flesh. "Locharbert boys hardly ever do the right thing. The minister is always complaining about it."

"Yes," said Peter, looking studious and trying not to be aggravated. "But in this case, the boy is a man, a man of means, and I think that changes things."

"It takes two to make a baby," Shefaline said, melting a gooey Brie onto her slice of bread. "George can look along for herself."

"Look *out* for herself," Peter said. "Besides, I'm trying to talk to Steve man-to-man."

Shefaline shrugged and bit into her bread.

Steve cleared his throat, but didn't meet anyone's eye. "Just for the record, this man of means doesn't even know if the child in question is his. The woman in question was seen with another man not a week after this man of means left."

Shefaline set her bread on her plate. "*Une pute, quoi*!"

Peter said, "That's not what I've heard."

"*Ah, bon*," said Shefaline, "and you believe everything you hear in this town."

"Well, no," said Peter. He glanced into his wife's face and realised for a fleeting moment that such scorn must have always been lying somewhere below the surface.

He turned to Steve. "I had no idea."

Steve smiled, though he didn't feel like it. He had hoped those who knew George better might claim she was incapable of this. Even he could locate in himself a serious area that would have nothing to do with the idea that George had slept with someone else so soon after he had left. But there was another part of himself that threatened to fall apart if George really was pregnant by him. It was his instinct to run: from his first wife, perhaps even his second. Running onto the next project was a natural reflex, one that had always worked, until it didn't anymore. Thoughts of making *Locharbert, the Movie* had been giving him reason to get out of bed these mornings. He could hear his feet beginning to hit that pavement.

After the table was cleared, Steve put his video into the machine and sat back on the arm of the couch, just as the tissue began to float, as if by itself from the pebbles on the shore to the roof of the Tinkers' shack. Tanners' filming didn't start until after Steve's exploration of Locharbert at night, but he had decided to keep his part, as a kind of prelude to the filming of the party and the people. He had edited out some repetition, but he had decided to keep Shefaline looking away from her husband like a figure in a painting by Renoir. He noted his hosts went quiet at that part, but they laughed at the scenes with Eli being sick at the Tinkers' feet.

Steve said, "I was thinking of doing a section on Scottish food and then editing in this part."

"You'd better not," said Peter.

Shefaline covered her mouth when the camera found Eli and Nicola in a passion on Steve's leather couch, but laughed when the goat took a run and butted the camera.

Steve had already watched the tape through a few times, but not with an audience. It took him back to the many screenings he had sat through, plunging into despair if the audience didn't seem to get what he was after, elated when they clapped or laughed in the right places.

When the video was over, he took no credit for his editing. Shefaline praised Tanner's eye for the unusual. Peter liked the flow of sequences.

Steve slid the video back into its box. "What if I did more of this? I was thinking I could start with a long shot of the town, then zero in on certain characters."

Shefaline clapped her hands. "Art in Locharbert!"

"I don't know," said Peter. "I wouldn't want it to explode in your face. These are very private people."

"I've been thinking we could start with you," said Steve, "since you look into everybody's window." Steve shifted to the edge of the armrest. "What if we introduced each character by coming through their window from your point of view."

Peter smiled. "Me? Well, I don't know."

"But you love films," said his wife.

Steve stood up. He hadn't felt this keyed up in a long time. "The Wallace brothers could be a sort of centrepiece. They know everything that ever happened in Locharbert. And then the postmistress, Queen of Gossip. Reverend Campbell, Secret Sinner. Who else?"

"Willy MacBrayne's the historian," Peter said.

"Devin Ally, of course," said Shefaline. "Everything runs through The Comm."

Peter cracked his knuckles. "What about my parents? Americans always like castles."

Steve ran his hands through his hair. "I could pitch it as a slice-of-life. Maybe I could bring in a small camera crew. But then it would start getting expensive. I'd have to pay the actors."

Peter nodded. "You would have to pay them something. Not much."

"I could maybe get a little seed money," he said, "but I won't get much for a quiet project like this. Bring in a few wealthy donors as executive producers, give them screen credit, a bit of the back end, play up the European angle."

Shefaline brought a bottle of Baileys Irish Cream and three glasses from the sideboard. "To Locharbert Films!" she said.

Steve took his glass and emptied it. "To Rose Cottage Productions!"

Peter threw his glass into the hearth. "And all who sail in her!"

Shefaline poured again, and kept pouring until Bailey's cream gave way to straight shots of Ardbeg. Peter brought out his guitar and they sang Scottish songs, none of which Steve knew, but all of which he gave his best. As morning spread out from the thin line beyond the hills, Steve stood by the window, the same window under which he and George had sat that first time with the rain streaming down, on that day when she moved with the small tinkle of bells on her dress.

He hadn't seen her for so long, and he had to keep pulling himself out of the kind of spiral that last time he almost hadn't managed to climb out of. He could feel the drinking threaten to take him over again, but he thought he could manage it if he had a project going. It was a sordid sort of dance, but he had pulled it off before: just enough of a habit to keep him on his toes, but not so as to make the project impossible. He had spent three months in Spain like that, and if the film hadn't bombed, it might have had its rewards. When the critics hit him, the drinking spiralled out of balance again and took him down with it. If only he'd been able to make the films he wanted, it would have gone differently.

Locharbert began to hold that promise for Steve. There would be no studio pulling the strings, turning his hand here, making his foot go there. He would be calling the shots. He had enough money to help finance a small project like this, and there was a trend already in play in the industry towards real-life drama.

He thought of the teenagers of Locharbert like Nicola, and how the project might give them something to stick around for. Steve McNaught was on a roll. It was what he did best. This kind of dance was what he specialised in.

CHAPTER TWENTY-THREE

No one standing in line at the Locharbert post office mentioned Steve McNaught's upcoming film. Actors, they knew, were paid in at least four figures, and everyone's mortgage stood to benefit. George MacBrayne was notably quiet, too, though everyone knew for different reasons. She had withdrawn from the town, even as she spent more time there, lurking behind her father's curtains, staring out at the buzz. People weren't walking in Locharbert anymore. People were scurrying. The Tinkers in their new coats were strutting.

The bakery had a whole new window display with braided breads and other things never eaten by the people of Locharbert. Davies the ironmonger, who used to sport the odd Loch Ness monster on his counter, had turned over a whole aisle to tourist knickknacks inscribed with *I Love Locharbert* or *Locharbert For Aye*.

The postmistress, Miss Delia Crawford, in case Steve McNaught should come in, had a plate of her own shortbread on the post office counter. School children were discouraged from it by a smack to the back of the hand.

George awoke in her old bed in her father's house, turned on her back and looked at the ceiling. A series of cracks in the plaster had been different things to her over the years.

When she first moved here with her father, they had formed the standard house drawn by all little children. This one even had smoke rising out of the stack. A home that could be counted on. In her teenage years, the lines became the parameters of a hockey field. In hockey, she played left back, so she knew where she would be standing, close to the goalie along the leftmost crack. As she grew older, the cracks on the ceiling mapped out Great Britain. She knew she would leave Locharbert in the end, and that she would travel south of the border, so her attention in those days was on the bottommost series of cracks. Now, as she looked at them, the cracks looked like faults in the plaster, separate from each other, nothing more.

She turned on her side around the hard stomach she still wasn't used to. The night before, watching *The Sound of Music*, and during the song "Something Good," she had felt life stir for the first time. She had heard women describe it as a flutter at first, no more than a butterfly wing. But this had felt exactly as it should, a very small baby doing somersaults. This morning as she stared at the ceiling, she slid her hand under the covers and felt her stomach roll inside her hand. These weren't other people's stories anymore. In her own red womb, she was alive in a new form of herself. She wanted to slip her hands inside to cradle this frail alien she already loved without having seen.

She had been hearing rumours about Steve and Nicola again, but they were easier to dismiss this time. Nicola had told her about Eli, so she knew Steve wasn't really in the picture. The rumours she had more difficulty with had to do with Rose Cottage Productions. For she believed that once Steve put the people of Locharbert on celluloid, the place would never be the same. And she counted on Locharbert being the same. It's what she had come home to after her years away. There would be tourists coming for their vacation's worth of "real life." But real life in Locharbert wouldn't exist anymore. Once the secret life of these people, and it was all secret in its way, was told, the vital throb of the town would bleed out.

"Have you told these things to the man?" Willy asked her.

She was hand-sewing the hem on one of her mother's maternity dresses, with difficulty, because she had never cared much for dressmaking.

"He doesn't understand," she said. "He comes from a place where there is no myth. There's no hum, because it's all so new and all so caught up in trying to prove how good it is. I've been there. I know."

George began to think she might walk over to Rose Cottage one evening and make her case. She still had Steve's T-shirt, and she knew what that meant. She wanted his hand on her belly when the life they had made stirred again. She wasn't fooling anybody, least of all Steve, standing there in his T-shirt implying the baby might not be his. His smile flashed quickly across her thoughts.

STEVE'S NOTION OF STARTING HIS FILM with a long shot of Locharbert had proven difficult to enact. First of all, he had had to hire a film crew from the Isle of Skye, but the equipment was more dated than Steve was used to. The second difficulty was the cast. At least one or two of the crowd would look into the camera. By the ninth take, and after a lot of shouting, they were all standing like statues. But at the last minute, Donal Wallace looked up at the helicopter and kept his neck craned. Donal Wallace didn't trust anything that flew without feathers.

Steve's budget had only allowed for one day's rental of the helicopter, and, since the light was fading, he had opted finally for a night shot with empty streets. He was happy with it in the end because it led nicely into his own footage of the tissue floating about the Tinkers' shack, which in turn faded nicely to a morning light where people were beginning to move about the streets again. He had to pay the police to cordon off Main Street; he paid other individuals to stay indoors. The farmers refused to be in his film, so Steve hired Iain Ally and Davies the ironmonger to stand on a street corner, wearing Wellington boots and flat caps, patting Peter Duart's dog. Nicola had a part, and the postmistress, when she had calmed down, was allowed to walk down the street as a passerby.

Peter Duart had shown up for the first day's shooting with a silk necktie, looking tired because he had not slept for the excitement. Steve had hired a makeup girl from Glasgow and had her staying above The Comm. She took Peter's necktie and masked the dark rings under his eyes with pan stick which didn't wear well in the salty dampness. In the end, Steve had to shoot Peter from behind as he rubbed a clean spot through the grime of the café window. The camera followed into the café to pick up some of the town's characters.

Steve shouted "Cut!" as was his habit. This was more like it. He set his camera aside and ate an ice cream dripping with raspberry sauce.

Behind the café, Steve shot the brothers rifling through the bins. They had to be looking right down into the rubbish, otherwise they were smiling too much. The costume lady thought they didn't look down-and-out enough in their new coats, so she had brought in clothes from the Red Cross shop, adding patches and frayed holes into the coats. They looked like clowns from the local circus. Steve called his friend Chip in L.A. The makeup girl went back to Glasgow. Production had to be stopped until Chip could tie up another project and get herself out to the highlands of Scotland.

She came up from Glasgow in a helicopter, which made Steve wince, but it brought the people onto the front green and gave them something to guess at. Was Chip a movie star? She certainly looked it. Or perhaps she was Steve's wife. By the way she ran at Steve and hugged and kissed him, she must at least be a girlfriend. George saw it all from the draper's window.

Nicola Ally proved to be a natural. At first Steve had only wanted her to stroll up Main Street turning the heads of the local boys. But he soon began to write in other scenes for her. He had written the script in two weeks, longhand because it felt more authentic that way, and he was constantly on the defensive against George's attack, even though he never saw her.

Through a clean spot rubbed by Peter Duart into the window of MacBrayne's, Steve filmed Willy standing by his Durex sign. In a later shot, he had Nicola slinking into the draper, and, in the next, she was seated on the front pew at a Sunday morning service. Reverend Campbell had already given him permission to film in the church. He only wanted fair warning, so that he could pull out his best sermon. Alasdair Campbell justified the filming with a handy text which ordered the disciples to *Go ye into all the world.* This was the only time in thirty-five years the Reverend had ever had the chance to reach out further than Locharbert.

Steve drove Nicola out to his house so she could put in a call to Eli. He was beginning to see Nicola differently these days. Of all the young actors he had worked with, she was the most eager and the most adaptable. Sometimes she could see where he was going even before he did. He began to think she wasn't as bad a match for his son as he had feared. He was even beginning to enjoy her company.

"See, I told you I was good," she said on the way out of town, where streetlamps faded back and the road was haunted by the shapes of trees. "Do you think I'll be famous, then?"

Steve laughed. "Being famous isn't all it's cracked up to be."

"Away," she said. She flicked the ashtray lid open and closed it. "It'd get me out of this hole."

"Going to college would get you out, too." Steve flipped the turn-signal on and turned down his drive.

"That'll be right," she said, getting out of the car. "I can just see me at university with specs on, walking around with a bunch of books, eating tofu."

Steve let her into the house. He still hadn't got used to being there without the boys. Nicola seemed like the next best thing. Steve poured her a lemonade.

She sipped noisily through a straw. "The problem with your film is," she said, "no one's going to believe I'm putting it out unless they see me actually do it. I mean, do I look like a slut?"

Steve dropped a few ice cubes into a glass and coated them with whisky. It's true he had come to think of Nicola that way, but now that he looked at her face, it was still a child's and enough like her father's to be guileless.

Nicola rested her hip against the cold polished countertop and twisted the ring Eli had given her around her finger. "Can I have one of those biscuits?"

Steve handed her a packet of Oreos Tanner had sent him. "Cookies," he said.

She bit into one, finished it quickly, then reached for another. "So how about if there's this scene where I'm snogging sneaky-like with this gorgeous bloke in a close."

Steve moved the cookies out of her reach. "Snogging?"

"I don't actually have to do any snogging. I can just make it look convincing. See."

She caught Steve around the neck and pulled his face against hers. He stiffened. She turned her back to him, passed her arms across her front and walked her fingers along her backside.

"See," she said, "from the right angle, it would look like something."

Steve laughed. "I get the picture."

After she had made her phone call, after he had hovered about trying not to listen to the details, after he had gone through the changes in the script with her, Steve drove Nicola back to her parents' house. He was on good terms with Devin these days. The lighting and sound crews were staying above the pub; folks were dropping in all day long for drinks.

Steve went into the Allys' house and stood in front of the electric fire nervously. Devin was at The Comm, and Anita wasn't as much on his side. She served him tea and buttered pancakes with jam, while he astounded the younger Allys by pulling 10 pence pieces from their ears. He drove home, mulling over Nicola's idea.

Steve had about four hours of film by now. He had sent a segment back to some friends in L.A., but they hadn't been able to make out some of the dialogue and suggested Steve would need subtitles. He had forgotten how accustomed he had become to the local dialect, but he knew subtitles would make the story drag. Nicola's idea of raising the stakes with a little sex was a worn formula he might well have to fall back on. He would have to hire a "gorgeous bloke" from Glasgow. He had wanted to steer clear of professional actors, but he had already hired a few young men from the drama school to play sailors when none were forthcoming in the harbour during the shoot.

The garden party he had filmed out at the castle had felt like a crowd of actors but had in fact been solely composed of the Duarts and their friends. Mrs. Duart had refused to let her son clean the windows in the background, but Steve had caught him on another day and would be able to edit him into the scene later. He also intended to slip the shot of the postmistress hurrying along the street into the draper scene. But all of this, Steve realised, was going to take proper machines, and, since editing was the crux of the filming process, he preferred to work with the people he had dealt with before.

GEORGE DROPPED ONE OF HER MOTHER'S maternity dresses over her head, then studied herself in the long mirror on the back of her father's wardrobe door. She didn't look much like her mother. The pictures of her mother that her father still owned didn't much resemble the memories George had anyway. George washed her hair and curled the ends into loose ringlets. This evening would be her coming out. Everyone knew she was pregnant, but not until she dressed the part and displayed it, would she acknowledge what they knew. Then it would all be done and there would be no more whispering.

As she stepped onto Main Street, she flicked her hair behind her.

Delia Crawford didn't stop as she passed. "There you are, Georgianna," she said, breathlessly. "I haven't seen you in ages."

George held her shoulders back. "No, I haven't been feeling all that well."

But Delia was already far enough away that she had to shout to make herself heard. "Cheerio just now."

George looked down at her stomach. It's true her bump was somewhat lost among the folds of the oversized dress, but the dress itself should have left no doubt. At the bottom of Main Street, she turned into the café, but there was no one there except Turo Caparella, who from behind his counter could only see her from the chest up. He might have noticed for a moment her expanded bust line, but his dark eyes gave nothing away.

"A ninety-nine," George said, "with raspberry."

It had been a long time since she had bought ice cream, and not since her childhood had she enjoyed the luxury of a chocolate flake in the top. The "raspberry" was just red syrup, but it turned the ice cream a pleasing pink as she licked the drips.

Down on the front by the concrete public bathrooms, George finished her ice cream while she watched a few children putting with an old golf iron and a deflated soccer ball. As a child, on evenings such as this when time stood still as it does for children, she had waited for crabs to take her bait in the rock pools beyond the front green. It took her father to come and call her home before she realised she was sitting in the dark.

Births, she felt, were like that. Ten hours compacted into one brilliant moment. Steve was like that. Those days and weeks with him had taken on their own self-designed rhythm, which had nothing to do with when shops opened or pubs closed.

George pulled her coat on as she started down the familiar path towards her shack. Free of the sickness of early pregnancy, and not yet burdened with any real weight, she felt supremely healthy and able to walk to the end of the mull if the whimsy took her. Her little child was swaying in its globe of water, aware of all her sounds, rocking itself to sleep.

When she came near to her house, her cats came running along the shore. There had been no need to come back and feed them, since rodents were abundant and, inside or out, they slept like all good cats curled inside themselves. She knelt beside them, tickling her fingers along their amber backs. She didn't need them as she once had. She walked them back to her house, let them in, and then kept walking along the shoreline until she came parallel with her rose cottage. The lights were on, the windows still curtainless. She had always envisioned red velvet curtains for that front window.

At the front door, she pulled the petals from a dead rose. She recognised Steve's voice from inside, but there was another, one she hoped she didn't recognise. And, yet, as she leaned towards the front window, she could clearly make out the back of Nicola Ally up against Steve, twirling his hair in her fingers. George's pleasant mood didn't stand a chance. She drew away to the side of the house where the goat nudged her arm in the dark. She smacked the leather of its back and pushed it away.

George went back to the window a few times, saw Nicola on Steve's phone, noticed Steve hovering attentively about her. She walked about the garden, snapping leaves off bushes, finally climbing inside the rhododendron bushes, as she had done as a small child.

When she heard the car leave, she went inside this house that was really hers. All new and wood-panelled, it wasn't her house anymore, with its leather, its appliances, a kitchen with maple cupboards and stone counters. Upstairs there were bunk beds; an enormous bed in the other room almost filled the entire space. She sat on it. It was firm, and these days she needed firm. But she didn't need Steve. She didn't need any more deception.

Downstairs she found boxes of empty bottles, whisky, vodka, half a bottle of wine on the counter, and two glasses, one with a straw. She sat on his leather couch and glanced through piles of papers. *As It Is in Heaven*. She lifted the title page and read an interview with Murdo Wallace. He was spilling the guts of the town, running off at the mouth like a burn in spate. And Steve was leading him like a little puppy to a dish of cream.

George stopped reading when she heard Steve's car. When he walked in, his eyes had to adjust for a moment before he noticed George with her handful of his papers.

"What in hell's name are you trying to do?" she asked.

He closed the door behind him with his foot. "Just trying to show things the way they are."

Her body felt rigid, her curled hair seeming now like something of a mockery. "And who stands to benefit?"

He lifted his hands. "Art."

Her laugh was bitter. "Don't you *art* me. What stands to benefit is your bank account."

Steve laughed. It truly was funny to think he would do anything but lose money with this venture. His accountant was already complaining about the drain on his capital. And here was George, suddenly from nowhere in his house in her big dress, threatening him with his own papers.

She turned to leave.

"Just for the record," he said, as she opened the door, "whose baby is that?" She turned with a look that told him he had volleyed the ball into the wrong court.

"Whose do you think, you bloody fool?"

He got to her and touched her arm. "Then where are you going?"

She shrugged him off. "I won't have anything to do with this, you know." She handed him his papers, as though they were old rags left by Tinkers. "As long as you're for this project, you're not for this place, and you're certainly not for me."

"I have to do this, George," he said. He sighed. "It's the best thing I've done. It's the only thing I've done that's real."

She grabbed his hand and led it to her stomach. "What's this, then?"

"It's trouble," he said. "I can make movies. But I make a lousy father."

He took his hand away. She left, pulling the door shut quietly behind her. He glanced at the two bottles of Laphroig on his fridge top and had drunk half of one before it started to register. By that time, he began to toast George. He even toasted her baby.

Steve called his sons, but it was early morning in California, so no one answered. He couldn't hear the slur in his voice as he left a message, but it came to him later, after the elation, when despair was setting in, that the father of John, Eli, and Tanner was nothing but a damn drunk. It was the sole thing in his life he was supremely good at. It was a prison he would never be released from, no matter how many crafts and useful things he learned to do on the inside. He was in for life, and the only way out was in a coffin.

He picked up the papers he had dropped on the floor. It was a good script. He didn't care about its viability in Hollywood. It had integrity, and it had heart, even though some of the characters in the end might not be able to laugh at themselves. It was a chunk of real life, what he had always been striving for; let George think what she liked about profit.

He drank up the rest of the bottle, then sauntered down the shore in the dark, looking for the Tinkers. There was a headwind, but by the time he reached their tent, he had lost the intention of seeing them and kept on going into town. He banged on the door of The Comm, but all was dark inside.

On the Front Street of Locharbert, Steve McNaught saluted and sang "The Star Spangled Banner". He sang a version of "Scotland the Brave" outside of MacBrayne's, where he was picked up by a policeman who had received a call. It was a policy of the police department to take disorderly drunken persons to the asylum for the night, since the small police station was not equipped with a soft room. Steve resisted arrest, which made the doctors up the brae decide that the American, about whom they were curious anyway, should spend the next day under psychiatric evaluation.

Steve knew the town would be talking about nothing else, especially since half of the town worked up here, and he kept recognising the nurses who brought him food on plastic trays and pills in plastic cups. The wife of Iain Ally was one of them. The husband of the clerk in the grocers was another.

Steve glowered at the ground in his tight disinfected room. They had taken his watch and his clothes upon entry, and he was sitting like any other disconnected person in thin hospital pyjamas that didn't close properly at the back. It was the only place he had been in since he came to Scotland with no draughts, just stale air holding the odour of other wards where patients were less continent. Still, he had little desire to leave, he told Chip when she came. He had broken down before and this was what he was best at. Screw the filming, screw the fathering, screw the screwing. The only thing he was truly good at was losing. Chip shook her head and left. She had her own crises, she said. She didn't need to come to Scotland to cater to someone else's.

Later that morning, a doctor from Pakistan told him the pills should help, but there was nothing more they could do for him in a place for crazy people.

Steve wiped the tears from his face. "What do I have to do to be 'crazy'?"

The doctor shook his head.

Steve was moved to a ward, where he was fed cups of tea and surprisingly non-institutional food. Not that it was good food, but it was common and designed to interrupt the patients' palates as little as possible. Steve found it all faintly comical, sitting in bed in a row of men, with his hospital tray across his lap, eating some manner of pie and the beans that were more or less the staple diet of the Scots. Under normal circumstances, the discovery of humour in his thoughts would have been enough to give him hope. But he was too far from real hope for it to make any difference.

He was watching a clock on the wall that was fifteen minutes slow, though time seemed irrelevant when he had nowhere to go and no one to see. He felt stuck like a pinned butterfly on a lepidopterist's display. A large nurse was pouring tea sloppily into cups set out on a cart. Ten minutes later, just as the tea in the cups turned tepid, he took his from a different nurse, little more than a girl with skin eruptions. Between the pouring of the tea and the cup being placed in Steve's hands, he realised he had not had one thought.

On his release form, under "destination upon leaving," Steve had left it blank. For all he had done to it, the cottage still didn't feel like his. The bottles on the top of the fridge did, but he was scared of them. He was too alone there, where the bottles had been his only friends. He knew they would be again.

The ambulance was to take him home. They gave him back his clothes and watch in the afternoon and placed his prescription drug on the pile. He didn't know what he was going to do when they dropped him off at the top of his drive. He watched fleets of nurses and trays of this and that, as though he were the conductor in an orchestra, signalling in different parts of a dissonant symphony. It was all well-staged. Everyone's life had its stage and its moments for walking on and off. Everyone had masks they used for a while until they turned them in for something else. Only his life had somehow moved off the stage altogether. He felt as though he was watching it from the audience. The play that was supposed to be him was going on without him.

A nurse helped him on with his jacket, the old denim one that had cost a small mint from Louis Vuitton in Beverly Hills, but which now looked about as old as he did. He couldn't decide if the other patients looked at him with envy or fear, as he sat on his bed, clothed, waiting for the ambulance.

"About half an hour," a nurse told him in a consoling voice. She handed him his last cup of lukewarm tea, the sacrament of his leaving. And then she brought another cup and a little table to set both on. She brought a plate of assorted biscuits, and then she brought Mrs. McPhealy.

Mrs. McPhealy was in her Sunday coat and hat. She was holding her handbag tight in front of her, as though it stood in danger of being grabbed at any moment.

The nurse said. "I'll tell the ambulance man you'll just be a few minutes late."

Mrs. McPhealy sat down at the table and looked at her cup of tea. Steve looked at his. He hadn't seen Mrs. McPhealy since he had visited the minister to get permission for filming a service, and then only the back of her. He hadn't talked to her since the day he left her house. He straightened the cuffs of his jacket and cleared his throat.

"Are you to stay in here for very long?" she asked.

Steve shook his head. "They decided I wasn't crazy enough."

He tried to smile, but his face wouldn't cooperate. Mrs. McPhealy was holding her hands tight around her handbag and definitely wasn't in the mood for tea or biscuits. The two cups sat at opposite ends of the table, slowly losing steam.

"And you?" Mrs. McPhealy asked, looking up and into his eyes. "Do you think you need to be here?"

Steve shrugged, something he had never done in Mrs. McPhealy's presence before. "It seems like I've made a mess of things, doesn't it?"

Mrs. McPhealy tutted. "I'm sure I've never heard a McNaught talk such utter nonsense."

Steve looked at her curiously. He had never seen this Mrs. McPhealy before. She wasn't standing over him, judging, but, as much as she was able, she seemed to be offering a shoulder.

"My son, Matthew, is here on a visit just now," she said, "so the house might feel a wee bit cramped. But I wouldn't like to think of you going back out to Achnarannoch by yourself, not until you're standing on your own two feet again."

Steve did feel weak on his feet. And how could he but accept this woman who had sacrificed much to walk past the church and visit him in a place for lunatics? He didn't tell her he didn't want to be any trouble to her. He didn't insist that he couldn't intrude. He took the offer, by standing next to the two cups of cold tea and offering his hand for her to stand up.

If she was pleased, she didn't show it, nor did she talk much on the way back down the brae. She asked him if they had fed him well. He didn't lie.

She tutted.

As they turned down Manse Brae, she told him he was welcome, if he felt able, to join Matthew for tea.

Steve didn't know if he felt able, but he located in himself a point of curiosity about Matthew McPhealy.

"Matthew is a vegetarian," she said, opening her gate. She said it quietly, as though being vegetarian were possibly equivalent to being insane.

Matthew McPhealy came out of the kitchen as soon as the front door closed behind them. In a house that had hitherto been occupied by short people, he seemed oversized, his clothes casual in a city way of still being smart. He stood over Steve, shaking his hand vigorously, and looking every bit like Reverend Alasdair Campbell, with his red hair and pale blue eyes with fair lashes. Matthew followed Steve into the visitor's blue bedroom, while Mrs. McPhealy went off to the kitchen.

As he had no luggage to set down, except the bottle of pills in his breast pocket, Steve set himself down on the edge of the bed.

Matthew leaned against the wall. "I was just whipping up a little gazpacho, if you feel like eating."

Steve hadn't heard the word gazpacho in so long, it made him want to weep.

Matthew turned to leave, but Steve called him back. "Why your mother's change of heart?"

Matthew shrugged. "Once you get past the fuss and nonsense, she's not a bad old bat."

After pie and beans and chips with everything, gazpacho was light relief to Steve's gastronomy.

Mrs. McPhealy had already eaten. She sat at the table and shook her head.

"Cold soup," she said. "Whatever next?"

They didn't expect Steve to talk, so he didn't. He just listened while they carried on mother-son banter about who in Locharbert had died since he was last home and who of Matthew's old friends Effie still saw down the street. Mrs. McPhealy had obviously given dessert some direction, for she appeared back in the living room where they were eating with a tray of ice cream sundaes.

"Matthew's partial to a dish of ice cream," she said.

"I bet he is," said Steve.

After dinner, Mrs. McPhealy instructed Steve to go to bed. She brought him a copy of *The Reader's Digest* and one of her cups of milky whisky brew. He read an article about the pituitary gland, then fell asleep with his feet on a hot water bottle. In the dark of the night, he awoke and found Matthew at the kitchen table playing solitaire.

"I can never sleep when I come back to Locharbert," he said. "After London, the dark is too dark."

Steve sat down at the table.

"So, how's the film coming along?" Matthew asked.

Steve pulled a face.

Matthew placed a red queen on a black king. Steve pointed out a black jack. He had been trying not to think about the filming.

He said, "We've set up a whole industry devoted to portraying life as it isn't. I thought people might appreciate a look at what is. But apparently it's not that simple."

Matthew started to laugh. He laughed jovially, like an old man, although he wasn't much past thirty. "I heard about the helicopter," he said.

Steve slapped his hand on his forehead. "Every time the camera panned in, there was Donal Wallace looking up like he'd seen a UFO." Steve sighed.

Matthew completed a run and turned the cards over.

"Anyway," said Steve. He stood up.

Matthew kept working on his game. Steve liked this man and wondered if he knew who his father was. He looked at the freckles on the back of his hand, and wondered if it even really mattered.

"I've been trying to find out," Steve said, "why my grandfather had to leave Locharbert."

Matthew glanced at the shadow in the glass of the kitchen door. He lowered his voice, but not so as anyone who wanted to hear couldn't. "He got a girl in trouble."

Steve sat down again. "He did? Who?"

"Some wild girl. She ended up in the asylum."

Steve rested his chin on his hand. "What happened to the baby?"

"Well," said Matthew, "in those days, being illegitimate, she was an outcast. Only fit for Tinkers, when you come to think of it."

Matthew started smiling. It was a nice smile, a broad smile, probably close to the minister's if Steve had ever seen that smile, which he hadn't.

Steve pushed back in his chair. "Tinkers? Do you mean like—you do mean like the Wallaces? Oh, my God, the Wallaces are McNaughts, aren't they?"

Matthew raised his eyebrows. "The tall and the short of it."

Steve went back to bed. He slept hard and awoke to the Hoover thundering under his bedroom door. He lay awake wondering why Murdo had said nothing of his kinship to Steve while he blethered on about the rest of the town's history: about George laughing at Devin Ally behind the school kitchens, about Willy MacBrayne and the postmistress among sacks of letters on half-day closing, even about Reverend Campbell and Mrs. McPhealy and the baby that was conceived between two pews in the Church of Scotland. Perhaps Murdo knew that at the end of the day the joke was not on them, but on the outsider.

Yon Steve McNaught, Hollywood director from Malibu, was never anything but a Tinker.

CHAPTER TWENTY-FOUR

When Steve McNaught left Locharbert, it was a day or two before the postman reported that the shopping cart he had set out for his mail was overflowing. No one seemed to be at home at Rose Cottage.

When Delia Crawford got the word, it took Anita Ally on lunch break four minutes and twenty-five seconds to carry the news up to Willy at the draper, and less than five seconds after Anita's departure for George to find out.

Willy shook his head. "You said he'd leave, right enough."

George stood against the light from the window. She let the sash go on the curtain, so that it fell across the light, dropping the room into darkness.

The puzzling thing for Devin Ally when he got the news was not that Steve McNaught had left, but that he had not said goodbye. Not even to Nicola. Her notions of becoming famous had evaporated without so much as an explanation. Even Eli's letters started to trail off. Devin had persuaded his moping daughter to put in a few hours behind the bar, which she did, but not with half the gusto she had brought to her role as the town floozie. Devin stood behind his bar, scratching his head with the opposite hand.

The postmistress had it on good authority, which everyone took to be her own, that the drink had driven him back to the kind of rehabilitation centre the people of Locharbert read about in glossy magazines and which could only be found in California. Drunks in Locharbert eventually came around by being hit repeatedly over the head by their wives. "Having sense knocked into him," was a phrase taken literally in these parts.

The postmistress knew how many empty bottles the dustbin men had removed from outside McNaught's door. Hell, one was only half-drunk, though the dustbin men had finished that off and no one was the wiser. But everyone had to pass through the post office eventually, and Delia found out the count was up in the thirties, not all whisky bottles, but near enough. Speculation was even made, though no one ever took credit for it, that Steve McNaught, as is the wont of strangers and people to do with stardom, had gone off to a lonely spot and there taken his own life. It was only a matter of time until his car would be found over a cliff or he would be discovered slumped over in his car, a revolver still in his hand.

Peter Duart was of the opinion that George had sent Steve packing, but, since George was saying nothing on the subject, this was an opinion he shared only with his wife. Shefaline was back to being the only foreigner in Locharbert, except for Caparella, and he didn't count. A good ice cream can excuse a man for many shortcomings. Shefaline felt betrayed and was of half a mind to retrieve her painting from Achnarannoch.

Davies the ironmonger said, "Good riddance," but what was he supposed to do now with all those mugs with *Sunny Locharbert* on the side? Those among the community who had told McNaught their secrets were of a mind with the ironmonger. McNaught hadn't paid them and had, no doubt, run off to avoid doing so. The money would have helped with the mortgage, the wives complained, while they knew their husbands would have laundered it through Devin Ally's operation at The Comm. The men wouldn't have minded the extra dram or two, and they did miss a man who had the gall to pick up and discard George MacBrayne.

On the subject of Steve McNaught, the three wee Wallaces were strangely silent and not much to be seen these days. Willy saw something in that, but he didn't care to speculate. At any rate, he wasn't about to mention Steve's name in George's presence. George was going about the business of being pregnant, one hand on her belly, the other on her back, eating the right things, taking her father's tonics, even smiling but only when she talked about the baby. Willy was more than happy at the thought of having a child around the draper's again, perhaps with the injection of American blood, a child less serious than Georgianna had been.

But as all news becomes old news, even in Locharbert, the topic of Steve McNaught faded, and the town began to signal in its meagre way the approach of Christmas. There was no decorated tree on the grass by the loch, no tinsel stretching from lamppost to lamppost; but the butcher had a few large chickens in his window, and the baker's display eventually shifted from braided breads to trays of mincemeat pies.

It was enough to bring a thrill to the schoolchildren let out for lunch because, although no physical Santa would ever appear in Locharbert, Santa of the imagination had now been given permission to emerge. It made the children work hard on their homework, the sooner to bring on Christmas holidays. It made the talk in the post office switch from Steve McNaught to the catalogues by which the people of rural settings do their shopping.

George MacBrayne fell in and out of gossip. It was said she had to enter shops sideways these days. She couldn't make it all the way out to her shack and had employed a schoolboy to bike out there every day to feed her cats, deprived as they were in the colder months of wild feed. As her earlier forays with much younger men were widely known, her precise relationship to the schoolboy was also explored. But, looking at George these days, it was clear even to the most insidious mind that the activity which had put her in this condition in the first place had ceased to be a possibility. So the people talked instead about New Years, which they called The Daft Days, because of what could happen then.

Mrs. McPhealy arranged the flowers in the church for Christmas, though every one of them had had to come up on the bus from Glasgow. It was costly, but it was her annual tithe, and Reverend Campbell would acknowledge it in the church bulletin.

Alasdair Campbell caught up with her in the vestibule. "I wonder if you wouldn't mind staying to help me with the communion glasses, Mrs. McPhealy."

It was a job the minister usually took upon himself. She nodded, took the trays of glasses and began laying them out in their holders. As she worked, Mrs. McPhealy trained a glance or two behind her, for the man seemed to be loitering, and it wasn't like him. He himself had preached about the evil of idle hands, and here he was standing at her back, wringing his.

When he cleared his throat, she jumped a little and patted her heart. He smiled and apologised.

"I was just wondering," he said, "if you had any idea why your American left so suddenly."

Effie felt the muscles in her shoulders and about her throat constrict. "I'm sure the embarrassment of being taken away by the policemen to the asylum was enough."

The minister said, "Hmm," then went about lurking again, moving things that were already in their rightful places.

Effie could feel him approach her back again.

"Nothing else?" he said.

"I'm sure I don't know," she said. "One evening he was there, and in the morning, he was gone. Never said a word."

Effie sighed. She missed her long-lost cousin, but she wasn't about to admit it. It seemed to her he had been doing better, even after Matthew had gone back to London. But Steve didn't go out walking of an evening anymore, just sat by the fire while she did her knitting. He had left a thank you note and three hundred pounds, which she kept in a drawer, not knowing if this was blood money. Not knowing gnawed at her bones, and there had been too much of that in her life.

Looking down at the sacrament glasses, each in its sacred hole, she knew that she couldn't hold herself in much longer. When she let out her breath, it came with a shudder. She sat down on the cushioned bench in the holy outer office of the Lord.

Alasdair stepped a little closer. "Whatever's the matter, Mrs. McPhealy?"

Mrs. McPhealy pulled her handkerchief embroidered with roses from the sleeve of her cardigan and dabbed the sides of her eyes. "Why is it you call me Mrs. McPhealy?"

And, because it was more than she had ever admitted, the tears turned from drips to a steady flow. Alasdair Campbell pulled a man-sized handkerchief from inside his cassocks and sat down on the bench beside her with a sigh. She took his hankie, covered her face and sobbed.

"Oh, Effie," he said. "Whatever have I done to you?"

Effie pulled the starched cloth from her face. She did more than look into his eyes hooded now by old age; she searched them.

"Did I do right by Matthew?" she asked. "Was Matthew the right name to give him?"

Alasdair nodded. "How could it not have been right to call him after one of the Lord's Apostles?"

She laid the minister's handkerchief on his knee, stood up and carried on with the glasses. Alasdair stood beside her, not a step or two away, his black cloth up against her knitted cardigan, watching her small fingers move adeptly between the holy glasses and the communion tray.

"I'm glad, Effie," he whispered.

CHRISTMAS CAME AND WENT with carols and hot soup at the church. The Tinkers never had any presents, but they had this. They promised Reverend Campbell to come more often, or even at all, to morning service, and then they sat on the church wall with their soup, swinging their feet, thankful for a cold but beneficent world.

When they wandered out to Achnarannoch and found Steve McNaught asleep upstairs, and Eli and Tanner in their beds, the Tinkers came back downstairs and slid a new video into the machine. This was the one Steve had made of themselves coming and going with a piece of tissue on the shore where their tent stood right enough, but where the light looked strange, not anything they had ever seen before.

"That was my tissue," Donal said.

Murdo said, "Away. You don't know that was yours."

"Aye, I do," said Donal, "I lost it."

Murdo shrugged. Donal was probably right. One tissue from the next was the kind of thing Donal could tell. It was bit like second sight, and no one should doubt that.

Steve came downstairs, scratching his new beard, rubbing his hands through his hair. "Hi, guys."

Murdo looked over. "It's yourself."

Donal and Doolie nodded, then went back to the television screen where the postmistress was fanning her cleavage with both hands.

"It is," said Steve. "It's myself all over again." He came into the kitchen and lit the gas under a kettle. "And, thank you very much, yes, I did have a pleasant flight, a little turbulence coming down into Glasgow, but nothing you couldn't handle."

Murdo squinted. He had no idea about turbulence, except what happened on Hogmanay.

Steve made his coffee, then sat on the arm of the sofa, while the butcher on the screen pointed to various meats with fingers red from the cold of his trade. It had taken Steve months to get to the final cut, but he was pleased with the result. It wasn't the most finished-looking film he had ever made, but that was sort of the point. He had dabbled a little with the lighting, but otherwise hadn't strayed far from the slice-of-life approach he had set out to achieve.

Later that day, Steve drove to the church, and parked his car on Manse Brae.

When Shefaline let him into the manse, her eyes opened wide. "*Salope!*"

Steve kissed her cheeks and hushed her quiet so he could surprise the minister. He found Reverend Campbell fussing in his study over next Sunday's sermon

The minister showed no surprise when Steve appeared at his study door.

"Steven, my man, come away in!"

Steve sat in the chair across the minister's desk, holding his video like Mrs. McPhealy clutched her handbag. He watched the minister's freckled fingers moving the pen across his paper, his lips moving.

"I need to get this sermon just right," he said. "The Sunday after Hogmanay I'll be wrestling with the devil himself to make myself heard." He rubbed his hands together. "Would you care for a wee cup of tea? I was going to have one myself."

Steve smiled. "That would be lovely."

Reverend Campbell tapped a bell on his desk, which brought Shefaline, as though she were a maid from yesteryear. She didn't curtsy, but took the order and came back with a tray spread with cups and saucers, a plate of chocolate biscuits, and a teapot. Steve winked at her, while the minister poured.

"Will you be having one yourself, Mrs. Duart?" the minister asked.

"No, I'll be going along," she said.

She folded her apron and hurried out, for after all, she was a wife of Locharbert and had news to spread.

Reverend Campbell took a sip of his tea and made a face. "Teabags," he said. "I'll never get used to the taste of the paper."

Steve needed to laugh. He was newly in from Los Angeles, where memory extended back only as far as the last Academy Awards. There must have been a time even there when teabags were a new fad, but it was so buried in other new fads and paraphernalia, it never crept near anyone's thinking.

The minister looked over his spectacles at Steve. "What can I do for you, young man?"

Steve held up his video. "That film I was making about Locharbert is finished. I'd like to show it to the town, and I was wondering if I could use the church hall this Friday."

The minister picked a chocolate finger off the plate and bit half. Something close to relish crossed his face.

Steve said, "It's called *As It Is In Heaven*." He sat up proudly. He was playing his ace.

Reverend Campbell passed the rest of the chocolate finger between his false teeth. "Do you mean to be quoting the Lord's Prayer, Steven?"

Steve said, "I do."

The minister couldn't quite make sense of it, but his mind was still with battling the devil.

"Aye," he said. "So long as it's not an X-rated film."

Steve took a drink of tea, trying to study the minister before his teacup had to go back into its saucer. This wasn't the same man he had spent what seemed like an entire year having Sunday dinner with at Mrs. McPhealy's. He hadn't ever seen his teeth before.

"Thank you," said Steve. He stood up. "I'll leave you to your sermonising."

The minister waved Steve back to the seat. "I've been of a mind to talk to you."

Steve remembered as a child being ordered a few times to sit on the opposite side of the school principal's desk, and this didn't feel much different. He sat back down, holding on to his video.

The minister turned a silver Celtic cross mounted on a base of onyx towards Steve. "Do you see this? It comes down from Saint Columba, who brought Christianity to these heathen shores."

Steve nodded. The cross with its Celtic engravings was more attractive than other crosses he'd seen, but then Steve didn't have much truck with crosses.

The minister turned the cross back to himself. "When Columba set foot on this land a millennium and a half ago, the heathen had already been here since time immemorial. It's why we have yon great stones standing up in the farmer's fields to this day. What brings a shiver to me, Steven, is the thought that the heathen will still be here when all the crosses are gone."

There was a tightness now on the minister's face. Steve didn't like to look. Nor could he think of what to say. It seemed to him that the removal of crosses, and all the shame that went with them, wouldn't be that bad of a thing. Steve looked at the man across the desk from him and tried to look understanding.

The minister was shaking his head. "There's a darkness on this land, Steven. Still," he looked up. "there's a light that lighteth every man. Every man knows what is right and what is wrong. I always hang on to the hope that sooner or later, each man will do the right."

Steve glanced at the door.

"Take a man like yourself," said the minister. "When you went away, you were having a wee problem with the drink, if I'm not mistaken."

Steve smiled. "I cannot deny it. But, as you say, eventually, a man will wake up and turn to the light."

The minister popped the other half of the chocolate finger into his mouth. "Well, I'm glad to hear it, Steven."

When Steve stood up to go, the minister waved him back down. "Another little matter." He finished chewing and cleared his throat. "Now I'm not saying that Georgianna MacBrayne is all goodness and light. Far from it."

"Reverend Campbell," Steve said, "It's true George is carrying my baby. A man can get himself into an awkward situation. I'm sure you know what I mean."

Steve hadn't come to throw his weight around, but he was cornered. When Reverend Campbell winced, it was not displeasing to him.

"We all pay for our sins," the minister said quietly. "Ministers and lay people alike."

He picked up his pen and went to write.

Steve stood up again. He went to the door. "Anyway, I have every intention of doing right by George MacBrayne."

Reverend Campbell nodded but didn't look up. "Good man."

Steve clicked his heels together, a formal salute and perhaps the wrong metaphor, but he did feel like a sergeant in the presence of a major. If he had exited quickly, he would have missed the minister's final words.

"Right enough, it can take some men a very long time to see the light."

Steve stood by the gate and caught his breath. He had only been back in the country half a day and he had already been forced to drop any mask or charade he had flown back over the Atlantic with. On the plane, he had been excited once Glasgow and the Erskine Bridge emerged from under the cloud. But now he wasn't sure about living his life this close to the bone. There was something to be said for living one step back from the veil, not having to strip naked every time you were asked a question. He put his hands in his jeans and walked down the road towards the drapers.

Willy MacBrayne showed more surprise to find Steve than the minister had.

He put a hand on Steve's shoulder. "We feared you'd put a gun to your head."

Willy led him up the dingy stairs to the apartment above and from which light shone as though they were on Jacob's ladder and Heaven hovered over their heads.

George had already heard Steve's voice and had gone to the window to look nonchalant when he arrived at the top of the stairs. She stood sideways to give him the full effect.

"Well, then," said Willy, "I'll leave you two alone."

Steve listened until Willy's footfall had disappeared from the stairwell.

He took a step forward. She didn't turn.

He said, "I was always coming back, you know. I just had to go and sort things out. I have been working on editing my film. It's good, George. Really good. I'm going to show it on Friday in the church hall. I think you're going to like it."

He took another step towards her.

She turned, but wasn't ready for the new beard, black and red by the sideburns. It took a moment for her to speak. "You didn't even tell me you were leaving."

"Right then I didn't think you cared." He smiled. "I guess I wanted you to miss me."

She wasn't quick enough on her feet these days to hit him, but her arm twitched as she turned away. "Well, I didn't."

He placed his hands on her shoulders. She hadn't meant to let him touch her, but she needed it more than she had needed anything since her mother left. His hands ran down her back and onto her stomach.

"Come back to the house with me," he said.

Willy made a noise at the bottom of the stairwell. They both glanced over, and when George laughed, he felt her belly shake under his hands, and then a little foot or hand, aroused by the shaking, rolled under his fingers.

"I'll be darned," he said. "There's somebody in there."

"It's Islay," she said.

He kissed her ear. "A girl? Don't you know I only have boys?"

George turned and laid her cheek against his beard. It hardly seemed like the same Steve. "Not this time, Sunshine."

His hands on her made her want to melt away. She closed her eyes and felt the warmth of the sun from the window on her back.

"Eli and Tanner came back with me," he said. "I'm filing for partial custody."

George stood back to get a better look at this bearded man masquerading as someone she once knew. The sunlight highlighted the red in his beard.

"About the film," he said.

But her mouth was already on his and she was edging him from the window to the settee. He watched the maternity dress unfurl over her head. With her swollen breasts hanging over her melon stomach she looked like an ancient goddess. He ran his finger around her darkened nipples.

"When are you due?"

She lowered his head against the side of her breast. "Three weeks. But I'm not made of china, you know."

Steve was cautious at first, then he forgot. She smelled a little different, a little milkier perhaps, but the memory of her skin was what had awoken him nights in L.A. when his whole life was a to-ing and fro-ing from the editing room. He hadn't known then if he would ever touch her again, and he certainly hadn't contemplated doing so on her father's couch. But for the next thirty minutes it didn't much matter where he was.

George knew Willy was still at the bottom of the staircase. It had become part of a consecrated narrative that she would rebuff this man if he ever had the courage to show up again. But the moment he laid his hand on her, all her objections floated off into fog. Afterwards, lying with Steve's head pressed against the side of her belly, she knew all these things would float back in eventually. But for now, there was only this moment, and none of the rest mattered.

CHAPTER TWENTY-FIVE

G eorge helped Steve and Tanner set up the church hall for the viewing of his film. Eli had effectively disappeared. Mrs. McPhealy, in the absence of any flowers, decked the hall with holly. Matthew was expected to arrive up from London for the viewing. She made millionaire's shortbread and invited the other ladies to bring in their baking.

Reverend Campbell brought out an old tea urn he had optimistically bought once with a view to holding church socials. *No Alcohol*, Reverend Campbell wrote with red marker on a sheet of cardboard and taped it to the door.

Steve had to make a run to Glasgow for the projection equipment, which he promised Reverend Campbell would subsequently become the property of the church. It made the minister whistle a Scottish jig as he helped to bring in the folding chairs. There was a collection of missionary films Alisdair had collected over time that now he would be able to dust off and show to his congregation.

There were other prospects in his future that had him whistling these days, but for now it was a secret. He had said nothing about it to Mrs. McPhealy, in case the word got out. Still, on the night of the Locharbert film, she did arrive with the top button of her tweed two-piece undone, and that had to mean something. That night, Reverend Alasdair Campbell stood at the door of the church hall welcoming the townsfolk in, as pleasant a man as they had ever seen in cassocks. No one missed the fact that, just visible between the hem of his trousers and his shoes, were a new pair of knitted grey socks.

Murdo, Donal, and Doolie knew the meaning of it, but they had already spotted the table of pastries and started to shuffle off in that direction. Mrs. McPhealy came over to stand guard.

Reverend Campbell had been put in charge of dimming lights, because only he knew where the switches had been hidden at some point in the past by a mischievous electrician. When the lights went out, Steve signalled to Tanner from his seat on the back row. Tanner started the film, then sat down beside George on the front row.

Steve could only see her from the back, but he was going to watch her every minute of the two hours the film was to run. Eli and Nicola appeared after the lights were out and sat next to Steve at the back. Eli had emerged the day before, angry at Steve because Nicola had suddenly announced she was saving herself for her wedding night.

"What's that got to do with me?" Steve had asked.

"She says she doesn't want to end up like George."

Steve had wanted to laugh, but Eli looked so unlike Eli. The wiles of women were beginning to take their toll.

Apart from the title *As It Is In Heaven,* there were no opening credits, just the camera panning from the sea into the darkened town and then the focus on Donal's lost tissue floating about the shore. The tissue (now digitally altered) danced up the shore, past the farmers who weren't really farmers, and into the street where Peter Duart was up a ladder outside the café. Peter was looking pleased because this was the first opportunity he had ever had to wash those windows, and the grime he wiped to make his peephole had needed no enhancing.

In the café sat Nicola Ally and her friends, nodding at a sailor who had just walked in for an ice cream. The sailor carried his ice cream outside where the raspberry dripped off and splatted like blood on the pavement. Peter's dog lapped it up, then ran around the back of the café to the Tinkers foraging in the bins.

The audience cheered and clapped. Peter Duart kept turning back from his seat and holding a thumbs up to Steve. They laughed at the postmistress's nervous talk to the camera from behind her desk, complaining about the proximity of her workplace to the pub.

"Many a man," she said, "has relieved himself in my doorway."

The crowd broke into cheers.

Someone shouted, "Ye should nae ha' been gawking, darling!"

This was unfair, but a foreigner had to expect it. The three brothers were smiling, because now Mrs. McPhealy was so distracted by the film, she didn't notice their hands quietly closing around her iced buns.

The crowd went silent at the part where Reverend Campbell stood in the mouth of Saint Columba's Cave, telling about the heathen darkness in the land, but cheered when he hovered at the back of Mrs. McPhealy and her church flowers. They hadn't known about Reverend Campbell's trip nine miles down the mull to Columba's sanctuary, but they did know he had fathered Matthew McPhealy.

Even George was smiling, though she lost it soon after when Willy was sneaking glances out his shop window and the postmistress was suddenly on her way somewhere in a hurry. Willy didn't seem to mind. He was sitting by the postmistress anyway.

A murmur of disapproval wafted over the crowd when the film moved on to Peter Duart's parents hosting their windy tea party. Toffs were always to be scorned because they brought it upon themselves.

The film cut to the butcher, who was pretending to show the camera cuts of meat, but was really telling stories about when his grandfather started the business and had to cater to the castle. He had been told to recount how Queen Victoria had once visited the castle, but he went with his own thoughts instead.

"Half the town used to work out at the castle, in the grounds and what have you. They used to house a fair number of maids, though they didn't stay maids for long, if you get my drift. Truth be told, half of Locharbert comes down from aristocracy."

From aristocracy to Tinkers, Murdo and his brothers were up next. Steve had edited out much of Murdo's blether, but they were funny little men just in the viewing. The best parts were their own: the teacakes they smashed on their foreheads, their toothless grins. When Steve had handed Murdo a bottle of Irn Bru and asked him to explain what it was, all three brothers turned away laughing. Steve asked them to showcase their new coats, but instead they opened them to reveal newspapers tied about their chests with string.

"Right enough," said Murdo. "It's been a wee bit chilly these nights."

Neither Donal nor Doolie spoke. They looked away, they looked down, they snickered down the sleeves of their coats. They weren't fool enough to expose themselves to this foreigner. Steve anticipated his American audience warming to these characters. In Locharbert, they lived and moved and had their being, and nobody even noticed them.

Steve glanced back at Reverend Campbell when the scene switched to the church service, but the minister's eyes were closed, listening to the words of his sermon, rather than watching Nicola Ally eying from her pew a schoolboy in a blazer who was really an actor from Glasgow.

Wives nudged their husbands when the camera went through Peter's peephole to the inside of the smoky Comm. Devin was behind the bar, reaching over to scratch his head. Nobody thought that was funny. When the real farmers at the bar turned away from the camera, the audience cheered. Nicola put in a good turn as a petulant barmaid. She turned to Steve in the audience and grinned; he waved.

When all was said and done and the lights came on, a little murmur passed through the audience. They clapped, they nodded. They came to Steve and shook his hand. They wondered where their pay was.

Steve had their money, though his own supply had dropped near depletion before he left. One of the first things he did when he got back to L.A. was to empty out one bank account down to the fifty dollars necessary to keep the account open. When he was finished editing, he had screened the movie before a group of his peers and one of the studios had thrown some money at the project. Not a lot, but enough for him to pay his actors and replenish his bank account. The money wasn't as important to him as the nod from the industry. It wasn't a film that would see wide release, but Steve had talked to some of the independent festivals, and things looked promising on that score.

George stayed in her seat until the hall was empty. Steve and Tanner folded the screen and left the projector at the back for the minister.

She smiled as Steve approached.

Steve clapped his hands. "Didn't I tell you you'd like it?"

"I like it," she said, "but that was never the problem. It's not what's in the film, but the film itself. Because if you take this heaven and put it on a billboard, it isn't going to be heaven anymore. Is it?"

Steve sighed. "Well, what do you want me to do with it? Burn it?"

If she had been angry, Steve could have defended himself. It's easier to throw a block against a strike. But he didn't know how to protect himself from this. George pulled her coat from the back of the chair and quietly left the hall.

Steve waved at Tanner standing by the door. "Come on, Boo."

"Didn't George like the movie?" Tanner asked in the car.

The trees were bare and bone white in the headlights. "Yes, she liked it."

"Then what's the matter?"

Steve turned into his drive. "Hell if I know."

But he did know. Left to himself, he could have reasoned his way out; after all, no one was complaining except George. What made her such an authority on the life of Locharbert, anyway? And hadn't he already done good for these people, at very least provided a point of interest? Nicola might have a career other than adding to the town's population. The Comm had done well by him. Everyone would have a few more coppers in their pockets. He had good reasons for being able to roll over and sleep that night. All he had done was paint a little red and dashing in a landscape of more subtle hues. But this wasn't just any other project. He needed this one. For himself.

Sleep was still lying heavily on him, when light filled his window the next morning. He could hear his boys playing cards downstairs. He rolled over and tried to slip back into a dream that was trying hard to get away. But there was an unusual quiet sitting on this day. When Tanner came up with a cup of coffee, Steve propped himself on an elbow.

"You've forgotten today's Mahogany," Tanner said. He set the cup on the bedside table. Steve noted the steam rising straight up, which meant the triple glazing on the windows was working. Still, it was cold.

"Hogmanay." Steve wrapped his hands around the cup and lifted it off the table. "I feel like I've been run over by a steamroller." Steve turned the alarm clock round to face him. "God, it's eleven o'clock."

Tanner sat down on the bed. "Is your movie going to be in the theatres?"

"Of course it is," Steve said. He put his lips to the rim of the cup and slurped the first hot mouthful.

Tanner flopped down by Steve's feet. "Eli says women are too much trouble."

"They are," said Steve. "A man spends his life trying to make two and two equal four. A woman isn't satisfied until she's made eight and eight come out to twenty-three. It's a losing game, son."

Tanner studied Steve while he finished his coffee. "George says we're going to have a sister. What if she's bad at math, too?"

Steve lay back down and looked at the ceiling, rows of neatly laid panels, one tongue into one groove side by side across his roof. "George doesn't know everything, you know. I've never had a girl yet."

Tanner got up and took Steve's cup. "It'd be kind of cool, though, wouldn't it?"

Steve looked over to the window. Something was very odd about this day. He could see the island of Islay, for one thing, sort of lit up, even though the wind was racing the clouds off the sea and over the shore.

By the time Steve had showered and was waiting by the car for his sons, the wind was rattling the sides of the new roof.

"Damn," said Steve. "Ginty must not have nailed that down properly."

They climbed into the car and drove to Locharbert, where they were hoping for lunch in the café. They parked the car along Front Street, then pushed along Main Street, which was strangely absent even of the dogs that generally loitered in the alleys. They didn't bother trying the café door, because the lights were out. They could hear trashcan lids lifting and dropping back in the alley. In the fields, the sheep were down on their knees for morning worship. But the town had slipped out of regular time into some slower species of motion.

"What the hell?" said Steve. "It's only Saturday."

They walked on, but not a shop was open. There were no closing signs in the window, as though it were simply understood that on this daftest of days, no one would leave their house until it was dark and harder for the spirits to catch them. Even the church was shut, all windows dark, with no sign of Alasdair Campbell pottering around, removing last Sunday's flowers from the vases in the window bottoms, straightening hymnals, or brushing leaves from the church steps.

Steve and the boys wandered into the graveyard looking for the name McNaught among the lichened headstones. They didn't know to stay inside like the people of Locharbert quietly sitting around their fires. They didn't know that the church had gone into hiding, and that the ghosts were already clearing their throats in readiness for a wild night. They couldn't see, but the hills were waking, as they had done once a year since the ancestors of this town lived in the ground and sent up their offerings in fire. When Steve looked up from a grave and saw the ironmonger's sign drifting past them on the wind, he took his sons to shelter on the shore with their cousins.

Between the church and the sea, between the late morning and the turning of the sun, before Steve and his sons even got to the shore, the wind had gathered new force and lifted the Tinkers' tent out of the pebbles and into the skeleton of a nearby tree.

Eli and Tanner ran back in the direction of the car. "Come on, Dad!"

Steve saw their mouths moving, but heard only the waves hammering the shore, the wind like a demented ghost inside his clothes.

"I'll be right there," he shouted.

He shielded his eyes against the strands of seaweed tossed by the air like a salty dried salad. There was no rain, but the clouds were just above his head, grey and roiling. He got to the tree where the tent hung and found the brothers huddled in the brush nearby.

"I'll drive you over to my house," he called.

Murdo shook his head. "The wind will be after your roof today, too."

Steve gestured for them to follow. They stayed put. Just in time, Steve ducked an old salted herring crate. He started to run and was breathless by the time he pulled the car door open and climbed in.

"This is wild," said Eli, smiling for the first time in days. "Do you think it's a hurricane?"

Steve started up the car. "Something like that."

Eli jumped up in the back seat and pointed. "There's George!"

Steve turned the engine off. George was crossing the road, the wind flapping in her trench coat, her hand gripping the strap of a shoulder bag.

The car door swung out of his hand as Steve jumped out. "Wait here."

Steve muscled his way along the pavement, but when he caught up with George, she kept on moving in the direction of the shore.

"Are you nuts?" he shouted. "There's things flying around out here."

She didn't answer.

He offered her a ride, but she kept walking, as though she'd fall over if she stopped.

When Steve climbed back into the car, Eli said, "You can't just leave her."

Steve flicked on the ignition. "I give up."

Tanner said, "Go and get her, Dad."

Steve let the clutch out and drove home.

WILLY HAD BEEN IN THE KITCHEN whistling, when George felt hot water rush down her thighs, soaking the mattress under her backside. The wind was rattling inside the lamppost at her window. Willy launched into "Flow Gently Sweet Afton".

George had stared at the cracks on the ceiling, and they all seemed like birthing cracks, waiting to bulge and break open. She had felt her stomach tighten, outlining the baby's back like cheeks sucked into cheekbones.

"Georgie." Her father tapped on the door. "Steve and his boys just went running up the road to the church."

He had gone off whistling "Coming Through The Rye." George ran over the words in her head. *But all the lads they smile at me.* It was something to focus on. *When coming through the rye.* She breathed into the tightening and loosened it. *Ilka lassie has her laddie.*

Her shack on the shore would be cold, especially with this wind. *Nane they say hae I.* She pulled her nightie up and wiped the fluid from her thighs and maiden hair. But the more she thought of her shack and the window and the heron, the more she knew she would have to get up and go. Walking was good for labour. She had walked many a woman through to the point of pushing. And then squatting.

Walking. Squatting. She had to get up and go before she couldn't walk anymore. *But all the lads they smile at me, when coming through the rye.*

Willy had been making lentil soup, thick and carroty orange, smelling like mushed peas. She dressed and slipped out of the door.

When she stepped out of the shelter of the shop door, the wind robbed her of her breath and sent her fighting for another. She couldn't go back, though. She needed the heron. She needed to know everything would be all right.

And then there was Steve standing in her path. She couldn't stop. She had to keep walking, walking until she had to squat, and, Lord, she didn't want to squat along the way. Murdo called out to her from the bushes, but she had to keep going.

IN THE LATE AFTERNOON, Steve fell asleep on his couch. Darkness crept down as he slept, and when he awoke, the only light was the glow of the fire on his face. Tanner was poking logs to make them spark.

The roof was banging even worse now, metal on metal. Beneath that, the wind sang under the door, and, as if in the distance, the goat was crying a high-pitched bleat.

"The lights are all out," Tanner said.

Steve pulled a jacket on and had to lean against the door to close it behind him. He got to the pen, whose gate had already been carried off, and fumbled with the goat's tether. Butthead wouldn't hold still, less daft than mad, and, once free, bolted, kicking up sand which flew back at Steve's eyes. Steve struggled out to the shore to see if George had managed to reach her destination. He could make out a low light, probably from candles.

"The wind must have taken out the lines," he said, leaning back against the door.

Steve picked Tanner's jacket from the back of the couch and tossed it to him. "What do you say we all go *first footing?*"

Tanner shrugged. "Will they have Coke?"

Steve had never been first footing, but Peter Duart had explained to him the custom of going from house to house to greet the New Year with neighbours over a dram. Or two.

"More like three," Peter had said.

Steve said, "Sure they will."

He called up the stairs for Eli.

"He went after Nicola," Tanner said. "I guess her math is getting better."

Steve knuckled Tanner's head in the dark. The car didn't start right up. Steve tried again. "Weird." He opened the bonnet, brushed away a pile of sand, and this time the engine fired.

CHAPTER TWENTY-SIX

When the Tinkers had seen George on the path, they didn't like the feeling they had around the joints in their toes. They weren't ones to mess with women, but in unison they thought they ought to keep an eye on this one. Without a word, they moved off together, trailing George MacBrayne in a fashion that would have normally caught her notice, but not on this Hogmanay with the sun on its downturn and with the noisy dead up and about their tricks.

They knew where she was going and arrived at her shack less than five minutes after her. She had the gas fire lit, but was sitting on the bed in her coat, beside her cats, her knees spread. They could see all this from the back window, because she was pointed towards the front. She had that screechy woman singing.

Donal tossed a stick at the heron by her wall; it flapped a few feet, then landed again. Murdo caught his arm when he reached for another stick.

Doolie's head was tilted into the wind, as though, if he just got the right position, he could tune into a different station. "Will we ask if she needs help?"

Murdo shook his head. "It's best not to bother a woman at a time like this."

Donal and Doolie nodded. They relied on Murdo for facts about women. Every now and then George broke the silence by speaking to her cats. The brothers were somewhat sheltered at the back of her house and one by one they fell asleep. It was dark before they awoke and heard George crying. She didn't have her coat on now, but she was in the same place. She was wearing a T-shirt and not a stitch below that, though the brothers could see nothing but her bare knees.

When Murdo noticed her wipe her eyes, he felt inclined to run for help, no matter what he had said to his brothers. Still, he remembered the way the farmers held back from a birthing dog or cow, and Murdo stood by his first assessment. Donal and Doolie were glad to hear it. They weren't used to women at all, and a crying woman left them confused and crying themselves. It made Donal wish he hadn't lost that tissue, but the back of his sleeve worked just as well.

George got up and let her cats out, then went back to her place on the bed.

Hogmanay is full of distractions. It's part of being daft. On Hogmanay, normally sane men had been known to strip naked and swim out to the seal-women. It was said in quiet corners, out of the reach of the church, that the people of Locharbert came down the line of the seal-people. Distractions of all kinds were abroad tonight, and by the time Steve and Tanner knocked on the Duarts' door, Peter was fairly caught up by the loveliness of his wife who had changed into a tight short dress and wrapped herself in a lacy shawl. He watched her body move within the cloth as she went to answer the door. He shouldn't have been surprised he had to share her tonight, but he greeted his guests with a little resentment.

Shefaline pulled Tanner to her side and laid her cheek against Steve's, exactly the place Peter wanted to be.

"You're the first," she said. "I made vol au vents."

Peter poured drinks and felt better. Shefaline said she had no Coke, but poured Tanner a glass of sirop de cassis. Tanner pulled a sly face at Steve. It looked like grape juice, but it surely didn't taste like grape juice. He sat on the floor by the fire and tuned out the adults' talk. The flames made the shadows in the small room dance, licked and lighted variously a shelf of books, a messy painting of mountains, a seagull floating on strings in a corner. It never felt dark this way in L.A. He never felt there this feeling of an animal in its cave, sheltered, but barely. He had shivered in the graveyard earlier in the day when the names carved in stone felt too noisy. He laid his head on his arm and watched the fire through the purple liquid in his glass.

"You can carry him upstairs, if you like," Peter said.

Shefaline yawned. "I'm sleepy myself."

Peter didn't feel tired. Hogmanay for him had always fallen at the end of Christmas break from boarding school. His parents, English by allegiance, if not entirely by blood, passed the festival over with sherry and one of those looks that carried disapproval of the common man and his revelries. But Peter had always suspected there was more to the night than sherry in tiny glasses and then coffee in china cups, because the workers at the castle had always had that night off and the next day to recover. He knew by the ruddiness in the cheeks of his father's man that Hogmanay held something of the unexpected.

His father would send the man off with, "Don't overdo it, Kenny."

He would chuckle, but, when Kenny had closed the door quietly behind him, there would be that look of superiority on his father's face. Peter had always wondered what made the farm workers whistle when Hogmanay was around the corner, even with hands raw from the outdoors.

He had finally found out about Hogmanay when he was working on the island boats. Hogmanay was a holiday because no one would go out on the water when mischief was abroad. They had drunk like all good sailors, among the company of the Gaelic people who lived without any sight of the mainland. But it wasn't until Peter bought the farmer's cottage near the ancient ruin that Hogmanay moved into full gear. Out at Killinochinoch, he was living among farmers, who felt the land as a fluid thing at the best of seasons, but at the approach of New Year, those bones, sunk and turning slowly into peat, turned up the nonsense, and a man could barely put a foot over them than they shifted and caused him to fall. The farmers told of such things, though Peter understood only the half, since it was half in Gaelic they spoke.

One farmer and then another arrived at the Duarts'. They came wearing kilts and sporrans and hovered by the fire, awkward, because this house was not as theirs. They tried one of Shefaline's vol au vents, then moved onto another house or farm where there were proper mince pies and Scottish music. This was the order of things. Steve observed all of it, chastising himself as long as he was able, for seeing only another movie in this. But how could he congeal a ghost onto film? How would he catch the hidden talk of farmers?

The old year gave over into the new. The bottle was empty. Shefaline fell asleep with her head against the arm of the sofa. The clock ticked on to two o'clock. With Tanner asleep upstairs and no Mrs. McPhealy to answer to, Steve had no inclination to move. The influx of first footers turned to a dribble then stopped. He felt himself rising to a standing position before he realised that Peter was helping him to do so.

"Fresh air," Peter said.

Steve slumped back into the comfort of cushions. Peter pulled him up again. "Come on, it'll do you good."

It was almost balmy outside now. Oddly quiet and redolent of nettles and firs. The wind had spent itself.

"Look at the moon," Steve said. "Damn female, taunting us from behind that cloud. She knows she's got us."

Steve pulled the collar of his jacket about his ears, as he followed Peter across boggy sedge out into the field by the house. The clouds had cleared, and the moon lit the path. The mud was hardening and glistening.

"Where are we going?" Steve asked.

When he craned his head back and looked at the clear sky, he didn't care that Peter didn't answer. When Peter stopped, he simply stopped, too. Below them a ring of stones held up a circular embankment.

Peter jumped down, only his head visible at the level of the path. He gestured to Steve to follow. But the cavern looked dark and overgrown. Steve hesitated at the rim.

"It's the last Stone Age dwelling undiscovered by the National Preservation Society. There would have been a turf roof over the top here. Jump down."

Steve lowered himself over the side and came down on rusted bracken. There was no one else in the dank sunken space, but it felt like he had interrupted an entire crowd.

The men were pensive, drowned out for the moment.

"The people hereabouts used to build fires on Hogmanay," Peter said. "They'd take turns jumping over them. It was a way of putting a full stop on the last year and starting something new. A sort of purification ritual."

Steve asked, "Why don't we build a fire in here and jump over it?"

Peter looked about them. "I'm afraid we're rather hemmed in. There's no room to run."

He fished around in his jacket pocket and came up with a small contraption that he placed in Steve's hand.

"It's an old flint from one of my ancestors. It used to be behind glass in the castle but I nicked it." Steve could see Peter's teeth grinning in the dark. "A small act of rebellion."

Steve crouched in the centre of the circle. For millennia in this field surrounded by ancient woods, the bracken had sprung every spring and curled back every winter; the feet of his ancestors had on a night like this worked a small groove into the sod as they moved back and forth about their fires. Above them this same moon had drifted in and out of thin cloud like a fleeting smile on the face of a lover.

CHAPTER TWENTY-SEVEN

George screamed. At first, she had thought she wanted to be alone, but now she was comforted by the knowledge of the heron somewhere out in the dark, and by the three Wallace brothers at the back of her house. During the pains, she wanted nobody touching her, nobody asking her if she was doing well. But in between times, she could have used a cup of tea or a hand on her shoulder. She had seen all this so many times before, but nothing could have prepared her for how it all felt from the inside.

She couldn't test herself, but she guessed she was probably about halfway to full dilation. She had no need to bear down yet, but a pressure was forcing itself heavily into her pelvis. She realised now that part of her had always suspected the women were faking their pain, overdoing it just a bit. But now it was her thrashing about, vomiting, and shitting; hers was the sudden alarm that all her guts were being mangled out. *Ilka lassie has her laddie. Nane they say hae I.*

George cried, because it felt better that way. It felt as though, if she shouted loud enough, the waves would turn back out of fear, that the god who designed this imperfect system of birth would relent and put her on the other side of it.

"What's she doing now?" Donal asked Murdo. He was the only one who had jumped up to the window when George screamed.

"She's throwing a book at the wall." Murdo sat back down between his brothers. "But I was fair worried there for a moment."

Donal and Doolie tucked themselves within the safety of their arms and went back to sleep. Murdo couldn't do the same. His had always been the job of caretaker. He settled back for a long wait and at first barely registered a light coming down the pathway followed swiftly by the rattling of a bike on the uneven path.

Murdo squinted into the blinding light until it clicked out and he could see a man leaning his bike against the wall, then bending over to free his trousers from their clips. Murdo sat back against the side of the house. It was only Willy MacBrayne.

When Willy closed the door of George's shack behind him, he looked at his daughter and shook his head.

George, easing the weight off first one buttock then the other, glanced over. "Don't just stand there looking glaikit."

Willy got to her just as another contraction brought a shout, which, if George could have seen, caused the heron to flutter and move a few feet off the wall. Stirring in his sleep for a moment, Donal saw it.

Willy tried to help George up. "Get up and walk."

George batted him away. "Not on your life. You're not moving me anywhere."

Willy sat down and folded his hands on his lap. George had been born in a Glasgow hospital, where fathers were kept in waiting rooms. The birth had been induced, so the doctor could be home in time for tea. The cervix hadn't opened properly and forceps were used. For the first part of George's life, her head looked like a dented dome.

George sighed after the passing of another contraction. "Willy, I need you to take a look."

"I'm looking," said Willy.

"No," said George, "you're going to have to look down there."

Willy stood up. "I will not."

Donal asked, "What are they doing now?"

Through the window Murdo saw Willy MacBrayne staring up between George's legs. "Never you mind."

"Do you see the head?" George said. She stopped to breathe into another convulsion.

Willy strained upward. "It comes and goes."

George sighed, another contraction over. "No cord on it?"

Willy stood back up. "Not even any hair on it."

George had had all kinds of hair when she was born. But a bald grandchild would do Willy MacBrayne just fine.

"You can wipe that smile off your face," George said, groaning.

Willy walked over to the kitchen. "I'll make you a wee cup of tea."

DAMP KINDLING WASN'T GOING to get in the way of the fire Steve was building at the edge of the sea. He was on a mission. He could see that George's lights were on. Butthead was wandering along the shoreline, scavenging among the seaweed.

It had taken many tries to get the flint to spark, but, finally, protected by the shield of his hand, a tiny glint had dropped into one of Mrs. McPhealy's firelighters. Steve quickly scrunched pieces of paper into balls and threw them in, laughing as they went up in a glorious blaze, sending up sparks into the night sky. Soon, the logs he carried out from the house were crackling over a glowing bed of embers. There was no wind now. No roaring in the ears. Nothing flying at the head. Whatever the imps and fairies had been up to was over now.

The paper Steve crinkled into loose balls was not newspaper, but leaves from the hard copy of his screenplay. Once the fire had got going, he tossed in the whole thing. And now he was fumbling in a box that sat beside him on the sand. Inside, were the reels of his film *As It Is In Heaven*. He dropped each one into the embers, setting up a horrible stink as they shrank and crinkled into nothing. Steve stood back and rubbed his hands against the heat.

"WHAT THE DEVIL ARE THOSE fools doing out there?" said Willy MacBrayne.

From the window, Willy could see the man on the shore become four, and then he watched them all taking turns jumping over the fire.

"I want to die," George said.

Willy turned back from the window. "It will soon be over."

George looked into his eyes, needing him to save her, because he was, after all, her father.

Willy handed her a cup of tea and laid his hand on her back. "I can't do this for you, Georgie."

George began to groan against the pain, but felt it turn into a push instead.

"What's the head doing now?"

"It's not going back in anymore."

"Thank God," she said.

STEVE BUILT UP THE FIRE with a few planks McGinty had left after the remodelling. It was getting harder to clear the flames, but he took a running jump, launched himself into the air, and landed it. He was clapping his hands with his Tinker relatives when he made out someone running towards them waving his arms.

He said, "What in hell?"

"The baby must be close," said Murdo.

"Aye," said Doolie. "It's been long in coming, right enough."

Donal asked, "When will it be time for breakfast?"

Willy MacBrayne stood back to let Steve pass, and then went to join the brothers by the fire. None of them said a word, just stood in a row with their faces towards the light creeping up from under the horizon.

STEVE TOOK A CLOTH FROM THE SINK and wiped George's face. He wiped his own face, too, but the tears kept coming.

"It burns!" George cried.

Finding her body slipping into a convulsive push, she slipped off the bed into a squat, which only brought the next batch of pains sooner. It burned and stretched, burned and stretched until there came a sudden release. Water gushed onto the floor at her feet.

"Stop blubbering," she said to Steve, "and get ready to catch."

Steve knelt down and softly touched the strange bodiless face emerging from the darkness. George let out a yell, then a push, and then in one second of expulsion his hands were filled with bluish pink flesh and cord and mucus and blood.

George fell back against the bed, panting.

Steve looked into the eyes of his baby. "God damn." He took a towel from a pile at his feet and wrapped the baby in a pink one. Steve laid his lips against the baby's head. "Islay. Just like you said."

George took the baby and held it against her breast. She looked down at her daughter's little face and smiled. It was Steve's face.

She said, "Looks like we've got another bloody Tinker on our hands."

When Steve wiped his eyes with his forearm, he ran a great smudge of charcoal across his cheeks.

George asked, "What on earth have you been doing?"

"Oh," he said, "just taking care of business."

"Business, is it?" she said. "Smells like a lot of smoke and mirrors to me. What were you burning?"

Steve broke into the kind of smile that made George want to forgive him even before his confession. But he seemed a bit jittery, and she was beginning to think she wouldn't like the answer.

"You'll be happy," he said.

Her eyes went to the window. There was a commotion going on out by the shoreline. "Try me," she said.

He knelt on the bed beside the woman and the baby girl. "*As It Is In Heaven* has passed over into history."

Tears leaked out of the sides of George's eyes. "Eejit!" She shook her head. "I was counting on the money from the film to do up the cottage."

Steve put both hands on the top of his head, went to the door, and kicked it. He said, "A man could die." He came back to the bed and he put his hands together as though he was praying. When more tears ran down George's face, he wiped them with the back of his hand.

"I didn't do it for you," he said. "I burned the screenplay and all the reels. I had to do this for myself."

George groaned and gave a shout as the placenta slipped out onto the bed.

Steve started to laugh. He wouldn't stop laughing, and it was the laughter of the gods, of Hogmanay and ghosts and ghoulies and of everything unseen.

Through her window George could see the first rays of morning outlining the islands. She leant down and kissed her baby's forehead, still sticky with vernix. Everything came around like this eventually: men and babies, Tinkers and fathers. It was all a gigantic birth, these tides of life, shuttling between pain and creation.

At the edge of the sea, the heron was waiting for the tide to bring in its breakfast. The world had slipped out of chaos and settled back into its groove. And today was going to be a good day.

EPILOGUE

Locharbert awoke from its daft night to a morning lit brightly by the sun. The sea was all a-glitter as Reverend Campbell padded out in his grey knitted socks to open the church doors and let the morning in. He slipped a few nails from his cassock pocket and held the paper against the door as he hammered them in. This was not a page from the newspaper or even a page torn from a film. Here were the banns that suggested the lady who decorated the church with her flowers, whom he had known since childhood, would not remain Mrs. McPhealy for long.

Delia Crawford hurried along Main Street buttoning her coat. She had been one of the first to hear how George MacBrayne's baby had arrived two weeks early, and into the hands of the American, if you like. Delia had to stop and catch her breath before she could draw the post office key from her pocket. People would be coming in early this morning.

The commotion out at Achnarannoch that night went into the annals of Locharbert. One of the Tinker brothers had caught fire, it was told, and had to be thrown into the sea. The other two joined in. Frolicking they were with nary a stitch on, and that on such a cold winter's night. The way it was told, the American had stripped down, too, and gone in after them.

"The things that go on in a wee place like Locharbert." Delia thrust the key into the hole and went into the post office for another day's business. She hung up her coat on its hook behind the counter, then smoothed her new cashmere sweater over her bosom.

"It's just the height of nonsense, so it is."

Enjoy more about
Mrs. McPhealy's American
Meet the Author
Check out author appearances
Explore special features

CLAIRE R. McDOUGALL was born in Edinburgh, Scotland, her family settling in rural Argyll's wild and rugged country-side, with its ancient ruins and standing stones. She studied philosophy for four years at Edinburgh University. After earning her MA, she spent four years on a Haldane scholar-ship to gain a Master of Letters at Christ Church, Oxford, studying Nietzsche. After moving to the United States, Claire worked as a journalist, before opting to pursue creative writ-ing full time. She has written eight novels and their attendant screenplays. She is the author of four published books: *Veil of Time* (Simon and Schuster 2014) *Druid Hill, Iona,* and *Hazel and the Chessmen.*

ACKNOWLEDGEMENTS

I am so grateful to Vicki DeArmon and Julie Park Tracey for rescuing this novel from its residence on the shelf. Sibylline Press is a little light shining against the enormity of corporate publishing, a place where the author is not a metric but a person with things to say.

One thing I do want to say is that this book in no way intends to denigrate the people in small-town Argyll where I grew up. They are anchors that hold me in place because they are welded to the land and to what is so without pretension.

Thank you to all who have encouraged me along the very long and winding pathway that has been my writing career to date. Thanks go, of course, to my husband, who burns the midnight oil to support this harebrained life I have chosen for myself. I am so grateful for my three creative and lovely children, who are my own very best creative efforts. A mention should also go out to my sisters Kathryn and Elisabeth and my cousin, Iain Edmondson, for their support. I would be remiss not to mention the real Steve (Ward) and Georgianna (Lilly), who, in an eerie turn of fate, and far from the setting of this story, went to the same high school in the same year, but never met.

And then there are the unseen hands: the deceased parents and those ancestors of the Hebridean Isle of Islay, who left impossible poverty under the Clearances but on whom I rely in some parallel dreamtime zone.

BOOK CLUB QUESTIONS

1. What is the theme of *Mrs. McPhealy's American*?

2. How does the author want you to think about these characters in small-town Scotland?

3. What does Steve McNaught think a new life in Scotland is going to offer him? Contrast this with what he actually finds there.

4. What role do the three tinkers play in the story? What is their value, both for the story and for Steve himself?

5. Contrast the women in Steve's life to date with what he encounters in Georgiana (George).

6. Why does George not want Steve to make the film about Locharbert? Is she right?

7. What characteristics of Mrs.McPhealy suggest she might be holding things in? Does she have any redeeming qualities?

8. What do the upperclass Duarts in the castle represent in the story?

9. Talk about the presence of Christianity/the church in the book.

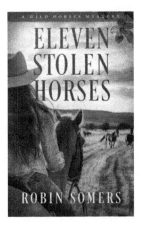

Eleven Stolen Horses:
A Wild Horses Mystery
BY ROBIN SOMERS

MYSTERY
Trade Paper, 306 pages (5.315 x 8.465) | $17
ISBN: 9781960573865
Also available as an ebook and audiobook

News reporter Eleanor Wooley wants to start her life over in the foothills of the Sierra Nevada but when her new best friend suddenly disappears, she finds herself in pursuit and in grave danger instead.

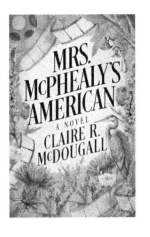

Mrs. McPhealy's American:
A Novel
BY CLAIRE R. MCDOUGALL

FICTION
Trade Paper, 344 pages (5.315 x 8.465) | $19
ISBN: 9781960573940
Also available as an ebook and audiobook

A one-way ticket to his ancestral home of Scotland lands beleaguered Hollywood director Steve McNaught at his distant relative's, Mrs. McPhealy's, in Locharbert where he's an immediate outcast and soon discovers that even love with a local can't save him.

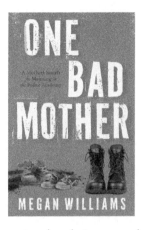

*One Bad Mother: A Mother's
Search for Meaning in the Police
Academy*
BY MEGAN WILLIAMS

MEMOIR
Trade Paper, 224 pages (5.315 x 8.465) | $17
ISBN: 9781960573858
Also available as an ebook and audiobook

A book for every mother who thinks
she is failing the test of motherhood.
Or thinks that challenging athletic feats
or professional achievements may be
easier than being a mother. That is—most of us. This is the thinking that landed the author in the police academy looking for win.

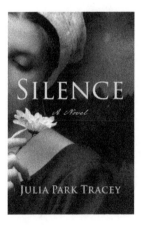

Silence: A Novel
BY JULIA PARK TRACEY

HISTORICAL FICTION
Trade Paper, 272 pages (5.315 x 8.465) | $18
ISBN: 9781736795491
Also available as an ebook and audiobook

A whiff of sulfur and witchcraft shadows this literary Puritan tale of loss
and redemption, based on this best-sell-
ing historical fiction author's own an-
cestor, her seventh great-grandmother.

For more books from **Sibylline Press**,
please visit our website at **sibyllinepress.com**